Mike took her hand what are you feeling right now?"

"Guilt," she answered, her voice thick.

"What else?"

"I'm scared."

"Of me?"

She shook her head. "No. Of me."

She finally raised her head to look at him. Her eyelashes clung together. Flakes of mascara mingled with the tears under her eyes. Slowly, cautiously, he brought his mouth to hers, and against her lips, said, "It's okay to be scared, Katie. It just means you're alive." Softly kissing the corner of her mouth, the hollow of her cheek, he tasted her tears. But she was pulling away from him.

"Don't do this, Mike."

"Why, darlin'?" He brushed a lock of hair away from her cheek.

"Please try to understand. Paul is the only man I've ever been with."

"Paul is dead, Kate." He was trying to understand, and failing. "You're still young. Are you going to keep yourself locked away from life forever?"

REMEMBER THE TIME

REMEMBER THE TIME

ANNETTE A. REYNOLDS

BANTAM BOOKS
NEW YORK TORONTO LONDON SYDNEY AUCKLAND

REMEMBER THE TIME

A Bantam Book/July 1997

ISBN 0-553-57652-6

Published simultaneously in the United States and Canada

Bantam Books are published by Bantam Books, a division of Bantam
Doubleday Dell Publishing Group, Inc. Its trademark, consisting of
the words "Bantam Books" and the portrayal of a rooster, is Registered
in U.S. Patent and Trademark Office and in other countries. Marca
Registrada. Bantam Books, 1540 Broadway, New York, New York
10036.

PRINTED IN THE UNITED STATES OF AMERICA

OPM   10   9   8   7   6   5   4   3   2

For Mary Ann Dolphin, my "idea gal" and one of the best friends a woman could have. Thanks for your faith. I couldn't have done it without you, no matter what you say.

To LTC Fred, who deserved a Purple Heart for putting up with me for all those years. Thanks for being . . .

A very special thank you to: Paul Rabbitt, my favorite male cousin on my mother's side, and rock-hound extraordinaire; Val Dumond, who helped me get the ball rolling; my agent, Julie Castiglia, for seeing the possibilities; and my editor, Shauna Summers, for leading me the rest of the way.

P.S. I love you, Mom!

REMEMBER
THE TIME

PROLOGUE

The front porch of the Victorian house provides the only relief from the afternoon sun. The threat of a thunder-storm will only make the heat worse, and the Shenandoah Valley of Virginia hunkers down to wait out the summer of 1977. Likewise, the three teenagers who sit sprawled on the porch in various states of heat prostration.

"Can it get any hotter?" Kate asks, her voice taking on just the slightest hint of a whine.

"Don't say that." Paul watches a fly take a desultory stroll across his forearm.

"Bet it's hotter than this in Arizona," Mike comments.

"But it's a dry heat," Paul and Kate say in unison. Paul looks down at Kate and they grin at each other.

No one on that porch doubts Paul Armstrong will be in Phoenix next summer. He is the golden boy of Staunton High School's baseball team. Making it to the majors isn't a pipe dream for Paul. His self-confidence will make it happen.

Kate groans as she raises her head from Paul's lap.

"Where're you going, Ms. Moran?" Paul asks, his fingers closing around her wrist.

"Get more tea."

"Ya gotta kiss me first."

"It's too hot," she moans, but they all know she doesn't mean it.

Both boys watch Kate's walk to the front door. Her cutoffs are short and her legs are long. Mike silently sings the praises of summer. The screen door slaps closed behind her and, for a few seconds, the relentless drone of the cicadas is silenced.

Mike feels a rivulet of sweat trickle down the nape of his neck. He looks over at his best friend. "How'd you get so lucky?" he asks.

Paul slouches lower in the porch swing, setting off a gentle rocking motion. "It's that Armstrong charm."

Mike snorts and shifts in the wicker armchair.

"Hey, we both had an equal shot at her." Paul's voice holds the hint of a shrug. "She picked me."

Mike remembers it differently, but says, "Yeah. I guess she's not as smart as she looks."

"I heard that, Michael Fitzgerald," Kate states, pushing open the screen door.

"Heard what?" Mike asks innocently.

Kate perches on the porch railing and rolls the cool glass across her forehead.

"You know I love you both. Just different."

"Please don't give me that 'I love you like a brother' routine. It wounds me," Mike says in what he hopes passes for mock pain.

The glass at her lips, Kate rolls her eyes at him then closes them and tilts her head back to take a long drink.

Her thick auburn hair is pulled back in a high ponytail, but a few heat-damp strands cling to her neck. Mike wants to lift them, blow on her hot skin. He wants to put his mouth there and taste her. The thought brings on the beginning of an erection and he guiltily glances at Paul.

When Mike sees those amused hazel eyes looking back at him he knows he's been caught.

ABANDONMENT
AND RUIN

CHAPTER

ONE

The initial assault on his body knocked the wind out of him. Gasping for air, he was swept along in _____ the tumult of the newly born river in the Arizona desert. Rocks pummeled him. One particularly jagged stone hit his leg with such force that it slashed his jeans and cut open his thigh. He could feel the warm blood swirling around him, contrasting sharply with the cold water. A small manzanita tree swept past him, caught his left arm, and pulled it back. He could hear the snap as a bone broke. The pain made him scream, and then there was nothing but numbness.

The thoughts that flashed through his mind were quicksilver and, in some ways, senseless. *There goes the season.* Followed by, *Kate's gonna be so pissed when she sees me.* And then, *I'm gonna have to buy Stu a new Jeep.*

A lethargy had come over him and the idea of sleep floated around his mind like a pleasant daydream. But there was something he needed to do. What was it? God, he couldn't think anymore.

Paul could hear something over the thunderous crashing of the water around him. It must've been Mitch. *Mitch is gonna be late. I'll have to explain it all to his wife . . .* Opening his eyes, Paul caught sight of the Jeep and remembered the most important thing. The thing he'd forgotten.

It took all the concentration he had left for him to reach out his right hand and grasp the side mirror. His legs—his whole body—were whipped backward by the oncoming water, and he screamed again when something hit his lacerated leg with the force of a twenty-pound hammer.

There it was! He could see his wallet wedged between the dashboard and the windscreen. If he could just reach his wallet, open it up, look at that photograph—he'd be able to find the strength to get through this. The decision he'd made earlier was too important to be sidetracked by a few cuts and bruises, or a broken arm.

He was only thirty-four years old. He was healthy and strong. Dying was not on his agenda. Not for a very long time. All his intensity—all the life he had left—went into pulling himself up to the open window.

But he never heard Mitchell's terrified shout. He never saw the boulder that crashed through the flimsy canvas roof of the Jeep, shattering the windshield, and his skull. He never got to hold the photograph hidden in the recesses of his wallet.

The search for Paul Armstrong and Mitchell Browder began at one P.M., immediately after the Maricopa County Sheriff's Department received the call from Kate Armstrong. Kate made the call immediately after Browder's wife phoned from the airport, complaining that her husband had failed to pick her up, and "I'm standing here with a cranky four-year-old and every damn toy she's got and five suitcases."

The search ended at 2:48 P.M. because Paul Armstrong and Mitchell Browder were just where they said they'd be.

The four-wheel-drive vehicle carrying a deputy and a member of the rescue squad sped along the dirt road. When they saw the unfamiliar sight of a river running through the desert, the deputy reverently whispered, "Flash flood," and immediately put in a call for an emergency vehicle. The two men breathed a sigh of relief when they spotted a man sitting on a large boulder. Their relief would be short-lived.

He fit the description of Mitchell Browder, and the deputy was about to cancel the call for emergency services when the stillness of the figure struck him. The two men got out of the car, not bothering to close the doors, and walked toward the lone man. He didn't move. He didn't acknowledge their presence. When the deputy called out his name, he didn't hear. He simply sat, staring at a point somewhere in the distance. When the man from the rescue squad drew closer he could see the mud caked on the man's clothing. When he stepped in front of him and repeated his name, Mitchell Browder slowly moved his head upward, revealing a face streaked with dirt and tears.

"Mr. Browder, where is Paul Armstrong?"

"He's gone," Mitchell answered in a hollow voice.

"Gone where, Mr. Browder?" the deputy asked in a patient voice. "Which way did he go? My partner will go find him and I'll stay with you."

Mitchell shifted his eyes away from whatever he had been staring at and turned them on the man who stood before him. They seemed to burn with pain and fear, and the deputy took a step backward.

And then Mitchell Browder said the words that stunned first the men standing in front of him, and then the entire nation.

"He's not far away. I watched Paul Armstrong die right over there."

Mitchell lifted a hand that felt heavy with the weight of his words, pointing to the nearly unrecognizable Jeep that sat buried in the muddy rubble of the flash flood, and then silent tears coursed down his face once again.

"He didn't stand a chance," stated the sheriff, thinking she was out of earshot.

"It was over very quickly," said a friend, who was also a doctor on call at the hospital, afterward.

"He didn't feel any pain," the coroner had pronounced, taking her hand.

Over and over again, the same meaningless phrases blew across her consciousness until she simply stopped hearing them. How the hell did they know? Although she had been spared the sight of his once beautiful now unrecognizable face, she had been forced to look at his battered body. A body that had been untouched by a surgeon's knife, despite thirteen years in baseball. It seemed to her that he had hurt very much.

Paul had tried to convince her to go with them that morning. But Kate was sick to death of everything to do with Arizona. She'd been married to Paul Armstrong, and consequently baseball, for thirteen years. It wasn't fun anymore. The constant moving, the road trips, the hundreds of hours spent alone, the limelight that Paul lived in as the Giants' phenomenal second baseman—all these things had worn her down. She'd almost not come to spring training this year. Almost. But at the last moment she'd changed her mind, knowing that separation from Paul would be even more devastating to their marriage. This was his last chance to make it better. Kate had done all she could. She didn't think she could live without him, but knew something had to give. And that "something" wasn't going to be her any longer.

And as she sat, dry-eyed, on the couch in the living room of her parents' Tempe home that night, surrounded by people who whispered and murmured and hovered, that was the one thought that assaulted her mind.

How am I supposed to go on without you?

It wasn't until the next day that she cried.

Mitchell Browder stood in front of her while she sat on that same couch. His eyes were bloodshot and he looked at her forlornly—helplessly. He held a small plastic bag that he continually passed from one hand to the other. When he finally began speaking, his words came out in torrents of pain.

"I'm sorry, Kate. I'm so sorry! I don't know what else . . ." He stopped and swallowed hard. "God, he was my best friend on the team. They just let me out of the hospital, and I wanted to come by and tell you how sorry . . . I don't know what else to say. It doesn't seem like enough. If there's anything I can do to help you . . . anything."

Kneeling in front of her, he held the bag out with both hands. When she didn't take it from him, he gently placed it on her lap.

"These are some of Paul's things. They forgot to give them to you at the hospital. They were going to send over some stranger to give them to you, but I wouldn't let them."

She tried to smile, but the effort it took was too great.

"He saved my life, Kate." Mitchell's voice broke. "He saved me and then he died. I'll never be able to repay him. I don't know what to do . . ."

And then this man, who had been through too many injuries to count, who was as tough as nails when it came to the vagaries of his career, began sobbing like a small child. His tears widened the crack in her heart, and she reached out for him.

They held each other for long minutes, and then she sent him away.

He was wiping his face with the back of his hand, standing in the archway that led to the hall, when he suddenly said, "The rose was for you. He wanted you to have it." Kate's grief-stricken eyes stared at him blankly, but he didn't want to have to explain any more and he walked away.

The bag he'd given her had fallen to the floor. As she reached for it, she saw where his teardrops had landed on the tiles. Tangible evidence of pain. Her fingers closed around the bag and she stood, knowing she'd never look inside.

Kate's mother found her in the guest room. There was a phone call for her. It was Mike Fitzgerald. Did she want to take it?

She hadn't even heard the telephone ring, but, yes, she wanted to talk to Mike. She always wanted to talk to Mike. He was the best friend she'd ever had.

And when she picked up the receiver and heard him say "Katie? Darlin'?" her loss hit her fully, and the tears finally came.

PRESERVATION

CHAPTER

TWO

"Homer? You up here?" Kate stood on the postage-sized stamp of a landing and waited. "_____ Homer?" The door to the tower room was half open and she reluctantly pushed it aside. "There you are."

He lay in the rectangle of weak sunlight the window admitted, a well-scuffed baseball between his huge paws. Kate knelt down in front of the black Lab. "You know I don't want you up here. It's a nice day. You need to be outside chasing squirrels or something." He gazed at her with liquid eyes, and she reached out to stroke his head. Kate's voice softened. "Hey, I miss him, too."

Her knees creaked as she stood, reminding her of the recent passing of her thirty-seventh birthday. "Getting old, Homer," she whispered, as she let her eyes slowly examine the contents of the room.

In two steps she was facing a set of shelves. Taking down one of the twelve baseball gloves, Kate slipped her left hand into it and punched the well-worn leather. Dust flew into the still air and sparkled in the shaft of light. She replaced the glove on the shelf and moved to a small chest of drawers. Her hands hesitated momentarily before sliding open the top drawer. She lightly passed her fingers across the fabric of a gray road jersey, feeling more than reading the appliquéd letters that spelled out his name and his number—five—in orange and black.

Resolutely pushing the drawer closed, she spoke to the dog once more. "Hey, Homer . . . remember the time he dressed you up and took you trick-or-treating?"

At the sound of his name, the dog's ears moved up a notch and he gave his tail a halfhearted wag.

"Think the socks are too much?"

Kate looks up from the book she's been immersed in to behold the sight of Homer wearing one of Paul's game jerseys. The dog's ears stick out of the two holes Paul has cut in one of his caps. White stockings with black stirrups encase his legs.

"You're not seriously taking that dog out into the neighborhood looking like that."

"It's Halloween. He shouldn't be deprived just 'cause he's a dog."

"Uh-huh." Kate looks into her husband's smiling eyes. "Was this your idea, or did you lose a bet to Mike again?"

"Actually, Homer heard a rumor that the Craigs were giving out Reese's cups this year."

At the sound of two of his favorite words—"Reese's cups"— Homer's tail begins sweeping the floor.

"Okay, but you make it understood that I had nothing to do with this."

Paul Armstrong leaves Homer's side. He bends down, cupping Kate's chin in his hand, and tilts her face until his lips meet hers.

"No way. The first words out of my mouth at every house are going to be, 'Katie made me do this.' "

"And who's going to believe that?" she asks, a smile tugging at the corners of her mouth.

He winks and turns to Homer. "C'mon boy. Let's go find a bag for all your goodies."

As they leave the den, she calls after him, "And he'd better not be wearing your cup!"

Later that evening, when the last of the neighborhood children have rung the doorbell, a knock on the front door surprises her. Turning the porch light back on, she finds Paul leaning against the railing. He lets go of the dog's leash, and Homer gallops past her and into the house.

"Hey, lady," he says, sleepy-voiced. His eyes insolently sweep down her body. "Trick or treat?"

Her legs felt weak remembering, and she clutched the sill of the window that she had been staring out of with unseeing eyes. Homer sat by her side, and when she let her hand drop, he nuzzled it. She didn't notice Mike Fitzgerald looking up at the house from his yard. Never saw him wave.

Time had a way of passing for Kate Armstrong that few others would understand. The rhythms of the year contrarily refused to conform. As soon as the last leaf was off the enormous beech tree that grew in her backyard, Kate began to feel as though she could breathe again. While spring—well . . . spring, with its promise of life, began the cycle of suffocation all over again. But the falling leaves, crisp days, and the smell of woodsmoke that drifted through the Shenandoah Valley weren't working their magic this year.

Stuck in a house she didn't want, with a dog who didn't want her, Kate neglected them both. Her parents were in Tempe, three thousand miles away. Paul's mother had moved over the Blue Ridge Mountains to Charlottesville, to live with her sister when Paul's father had died. Paul's sister had left Staunton, too. Patricia's misplaced values made her believe that Charlottesville, with its university and horse farms and aura of Thomas Jefferson, somehow rubbed off on her socially. She had married one of the ubiquitous lawyers that the

University of Virginia churned out and couldn't be bothered with a run-down Victorian house in a town like Staunton. The house was left to Paul, and because it was the home he grew up in, Kate couldn't bring herself to leave it. But she couldn't bring herself to love it, either.

Paul Armstrong had died two and a half years ago, and the only thing Kate had shown any interest in since then was his grave. She could be found there once a month, pulling up weeds, placing fresh flowers in the two cement urns that flanked the large stone. Sometimes she would sit under the beech tree that protected the family's plot and read. Other times, if it had been a particularly bad month for her, she would talk to him. The taking of his life had taken hers. This wasn't something she consciously understood. Friends stopped calling. They'd heard "No thanks, I just don't feel like it" one too many times.

The girl who had loved life became the woman who suffered through it. She had been alone too long, but didn't realize that loneliness had made heavy inroads to her soul.

Kate now sat at the top of the stairs, elbows on her knees, chin in her hands.

"God, I'm bored." She was talking to the dog again. Not a good habit. "And it's only eleven o'clock, Homer. What are we going to do the rest of the day?"

Kate looked at the list she'd been holding when Homer had sneaked upstairs. There were at least twelve items written in her shorthand. Of the twelve—some of which were: *dust dwnstrs, rake lawn, p-u dry cl,* and *swp kitch flr*—the only one that had been crossed off was *chg bulb over stv.* She'd made the list two weeks ago and looked at it daily, and once again, it overwhelmed her. She stuffed it in the pocket of her shirt.

Footsteps sounded on the front porch, and Kate

groaned as Homer shot past her and rocketed down the stairs, barking hysterically.

"Homer! For God's sake!"

She reached the bottom of the staircase in time to see the mail drop through the slot in the door, and the dog trample it in an attempt to shove his snout through the brass oval. Pushing him aside, she muttered, "Why do we have to do this every damn day?" and rescued the pile of catalogs and envelopes. She carried them into the kitchen and dropped them on the table. The obvious junk went directly into the trash, while a Neiman Marcus preholiday catalog was tossed into a basket. She'd look at it later. Jamming the bills from the gas and phone companies into an already-full napkin holder that served as her accounts payable file, she found two actual pieces of mail. One was what was left of the monthly pension check she received from the baseball commission after debts had been served. She hated those things, and despite needing the money, it sometimes took her months to deposit them in her account. Kate stuffed this one into a small drawer by the phone, then went back to the table and picked up the hand-addressed gold-colored envelope with the blue borders. She didn't have to turn it over to know the flap would be embossed with her high school's crest. And she didn't want to open it, knowing it was the announcement for the dedication of the new gym in Paul's name. Instead, she put it back on the table, not wanting to think about it, or the twenty years that had gone by at the speed of sound.

She rotated her head from left to right in an attempt to rid herself of the stress that suddenly had her neck muscles in knots.

Kate went to the phone and dialed.

"Sheryl? Hi. Think you can work me in today?"

CHAPTER

THREE

A small breeze stirred the branches of the maple he stood under and a few die-hard leaves that had held on slowly fluttered to the ground. Mike captured them in the tines of the rake and bent to the task of bagging what was left of fall.

An Indian summer day had brought him out to finish the last of the yard cleanup, and the Victorian house across the way had snared his attention, as it had for the past three years.

The house had stood its ground for over ninety years. Today, against the backdrop of a pale blue November sky, the thin sunlight exposed many of its flaws. The white paint curled away from the porch columns and the eaves, revealing a gray patch here, or another layer of white there. One of the drainpipes had detached itself from a corner, probably during a recent storm, and it leaned away from the house waiting for the next sharp gust of wind to finish the job. A storm window from the second floor had fallen out, landing on a boxwood hedge that had the scraggly look of a GI with a bad haircut. The hedge was probably as old as the house, and equally neglected.

Mike Fitzgerald leaned on his rake, turned his gaze upward, and flinched as his eye caught the final blow to his sensibilities. Several fish-scale shingles were missing from the cornice, giving the house a jack-o'-lantern grimace. He'd been out of town for only six days. Kate's house was falling apart and winter was coming—both at an alarming rate. He could see all this, and more, from the back corner of his own lot.

He saw movement in the window of the small tower and thought she was watching him. He put his hand up in a tentative wave, a little embarrassed that he'd been seen, then turned back to the pile of leaves.

Mike had just finished hauling the last Hefty bag full of leaves to the curb when Homer began his daily defense of Frazier Street against the dreaded mail carrier. Shaking his head, he made his way across the side lawn, picked up the rake and entered what passed for a garage in 1910. Too small to hold a car any larger than a VW bug, he used the gray stuccoed building at the corner of his lot as an oversized toolshed.

As he was closing the double doors he heard a car start, and then Kate Armstrong turned the corner in front of his house and drove off down the street. Without a second thought he went back inside the garage and retrieved his rake. The day was too nice to waste indoors, and he enjoyed helping her out when he could.

He started at the far corner of her small front yard and had already amassed three large piles of leaves when he heard a shout.

"Package for you, Mr. Fitz!"

Turning, he saw the mailman had finished the upper part of the street.

"Thanks, Ray. Be right there."

They met in the middle of the road.

"Quite a bundle for you down at the post office," the postman said, handing Mike a small box along with the regular mail. "Glad to have you back."

"Good to be back, Ray."

"Any more old buildings that need saving?"

Mike smiled. "Even if there are, I'm sticking around here for a while. I have an old building of my own that's crying out for attention."

"I hear that," Ray Halpern chuckled. "With winter comin' on, the missus has a long list of 'honey-do's' for me." He took Mike's smile as an invitation to go on. "See you're helpin' out Mrs. Armstrong." He paused, shaking his head slightly. "Sad thing."

Uncomfortable with the turn the conversation was taking, Mike nodded in agreement. "Yeah, and I'd better get back to it. Thanks again, Ray."

He turned the package over as he walked back to Kate's yard. The return address was from the historical society in a small town in Oregon. Probably a gift. As a part-time advisor for the National Trust, he'd spent three days there on a consultation with the local preservationists back in July. Originally based in Richmond, his company now worked out of two large offices in the Historic Staunton Foundation. Between lectures and consults, Mike was seldom home, but when he did manage to alight, he was happy to let the folks at the foundation pick his brain at no charge. His standard fee was nothing to sneeze at, but the people who hired him always felt the need to send something, and so he had gathered quite a collection of bric-a-brac that he stored in one of the many empty rooms in his house.

Mike's degree was in architecture, but his minor in preservation was what had finally shone through. He loved the old buildings he'd grown up around. He had an innate understanding of what was right and wrong for the remodel of a house; or the new use of a theater built in 1915. He could sense a client's smallest concern and still convince them that keeping the old was almost always preferable to razing and rebuilding. And then he'd show them why: financially, esthetically, and finally, in personal pride. His restorations were flawless, but Mike engaged the clients in such a way that in the end *they* received the accolades for their foresight.

Mike placed the box which contained the latest addition to his thank-you gifts on the lawn and leaned against the beech tree as he flipped through the rest of the mail. Opening the dedication announcement, he saw his class year in one-inch boldface and chuckled. How could twenty years have gone by? Then it occurred to him that if he'd gotten one, so had Kate. And it would be painful for her. And that was painful for him.

He dropped the stack of envelopes next to the package and closed his eyes. He'd have to call Donna Estes to find out what the committee was planning for the dedication of the new gym. Paul Armstrong was one of Staunton's local heroes and the high school never passed up a chance to capitalize on his name. Kate would be expected to attend, and Mike knew what her reaction would be.

Sighing, he pushed himself away from the tree and picked up the rake. He finished raking and bagging the leaves, then let himself into Kate's backyard through the side gate with the intention of doing a little more work, but Homer had other ideas. The dog had been sleeping on the back porch. At the sight of Mike, he let out a small yelp, leapt up and bounded toward a ball he'd left under a shrub. Dropping it at Mike's feet, he gazed up at him expectantly.

"Homer, I don't have time for this," Mike said, but he picked up the ball anyway and tossed it across the large yard. He didn't get any more work done as the dog tirelessly retrieved the ball for the next half hour.

Stalling didn't help. Kate still hadn't returned when he let himself out of the gate and picked up his mail. Homer's whining followed him back across the street.

CHAPTER

FOUR

"You wanna talk about it?" Sheryl Keller's strong fingers found a knot the size of a walnut near _____ Kate's left shoulder blade. She dug into it, trying to ease it away.

The pain caught Kate by surprise and, with a gasp, her eyes flew open. Voice muffled by the doughnut-shaped pillow her face rested in, she asked, "How do you do that?"

"What?" Sheryl kept working the knot until she felt it break apart.

"Find the most painful spot and then torture me with it—that's what. I don't know why I come in here thinking a massage is going to relax me."

Practiced hands moved across Kate's bare back until they homed in on another knotted muscle. "You didn't answer my question," Sheryl said.

Kate grimaced as she felt another small tendon pop into its rightful place. "You're not the only massage therapist in town, y'know."

There was a smile in Sheryl's voice as she worked a fresh handful of oil into Kate's tight shoulders. "Yeah, but I'm the only one who doesn't charge you."

Kate grunted.

"Well?"

"Well, what?" Kate asked.

"What brings you here in this sorry state of clenchitude?"

"I came for a massage, not a therapy session." Kate spoke a little too sharply and regretted it instantly.

But Sheryl wasn't put off. She'd known Kate a long time—twenty-one years, to be exact—and knew the latest manifestation of her personality. Paul's death had brought on a pitiful state of melancholy the first year, which blended well with the later state of inertia. Now, closing in on the third year of his passing, bitterness had crept in. It was a shame because, just before his accident, Kate had seemed to be coming to some kind of positive place within herself. Changes had been in the air.

"Nice weather we're having," Sheryl said in an exceedingly chirpy voice.

"If you must know, I got the announcement about the new gym . . ."

"And you figure Donna, that perpetual cheerleader, has something big planned to honor Paul, which means you'll have to be there for it."

"Yeah, something like that." Kate's voice hardened. "And I refuse to be put through it."

"Hey! You just undid everything I've been trying to fix for the past half hour." Covering Kate's back with the sheet, she said, "Turn over. Let me work on that steel rod that passes for a neck."

Sitting behind Kate, Sheryl cradled her head with one hand and began slowly stroking the tendons in Kate's neck. She spoke softly. "Mike will be there for you. You know that. He won't let you face it alone."

"Your brother is never around long enough to buy milk. What makes you think he'll be here for the dedication?"

"He'll be there for you, and Paul, no matter when it is. When is it, anyway?"

"I didn't look." Kate winced as Sheryl found another tender spot.

"You haven't been doing those neck stretches I showed you."

"No, but I promise—"

"Promise you will. I've heard that before." Her fingers moved to Kate's temple. "Have you been in the shop lately?"

Kate shook her head slightly. "Now you're trying to give me a headache. Is that it?"

"Nope," Sheryl answered, all innocence. "I just wondered if you'd gotten in any pieces I'd be interested in. That's all."

"You're a terrible liar, Sherry."

"Okay, so maybe I wondered what you do with yourself all day, every day."

"I do enough. Can we change the subject?"

Sheryl stood and moved to Kate's right side. Uncovering her arm, she began working on her bicep. Kate opened her eyes and was struck anew at how physically different Sheryl and Mike were. They were like a photograph and its negative. Sheryl had inherited her mother's honey-colored hair and brown eyes, while Mike had his father's black Irish hair and clear, gray eyes.

Sheryl caught her looking and smiled. The smile was Mike's. "Did I tell you Matt is back for the winter?"

"Isn't he going back to school?"

Sheryl hesitated, turning her attention to Kate's forearm. "He's decided to take a semester off."

"Oh. How did he like Charleston?"

"Savannah."

"Sorry—Savannah. How did he like it?"

"Well, I think he enjoyed spending the summer with his dad, but he's glad to be home for a while. He's going to be doing some work for Mike."

"Hope I finally get to meet him. How old is he now?"

"Twenty this April."

Kate sighed. "I can't believe you have a son who's twenty years old. And I still can't believe I've never met him." Sheryl was only two years older than Kate. Where did the time go?

"Yeah, I feel like I'm in early retirement. I see all these other women waiting till they're in their thirties to have kids and I think I did the right thing. God, I'd hate to be raising a teenager in my fifties."

"Yes, you were lucky."

Sheryl stole a glance at Kate's face and knew it was time to move on to other topics. "Had enough?"

Kate raised one eyebrow in a perfect imitation of Vivien Leigh's Scarlett. "Isn't it funny how I come in here feeling like I've been in a fight, and leave feeling like I lost it?"

"Go home. Take a hot bath in some Epsom salts. The pain'll go away," Sheryl said with a smile as she left the room.

Kate stayed on the table for a few more seconds. As she pulled the sheet aside, she whispered, "The pain never goes away, Sheryl."

Not wanting to go home, and not wanting to deal with humanity in general, Kate wound her way through the tiny maze of one-way streets that made up Staunton. She drove past the turn for her house until she saw the entrance to Gypsy Hill Park, then turned into the gate. Slowly guiding the car past the duck pond, Kate was pleased to see only two other cars stopped along the edges of the park. She pulled into a space and turned off the engine. A little girl and her mother were feeding the ducks and geese at the far end of the pond. What seemed like hundreds of waterfowl packed themselves together near the fence, and the quacking was deafening as the little girl tried to keep up with the demand for more bread. Kate could see the look of delight on the child's face. She turned and walked the other way.

Gypsy Hill Park was situated on a long, thin strip of

land that had been bought by the city at the turn of the century. The thick carpet of red, yellow, and brown leaves that Kate sank into with every step attested to the fact that the founders had planned well. The cedars provided the only patches of dusky green at eye level, while the grass, where it was visible, was the brilliant shade that comes just before the first frost.

Hands in the pockets of her light jacket, Kate strolled past the municipal pool, emptied and covered. The tiny train that children rode in the summer, with its shrill whistle and chugging sounds, had been put in its shed, and the oval track had disappeared under a layer of leaves. Then she came to the Little League field.

Idly running her hand along the chain-link fence as she walked around it, Kate stopped when she reached the other side. The only stand of metal bleachers beckoned her and she sat. Four years ago Paul had donated the bleachers and an electric scoreboard, and her head filled with the sounds of hundreds of children pushing and shouting to get near Paul as the dedication took place. Her eyes, on the other hand, filled with tears. There was nowhere in Staunton she could go without a memory crowding aside any pleasure. She angrily swiped at her cheeks with the back of her hand and stood.

Damn baseball! She wanted to scream it at the top of her lungs. Baseball had taken away her husband in every sense. He'd never been around when she needed him. Always on the road. There had never been any permanence in their lives. They'd divided their time among three cities: Phoenix in the spring, San Francisco in the summer, Staunton in the winter. They were never in any of them long enough to really settle in. This wasn't something she'd considered in the beginning of their life together. And in the end, he'd died because of baseball. Paul would still be alive if spring training hadn't taken him to Phoenix. If he hadn't been friends with Mitch

Browder. If Mitch hadn't been into rock collecting. If, if, if . . .

Kate hated the game with all her soul. It was an active, festering boil of a hatred that seethed just below the surface of her every waking moment, whether she admitted it to herself or not. It was a primary focus in her life.

Walking quickly now, Kate made a beeline back to her car. She knew the bandstand was up ahead, its back to the duck pond. She didn't want to see it. Didn't want to deal with those memories, either. And so she dredged up bad ones. By the time she reached her house, bitterness was beginning to bore a hole into her skull. Kate couldn't wait to dam it with a couple, or twelve, aspirin.

CHAPTER

FIVE

Kate left the car parked in front of the house and went up the front steps. A piece of pink paper _____ tacked to one side of the door fluttered in the afternoon breeze. She didn't bother looking at it, but simply snatched it from its tiny anchor. In one fluid motion she had crumpled the flier, stuffed it in her handbag, put the key in the lock, and let herself in.

The house was so quiet she could actually hear the blood rushing through the veins in her head. As she got closer to the kitchen, another sound, more familiar and possibly more annoying, reached her ears. The faucet was dripping again. Dropping her purse on the table, Kate reached for the economy-sized bottle of aspirin she kept on a lazy Susan and shook out three tablets. She stared at the white pills in her palm, shrugged, and took one more from the bottle. The cupboard she kept the glasses in was empty. The dishwasher was full, and needed running.

"Shit."

Kate picked up a mug that had held coffee two days ago and made a face. Finally, out of desperation, she opened another cabinet and took out a glass measuring cup. Filling it with water from the tap, she swallowed the tablets, and then watched as the interval between drips grew shorter.

"Oh, I *really* need this," she said to herself, flinging open a drawer and pulling out a pair of pliers. She tightened down the faucet handle and the drops of water came to a stop. Satisfied with her handiwork, she tossed the pliers back in the drawer and went into the den. She found a Fred Astaire movie on television and curled up on the sofa.

The breeze blowing in from the open window had turned chilly and it woke her. The stiffness in her back brought an involuntary groan, a sound she never remembered making when she was younger. Like gray hairs and laugh lines that suddenly appeared in her midthirties, so these new noises came, too.

The telephone that sat on the end table jangled. It was an old rotary phone from the forties, and she always swore she could see it wiggle and dance as the bell rang. Her cartoon phone. When she picked up, there was no one on the other end. This was a regular occurrence. The C & P Telephone Company, which stood for Chesapeake and Potomac but which most residents called Cheapskate and Poky, also seemed to date back to the forties. Kate hung up and waited for it to ring again. And it did.

"Kate? It's Mike. Didn't you see my note?"

"What note?" She could tell by the silence that Mike had closed his eyes in annoyance, and she said, "I heard that."

"I left a note by your front door."

"Where?" She continued to bait him.

"On a pushpin right next to the door. It was on a pink flyer for the SPCA Thrift Shop."

"I guess I didn't realize it was something important. What did it say?"

He picked up her mood. His voice, a well-moderated

blend of East Coast inflection with just a touch of Virginia gentleman, took on a slight Irish lilt. Kate called it his leprechaun voice. "They're havin' their annual half-off sale this weekend."

"What are you talking about?"

She didn't seem to be amused. He must have misjudged her. "Never mind. The gist of the note is that Homer is over here visiting me."

She sighed. "I thought it was a little too quiet."

"He got through that hole in the fence again. I can fix it for you, if you want." There was no reply. "Or not. Do you want me to bring him over?"

"If you must."

"I'm afraid I must. Are you decent?"

She smiled at that. It was a very old joke between them. "Never. Come on over."

Kate was still sitting on the couch when the front door opened four minutes later. She heard Homer's toenails scrabble across the hardwood floor of the entry hall as he raced to the kitchen, and his food bowl. He never understood why it wasn't perpetually full.

Mike's voice reached her. "Kate? Where are you?"

"In here."

"Where?"

"Just follow the sound of my voice."

"My, we're in a good mood," Mike said, entering the den. He took in her rumpled shirt and puffy eyes. Her dark auburn hair, which usually hung in gleaming waves to her shoulders, had been pulled back in a barrette that now stuck out at an angle. Wisps of hair had escaped and formed odd cowlicks. "And you got all dolled up just for me. You really shouldn't have."

"Nice to see you, too." As she spoke the words, her hands went to the barrette and removed it. She ran her fingers through her hair. "I was taking a nap."

Mike leaned against the built-in bookcase and folded his arms across his chest. "Late dinner for two last night?"

Kate eyed him for a split second, then retorted, "Yeah, me and David Letterman."

"Y'know, if you actually went to sleep before two A.M. you wouldn't wake up feeling like crap every day."

"Don't start, Mike. And not that it's any of your business, but I do go to sleep before two A.M."

"Falling asleep on the couch with the TV on isn't what I'd call getting a good night's sleep."

Almost too weary to argue, Kate fixed him with a look that would crumble stone. "I don't need another mother, thanks. And how the hell do you know where I sleep?"

"I got in late last night. Saw the light."

"What is it with you Fitzgeralds? If you're going to lecture me like I'm a child, then you can go home now."

Not wanting to be banished, he unfolded his arms and held them up in surrender. "Hey, I'm sorry. Can we start over?"

Kate looked down at the carpet. "Yeah, sorry. It's been a bad day." Her head came up and she tried to smile. "I could use a cup of coffee. Want one?"

Mike angled his body into one of the kitchen chairs and, with his foot, pulled another chair toward him and propped his long legs on it. Homer, always glad for any company, sat at his side and let Mike scratch his head.

Kate measured coffee into the filter and then took the carafe to the sink. Forgetting the cold water tap was practically welded shut, she grunted when it wouldn't turn. Swearing under her breath, she set the pot down to free both hands. It still wouldn't budge and Mike, hiding a grin, asked, "Can I get that for you?"

"Thanks, but I can do it," she answered, removing the pliers from the drawer again.

He shook his head, but didn't say anything.

Once the coffee was perking, Kate realized she still hadn't started the dishwasher. Pulling two mugs out of the top rack, she began washing them.

"Are you sure this isn't too much trouble? We could always go to the Beverley."

Kate turned and gave him a warning look as she dried the mugs with a paper towel. All the dishcloths were in the dryer.

Setting a mug on the table next to him, she asked, "You take milk, right?"

He nodded and watched her open the refrigerator. She stood in front of it for what seemed a very long time, and Mike suddenly understood why. "Hey, I can drink it black if you're out."

"No!" Her voice wavered momentarily. "No, I must have something you can use."

Mike's legs slipped off the chair and he sat up. "It's okay. Really."

She had closed the door, and moved to the cupboards, her hands pushing aside cans and jars. Mike stood as she began frantically pawing through drawers. When her fingers closed around a small packet, she felt triumphant, until she saw it was a Wash'n Dri. Slamming it down on the counter, the tears finally came. Mike's hand on her shoulder made her flinch.

"Stop it, Kate. Forget it."

"I know I'll find something," she said between sobs.

"Katie, darlin', I can't stand to see you like this."

Her voice took on a hard edge. "Then go home, 'cause this is what I am now."

It took all the strength he had not to pull her to him. "I don't think you need to be alone."

"I think I know what I need."

"Christ, but you are pigheaded." He took a deep breath. "Do you really want me to go?" he asked, not wanting to hear her answer.

She nodded. "Yeah—go."

He stared at the back of her head before turning away.
He left the way he came. It took her a few moments to
realize she'd forgotten to thank him for bringing Homer
back. Picking up one of the two clean mugs, she flung it
across the room. It hit the stovetop, shattering. Homer
slunk out of the room, leaving her alone. It was what she
wanted, after all. Wasn't it?

CHAPTER

SIX

He had loved her—no, make that obsessed over her—for as long as he could remember. It was _____ their junior year. She had walked into their English class that first week of October—her family had just moved to the area—and she captured the heart of every male in the room.

The teacher introduces her as Kathleen Moran and asks her to tell the class a little about herself. With a tremendous amount of poise, she walks to the teacher's desk, puts down her purse and books, and speaks.

"Hi. I just moved here from Oklahoma but I was born in Pennsylvania. My father just retired from the army and we're in Staunton because he's going to be teaching at the military academy. This is the eighth school I've gone to, but so far it seems like the friendliest." She looks at the faces watching her and notices a familiar one. It is a girl named Chris who lives across the street from her. They have already spoken and so she focuses on her when she says, "I've lived in five states and one foreign country but I've never seen any place as pretty as Staunton. And, by the way, everyone calls me Kate."

Her smile encompasses the entire room. It is impossible not to smile back at her. The boys have seen all they need to know *about Kate Moran. Their minds are filled with ideas on how to make this auburn-haired beauty feel welcome. The girls' minds, however, are filled with other, less-than-charitable, ideas. And yet they find themselves smiling at her, too. Chris, Kate's first acquaintance, has already spread the word about this new-comer but nothing has prepared them for what she looks like. Chris's assessment of the situation had been, "You won't like her when you see her, but once you talk to her she's pretty cool."*

The teacher waits for the whispers to subside, then says, "Maybe you can tell us some of your interests."

Kate has already picked up her belongings from the teacher's desk and is walking toward an empty desk, when she tosses off, "Oh, I like rock music, reading, antiques. But I love baseball." She carefully slides her miniskirted body into the seat. All male eyes move their field of vision down a foot. "Especially the San Francisco Giants." Kate takes a pencil out of her purse, opens her spiral notebook and looks up at the teacher expectantly.

"Yes. Well. Thank you, Kate." He has to physically pull himself away from her dark blue eyes. "We're glad to have you here."

Paul Armstrong leans forward and taps Mike on the shoulder. The two have been best friends since the third grade, and Mike knows what Paul is going to say before the words are out of his mouth.

"I think I'm in love," Paul whispers. It is his standard remark, made in his usual offhand way. This time he means it.

"You and me both, bud. Think she can handle the Dynamic Duo?" comes Mike's conditioned response. He keeps his voice light, but his heart feels heavy. He really wants this one, but Kate Moran seems to be made for Paul. And they agreed a long time ago not to let a girl get in the way of their friendship.

What did they know at the age of sixteen? They were young and stupid. And in the end it didn't really matter anyway. Kate had come into the lives of Paul and Mike not knowing the rules, and when Paul Armstrong saw her that crisp October day, the rule book got tossed out the window.

Mike held a glass of J & B as he stared out the bay window in his bedroom. With all the leaves off the trees, he had a clear view of her house. The only light he could see came from the den. It seemed to be the only room she used anymore. His sister had told him that she hadn't slept in the bedroom she'd shared with Paul since his death. Kate kept her clothes there and used it as a rather large dressing room, but that was it.

There was a living room and dining room. Both were formal. Packed with antiques that Kate had collected throughout her travels with Paul, they reminded Mike of some of the historic homes he'd visited. Filled with beautiful furnishings, but never used, they seemed like stage settings waiting for the players to make their entrance and bring them to life. Paul and Kate used to give legendary parties. Now, no one entered those rooms.

She had two guest rooms on the second floor. They were at the back of the house and he guessed she slept in one of them, when she wasn't using the couch in the den. Like most Victorian houses, it had one very large bathroom on the second floor, and a very tiny WC on the main floor. And, finally, there was the little tower room. He'd been in it only once, when he and Paul had moved some old boxes of papers out of the den. It had been in the dead of winter and they could see their breath as they piled the five years' worth of tax paperwork in a corner. At the time it seemed that the room contained all the usual things people had in their attics . . . Christmas decorations, old clothing that no one wanted, a shelf covered with magazines and broken things that needed mending but no one ever got around to.

Mike brought the highball glass to his lips and sipped the scotch. The ice had melted. It tasted like warm medicine and he grimaced. Finishing it in one gulp, he turned from the window and went back downstairs to wait for Sheryl and his nephew, Matt. He hadn't seen the boy in nearly a year and he was looking forward to it. He had wanted to invite Kate over, too. That was, rather apparently, out of the question.

He was in the kitchen fixing himself another drink when he heard the front door slam and a shout. Smiling, Mike shouted back, "In the kitchen!"

A tall, well-built young man appeared in the doorway with an astonishingly similar smile on his face.

"Christ, did you get taller?"

Matt grinned. "No—I think you're shrinking."

Mike snorted as he put an arm around his nephew. "Where's your mom?" he asked, handing Matt a Coke. He motioned for him to sit at the table.

"She said to tell you she'd be here later."

"So." Mike sat across the table from Matt. "Judging from your stats, you had a pretty good season."

"Pretty good? I ended up hitting two-ninety and change with eighteen home runs. I only made three errors! I'd say that was damned good."

Mike smiled. His cockiness reminded him of Paul. "Like I said. Pretty good . . . for single A ball."

"Thanks for your support, Uncle Mike."

"So, is this it? Are you convinced this is what you want to do?"

Matt nodded emphatically.

"It's a hard life, Matt. There are a thousand other guys like you, all saying the same thing."

Matt's face took on a stubborn set. "There may be a thousand other guys out there saying it, but I'm gonna do it. I'll be one of the best second basemen in the majors some day. Count on it."

Mike rested his chin in his hand and stared at Matt for a moment before asking, "What does your dad think?"

"He's all for it."

Mike suspected as much. Since the divorce, if Sheryl said "black," Dan said "white." And Sheryl was pretty much saying "black" about Matt's baseball aspirations. Mike took a fence-straddling approach to the whole situation. The boy obviously had a talent for the game, but Mike also knew how tough it could be. He loved his nephew with all his heart. But more than that, he liked him.

Matt was a bright, hardworking, good-hearted kid. As a son, he was every mother's dream. As a young man, he was every daughter's fantasy—and every father's nightmare. He was a great-looking, self-assured jock with brains. Since his fourteenth birthday, Matt had had to beat the girls off with a bat. Sheryl was constantly amazed that the boy didn't take advantage of his obvious charms. She jokingly attributed this to his "excellent upbringing by a totally emancipated woman."

Matt interrupted Mike's thoughts, saying, "So, you're gonna talk to Mom about it, right? Make her understand it's real?"

"You're only four quarters away from your degree. Are you still planning on taking classes this winter?"

Matt nodded.

"Okay, I'll talk to her. But she's not the only one who wants you to finish school. Understand?"

"Yeah, but Paul Armstrong never finished school."

"And he always wished he had." Mike's voice took on a wistful tone. "I'd give anything for him to see you now."

"Are you two talking about Paul again?" Sheryl Fitzgerald Keller had let herself in the front door and heard their voices in the kitchen. Draping her purse over a chair, she opened the refrigerator and took out a bottle of Evian water. "You're gonna have to find another topic of conversation when Kate gets here. Where is she, anyway?"

"Not coming," Mike said, taking a large swallow of scotch.

"Why?"

"I never got around to asking her."

The subject was closed as far as Mike was concerned, but Sheryl persisted. "Well, why the hell not? We were just talking about her meeting Matt today."

"Let me put it this way. After she threw me out, it just didn't seem like the thing to do."

Sheryl's eyebrows went up a fraction of an inch before she went to the phone.

"Don't do it, Sheryl. She was in rare form today."

Matt was watching the two of them. He finally interrupted. "What's the story?"

Mike looked at Sheryl, then back at Matt.

"It's too long to get into right now. Just remember that when you *do* meet Kate, the subjects of Paul and baseball are off limits."

"Oh, man! That sucks! She must have some great stuff of his."

"Well, if she does, I've never seen it around the house. So forget it."

Matt was crestfallen. He'd envisioned long conversations about her part in Paul Armstrong's life. Wonderful stories about incredible plays. Gossip about all the players. A chance to see all his awards. Maybe she'd even watch a game tape with him.

He was about to enter another plea, when Mike cut him off. "I mean it, Matt. Not a word."

Sheryl had been listening quietly, a frown on her face. "You treat her like she's some delicate flower. It's been nearly three years, Mike. Someone needs to give her a swift kick in the ass. Bring her into the world again."

"Hey! Don't tell me how to deal with Kate. I know what she needs, and it isn't a kick in the ass."

Sheryl grinned. "Yeah, I know what she needs, too.

But I didn't want to say 'a piece of ass' in front of my young and impressionable son."

Matt groaned, while Mike exclaimed, "Sheryl, for God's sake!"

"Speaking of which, I saw *your* car parked outside Susan Lake's place a couple of weeks ago. About seven A.M."

"God, I hate small towns," Mike said in disgust.

"And speaking of getting laid, guess who asked me out today?"

Mike glanced at his nephew, who seemed to be taking the conversation in stride. "I can't."

"Randy 'God's-Gift-to-the-Maidens-of-Staunton' Shifflett."

"I hope you had the good sense to turn him down."

"Who's Randy Shifflett?" Matt asked, perceiving the beginning of a good story.

Ignoring her son's question, Sheryl said, "Hey, those two car dealerships make him some good money. So he takes me out to a fancy place for dinner. What's wrong with that?"

"He's a piece of slime, that's what's wrong with that," Mike said.

"Who's Randy Shifflett?" Matt persisted.

Mike turned to his nephew. "I just told you. He's a piece of slime."

"Come on, Uncle Mike . . ."

Sheryl was laughing now. "Hey, Mike? Remember the time you and Paul pantsed him at my birthday party?"

Matt grinned. He knew he was about to be rewarded, but was disappointed when his mother picked up the phone instead. "Hey! I wanted to hear this."

"In a minute . . ." Sheryl punched in Kate's phone number as Mike glared at her.

"I can guarantee she's not going to answer," he stated.

CHAPTER

SEVEN

K ate sank deeper into the warm, sudsy water, ignoring the ringing telephone. A plastic bath _____ pillow cradled her head and a damp washcloth covered her eyes. Raising an arm heavy with water and the effects of approximately one quarter of a bottle of 1991 Vouvray, she blindly groped along the windowsill, searching for the glass. Kate's slippery fingers closed around the stem, but the glass popped through them like a peeled grape and landed in the water with a soft splash.

"Crap."

She sat up. Letting the cloth fall onto her stomach, Kate reached across the long expanse of the tub and made several failed attempts to grasp the glass. The bathtub was big enough to do water aerobics in; big enough for her and Paul to stretch out in; big enough to make love in. Now, the claw-footed behemoth was only big.

The phone stopped ringing just as she held up the glass in triumph. "And on her fourth attempt, Kate Armstrong shoots and scores!"

Kate wiped the glass off with a nearby towel, refilled it, and drank deeply. A shiver sent her free hand to the hot water handle. As the scalding water mixed with the tepid, a warm river flowed between her thighs, surrounding her like the afterglow of an orgasm. Kate sank back into the water until it covered her shoulders. The only sound was an occasional tapping from the radiator.

She hears a tapping noise at her bedroom window and looks up from her English homework. The only light in her room comes from the study lamp. The shades are pulled down and she can see the silhouette of the dogwood tree's branches whipping back and forth in the wind. Kate turns back to her essay but finds she can't get too excited about comparing the styles of Hemingway and Steinbeck at the moment. She's managed to write two paragraphs on the subject. The rest of the page is filled with doodles. She has written Paul's name in all its variations. Hearts filled with P.A. + K.M. appear in each corner. She's even tried "Katie Armstrong" and "Kate Moran Armstrong" and "Paul and Kathleen Armstrong."

Is she at the Friday-night dance like everyone else? No. She's stuck in her room doing homework. Grounded for the weekend for the first time ever. And just because she'd come home from a date with Paul a lousy forty-five minutes after curfew. The argument with her father had been short and to the point.

"Do you know what time it is?" Jim Moran stood at the foot of the stairs, arms crossed.

"I take it it's after eleven," she'd answered, just a little too smartly.

"It's eleven forty-five."

"God, Dad. I'm seventeen years old!"

"Right. That means you're old enough to tell time."

She probably could've gotten away with it, but she took it that extra mile.

"Well, why don't you requisition a walkie-talkie? That way you can give me a five-minute warning."

From his porch, Mike watched Matt and Sheryl drive away. He slowly sank onto the small cedar glider and looked out at the clear night sky. Out of the corner of his eye, he saw one of the neighbor's kids leaning out of a window. He heard whispered voices and a giggle. Mike smiled ruefully as he closed his eyes, letting the memory come.

He taps at her window more insistently. When the shade rolls up, Kate jumps and clutches at her heart. Mike peers in at her, smiling. He gives a little wave and motions for her to open the window.

"God, Mike! You scared the hell out of me! What are you doing?"

"I'm your chauffeur to the dance."

"What are you talking about? You know I'm grounded," Kate whispers. *"And keep your voice down."*

Mike grins. "I also happen to know your mom and dad are going out tonight."

Suddenly, there is a knock on the door, spinning Kate around. Her mother's voice says, "Kate? We're leaving now."

The doorknob turns.

Kate blanches and hisses at Mike, "Get down!"

The door opens and Mary Moran finds her daughter sitting at her desk, pencil in hand. "We're leaving," she repeats. "I don't know how late we'll be. You know what happens when your dad gets together with his Army buddies."

Kate steals a glance toward the window, then smiles at her mother. "Don't tell me it's already been a month since the last Retarded Colonel's Club meeting?"

Kate's mother chuckles at the pun. "Don't you ever let your father hear you say that."

"You're the one who came up with it."

"And I'll deny it."

Kate thinks she'll give it one more shot, and she asks, "Mom, couldn't I just go to the dance for a couple of hours? I promise I'll be home by nine-thirty. And I'll stay in the rest of the weekend."

Her father appears in the doorway. He is slipping into his jacket. "Not on your life," he states.

Kate's mother shrugs.

"Well," Kate says. "It was worth a try."

"That's true, Katie. Never stop trying." He smiles, taking his wife's arm.

Kate waits until she hears the car start before turning back to the window. Mike pops back into view. "Put on your red dress, mama, 'cause we're goin' out tonight."

"You're crazy."

"Look, Kate. You wanna go to the dance, or not?"

"Well, yeah," Kate replies warily.

"So hurry up and get dressed. I'm taking you."

Twenty minutes later Kate sits in the passenger seat of Mike's '67 Mustang.

"If I get caught, I'll be grounded for life. You realize that, don't you?"

"Stop worrying." They are stopped at a light. "By the way, you look great in that dress." He says it casually, trying to keep his eyes off the shapely expanse of Kate's thighs.

"Thanks, I hope Paul likes it."

Mike's jaw tightens and he pulls into traffic a little too quickly.

"Aren't we going to pick him up?" Kate asks, as Mike drives past the turn to Paul's house.

"He's at the dance. He doesn't know I'm bringing you. It's my little surprise."

"Oh, Mike! What a sweet thing to do!"

He feels himself grow hot and is thankful the car is dark. "Yeah, well, I got sick of watching him moon around all afternoon."

They turn into the parking lot of the school and Mike shuts off the engine. He turns to Kate. "Well, here we are."

"Where's your date?"

"I wasn't planning on coming so I didn't ask anyone."

"You're coming in, aren't you?"

He nods. It's difficult, but he manages to say, "You'll save a dance for me, right?"

Kate leans over and kisses him on the cheek. He's never been this close to her. It's torture.

"Of course I will," she answers, smiling into his eyes. *"You're the best friend I've ever had."*

Mike had been asleep for approximately half an hour when Kate called to apologize.

His voice rough with sleep, he said, "It's okay, Kate. I understand."

"No. It's not okay, Mike. I don't know why I act this way."

"Get some sleep, Katie. If you're up before ten tomorrow, I'll take you out for breakfast. I want to talk to you about your house."

"Mike?"

"Yeah?"

"You're the best friend I've ever had. You know that, don't you?"

"See you tomorrow, Kate."

He gently let the receiver drop into its cradle. On his back, in the dark, he brought his forearm above his head and closed his eyes. Somewhere in the recesses of his mind he could hear the first bass notes of a Temptations' song. He drifted back to sleep dancing with a seventeen-year-old Kate in his arms, the refrain of "My Girl" echoing through his head.

CHAPTER

EIGHT

K ate knocked on the back door, then let herself into the small mud porch that in turn led to the _____ kitchen. "Do I remember right? Did you ask me out to breakfast?"

Mike sat back from the table and put down the newspaper. "You do, and I did."

"Oh, good," she said in mock relief. "I was afraid I'd dreamed it. Do I smell coffee?"

As he poured her a cup, Mike asked, "How are you feeling this morning?"

She cupped her hands around the warm mug and with a touch of irony said, "I can't be sure, not ever having experienced the feeling, but I think I'm a little hungover."

Mike chuckled. "Yeah, that must've been someone who looked a lot like you whose head I held while she lost her cookies at the side of the road. Several times."

"God, weren't we stupid?"

"That we were," he said, turning to the oven. "Take your coat off and stay awhile."

"I thought you were taking me out to eat."

"You're out and you're about to eat."

"I see," Kate said with a smile. She sat at the table and pushed the paper aside. Mike set a plate in front of her.

"Eggs Benedict! Jesus, Mike . . ." Kate put a forkful in her mouth and closed her eyes in bliss. "This is delicious. You're gonna make some woman a terrific wife."

"Having utterly failed at being a husband," Mike stated, joining her.

"Allison wasn't good enough for you." Kate grinned. "What about that artist you were seeing? What was her name? Eleanor something-or-other . . ."

"Pleasant."

"Yes, she seemed nice."

"No. Pleasant was her last name."

Kate thoughtfully chewed a bite of English muffin. "What happened?"

"She moved to Charleston. We still talk." Trying to steer the conversation in another direction, he asked, "More coffee?"

"Just talk?" Kate kept on.

"If business throws us together we do more than talk. Okay?"

"I'm sure Sheryl said you were practically engaged," Kate mused.

"Sheryl talks too much. Besides, I didn't ask you over here to discuss my personal life, as fascinating as it may be."

"Sorry. What *did* you want to talk about? I've forgotten."

"Your house, Kate. It's falling apart around you. I'm sure you've noticed."

"I have. Reminds me a lot of me." She grinned.

"Not funny," Mike said, although he tended to agree with her. "Some morning you're going to wake up with the sun in your eyes, and it won't be coming through the window."

Kate sipped her coffee, then said, "I can't keep up with it, Mike."

"Do you plan on staying there?"

"Where else would I go? I can't sell it."

"Why?" He looked at her hard.

Her eyes shifted to a point somewhere over his shoulder. "Well, I just can't. That's all."

Mike knew enough to leave that one alone. "Look, Kate. Winter's coming and the damage is just going to get worse. I'm about to make you an offer you can't refuse."

Her eyes found his again. "What's that?"

"I'll do the work for you. No charge. I'm going to be here for a couple of months and I've got Matt to help me. It's a crime to let that place go the way you have. What do you say?"

"I say, what's the catch?"

"No catch. I'll go over the whole place. Do an evaluation. We'll do the worst first."

Kate chewed her bottom lip for a moment. "I can't let you do all that for nothing. You know that. And I repeat, what's the catch?"

Mike took a deep breath and pretended to think. "Okay, how's this? I need some help cataloging the furnishings at Cobble Hill. They're doing a major restoration, which means stripping the house and storing everything."

Without hesitation, Kate said, "I can't."

"Oh, I think you can. It's just a question of whether you will or won't." Mike watched her face take on that familiar stubborn set.

"Is this some plan that you and Sheryl cooked up? Get Kate back on her feet?"

"Well, I see it as a barter, plain and simple. I can really use your expertise. I can't help the way you choose to look at it."

She was wrestling with it. *Good*, Mike thought. *A small guilt trip can't hurt the cause.*

Kate finally said, "I'll think about it, okay?"

He nodded.

"I'll let you know in a couple of days."

"Fine." Mike stood. "Did you have enough to eat?"

Kate handed him her plate. "Yes, thanks. It was wonderful."

Mike set the dishes in the sink and, with his back to her, asked, "Do you have a couple of minutes?"

"Sure."

"Good. I wanted to show you the bedroom. It's finally finished and I think there's a piece in there you'll really appreciate."

Mike had bought the gray-stuccoed Craftsman home three years ago. He'd paid next to nothing for the 1910 gem. Aside from a bad roof and years of neglect, it had survived the whims of renovation. All the interior woodwork was original and unpainted. The built-in sideboard in the dining room, the inglenook with its bench seat, the tiles around the fireplaces in the living room and master bedroom—all had been left untouched.

Mike had replicated the original forest-green roof and painted the exterior trim the same color. The covered front porch that ran the width of the house also had the same sloped green roof and a gabled entry. The stucco had cracked along the face of the porch and Mike had done the patch work himself. And then he'd tackled the interior. It had taken him nearly two years to finish it to his satisfaction. Furnishing it came next. Gustav Stickley, one of the founders of the American Arts and Crafts movement, could have walked into Mike's house and felt at home. It was *that* authentic.

Kate followed him down the hallway and up the stairs, saying, "Don't tell me you finally found that Stickley wardrobe you'd been hunting for?"

"Better." He stood aside to let her enter.

"Better? How is that possible?"

He pushed the light switch and listened to her intake of breath. She quickly walked to a medium-sized oak wardrobe and ran her fingers along the inlay.

"A Crafters?" She bent down to inspect the brass

handles. "God, it's beautiful." Then she looked around the room, her eyes stopping to caress each piece of mission-style furniture.

Kate was enthralled by the bedroom. She'd been in it only one other time, when he'd first moved in, and she was stunned by the transformation. Kate walked the perimeter of the room, her hand lovingly stroking each piece, her eyes soothed by the warm light that reflected off the honey-colored furniture.

"Mike," she said in hushed tones. "It's perfect."

"Almost," he said, watching her.

She continued her exploration and, almost as an afterthought, asked, "Almost? What else could you possibly need?"

His heart beat faster, and he nearly told her then, but she looked over at him and smiled and he knew he couldn't do it.

"It's perfect," she repeated.

"Glad you like it."

Kate sat on the bed and leaned back on her arms, letting her feet dangle above the simple design of the small wool rug. "If I lived here, I'd never leave this room."

The room suddenly got warmer and Mike propelled himself away from the wall he'd been leaning against. "I've got a spot I'm trying to fill in the den. Care to give me your opinion?"

"Sure." Kate hopped off the bed. "Lead the way, bwana."

"Y'know," Mike was saying as they walked down the staircase, "I ran into Cindy a couple of weeks ago. She said the shop is doing pretty well."

"Amazing, isn't it? I don't remember the last time I was in there."

"Funny, she said exactly the same thing." They had entered the room Mike used as his study. "Have you become the silent partner?"

"No comment."

On her thirtieth birthday, Kate's love of antiques and innate sense of style finally came together.

"Rise and shine, birthday girl," Paul whispers in her ear.

She mumbles something and burrows deeper under the comforter.

"Come on, you lazy woman."

"What time is it?"

"Time to get up." He rips the covers off the bed, exposing a naked Kate to the brilliant October day.

She groans and covers her face with her hand. "Have a heart, Paul. I was up till three."

He stands next to the bed. "So was I."

"But you didn't drink a whole bottle of champagne by yourself." She squints through her fingers at him. "And you're still mad, aren't you."

"I guess I didn't know they were holding auditions for the Solid Gold Dancers right here on Frazier Street."

Kate groans, remembering the spectacle she'd made of herself at her birthday party. "Why didn't you stop me?"

"You were a full three sheets to the wind. There wasn't much I could do."

"I'm sorry," she says. "I didn't mean to embarrass you."

He finally sits next to her. Runs a hand down her thigh. "I've gotta admit, it was pretty sexy."

She savors the feel of his fingers on her skin. "I did it for you," she whispers.

"Well." He bends to kiss her shoulder. "I just wish you'd saved it for later. Good thing I got to you just as you were taking off your jacket."

"Thank God for that," she mutters. The velvet bolero she'd worn not only covered the lacy, sleeveless bodysuit with the low-cut back. It also covered her spine.

"You don't need to be ashamed of it, Kate." Paul lifts her hair and places his lips on the nape of her neck. "It's what

makes you real." His finger slowly traces the scar that runs, like a pale zipper, down the length of her back.

The scar has been a part of her existence since she was twelve years old, and she hates it. It was a product of surgery to correct a curvature of the spine. After the operation, she'd had to live in a body cast for nearly a year. She'd been subjected to ferocious teasing because of it. The only good thing about it, as far as Kate was concerned, was her perfect posture. Other than that, the scar meant nothing but humiliation. But Paul sees what she refuses to see—that it has made her strong.

"I just don't want the whole world to know about it. Is that all right with you?" She's turned over, only to get caught in the gaze of his hazel eyes.

He smiles. "Your secret's safe with me. And if you don't get up right now and get dressed, you won't get your present until tomorrow."

"Why tomorrow?"

" 'Cause that's when I'll be done making love to you."

"Is that a threat?" Her hand travels up his hard thigh until she can feel the start of his erection through his jeans. "Or a promise?"

Some twenty minutes later, as Kate lies listening to the slowing of her husband's heartbeat, she hears voices and the slamming of a car door outside. She's forgotten that Mike and his current girlfriend have stayed the night, not wanting to drive back to Richmond after the party. All Kate wants to do is spend the day in bed with Paul, a rare occurrence these days. "Shit," she murmurs under her breath.

"Not your usual reaction." Paul slowly lifts himself away from her. "By the way, Mike's already up."

Kate closes her eyes in embarrassment. "I can't face him."

"He took it pretty well," Paul says, yawning. "It's Sandra, or Susan, or whatever her name is, that seemed a little bent out of shape. But what can you expect from a theology professor?"

Kate reaches for Paul's arm. "I thought you were going to make love to me until tomorrow." But he's already pulling on his underwear.

"*Don't you think you'd better say bye to Mike?*"

Kate slowly sits up, her head pounding, and wonders how much time will pass before the next time she and Paul make love. "Can't we just stay in here until they leave? This was so nice . . ."

His back to her, he zips up his pants. "What about your birthday present?"

She could say, "All I want is the old Paul back," but realizes she doesn't know who that might be. And so she says, "Tell him I'll be down in a few minutes."

An hour after Mike and Sharon drive away, Kate sits in her car, one of Paul's ties covering her eyes in a makeshift blindfold. As Paul opens the door for her, she says, "I can't believe you're putting me through this with the massive hangover I've got."

"I think you'll find it was worth it," Paul answers, taking her arm and helping her out of the car. He places something in her hand. It feels like a key. "Ready?"

She nods, and he removes the blindfold.

They stand in front of a two-story town house on Frederick Street. The simple Victorian building has recently been painted a pale seafoam green with white trim. The realty sign has a SOLD *sticker slapped across it. A painted wooden sign hangs from the porch. It reads:* Remember the Time.

She doesn't know what to make of this and turns to Paul, a question in her eyes.

"You're now a member of the Staunton business community." He faces her and puts his arms around her waist. "Happy birthday, baby," he says, kissing her.

The shop had done well. Well enough for her to hire full-time help during the baseball season, when she and Paul lived in San Francisco. Well enough for Cindy Peters, Kate's assistant, to buy into the business and become Kate's partner. And well enough for Cindy to hire part-time help, because Kate rarely showed up after Paul's death.

But it had never felt like hers.

Kate's dream of owning an antique shop had come true without her having to lift a finger, and she'd resented the hell out of Paul for that. He'd found the building, bought it, picked the interior and exterior colors. He'd had all the renovations done. He'd said, "All you have to do is fill it up with stuff to sell."

She'd felt like a child whose school project had been usurped by well-meaning parents; as if they were the ones being graded. Paul had taken her dream out of her hands, made it reality, and in so doing, had taken away all the joy it should have brought. She had felt no sense of achievement. It was just another gift from Paul that wasn't really hers to keep. Another bribe to placate her. As if the shop could ever make up for his infidelity.

But she'd smiled at him. Pretended she was thrilled. It wouldn't have done any good to do otherwise.

It seemed she had nothing that was her very own. Except that damned scar.

Now she watched as Mike spread his arms and indicated a five-foot space of empty wall in his study. "When I mentioned to Cindy that I was looking for a small sideboard, she said she'd try and locate one for me. I want to put it here."

"Does it have to be a sideboard? I mean, couldn't you use a small bookcase more?" She eyed the stacks of books pushed against the wall, some of them three feet tall.

"But I've got this lamp I really want to use." Mike walked to a cabinet and bent to open the bottom door. "And I don't think it'll fit on a bookcase." He pulled out a copper lamp base and set it on the floor while he continued searching for the shade. "What do you think?"

Kate didn't reply. She was suddenly, inexplicably fascinated by the jeans he wore. Well-worn, they looked as soft as chamois. They fit him loosely, but when he bent over they became a second skin.

Mike located the mica shade and attached it to the base. "Kate?" He looked over his shoulder.

"Huh?" Kate's eyes lifted. "I'm sorry, Mike. What did you say?"

"Do you think it'll fit?"

She thought it over for a moment. "Oh! You mean the lamp?"

"What else would I mean?"

Kate smiled and shook her head. "Nothing. Yes, I think it'll fit." She paused. "Did anyone ever tell you you have a very nice ass?"

Stunned, Mike sat back.

Kate grinned. "Don't tell me you're blushing?"

A beat passed, and then Mike said, "As long as I've known you I'm constantly amazed by the fact that you never engage your brain before you open your mouth."

"I was just making an observation."

"How am I supposed to take that observation?"

"It was a compliment. What did you think it was? A come-on?" She laughed, and wondered herself why she'd said it. "Just say 'thank you.' "

"Gee, thanks, Katie," Mike said, standing. "Means a lot coming from you."

"I can't believe no one in that harem you've had has ever told you that before."

"Not that it's any of your business."

They walked out of the house together. Mike accompanied her to the street, where she thanked him again and continued toward her own house. She slowed down and then stopped in the middle of the street. Turning, she said, "I've decided."

He waited to find out what she was talking about. With Kate, it could be anything.

"About the house, I mean. I want you to do it for me."

He knew better than to show his elation and, so, in a businesslike tone said, "Good. I'll come by tomorrow morning and we can see what needs to be done."

She turned and raised her arm in a wave.

CHAPTER

NINE

K ate entered the house and fought down a feeling of panic. She shouldn't have said yes to Mike. _____ She should have pretended to think it over, as she'd originally planned, and then told him no. She didn't know what had come over her. Now it was too late. She'd committed herself.

What was today? She checked the calendar with its color-coded dots that ordered her life. Red meant call Cindy at the shop. Blue was garbage day. Green was the day Homer got his heartworm pill. Yellow told her that the Orkin man was coming for the monthly spraying. On and on they went. A Technicolor march of time in a gray life.

Her finger landed on Thursday, with its black dot.

With the last of the weeds pulled, Kate sat back on her heels and brushed off her hands. There had only been a few this time, and she dropped them into the paper bag she'd brought with her. The yellow lilies she'd placed in the urns last month were unrecognizable and she pushed them into the bag as well. Reaching into the basket she always brought, Kate took out the plastic gallon jug of water and emptied it into the urns.

Her stop at the florist shop this morning had yielded two dozen strawflowers and two large stems of sea holly. They followed the water into the vases. Finally, with a sponge she'd dampened with a little of the water, she wiped off the smooth granite stone. As always, she silently read the few words engraved on it.

Paul Allen Armstrong, Jr.
Born—June 6, 1959 Died—March 11, 1994

Died March 11, 1994. The words circled in her mind, an endless tape loop of bad dreams and rainy days. Tragedy. The cemetery was her cathedral and the gravestone her confessional.

Kate sat against the giant beech. It was the only tree whose leaves still clung to its branches. She gazed across the gentle hills of Thornrose Cemetery. Sunlight glinted off marble and granite. She was alone. Closing her eyes, she began talking, always with the same six words.

"Baby, I miss you so much . . ." Today she intoned them like well-rehearsed dialogue. She knew her lines inside and out, but after countless performances they'd begun to lose their meaning for her. Instead of the heartfelt plea they'd been, they'd become just words.

"Baby, I miss you so much," she repeated, trying to recapture the anguish she'd felt that first year of his death. "I had some really bad days this month . . ."

As Kate "spoke" to Paul, she tried to conjure up an image of his face. It got harder all the time, frightening her. But, finally, there it was. Clear, hazel eyes peering out from under an impossibly thick fringe of golden lashes. Even in his twenties, his eyes crinkled at the corners when he laughed. In the summer, his light brown hair and eyebrows became gilded by the sun. He'd always kept his hair short, but not cropped. He'd had to contend with a slight wave in it all his life. His ears lay flat against his head, showing off the strong lines of his jaw. His mouth had a perpetually amused lift to it. His lips were remarkably sensuous. When he smiled, he revealed teeth that were the product of thousands of dollars' worth of orthodontia. His smile also revealed the dimple on the right side of his cheek.

She could see it all now, and she smiled back at the portrait that her mind allowed her to view.

"Hey, Katie! Look at this!"

She follows his voice into the living room of the hotel suite where the Giants have put them up. He has pulled the heavy curtains to reveal a sparkling view of San Francisco Bay, the twin red towers of the Golden Gate Bridge just visible above the buildings that surround the Embarcadero. Draping his arm over her shoulder, he points out Alcatraz Island to her.

She smiles at his excitement. "Where is it?"

"South of here," he answers, knowing she means Candlestick Park. "God! Can you believe we're really here?"

"I'm not surprised," she says, putting her arms around his waist. "You're a great ballplayer. Anyone can see that."

Paul has gone from single A ball to triple A ball to the majors in two seasons. He is a phenomenon that has made the Giants' scouting staff look like geniuses, and the Giants' owner wet his pants. At the tender age of twenty-two he is the Giants' starting second baseman.

Everything comes easy to Paul Armstrong. Not that he doesn't appreciate it. He does. But he's also come to expect it.

Raised in an upper-middle-class home, with a father, mother, and sister who have always looked on him as their All-American Golden Boy, he can do no wrong.

Paul Allen Armstrong, Sr., made his money through hard work and good business sense. The small sporting goods store he'd started has turned into a small empire that stretches across Virginia and Maryland. Paul had worked in the Staunton shop since the age of twelve. His parents supported his baseball habit that began in Little League. When coaches started telling his father the boy had real talent, he focused all his energy on helping his son, and the boy had come through.

He had the satisfaction of seeing his son conquer high school ball and, on the basis of excellent grades and incredible ability, win a scholarship to James Madison University. Paul was drafted by the San Francisco Giants in his first year.

Women hovered around Paul like hummingbirds around an irresistibly bright flower. He'd chosen Kate for her independence, her wit, her beauty, and her love of baseball. His personal life-plan, which he'd explained to Kate more than once, called for a major league career, a wife that would be the envy of every man, and a couple of kids, one of which would hopefully be Paul Allen Armstrong III.

Now, as he stands at the window of the hotel, she knows he sees it all falling into place. Turning his head, he places his lips against Kate's ear. "Let's make a baby."

Kate buries her face in his neck, suddenly shy. They've been married only a few months and their lovemaking still seems like a forbidden pleasure, after all the years of holding back.

He gently pushes her away and kisses the corner of her mouth. "C'mon, Katie," he whispers. "Let's do it."

Kate opened her eyes and shivered. The sky had become streaky with clouds. While she'd daydreamed, the Indian summer had crept away on tiptoe, leaving behind the sharp breath of winter. The change was in the air she took into her lungs, and it frightened her.

It had happened slowly, this fear of change. So slowly she hadn't been aware of it. It began in the fourth year of their marriage, when she'd say things to Paul like, "I don't want to try that new restaurant. Can't we just go home?" Or she'd make excuses not to meet a new team wife. When the team fired one of the coaches she had been more upset about it than Paul. That had been the year they'd bought a very expensive, very luxurious con-

dominium with a panoramic view of San Francisco and
the Bay.

It wasn't Kate's idea. She didn't mind the apartment
they rented for the season. They occupied the top floor
of an Italianate row house on Bush Street. The landlords,
an unobtrusive gay couple who lived below them, always
held the rooms for them at the beginning of the season.
Kate loved the house, dressed in slate blue with white
and cinnamon trim. She loved being able to walk out the
door and catch the electric streetcar to all her favorite
junk shops. Far from home, she really loved the sense of
stability the neighborhood gave her.

But Paul was a star, making money they couldn't have
imagined the first couple of years they were married.
One afternoon, on an off day, he'd driven her downtown
on the pretext of sightseeing near the wharf. They'd
ended up in front of a towering glass and steel mon-
strosity called the Pier 51 Towers.

"Why are we stopping here?" Kate asks.

*"The Breedens bought one of these and they invited us up to
see it," he replies, walking her to the entry.*

*A doorman dressed in a maroon jacket and matching cap
opens the heavy glass door for them. The lobby is all marble
and brass. Two of the biggest ficus trees she's ever seen flank the
elevators.*

*"Pretty fancy," she whispers, as the elevator doors silently
slide open. What she is thinking is,* Pretty pretentious.

*They enter the glass box that takes them to the thirty-fourth
floor while giving them a view of the harbor. Paul and Kate
don't speak during the short ride.*

*Sue and Jimmy Breeden greet them at the door, eager to give
them the grand tour of their new home away from home.
Secretly hoping this won't take long, Kate makes all the appropriate admiring noises. She loathes the cold feeling the glass and
marble and granite give her. The kitchen reminds her of an*

operating room, with its stainless steel sterility. Yes, the view is spectacular, but can a person really live here?

As the door closes behind them, Paul asks, "So, what do you think?"

She shrugs. "It's all right for some people, but it's not me."

"You didn't like it?"

The expression on his face gives her the first warning sign.

"No. I didn't. Did you?" They stand in the middle of the echoing hallway. Kate turns to face Paul. "Did you?" she repeats.

"Yeah, I did. A lot."

"Really?"

He tries a different tack. "Look, Kate. I think it's time for us to buy some property."

"And you think this is where you'd like to live?" She is incredulous.

"Let's go have lunch and talk about it."

Sitting in one of the many seafood restaurants along the wharf, they have their first real argument as husband and wife. In the end, tired and angry, Kate gives in when Paul says, "It's my money and I say we buy it."

They had moved in three weeks later.

That had been a bad year for Kate. She'd blamed it on the condo. It didn't feel right. It wasn't "home." She remembered how she'd yearned for the familiarity of Staunton. And of Mike. His phone calls always seemed to come at the moment she was at her lowest. But her calls to him were only made when she felt really good. It would have been too humiliating to complain about her life. Even to Mike.

She had to mask something she was growing more afraid of as the years went by: that she had made a mistake in marrying Paul. The niggling thought that maybe they weren't the perfect couple bored into her brain like a small worm that had found its way into an apple. It couldn't be seen from the outside, but the damage was done.

Feeling displaced made her cling to Paul, because he was the only stability she could find, and Kate slowly gave her life over to him. She unconsciously began relying on him for everything. It made her feel safe, this perfect world filled only with Paul and his career. *His* condo. *His* house. *His* friends. Even the puppy he bought for her became his. And truth be told, it was the way Kate had wanted—needed—it.

Nineteen eighty-four was the year her father retired for the second time and her parents moved to Arizona. It was the year Paul's father died, and Paul's mother moved to Charlottesville, leaving them the house in Staunton. It was the year Kate discovered she couldn't have children. And if all that hadn't been bad enough, it was the year Paul started lying to her. She didn't discover that until later. But once she had, a small part of the old Kate resurfaced. The Kate whose strength had diminished began speaking out a little more with each of Paul's deceptions, until the time came that she presented an ultimatum. A few months later, Paul was gone, and that old Kate disappeared again.

Since his death, every day was an unknown. She began stripping her life of everything that could possibly upset her balance, until she'd ended up with the bare bones of an existence. Her calendar ran her life. And now, the thought of fixing the house, with all its upheavals—with Mike and Matt storming the castle walls—scared the hell out of her.

Kate left the cemetery unnerved because her visit with Paul hadn't calmed her. It always had before.

RENOVATION

CHAPTER

TEN

Kate sat at the kitchen table paging through a catalog. She could hear Mike's footsteps above her, _____ as he moved around the guest room checking it with his usual thoroughness. He'd already been there an hour and still wasn't finished with the top floor. Sighing, she raised her eyes to the ceiling and nervously tapped her fingernails on the mug of coffee that had now grown cold.

A few minutes later, notebook in hand, Mike entered the kitchen. "I'm going up on the roof now. I want to check it before it starts raining."

Kate glanced out the window. The sky was a threatening deep gray. She didn't like the idea of Mike on the steeply sloping roof, even on a good day. "Be careful, please."

He grinned. "Worried about my very nice ass?"

"No. Mine," she said. "If you fall off, I'm the one your family will sue."

"Oh, well, wouldn't want anything to happen to *your* very nice ass," he said, walking past her and out the back door.

Kate stood and walked to the sink to pour out the coffee. She watched Mike stride across the backyard toward the garage. The wind had picked up and the heavy flannel shirt he wore unbuttoned over his T-shirt billowed behind him. He disappeared into the small building and came out a few seconds later carrying a ladder. Homer had joined him, trotting by his side, and then they both vanished around the side of the house.

With another sigh, Kate turned and leaned against the counter. With Mike popping in and out she was unable to concentrate on the book she'd begun reading the night before. She didn't feel right about just sitting in front of the television like a sofa spud while Mike was working. Desperate for something to do, she decided to cook.

Kate's culinary skills ranked somewhere just above high school home ec class. She had only two "specialties." One was a killer spaghetti and meatballs recipe she'd cajoled from her aunt. The other was corned beef and cabbage. Even Kate couldn't screw those up. She heavily supported the local restaurants, and her freezer was stocked with every imaginable prepackaged frozen-food product.

Since she didn't have any corned beef on hand, she pulled a package of hamburger out of the freezer. Setting the microwave on defrost, Kate gathered the rest of the supplies she needed for the spaghetti sauce. Then, putting a cassette tape into the boom box she kept in the kitchen, Kate went about her task to the sounds of Bruce Hornsby.

"Smells good."

She hadn't heard him come in and his voice startled her. Kate turned from the pot she was stirring. Mike stood in the doorway, mopping his face with the tail of his shirt.

"You're wet," she said unnecessarily.

"Happens when it rains."

Kate handed him a kitchen towel and for the first time noticed the smell of wet earth coming through the open window.

As he dried off his hair, Mike said, "Is that Kate's famous spaghetti sauce?"

She went back to the stove. "It's the only thing I'm famous for."

"I wouldn't say that."

He was behind her, peering over her shoulder. Kate brought up the wooden spoon, blew on the thick sauce, and offered Mike a taste. He was so close she could detect the faint aroma of the sandalwood shaving soap he used.

"Ummm. Good stuff."

"There's plenty. Want to have dinner?" she asked, before she could think about it.

His eyes widened slightly. "I'd like that." And knowing Kate's weakness for good wines, he added, "I have a couple of bottles of a really nice Chianti a client gave me."

Kate nodded, suddenly ill at ease.

Mike noticed, and quickly said, "Well, I'll get back to work. I need to check the attic. I'll finish up outside when it quits raining."

"The attic?"

"The attic, the tower. I need to check for leaks."

"No!" She realized she'd said it a little too emphatically, and tempered her voice. "I mean, why don't you check down here first?"

"It's raining now, Kate. It's a perfect time to check the rafters."

Thinking hard, she answered, "I'm not sure where the key is to the tower room. I'll have to look for it."

"Fine." He looked at her, wondering what was in that room she didn't want him to see. "I'll start in the attic." He gave her a smile. "And thanks for the dinner invite. I could use the company."

Back on the second floor, Mike walked past the four steps that led up to the tower, but his curiosity got the better of him and he backtracked. Checking to be sure

Kate hadn't followed him, he climbed the stairs, keeping to the left to silence any telltale squeaks. Turning the doorknob, he found she was telling the truth. It was locked. He went down on one knee and peered through the keyhole, but all he could see was the window on the opposite side of the room. Whatever she was hiding would have to remain hidden. He wasn't going to force her to open it.

In the hallway again, Mike reached for the rope attached to the folding stepladder that allowed entry into the attic space. The trapdoor opened with a metallic groan, and a shower of dust fell on his head. Shaking it off, he pulled down the ladder and began climbing. A sneeze shook him as he entered the dark attic.

He played the small beam from his pocket flashlight around the cavernous space until he located a bare bulb fixture, but when he tugged on the chain nothing happened. Cursing, he lowered himself down the ladder once more.

Standing at the top of the stairs, he shouted down, "Kate!" No answer was forthcoming, so he continued down. "Kate?"

Mike popped his head into the empty kitchen. Shrugging, he walked toward the pantry, hoping that was where she kept her spare lightbulbs. He got lucky. Picking out two sixty-watt bulbs, he reached out to turn off the light when he noticed a key hanging near the switch. It was an old-fashioned brass skeleton key and he knew which lock it opened, but he left it there.

As he was walking down the hallway, he heard the back door close. "Kate?" She appeared in the kitchen doorway. "I took a couple of lightbulbs out of the pantry."

"Fine."

"Did you find that key?"

She shook her head. "I really don't know where it is,

Mike." Her lie caused her to look away from him. "Just forget about the tower. I'm sure it's fine."

"You're the boss."

Once in the attic again, he screwed in the bulb. The weak light pooled in the center of the attic, unable to penetrate the blackness that lingered in the corners. The floor creaked under his weight as he walked the narrow path left between boxes and suitcases and trunks. There were no real windows in the attic. The two vents on either end of the space, if viewed from the outside, resembled small gothic windows covered with a tracery pattern. From the inside, the tracery allowed air into the attic, and small pinpoints of light on a sunny day. Today, they were nearly invisible.

His tiny flashlight wasn't going to do the trick. Mike made his way back to the attic's opening and called down to Kate. She finally heard him after his third shout and was soon standing at the foot of the ladder.

"You bellowed?"

"Sorry to drag you up here, but I need a good flashlight."

"It's in the kitchen. Be right back."

He sat down to wait, dangling his legs through the trapdoor. His eyes settled on a stack of boxes. They were marked TAXES in thick black felt pen, followed by the year. He was surprised to see the dates going back as far as 1984. These were the boxes he and Paul had put in the tower room years ago. Had she moved everything out of that room? By herself?

Her voice brought him back. She was climbing the ladder. Mike reached between his legs and took the flashlight from her. "I'll try not to bother you again."

"No bother. Find anything interesting?"

"No," he said, standing. "Not even a bat."

She still stood on the ladder, her head and shoulders above the floor now. Mike had disappeared into the shadows. The flashlight's beam moved over the rafters. She heard him grunt.

"What?"

"There's a small leak over here." The light moved to the floor. "No damage, though."

He continued his search while Kate rested her chin on her arms. He found one more wet spot near the front of the house.

"You got lucky," he said. "Looks like the outside needs the most work." Stooping, he traced the electrical wiring with the light. "What time's dinner?" he asked, continuing along the side of the room. He discovered mouse droppings and a little fraying around the insulation of one of the wires that ran along the floor. He made a mental note to wrap them. "You have a mouse. Want me to set out traps?"

"No. Live and let live. How's six o'clock?"

"Great," he said, straightening up. "You move all this stuff by yourself?"

His casual question caught her off guard, and she answered without thinking. "Well, yeah, who else?"

Hunkering down in front of her, he said, "Katie, I know you know where the key is. If you value what's in there, why not let me take a look? Make sure there aren't any problems."

Stiffening, she pushed away from the frame of the trapdoor and disappeared.

Mike closed his eyes in frustration. "Come on, Kate. I promise I'll only check the roof and wiring."

"No," she stated like a three-year-old.

He heard her footsteps fading away down the hallway, and then a door closing firmly.

Kate flung herself onto the overstuffed chair, crossed her arms over her chest, and stared out the window of the guest room. The rain was falling steadily now, creating a hypnotic pattering sound. It was a sound she'd forever associate with aching muscles and an overwhelming feeling of loneliness.

The day of Paul's funeral is overcast, but the rain that threatens holds off for the memorial service, which has turned into a standing-room-only media circus. Kate sits at the far end of the front pew, eyes lowered to her hands folded in her lap. To her left sits her mother-in-law. Margaret Armstrong sniffles into a lace handkerchief, while her daughter and son-in-law, sitting to her immediate left, stare straight ahead. Kate already feels the family moving away from her. She no longer matters.

Mike sits directly behind Kate, his hand resting on her shoulder. She longs for the reassuring bulk of her father, but complications from the flu have landed him in the hospital with pneumonia, making travel from Tempe impossible.

The baseball faction is well represented. Spring training has come to a halt so that teammates can attend the service. The townspeople of Staunton have shown up in droves, and about one hundred people stand outside the chapel, waiting to pay their respects. The newspaper, magazine, and television reporters haven't been allowed inside the chapel, and so spend their time trying to catch snippets of something newsworthy as more and more mourners try to enter the stone building.

The whispering inside the chapel swirls around her, building to a crescendo of voices, creaking pews, and the organ music she's always hated. Kate, shell-shocked and dry-eyed, stares at the coffin, unable to comprehend the fact that her husband is lying inside.

Suddenly, the room grows quiet, and the priest begins the service. Kate, lulled by his voice, loses herself in the dolorous tones. Her vision blurs as she gazes at the flowers draped over the casket. She doesn't hear a word he, or the other speakers, have said. She is surprised when Mike shakes her shoulder and whispers her name into her ear.

Standing, she moves away from the pew, and the whispering

begins again. Smoothing the front of her skirt, she wavers, and Mike quickly stands and takes her arm. They walk down the side aisle, the rest of the family following, toward a room at the back of the chapel where they will wait until it is time for the private graveside service.

Kate walks to the back of the cozy, paneled room and sits in an armchair, its comfort lost on her. The black suit she wears accentuates her pale beauty. Her auburn hair falls in glistening waves around the collar. She wears a brimmed hat with a veil that she now lifts back. Mike is at her side with a cup of coffee and she takes it from him without a word. He sits on the arm of the chair and she is grateful for his presence.

She gazes at the bookshelf across the room. Tears leak out of the corners of her eyes, and she tries to blink them away.

Mike puts his arms around her, and she suddenly says in a quiet, choked voice, "I can't go through with this, Mike."

"I'm right here, Katie. Not much longer."

"I can't do it," she whispers again, then she buries her face in his jacket.

At the graveside, Mike holds on to her arm for the short prayer, and then drives her home. Paul's family has already left for Charlottesville, leaving Kate alone in the house once again.

Mike sees Kate to the door. "Do you want me to come in? I can stay with you tonight."

She shakes her head. "I'm going to go lie down. I'm really tired." Then, realizing that not only has she lost her husband, but Mike has lost his friend, she puts her arms around him. "How will we ever be the same?" she asks, her voice trembling.

"Come on, darlin'. We'll be okay," he says, accepting her embrace. "You know where I am if you need me."

She pulls away and quickly steps into the house.

She has slept the whole afternoon and well into the evening, when she is awakened by the sound of rain pounding against the window. Disoriented, she sits up in the guest bed and switches on the lamp. She is still wearing the black suit, and begins peeling it off. She balls it up and shoves it into a wastebasket.

Wearing only her panties and bra, she walks down the hallway to the master bedroom. Kate hesitates before opening the door, but once inside she strides purposefully to the closet and finds a pair of jeans and a sweatshirt.

And then she goes up to the tower room and begins moving out every box—every piece of junk—that is in it. It takes her well over an hour, but soon she has everything piled beneath the attic trapdoor. Another hour and she has it all in the attic. Her muscles scream for relief, but she doesn't stop.

She goes from room to room, carrying a large box, removing everything that is Paul's. When the box is filled, she carries it to the tower room, unpacks it, and starts all over again. Sometime around midnight, she finishes.

Kate is standing in the center of the room. All his clothing has been carefully folded and placed in a small trunk. His uniforms take up the five drawers in the chest. His equipment is organized on a metal shelf unit. Shoes sit in a row along one wall. All the little things—jewelry, shaving items, cologne, soap—have been arranged in a carved walnut box that rests atop the chest of drawers. His awards are hung on the wall, in any empty space she can find.

Turning off the light, she closes the door and locks it. She hangs the key in the pantry before going into the den. Not bothering to turn on the light, Kate lowers herself onto the couch, fully exhausted. She falls asleep seconds later and doesn't wake up till the phone rings at eleven o'clock the next morning. Rain drums against the house, and as she gets up to answer the call, her legs nearly fly out from under her. Her thighs ache. Her back and arms are stiff and painful.

The caller is a teary Sheryl, apologizing for not being at the funeral. It had been impossible for her to come. Kate listens to Mike's sister ramble on about the divorce, and how she was just finishing up massage school, and Matt's SAT's were yesterday, and they just couldn't get away, and she was so sorry.

Kate is tired and in pain, and she simply says, "It's all right, Sheryl. I know you cared."

"I just wish I had been there for you," the other woman says, *a fresh spate of tears audible over the wire.*

Kate hangs up and wearily makes the climb to the second floor and the bathroom. The hot shower takes away some of the pain in her muscles, but not the ache in her heart.

Mike stood outside the guest room door, unsure of what to do. She'd been in there for nearly two hours. He'd finished the downstairs a few minutes ago and just as he was about to knock he'd heard her sniffling. He continued to stand there, his arms raised, and a small grimace crossed his face when he heard her blow her nose. Deciding that disturbing her was the best thing to do, he finally rapped on the door. "Kate? Just wanted to let you know I'm done." He put his ear to the door, waiting for a response. He heard her walk to the door, but she didn't open it.

"Okay. Thanks, Mike. See you at six."

He hesitated, wanting—no, needing—to comfort her. Instead, he drew in his breath, and said, "Yeah. Six. I'll be the guy with the two bottles of wine in his hands and the smile on his face."

CHAPTER

ELEVEN

They had eaten in the kitchen and had consumed most of the first bottle of Chianti. Mike, wary of Kate's mood, kept the conversation centered on the house and the work to be done. She didn't hide her consternation well when he told her they could start on Monday, just two days away.

As Kate rinsed off the plates and put them in the dishwasher, Mike wondered if he was supposed to get up and leave. It was early, but he still had that second bottle of wine and he desperately missed the long talks he and Kate used to have. When Paul was still alive, Mike would drive up for a weekend visit during the winter months. Paul took full advantage of the fact that he didn't have to work the night shift, and would go to bed early, leaving Kate and Mike chatting till the wee hours. A few times Mike had even brought his girlfriend of the moment. She invariably got bored with the subjects of antiques and old houses and wouldn't bother to hide a yawn once either Kate or Mike would say, "Hey, remember the time . . . ?" Annoyed, the woman would eventually find her way to the guest bedroom, while Kate and Mike sipped wine and reminisced.

Now, remembering was too hard for Kate, but Mike's need for her was even more excruciating. For too many years Paul rightfully stood between Mike and his love for Kate. And Mike respected that, even though it had been Paul who had thrown away the rule book the two boys had developed in the course of their friendship. They had both seen Kate and had both understood she could shatter the stone their book was written on. Mike's loyalty to Paul couldn't be budged in the old days. When it became Paul and Kate, his loyalties weren't divided. Not at first. But when he began seeing the changes that Paul's lifestyle had made in Kate, there was no doubt in his mind who needed his friendship more.

Paul was gone now. And Mike, who would have gone though his entire life never showing her how he felt, now wanted her to know. And the only way he knew how was to slowly, carefully peel away the layers that were Kate's pain, until he reached the smooth plane of her heart that wasn't scarred.

"Now what, Kate?" he asked.

"Now," she said, wiping off her hands. "We finish that other bottle of wine."

He didn't realize he'd been holding his breath, and he let it out slowly.

Kate sat on the sofa, her back against the arm, her legs stretched out in front of her, while Mike settled into the armchair. The only light in the den came through the intricate glass pieces of a Tiffany lamp that sat on the table behind the couch. Her prized possession. Paul had given it to her on their sixth anniversary.

It had been much too extravagant. She had teased him about it, saying, "Either I was very, very good or you've been very, very bad." She had later discovered that she'd been right on both counts, but by then it was spring, the road trip long forgotten, and he'd sworn he couldn't even remember the woman's name. Nothing unusual—nothing ninety percent of the other baseball wives hadn't lived through and survived.

Mike, a small smile on his face, watched Kate reach up and trace the iris design.

"It's still a beauty," he said, remembering the frantic call he'd gotten from Paul. "I need something really special," he'd said. "A guilt gift," Mike later said, after Paul had spilled his guts about the affair. Mike made the suggestion, and when Paul balked at the price, Mike had asked, "She's worth it, isn't she?"—secretly pleased that he could stick it to Paul just a little bit. He'd found the Iris lamp on one of his trips to New York and had it delivered to Paul in time for their anniversary, and Paul had paid the $12,000 tab with relief.

"I've been dying to know . . . where did you ever find it?" she asked.

His eyebrows lifted in surprise. "How did you know?"

"Oh, come on, Mike. Where would Paul have even begun to look for something like this? It's got Michael Fitzgerald written all over it, and I thank you." One corner of her mouth lifted as she added, "We both know why he agreed to buy it, and it had nothing to do with our anniversary, so you can tell me."

"Sotheby's," he finally said. "What else do you know, Katie?"

She shrugged, taking a sip of the dark wine. "You'd be surprised."

"So surprise me." He got up to refill her glass.

"Well, I know you're trying to get me drunk."

He laughed as he sat back down. "Katie, darlin', I happen to know it takes a whole lot more than a bottle of Chianti to get you drunk."

Her smile was sly.

"What else?" he pressed.

"Ummm, let's see . . ." She paused as if in deep thought. "I know that the women you date think you're incapable of making a commitment."

"Who've you been talking to?"

"I think the last one was the one who cornered me in your kitchen during that Fourth of July barbecue last year. That dark-haired woman. Summer? Spring?"

"Autumn," Mike answered curtly.

"Right! God, I can't believe you went out with someone named Autumn. Anyway, it was Autumn this time, and she says—"

"What do you mean, 'this time'?"

"Just what I said. She wasn't the first. *Anyway* . . . she says, what does a woman have to do to get Mike Fitzgerald to commit? And I said, wait till hell freezes over. She didn't seem to appreciate my standard reply."

"I can see you're enjoying this, but what would you say if I told you I'd already made the big commitment?"

Kate was thrown off balance, and instead of even pretending to be happy for him, she challenged him. "Who to?"

"Wouldn't you like to know," he stated. "Christ, how did we get on this subject?" Mike stood and walked to the bookcase, as the lighthearted mood evaporated.

Rain pattered against the window. For a moment it was the only sound in the room.

Kate broke the silence. "Mike? Are you very lonely?"

He turned to stare at her. "Yes, I am. Aren't you?"

Her hand came up to cover her eyes, and in a husky voice she said, "Yes, I think I am."

Kneeling next to the couch, he took the glass of wine from her right hand, and drew her other hand away from her face. "Come here, darlin'." He folded her into his chest. "Kate, nobody should be alone if they don't want to be. But you've shut everybody out. I know you loved Paul and I know you always will, but you've got to make room for other people in your life."

She listened to his comforting voice and felt his heartbeat. "Here's what else I know," she said against his arm. "You're a very nice man, Mike Fitzergald."

He closed his eyes, wanting to hold her like this for the rest of his natural life, but he pushed her away. "Here's something you don't know. I came over here tonight to talk to you about the dedication."

She brushed a knuckle under her eye. "I take it back. You're not a very nice man."

Mike sat cross-legged on the rug in front of her. "Sheryl talked to Donna Estes. The committee is planning a tribute to Paul. You need to be there to unveil the plaque they're going to install on the new gym. It's going to be named after him."

"Oh, Christ . . . will this never end?"

"Maybe you can make it end, Kate. What you say at the dedication could finally put this all to rest."

She tipped back the glass, and drained it. "When is the damned thing?"

"March eleventh," he answered quietly.

"God in heaven, why are they doing this to me?" she wailed.

"Kate, I'll be there with you. We'll get through it. And it will be over and done with." *And maybe we can all get on with our lives, with Saint Paul put to rest.*

Kate was hugging her legs, rocking to and fro, her head buried in her knees. In a muffled voice, she said, "I can't think about this now. I don't know yet. Please tell Donna for me." She lifted her head to look at him. "Please?"

Mike shook his head. "Not this time, Kate."

Saying no to Kate was one of the hardest things he'd ever had to do. He'd watched as she'd gone from vital Kate Moran to needy Kate Armstrong to "Paul's wife," with nothing left that resembled the girl he'd grown up with. He didn't want to watch anymore.

"It's time to take control of your life again, Kate. You just got done telling me you're lonely." Mike stood up. "You're the only one who can do something about that."

Kate stared at him openmouthed. Never one to back

down from a challenge, Kate reached across the couch and jerked the phone off the table. "What's Donna's number?"

Reaching under the end table, he withdrew the *Reader's Digest*-sized phone book and tossed it in her lap. "Look it up." He strode to the door. He could hear Kate paging through the book, cursing him under her breath. "Thanks for dinner, Kate." And he was in the hallway.

As she dialed Donna's number, Kate shouted at him, "Who is this woman you've committed yourself to? Because you can't call that two-minute marriage to Allison a commitment!"

Mike couldn't stop himself from shouting back, "It's you, Kate! Just you!"

The front door slammed.

CHAPTER
TWELVE

Mike barreled through his back door as if the hounds of hell pursued him.

———— "Jesus H. Christ, Fitzgerald! What the hell came over you?" he yelled at the kitchen walls.

There was no answer to his anguished question, only the sibilant sound of the icemaker refilling.

"What kind of a stupid-ass thing was that to say?"

He wished he could turn back the clock . . . just get that last hour back in hand and under control. If only she hadn't brought up Allison. Sweet Allison, who had put up with so much. What a shit he'd been.

He was still living in Richmond at the time. They met at a two-day preservation seminar he was teaching for the University of Richmond in the summer of 1991. When Allison Barclay walked into the conference room he'd glanced up from his paperwork and found himself staring. She was a petite woman with long strawberry-blond hair. Fair-skinned, blue-eyed. Any resemblance to a Southern belle ended there. She was incredibly confident and, he found a little later, extremely outspoken. Mike was drawn to her from the start, but for the life of him couldn't figure out why. *Not my type* kept running through his mind. And yet, there was something. He couldn't put his finger on it. Her smile? Her attitude?

During the afternoon break, while the smokers headed for the outdoors, Allison had perched on the end of the twenty-foot conference table and asked, "So, do your interests run to· *everything* old?" He'd looked up from his papers, startled. His heart beat a little faster as he'd grinned and replied, "No. There's something to be said for the novel and untried." Her eyes never left his as she'd said, "I deeply believe in novelty."

They'd hit it off instantly, and before the seminar had ended the next day, he had asked her to dinner. God, she'd been amazing. Bright, funny, beautiful. As he sat across the table from her, he'd almost told her about Kate. Thinking back on it now, it would have been for the best. Maybe if he'd said something then, the aura that surrounded Kate would have been diffused into a somewhat less volatile mixture. Maybe Allison would have understood a little better what she had gotten herself into. And maybe things could have turned out differently.

Mike remembered being surprised he'd never seen her before. His offices were down the block from the Virginia Museum of Fine Arts, where she was a research assistant. As a member, he liked eating his lunch in their courtyard restaurant, sometimes twice a week. She explained she'd only been with the museum for two months and went home for lunch. They exchanged phone numbers, and he called her the next week. Three weeks later, she gave him the key to her apartment, since he was spending most of his nights there. His own town house in Richmond's Fan District became a stopover. He'd taken her there only a few times.

A couple of weeks later, while they were lying in bed, Allison had asked point-blank, "Do you love me, Mike?"

"Didn't I just prove that I do?"

"Wrong answer." She rolled over to look at him. "Why can't you say it?"

"Okay, I love you."

"Oh, very romantic." But she'd smiled. "Why don't we move in together?"

"I thought we practically had."

"The operative word is 'practically.' Wouldn't we be more comfortable at your place? It's so much bigger, and it's going to waste. Don't you miss it?"

He tried to keep his voice indifferent, but the trepidation crept out. "Are you saying you want to move in with me?"

Allison heard the unspoken misgiving and ignored it. "Yes, I am. It's easier for me to give up my apartment than for you to sell or rent out your house." Her fingers traced the hard, tanned bicep of his upper arm, glided across the dark, silky hair of his forearm, and came to rest on his knuckles. "What do you say, lover?"

By August first, she'd sublet her apartment, stored most of her furniture, and moved into his town house. He helped her carry in the three suitcases and fifteen boxes, and watched her unpack into the spaces he'd made for her.

Mike found he enjoyed the arrangement and the domesticity. He could almost convince himself that he'd forgotten Kate, with Allison to hold every night. Their lifestyles meshed well. His short business trips, which had always been reprieves from his lonely life, became even more pleasurable because he had Allison to come home to.

Mike wasn't proud of the fact that he'd gone through women like Sherman went through Georgia, but he didn't think of himself as a user. He was truly looking for the right one. Unfortunately, none of them could match his ideal—his Kate. When he could see things weren't going to work out, he'd always been honest with them all, even though his candor had usually ended up hurting them. But Allison seemed to almost fill the place in his heart he'd reserved for Kate Armstrong.

And so by September first he'd asked her to marry him. Their wedding was a civil ceremony. He didn't tell Sheryl till the next day, when they drove through Clinton, Maryland, on their way to Washington, DC. "It'll be a working honeymoon," he'd warned Allison. "You consider that work?" she'd jokingly pouted.

His parents never even got to meet her. By the time Mike was able to get away to Tampa to see them, he and Allison had already split up.

He'd never brought up Kate or Paul. He avoided the subject of his hometown when he could. But the Armstrongs were due back in Staunton in a little over a month, and he knew it was just a matter of time before Kate invited the newlyweds for a visit.

Mike wanted this marriage to work. And then they'd gone to that damned New Year's Eve party.

"You know Paul Armstrong?" Allison asks in amazement.

She holds up a framed photograph of Paul and Mike that Kate had taken the year Paul won the Gold Glove award for the first time. Allison rarely enters his study while he is working, and never comes in when he isn't there. Her respect for his privacy is one of the things he really appreciates about her.

"We grew up together."

"Wow," she says, putting the frame back in its place on the library table. And then she spots the only photo of Kate he allows himself to display. Actually, it is one of her wedding photos. Kate and Paul standing on the steps of Saint Francis Catholic Church, with Kate looking at Paul, and Paul laughing into the camera. The picture serves as a reminder that she really does belong to someone else, and that someone else is his best friend. It is a humbling experience every time he looks at it.

"Aren't they the perfect couple?" she exclaims. "They're both gorgeous."

Mike says nothing. Instead, he takes Allison in his arms and kisses her desperately.

When Paul calls in December it is only the third time they've talked that winter.

"What's up, bud? We haven't seen you in ages."

"Work's keeping me pretty busy," Mike answers.

"Yeah, work and Allison. Am I right?"

"When you're right, you're right."

"Well, you and Allison need to get yourselves over here for New Year's Eve. Kate's planning a big one. It's 'come as your favorite movie character.' We're giving out prizes for best costume, and best performance."

Mike winces. "Best performance?"

"Yeah, everyone has to do a scene from the movie their character's from."

Now Mike groans. "Who are you going as?"

"Crash Davis," Paul answers, naming the down-on-his-luck baseball player Kevin Costner has made popular in the movie Bull Durham.

"Quite a stretch for you," Mike states sarcastically. "Don't tell me Kate's going as Annie Savoy?"

"She told me not to tell. So, we'll see you in a couple of weeks. Can't wait to meet Allison."

Suddenly Kate's voice comes on the line. "Yeah, and I hope she's more fun than that Marla."

"Mara," Mike corrects her. "And the woman I'm married to is named Allison. Can you try and remember that? Al-li-son."

Kate's throaty laugh makes him weak.

"Remember what I told you," Mike says as they pull in front of the Armstrongs' house the afternoon of December 31. "Don't take anything Kate says or does too seriously."

"Stop worrying. This is going to be fun."

Mike steps out of the car, muttering, "Yeah. Fun."

Paul meets them at the door, and as Mike introduces Allison he sees a look of incomprehension cross his friend's face.

Allison enters the house, and Paul draws Mike aside and says, "Not your usual type." Mike knows what he means is, she's not like Kate, and he replies, "You're wrong."

The two men find the two women face-to-face in the hallway. They have already introduced themselves and are shaking hands. Mike watches Kate's face, concerned at what he sees.

Kate's scrutiny of Allison is unnerving. He isn't sure, having never seen it before, but he thinks it is a look of jealousy. And for the life of him, he can't understand why. But when Kate sees Mike, her face lights up and she is suddenly coquettish. Almost possessive in the way she takes his arm; the way she kisses his cheek. And then he knows they are all in trouble when she whispers, "I've been practicing my performance for two weeks. I'm betting you'll like it."

Mike attempts to smile, as he hisses back, "Kate, I'm warning you, don't fuck this up for me. I've already told her all about you and your parties."

She stands back, grinning. "Let me show you up to the guest room, Allison. The party starts at eight, so we have plenty of time to get to know each other." Kate takes her arm and leads Allison up the stairs, saying, "I can't believe Mike is finally married."

Mike has wandered downstairs a little past seven and is fixing himself a drink when Paul joins him.

"You'd think there would be a time in your life when you wouldn't want to wear a baseball uniform," Mike comments.

"Yeah, but look how good I look in it."

Through his connections, Paul has gotten an authentic Durham Bulls home uniform and has had the number 20 sewn on the back. It is the only time he hasn't worn the number he started the majors with—5.

"You look pretty sharp, Marshal Kane."

Mike does his best Gary Cooper "aw shucks" grin and lifts his black Stetson with his middle finger. The gesture isn't lost on Paul.

When Allison saw Mike's outfit from High Noon *for the first time just a few minutes earlier, she seductively circled him, eyeing the long-sleeved white shirt, black vest complete with star-shaped badge, the tight black jeans and black boots, and had growled. His gun belt rode low on his hips and she pressed up against him, saying, "Is that your gun, or are you just happy to see me?" Allison wore only a merry widow and stockings. He had replied, "A little of both, ma'am."*

Now, Allison's voice asks, "Well, what do you think, boys?"

The two men turn. Mike's face breaks into a broad smile that wavers when he hears Paul say, "Uh-oh."

Mike tears his eyes from Allison, who is walking into the living room, and looks at Paul. "What do you mean, 'uh-oh'?" And then he sees Kate coming down the staircase, and he distinctly says, "Oh, shit."

Two gorgeous, redheaded women. Two strapless, curve-hugging, floor-length, slit-to-the-crotch, black satin dresses. Two pairs of long black satin gloves. Two pairs of black ankle-strap high heels. Two "Rita Hayworths." Two Gildas. And two pairs of stunned blue eyes.

Kate is the first to break the awkward silence, when she throws back her head and laughs. "Great minds think alike!" Mike, preparing himself for the worst, is relieved when Kate puts her arm around Allison's waist and says, "Are you the two luckiest men in the world, or what?"

Mike takes his eyes off Kate to see how Allison is taking it, and he can see she isn't taking it well. He honestly thought it would have been the other way around. Mike quickly goes to Allison, who has wriggled out from Kate's hold on her.

"You look amazing," he says, kissing her on the lips. "The wig is the perfect touch."

She looks up at him, eyes narrowed slightly, and mouths the words, "I don't believe this."

He shrugs, whispering, "This is going to be fun. Remember?"

But his eyes stray to Kate and the amount of skin she is showing. Something is different about her, but he can't put his finger on what she's changed.

By the time the guests start arriving, Allison's discomfort has subsided. Each time a new couple comes in the door, the talk *centers around their costumes, and by nine o'clock the house on Frazier Street is filled with people talking, eating, laughing, and dancing. The two Gildas have become the clichéd joke of the evening, when nearly every person who is introduced to Allison says, "Haven't we met somewhere?"*

The insanity begins in earnest when Kate announces the start of the auditions. After an hour of hilarious renditions of scenes that go from Gone With the Wind *to* The Godfather, *Kate yells, "Take five, everybody! I think I wet my pants," and she turns the stereo up again and goes into the kitchen to put a fresh batch of hors d'oeuvres in the oven.*

Allison, sitting on Mike's lap during the entertainment, says, "I'm going to see if she needs any help."

Allison enters the kitchen and asks, "What can I do?"

"Oh, good! A helper." Kate straightens up, closing the oven door. "Could you get the rest of the vegetable platters out of the fridge?"

Allison is removing the plastic wrap from the trays when she notices Kate standing at the counter, preparing another bowl of chili dip. "Don't you want to put on an apron?"

"There's an idea," Kate answers, holding up hands covered with the cheese she is grating. "Would you mind tying it on for me?"

Allison stands behind Kate. "You've got something on your dress back here." She starts to brush at the tan-colored stain that has appeared where the zipper starts on the dress. Kate whirls around, startling her.

"Would you mind doing this? I'll take care of it." Kate rushes out of the kitchen and nearly knocks over Mike in the hallway in her hurry to get upstairs.

"Kate? What's wrong?" His words bounce off her retreating back. Puzzled, he pokes his head into the living room and catches Paul's attention. "Kate just ran upstairs and she looked panicked."

"I'll check on her. Thanks," Paul says, hurrying after his wife.

Allison appears in the doorway, a questioning look in her eyes.

"What happened?" Mike asks.

"I don't know. I noticed a spot on the back of her dress, and she went nuts."

Paul comes down a few minutes later, and Mike seeks him out. "Is she okay?"

"Yeah. Everything's fine. Don't say anything, okay?"

Kate enters the living room moments later wearing a black silk shawl, and it is then Mike realizes what has been nagging at him about Kate's dress. It's strapless, and although higher in the back than Allison's, it still shows about six inches of her upper back, something he's never seen before. And there is something else he's never seen. Her scar. He's known about it for years, and knows she never wears anything that would reveal it. And he hasn't seen it tonight, either. She has covered it with body makeup. That is the stain Allison has seen.

Mike notices Allison working her way through the crowd toward Kate. Moving quickly, he grasps Allison's arm before she can reach Kate. Without preamble, he states, "I'll tell you later. Don't say a word."

But the evening has been ruined for Kate. He can see it on her face and in the subdued movements of her body. Allison watches in hurt wonder as Mike leaves her side to go to Kate.

"Did you save a dance for me, Katie?" Mike asks, running a gentle hand over her hair.

And it is then that Allison knows she has a rival in Kate, and that Kate doesn't even know it. Allison can't take her eyes off Mike as his arm circles Kate's waist, and she melts into his body. They both have their eyes closed, but she can see them whispering to each other. Allison looks for Paul in the crowd, wanting to see his reaction, but she is disappointed when he watches Kate and Mike for a few seconds with a grin on his face, and then goes back to the conversation he is having with three other men.

When they've finished their dance, Kate's spirits seem restored, and Mike watches in amusement as she asks for quiet.

"*Jerry? We haven't seen your performance yet, and I'm sure everyone is dying to know what scene you're going to do from* True Grit. *Why don't you start the next round?*"

Jerry Springer, the second-string catcher for the Giants who comes from nearby Waynesboro, quickly says, "*What about you, Kate? I think the hostess should lead off the second half.*"

His suggestion is met with voices raised in agreement and clapping. Kate looks at Paul across the room and he gives her an encouraging nod. Her eyes sweep the room, then she grins and gives a "*what the hell*" shrug.

"*Okay, let's get this over with.*" She looks at Allison. "*Care to join me?*"

Allison shakes her head. "*No. I don't think I can compete.*"

Kate moves to the far wall, takes off the shawl, and faces the crowd. "*All right, Paul. Hit it.*"

The music starts and Kate begins her husky-voiced rendition of "Put the Blame on Mame," doing a perfect imitation of Rita Hayworth's pouty, provocative burlesque. Their friends roar as she slowly peels off a glove, trails it over Mike's head, and drops it in his lap. As she seductively glides through the movements of the number, the other glove comes off, ending up in Lou Whitley's outstretched hand. She bends forward, placing her hands on her thighs, revealing milky-white cleavage. She sings through a curtain of fiery hair, one smoky blue eye gazing at her audience. When she finishes with arms up and one shapely leg peeking out of the expanse of black satin, those who aren't already standing, leap up to join the applause.

Winking at Mike, Kate grabs her shawl on her way out the door.

Allison downs the gin and tonic she's been nursing during Kate's number, and holds out the glass to Mike. "*I'll be right back.*"

Allison finds Kate on the mud porch, the back door wide open.

Kate smiles. "*Needed some fresh air.*"

"*I can imagine,*" Allison responds. "*I could use a little myself.*" She pauses, then says, "*That was quite a performance.*"

"*Thanks,*" Kate answers. "*It would've been a kick to do it together.*"

Kate's words seem genuine to Allison, but she still asks, "*It was a performance, wasn't it?*"

Kate turns. "*What do you mean?*"

"*Nothing,*" Allison says as she looks into Kate's eyes and sees genuine puzzlement. "*Kate, can I ask you something?*"

"*Sure.*"

"*It's about Mike. What's the longest relationship he's had?*"

"*Probably the one he has with you. I guess hell finally froze over.*" Kate's grin disappears at Allison's frown. "*Hey, I'm sorry!*" She runs her hand down the other woman's arm. "*It's a very old joke. He's lucky he found you.*"

The champagne starts flowing around quarter to twelve. Allison drifts from room to room searching for Mike. She finally finds him in the backyard playing catch with Kate and Homer while Paul looks on from the back porch. Kate has slipped a sweater on over her dress and has taken off her shoes. Allison can see Mike's breath in the backlight of the floods in the trees. They are both laughing, as they tease the dog with the promise of a tossed ball.

Allison leans on the railing next to Paul. "*Do I remind you of her?*"

"*Does it matter?*" he asks.

"*I hope not,*" she says softly.

They both watch in silence for a few minutes, then Allison asks, "*It doesn't bother you?*"

"*What's that?*" Paul asks, never taking his eyes off Kate.

"*That he's in love with your wife.*"

Paul chuckles. "*Everyone loves Kate. Besides.*" Paul glances at Allison before turning his attention back to Kate. "*It shouldn't bother you, either. He married you, didn't he?*"

There is a groundswell of noise billowing out of the house and the screams of "*Happy New Year*" reach their ears. Kate runs to Mike and flings her arms around him, as he lifts her *into the air and swings around. When her feet are back on the ground, she pulls his head down and kisses him. In seconds, Kate is running toward Paul. She reaches the railing and smiles up at Paul, saying, "Happy New Year, baby. God, I love being home!"*

Paul reaches down, scoops her up in his arms, and brings her over the railing. Still holding her, he brings his lips to hers for a hungry kiss. As Paul carries her into the house, he says over his shoulder, "See you guys in the morning . . . Happy New Year!"

Mike is still standing in the middle of the yard. He hasn't noticed Allison come out, and is now surprised to see her. He hurries to the porch. "Alli! I didn't know you were out here."

"Obviously. Happy New Year, Mike."

"Happy New Year, Alli." He leans forward to kiss her, but she backs away.

"What's this about?" he asks.

"Can't you guess?"

He draws a breath. "I warned you about Kate."

Allison locks her eyes with his. "But you didn't warn me about you. I'm going to bed."

Mike sees the party out to its bitter end. The last couple departs around one-thirty, leaving Mike to turn out lights and lock doors. As he pads past Paul and Kate's door in bare feet he can hear their bedsprings creaking, but no other sounds come through the thick walls and heavy door. He's heard it before. It always tortures him.

Mike slips into the guest room. Allison has left the small art-glass lamp on and it casts an amber glow in the far corner of the large room. He undresses quickly, turns off the light, and makes his way into the four-poster bed. No movement comes from Allison's side of the mattress, but he knows she's not asleep.

"Alli?" he whispers, tentatively touching her shoulder. There is no response. "Alli, please?"

Her voice is rigid with anger. "What is it, Mike?"

He moves closer to her, kissing her hair. She stiffens when he tries to pull her next to him.

"I will not be your substitute for her," she says through clenched teeth. "I will not be your second choice." She hears him sigh and tears spring to her eyes. "Have you ever once made love to me when she wasn't in the bed between us?"

A few seconds pass before he says, "I'm sorry, Allison. I was really hoping . . . I wanted it to work. For what it's worth, I love you."

"But not enough to make you forget her."

Mike was in Williamsburg on a consultation with the College of William and Mary the day she moved out. He knew she'd be gone when he came home, but the quiet house hurt just the same. Paul had called a few days after the party. When he'd asked after Allison, Mike told him she'd gone. There had been a long silence on the line. Paul finally said, "You wanna talk about it?" But Mike had declined. "Okay, buddy. But it's a new year. It can only get better, right?"

His divorce became final just six months later.

Now, turning off the lights in his kitchen in the house on High Street, Mike muttered, "Yeah, right," remembering the next few years. "You really called it there, Paul."

Forgetting to lock the door, he went upstairs to bed.

CHAPTER

THIRTEEN

K ate held the phone to her ear as Mike's departing words echoed through her mind. *"It's you, _____ Kate . . . Just you."*

She'd been staring, dumbfounded, at the door Mike had walked out of when Donna Estes said, "Hello," for the third time. Kate was finally able to speak and she said, "Sorry, Donna. I'll have to call you back," and hung up the phone. Kate sat for a few seconds longer, then, out loud, asked herself, "What did he say?"

Kate sprang off the couch and paced the room, muttering to herself. "What did *that* mean?" She whirled toward the telephone and grabbed the receiver, then slammed it back down. *No! I will not call you!* Her wine glass still held some of the ruby Chianti and Kate polished it off as she stalked out of the den toward the kitchen. The dinner dishes were still piled in the sink and she tackled them with a manic fervor, but the work didn't silence Mike's words. Kate rinsed the final plate and, drying her hands on her jeans, deliberately strode down the hallway and out of her house.

She didn't bother to knock on his back door. Kate flipped on the kitchen light and swept through the house. "Michael James Fitzgerald!" she shouted, climbing the stairs.

The light came on in the bedroom, and she heard him say, "Jesus! Kate?"

Before he could move, she was in the room. "How *dare* you say something like that to me and then walk out!" Mike sat up in his bed, bare-chested. "And what the hell did you mean by that?" she demanded.

"You're a big girl, Kate. You know what I meant." He leaned back against the headboard.

"You get out of that bed this instant. I can't talk to you like this."

He didn't move.

Her voice lowered, her words measured, she said, "Will you please get up."

Mike shrugged and threw off the covers. Rising to his full six feet, he stood in front of her wearing nothing but a pair of navy blue briefs.

Kate blushed violently, and she hissed, "Put some clothes on!"

His eyes narrowed. "You walk into my bedroom uninvited, you take the consequences."

"Thanks for the warning," she stated. "I'll be in the living room."

His voice followed her into the hallway and down the stairs. "And miss your chance to see my very nice ass up close and personal?"

Kate yanked open the draperies and stared, unseeing, into the dark street. Her thoughts moved at the speed of sound. Her heart beat heavy and fast.

The sight of Mike nearly naked had taken her breath away, but she wouldn't admit it, even to herself. Instead, she tried to focus on the known feelings: outrage and fear. But she couldn't pretend any longer. The quiet voice that, through the years, had whispered, *"You've made a mistake,"* was suddenly screaming to be heard. *"It's been Mike all along."*

Her hands flew up to cover her ears, as if that could block out the sound. She grew hot again, but this time with guilt. Mike's footsteps on the stairs warned her, and she lowered her hands to grip the windowsill.

He sauntered into the living room a few seconds later. Flopping into a leather armchair, he said, "Let's talk."

She turned from the window. He'd put on a pair of jeans. The faded denim shirt he wore was unbuttoned. His feet were bare. It was a moment before she could speak normally. "Explain to me just exactly what you meant."

"I meant just what I said. You're the woman I committed myself to a long time ago." His eyes held hers. "God help me." She took a step toward him, stopped, and a look of confusion crossed her face. "What? Kate Armstrong speechless? I don't believe it."

She sat on the ottoman in front of him. Slowly, as if trying to work it out in her mind, she said, "What you mean is, you're my friend, and you feel obligated to take care of me."

"What I mean is, I love you." His voice didn't yield to the wistfulness he felt. It was stone.

But Kate refused to hear the words the way he meant them. "I love you, too, Mike. You know that."

His jaw tightened. "As a friend," he said.

"Of course," she said, trying to sound convincing. "You're my best friend."

"Okay, Kate. You believe what you want to believe. But it's getting harder and harder for me to be just your friend anymore." He paused. "You asked me if I was lonely. Why?"

Kate looked into his gray eyes with their frame of dark lashes and was frightened by what she saw. She quickly stood. Mike took her wrist, and repeated his question.

"I—I don't know. It's just that lately . . . Mike, I feel so lost." Her voice had dropped to a whisper. "And I can't remember him anymore. Not really. I can't even remember what it felt like when we made love." Her eyes filled.

He was standing in front of her now and he took her other hand. His voice softened. "Katie, that's God's way of telling you to start feeling something new." He placed her hand on his chest. "Can you feel my heart beating? It means I'm alive."

She stared at his hand covering hers. Her pale skin pressed against his tanned chest felt right. Too right. The tears spilled over her cheeks.

"Kate, what are you feeling right now?"

"Guilt," she answered, her voice thick.

"What else?"

"I'm scared."

"Of me?"

She shook her head. "No. Of me."

She finally raised her head to look at him. Her eyelashes clung together. Flakes of mascara mingled with the tears under her eyes. Slowly, cautiously, he brought his mouth to hers, and against her lips said, "It's okay to be scared, Katie. It just means you're alive, too." Softly kissing the corner of her mouth, the hollow of her cheek, he tasted her tears and savored them, a salty delicacy. But she was pulling away from him.

"Don't do this, Mike."

"Why, darlin'?" He brushed a lock of hair away from her cheek.

"Please try to understand. Paul is the only man I've ever been with."

"Paul is dead, Kate." He was trying to understand, and failing. "You're still young. Are you going to keep yourself locked away from life forever?"

She didn't answer him, and he finally said, "Go home, Katie. Think about what I said. You know where to find me. I'll always be here for you. You must know that after twenty-one years."

She took her hand from his and left him standing in the living room. Mike couldn't help thinking about the tower room. If he could only penetrate those walls that surrounded her secret place, he felt sure he could set Kate free.

He ran a trembling hand through his hair, the ache for her worse than ever.

Kate lay in bed, confused and afraid. Mike's closeness had let loose a feeling she'd reserved only for Paul. It had been so long that she thought she'd forgotten what it was like to want to be touched. But Mike's lips on hers—that brief kiss—brought it all back. The few times Kate had allowed herself to become lost in the memory of Paul's lovemaking—when her hand would slip down between her legs—had left her feeling so desolate that she'd even denied herself that small release anymore.

Now she didn't know what was going on inside her. The little voice said, *"It's time to admit the truth."* But at the moment, Kate didn't want to listen. And so she questioned it.

This need she felt: was it real, or was she simply, and finally, lonely? And was that a good enough reason to go to Mike? It hardly seemed fair to him. He wanted so much more from her. He deserved so much more. And if she were truly his friend, she'd make him see that. Friends were supposed to tell friends when they thought they were making a mistake, weren't they?

But Kate suddenly recalled the warmth of Mike's chest under the palm of her hand, and she involuntarily gasped.

Paul took Kate's virginity on their wedding night. The years leading up to that night had been difficult, to say the least, and Kate had always been amazed at Paul's self-restraint. Not that he didn't try. Not that he didn't push it as far as he could. On those occasions, when he'd beg her, it didn't take much more than a few strokes of her hand to bring him off.

Paul Armstrong liked—no, loved—the idea that Kate was his and no one else's. Never was. Never would be. Along with all his other talents, he was an accomplished lover. It didn't occur to Kate to wonder how he'd become so accomplished. Like many women, she assumed that a man just knew what to do. That it was an inherent ability. And Paul didn't shake that assumption. When they'd talked about sex, usually in the backseat of Paul's car after another window-steaming necking session, the questions Kate asked were vague and fairly innocuous. "What does it feel like when I do this?" "How many other girls have you done this to?" She took it for granted that he'd done most of it before. Except for the big "It."

A little shy when it came to talking with Paul about his experience, she had no qualms about asking Mike. And Mike, trying to be true to Paul and Kate at the same time, would answer with vague references to other girls, always assuring Kate that she was the one Paul loved, so what difference did it make what he'd done before. "But has he ever slept with anyone?" she'd insist. And Mike would answer as truthfully as he could, "No, he's never slept with anyone." Kate placed all her trust in them both.

In her bedroom, with the door locked, Kate had pored over a well-worn copy of *The Joy of Sex*. She thought she knew all there was to know about making love. But nothing prepared her for the night of January 6, 1977.

Nervous, but not frightened, she steps out of the bathroom of their honeymoon suite wearing the peach silk gown she's ordered from Victoria's Secret. Paul sits on the edge of the bed, and holds out his hand to her. Accepting it, she lets him pull her down to the bed, and then he stands and removes the royal blue satin robe she's given him. Kate has never seen him completely

naked, and she can see he feels at home with his body. It's perfectly proportioned. An athlete's body.

He sits next to her and his eyes drift down the length of her
and back up, to meet her eyes with a smile. "God, you're beautiful," he says, his fingers tracing the skin just above the bodice
of her nightgown.

Kate feels a moistness between her legs, and a surge of heat
somewhere deep in her belly. Reaching up, she pulls his head
down to kiss him. His tongue delicately explores her mouth
and she moans. The months they've been apart, while he
played in the minors and then winter ball in Mexico have left
her senses deprived. This is a new Paul, this man who takes
his time. There is no sense of urgency to his attentions. He
seems content to tease and stroke and kiss until she can't take
it anymore.

Her own hands pull her nightgown above her hips, as she
begs him, "Please, Paul. I can't wait anymore."

"That's what I wanted to hear," he says.

His fingers open her, and she feels the first insistent pressure
of his penis. She opens her legs to accommodate him, and gasps
as he pushes against her. The pain is sharp and she cries out, as
he slips in deeper.

He was holding himself above her, and now lowers himself
until his mouth touches her ear. "Bear down, Katie," he whispers. "We're almost there. I love you."

And Kate pushes, allowing him to fill her completely. He
doesn't move until he feels her muscles relax, accepting him, and
then he begins a slow rhythm. It doesn't take him long to come,
groaning her name against her neck. He holds himself inside her
for a long time, and then slowly pulls out, watching her grimace
in pain.

Holding her face, he traces his thumbs over her cheekbones, as
he says, "I'm sorry, Kate. It'll get better. Trust me."

"I know," she says with a shaky smile. "I do."

"I'll be right back."

She can hear water running in the bathroom, and he comes
back out with a washcloth and towel. The warmth of the cloth

soothes her and she closes her eyes, as he gently washes the blood from her thighs and towels her off. He bends to kiss her belly. His fingers outline her hipbones and then slowly caress her hips and buttocks. He kisses the tops of her thighs, and she sighs. His hands move to her knees, slowly pushing them apart, and his lips find the velvety skin that is the inside of her thighs. He softly bites the smooth flesh and he hears her make a small noise. Raising his head slightly, he sees her eyes open, a look of embarrassment on her face.

"It's your turn, Katie."

Her eyes widen as she understands what he means to do, but before she can protest, his warm mouth surrounds her. This is heaven, this liquid stroking, and she closes her eyes again and gives herself up to him. The room fills with her soft moans. She wants more and pulls her legs up. He devours her.

Kate's hands find their way to his head, urging him to go deeper. "Oh, Christ! Christ, Paul . . ." Her body has gone rigid and then the waves of her orgasm begin.

The sounds she makes are primal. Paul has never heard anything like it and Kate has never felt anything like it. And then he hears her say, "Paul, I want you inside me."

He covers her with his body, entering her, whispering, "Oh, Katie . . . you are amazing."

She lost track of how many times they made love that first night. The next morning she wakes before Paul. Kate looks over at his long, lean body draped across the bed. He is dead to the world—utterly at peace. He is beautiful, and he's hers.

She grows warm remembering the things they've done. God, it had been wonderful. Everything she'd hoped. Kate yawns and stretches, smiling. Then she quietly slides to the edge of the king-sized bed, puts her feet on the plush carpet, and tries to walk to the bathroom.

"Oh, shit," she says through clenched teeth.

Her thighs feel like rubber, and what is going on between her legs? She feels like she's on fire. She begins cautiously waddling the twenty long feet to the bathroom, when she hears Paul *chuckle. Kate stops and turns. "What are you laughing at? You did this to me."*

"I didn't hear any complaints at the time."

She makes a face at him and continues on her journey.

Returning to the bed takes nearly as long, and as she climbs in, Kate sees his erection. In mock terror, she says, "You put that thing away! It's a lethal weapon."

Paul scrambles across the bed and pins her down, while she screams and pretends to faint.

"Now I have you right where I want you," Paul says, biting her neck.

Kate opens her eyes and smiles. "This is right where I want to be." She takes his face in her hands and looks into his hazel eyes. "I love you, Paul. Thank you for being so patient. I know it's been hard for you."

He runs a hand over her shoulder and down her arm and, in a husky voice, says, "Baby, you were worth it."

"Paul?"

"Hmm?" He takes his eyes off the curve of her breast.

"We'll always be together, won't we?"

"Always?" he repeats lightly. "Man, that's an awful long time." Then he sees she is serious. "Katie! I promise. Always."

For Kate, life with Paul had been about trust, with a capital *T*. She'd trusted him to love her. Period.

She hadn't seen his body before their wedding night, and he hadn't seen hers. The two-foot-long scar down her back, which she hid from everyone, was the ruler with which she measured trust. By the time she'd reached high school, only two people that mattered knew about the scar: her parents.

Kate viewed the scar as a flaw. A constant reminder that she was somehow different from everyone else. She'd watched with envy as the other girls in her eighth-grade gym class importantly hooked their white cotton bras around their chests, while she sat on the sidelines, her upper body constricted by plaster and gauze. In high school she still only filled an A cup, and she blamed the body cast for stunting her growth. She couldn't seem to see past her small breasts and disfigured back.

Her classmates envied her fiery beauty. Her teachers couldn't praise her work enough. They couldn't know that her self-assured spirit was a cover. Kate never thought of herself as attractive and didn't believe the compliments she received, despite her gracious thank-yous. And she just knew that the boys who wanted to go out with her wouldn't give her a second look if they'd known about the scar and her barely-there breasts. She felt like a fraud in a 36B padded push-up bra.

Kate didn't tell Paul about the scar until the night he asked her to marry him. She'd actually cringed as she'd said, "There's something you need to know about me, and I'll understand if you want to back out." But he'd grinned, saying, "If I had the scar, would you stop loving me?" "No," she'd answered. "Well, then quit being such a doofus, and say yes."

Paul didn't care that it was there, just that it was part of Kate and that it had hurt her. On their first night together, it took much coaxing on his part, but he finally got her to turn over. It was an angry-looking mark, nearly two inches wide. "Katie," he'd said. "You must've been incredibly brave to go through this. If I had known you then, I would've told you how proud I was of you." And then he'd kissed the length of her spine, bringing tears to her eyes.

Kate lay in her bed thinking about the blind trust she'd placed in Paul. Even when he gave her cause to lose faith in him, she never wavered. She became like a dog, beaten by its master only to wag its tail in acceptance the next time it was stroked. As hard as she tried to break the habit, Paul always came back to stroke her. And she always accepted him, because her doubt in her decision to marry Paul—that maybe she was *still* a fraud—brought with it guilt and, ultimately, refutation.

The little betrayals never meant as much as his love for her. Of this, she was certain. But that much trust had taken so much out of her. After his death, it was hard keeping the faith. God had let her down. So had Paul. But Kate saw where her loyalties lay and she preferred to blame God. It was easier than admitting she'd made an enormous error in judgment.

And now, she didn't want to put her trust—her Self—in anyone's hands again. Kate knew it wasn't Paul's memory she was trying to preserve, but her own. Mike had just scared the hell out of her. Why was the truth so much harder to believe? She wanted to go back to that safe place called Denial.

Coming to a decision, she reached over, turned on the lamp by the bed, and picked up the phone.

CHAPTER

FOURTEEN

M ike was still awake when the phone rang. He quickly picked it up, hoping to hear Kate's _____ voice, but it was his sister.

His disappointment was obvious, and Sheryl said, "Don't tell me you're sitting there pining away over Kate again? Jesus, Mike. You're a grown man. Ante up or fold."

"Thanks, Sheryl. I can always count on your understanding nature. And for your information, I laid my cards out on the table tonight and got the crap beat out of me."

Sheryl was stunned. "You actually told her how you feel? My hat's off to you, Mikey. I take it she didn't leap into your bed?"

"I hope to God Matt's not sitting in the room listening to this conversation."

"No, he's out with some friends. Your secret is safe with me. Hang on." He could hear the teakettle whistling, and the sound of silverware against china. "Okay, I'm back. Tell me the whole sad story. No, wait. Let me guess. She doesn't want to sully the memory of Paul Armstrong, the savior of Staunton."

Annoyed that his sister could reduce his agony to a few

sharp words, no matter that she was probably right, Mike asked, "Why do you find this so fucking amusing?"

"What I find amusing is Kate's loyalty to that guy. Yeah, he was good-looking and bright and a great base-ball player. But he was a shit."

"That's a little strong, isn't it? He really did love her," Mike said in programmed defense of his friend.

"Okay, I'll amend that. He was a lovable shit. Look what he put her through."

Not sure how much his sister knew, Mike was careful with his reply. "The bad investments weren't totally his fault. That so-called financial manager had a lot to do with that."

There was a moment of silence on Sheryl's end, then she said, "All that woman had left when he died was the house, the rest of that year's contract money, and the dog. I think he knew what was happening. Thank God the shop was in her name." There was a clicking noise on the line. "Hold on. I've got another call coming in."

Mike didn't have to wait long.

"Mike? I've got Kate waiting. Do you want me to tell her I'm on with you?"

"No," he replied, wishing he could tap into their con-versation. "And be nice."

"Have a little faith in me, Mike!" Sheryl said and hung up.

"Where have I heard that before?" Mike asked him-self as he dropped the receiver into its cradle.

Mike sat back and his eyes focused on the leather and oak morris chair across from him. He could almost see Paul sitting forward at the edge of the seat, saying, "Have a little faith in me, man."

It was late winter, 1994, and Mike was still living in Richmond. Already irritated that Kate hadn't come with

Paul this time, Mike snorted. "I work hard for my money."

"What, like I don't?"

Mike rolled his eyes. "You play a game, and you get paid."

Paul grinned. "Yeah, I'm a lucky guy. So, how about it? Think you can come up with twenty thousand?"

"Oh, I can come up with it. I'm just not gonna give it to your pal to buy some junk stock. And if you used your brain, you wouldn't do it, either."

"You're being more than your usual retentive self today. What's your problem?"

Mike's problem was that he'd been counting on seeing Kate one more time before the Armstrongs headed west for spring training. It had become a tradition since Paul had entered the majors. Every year, the three of them had gotten together the week before Paul had to report. When Paul showed up on Mike's doorstep alone, the first question out of Mike's mouth had been, "Where's Kate?" Paul told him she hadn't been feeling well, and for him to go on alone. It didn't sound like Kate. The letdown was like getting your mouth set for prime rib and finding out the last piece had just been ordered by the guy at the next table. Nothing sounded good after that.

"You're my problem," Mike answered. "Does Kate know about this latest 'sure thing'?"

"I mentioned it to her."

"Did you mention you've already sunk fifty grand into that black hole of a country club?"

The muscle in Paul's left jaw tightened. "I know you'd like it if it were the other way around, but Kate's *my* wife. I decide what she needs to know. Besides, you had a wife of your own. Remember?"

"This isn't about me and Allison." Mike didn't see any sense in stopping now. The conversation had veered out of control. "Do you think Kate needs to know about the women you've been fucking on the road?"

"She knows. She got over it. How come you haven't?"

"Bullshit, she knows!" Mike exploded. "The only one she knows about is the first one. And that's 'cause she guessed and you had to come clean!"

"I don't have to explain it to you, pal. That's just life on the road."

"What a convenient excuse," Mike said sarcastically.

"Okay, so she doesn't know. So what? It's not hurting her, is it?"

"You're a class A prick. You know that, Armstrong? If I had thought for one minute you'd end up treating her like dirt, I would've done my best to make her mine."

"You didn't stand a chance."

The venom of Paul's statement caused Mike to sit back abruptly. He stared at the man he suddenly didn't know and tried to get a handle on his fury.

Finally, he asked. "Why do you do it? Kate's the best thing that ever happened to you."

"Look, she didn't exactly hold up her end of the bargain."

"What are you talking about?" And then the light dawned. "Are you trying to tell me that because she couldn't have kids—couldn't give you a son—that you feel it's your right to do whatever the hell you please? Oh, that's rich! She didn't do it on purpose, y'know. She didn't plot to marry you knowing she couldn't have children and then spring it on you a few years down the road." Mike remembered the agony she'd gone through. She had been terrified of telling Paul what the doctor's final words on the subject had been, and so she'd called Mike. And he had told her that Paul would understand.

Paul stood and now walked toward the window. "It's not just that. She's not the woman I married. She's changed."

"Sure she's changed. So have you. She's doing everything she can to hold on to you."

"Well, she's suffocating me, Mike."

Mike drew a deep breath. "You want out?"

Paul shook his head. "No, we've been together too long. I still love her, Mike."

"Then what? You want Kate, and you want everyone else who's willing to spread their legs for the great Paul Armstrong? Is that it?" When Paul didn't answer, Mike's eyes narrowed and he shook his head in disgust. "The Prince Charming of Baseball. What a joke."

Paul turned away from the window and fixed his eyes on his friend. "You're pathetic. I don't need this shit from you. You want to apologize, you know where I'll be . . . *pal.*"

Mike was on the phone with Kate the moment Paul walked out the door. "Paul said you were sick. How are you feeling?"

"I'm surviving, but I'm really tired."

Her voice was hoarse and he could tell she'd been crying.

"What's really wrong, Katie?"

"Just a cold. That's all."

But he knew what it was. "You told him, didn't you."

"It was awful, Mike." Her voice broke and a sob escaped, but she held herself in check. "I tried to be calm. But he kept denying there were other women." Her voice rose. "He just kept lying to me! Even when I pointed out the evidence, he acted like I was some kind of lunatic, imagining it all."

"You knew he would, Katie. We talked about that."

"I know," she said softly.

"What about the money?"

"I tried to follow the script you and I worked out, Mike. I really did. I told him that I needed to be included in all financial decisions from now on, but he said his advisor would take care of it."

Mike winced, not knowing what to tell her anymore. If she got angry enough—fed up enough—would she finally leave Paul? "What did *you* say?" Silence. "Kate?"

She answered so softly he had to jam the phone against his ear to hear her.

"I told him that if he couldn't be honest with me, I couldn't live with him."

Mike stayed silent, afraid his voice would give away the soaring hope he felt. Christ, she could probably hear his heart pounding.

"I told him to go to Phoenix without me."

She began sobbing. He had to say something. "Katie, please . . . stop crying. Tell me what Paul said."

"He . . . he yelled at me. Said he didn't know who I was anymore." Silence. Then, "And I screamed back at him that I didn't know who I was anymore, either."

"I know it was a hard thing to do, but it was time."

"I know," she whispered. "Did he . . . did he say anything to you?"

"No."

"Nothing at all?"

Mike cradled his forehead in his hand and closed his eyes. "He said he still loves you."

Paul had flown to Phoenix alone and spent his first ten days there trying to convince her to join him. In the end, Kate had relented. She'd called Mike and, almost apologetically, told him of her decision. "I have to go, Mike," she'd said, as if seeking his approval. "He wants to try to work things out. I need to see his eyes . . . to see if he really means it, y'know?"

"Stay tough, Kate," Mike had said, his heart breaking. "I'll see you in October." He'd paused. The vapor of a decision had now become a solid, and Paul's words came back to him. *"You didn't stand a chance."*

His last words to her before she left for Phoenix were, "Tell Paul I'm . . . No. Just tell him I'll call."

But he never made that call. And he saw Kate much

sooner than October, because Paul was dead two weeks later.

Mike's fist came down onto the arm of the couch, making an unsatisfying thud. What the hell did faith mean to him anymore? Guilt was the new watchword. His own guilt was the reason he more than understood what Kate was going through—and why he'd been so patient with her. But it had to end. He knew he could never take back the words he'd said to Paul. He wanted to move ahead. And he wanted Kate to make that journey with him.

When the phone rang again that evening, he knew it was Sheryl, ready to pick up their conversation where they'd left off. He wasn't in the mood and he let it ring until the machine picked it up.

"I know you're there, Mike." She waited. "Okay, so don't pick up. I just want to let you know you owe me one. Kate called to tell me she wanted out of your contract, and I convinced her that whatever had happened between the two of you, she still needed to get that damned house fixed. Believe me, it took some doing. So, in case you had any doubt, you guys are still on for Monday. Say thank you, little brother."

CHAPTER
FIFTEEN

K ate had just finished drying her hair when she heard a loud metallic clattering outside, accompa-_____ nied by Homer's barking. She hurried to the bedroom and peered out the window. Then she swore to herself. She'd gotten up early in hopes of getting out of the house before Mike arrived. She even had a note written and ready to pin to the front door, telling him she'd be gone for the day. Too late.

By the time Kate put on what little makeup she wore, her anxiety level had risen considerably. When Mike rang the doorbell, her unease at seeing him again caused her heart to pound and she felt herself grow hot with embarrassment. He rang the bell again as she was coming down the stairs, and she heard him shout, "Kate? It's just me. Open up."

He stood on the porch looking nearly as uncomfortable as she felt. Kate stood aside to let him in. "You're early."

"Sorry. Habit."

They stood in the hallway for a few seconds and Mike finally said, "Just wanted to put my thermos in the kitchen." He held up the metal container as if to prove he had a valid excuse for being in the house.

"Be my guest," she said, waving him on. She was

a few steps behind him, when she asked, "Where's Matt?"

"He's on his way."

Mike set the thermos on the counter and turned to face her. "Why are we acting like strangers?" She shrugged, her unease still evident. "I'm sorry if what I said last night made you uncomfortable, but I had to let you know how I feel."

"Not now, Mike. Please."

"Right," Mike said shortly. "Not now." He brushed past her. As he stepped outside, Matt was pulling up to the curb.

Kate was trying to form an apology, but she hung back in the doorway to watch Mike trot down the steps to meet his nephew. The two stood talking with their heads bent together. Matt's short hair, the color of walnut shells, contrasted with Mike's. The younger man, with his faded jeans slung low on his lean hips, subconsciously aped his uncle's gestures. She could see the similarity of their builds and, whether from genes or hard work, they were both in great shape. Kate surprised herself by noticing.

Matt lifted his head for a moment and scanned the roof before pushing up the sleeves on the jersey he wore. His forearms were strong and tanned. Kate was still staring at him when she realized Mike was speaking to her. She stepped out of the protection of the entry.

"Kate, this is Matt."

She held out her hand to the handsome young man.

"It's nice to finally meet you, Mrs. Armstrong."

"Kate. Please."

She looked up into his face and was startled by a pair of eyes the color of dry pine bark—not quite brown, not quite gray. The clear irises were rimmed in black, further setting off their hazel color. His mouth was smiling the patented Fitzgerald smile. She felt as if she'd known him forever, and she smiled back.

Matt was still holding her hand, when she said, "Well, I'll let you guys get to work."

He quickly released her, and watched appreciatively as she made her way back up the cement walk. "Nice," he stated.

Mike, misreading his nephew's comment, answered, "Yeah, she's a great lady."

Matt bent to pick up the toolbox. "Man, she's one *hot* lady."

Mike looked up from his notebook, startled.

"Don't tell me you never noticed," Matt said, grinning.

Mike casually shrugged. "We grew up together," he said by way of explanation.

"So. What?"

"So." Mike turned and walked toward the ladder he'd left on the lawn. "I guess I think of her as a sister." He wondered if Matt was buying this.

"Hey, if it were me, I'd be thinking second cousin twice-removed."

Mike headed off in the direction of the backyard. "I'm not paying you to think."

Matt made a face, and followed his uncle.

CHAPTER

SIXTEEN

The work had been going well. On Thursday, as Kate left the house for a lunch date with Sheryl, _____ she circled the house until she found the ladder and Mike.

"I'm leaving," she called up to him. "Is there anything you need while I'm out?"

"Just your smile, darlin'," he shouted down.

"That Irish charm will take you only so far in life, Michael Fitzgerald."

He grinned as she turned and headed for her car, raising her arm in a wave. Mike went back to replacing the fish-scale shingles in the cornice.

"Hey! Uncle Mike?" Matt's shout reached him from the other side of the house. "Can you come here a minute?"

Mike looked up at Matt, who had been working on the eaves under the tower and now stood next to the window. "What? You find some rot?"

"No. Something a lot more interesting. Come on up."

Kate leafed through the June 1989 issue of *House and Garden* as she sat in Sheryl's living room, which doubled as her waiting room when she had clients. She heard voices coming down the hall. One sounded suspiciously like Donna Estes's, and she quickly put down the magazine and jumped up to make a run for the bathroom. She wasn't fast enough, and looked into the pert face of the ex-head-cheerleader.

"Kate!" Donna exclaimed. "What a coincidence. I was just telling Sheryl I needed to call you. And here you are!"

"Donna," Kate said evenly, eyeing Sheryl over Donna's shoulder. Sheryl gave Kate a shrug, conveying her deepest sympathies.

Donna, oblivious to the silent signals, said, "You baffled me with that phone call the other night. Was there something you wanted to tell me?"

Kate was the one who looked baffled. "Phone call?"

"Come on, Kate. I know we're all getting older, but surely you remember calling me?"

"Oh, Christ, I'm sorry, Donna." The other woman flinched at Kate's choice of words. "Listen, can I call you later?"

Sheryl picked up the cue and took Donna's arm. "Kate and I were just going out." Donna's head was bobbing up and down as Sheryl showed her out the door.

Sheryl held up her hands before Kate could lay into her. "It's not my fault. My regular client canceled this morning and Donna just walked in. I couldn't turn her down." Kate made a face. As they were walking out the door, Sheryl asked in a conspiratorial tone, "Do you suppose she puts on her outfit and Bill puts on his shoulder pads, and they play the Football Captain and the Cheerleader?"

Kate snickered. "That's a scary thought."

"It sure is. I've been under the bleachers with Bill."

Kate's laughter pealed out across the street.

Mike, his hands shading the sides of his face, peered into the window of the tower room. "Oh, Christ," he said softly, as he stared at the shrine Kate had built to Paul.

"Amazing, huh?" Matt said excitedly. "She's got all his stuff in there! How do I get in?"

"You don't," Mike answered, straightening up.

"Oh, come on! Can't I just sneak in—take a look?"

"Not without Kate's permission."

"How am I supposed to get her permission if I can't talk to her about Paul Armstrong?"

"I guess you're stuck between a rock and a hard place, Matt, m'boy."

"I bet I can get her to show it to me."

"You say one word to her about this and you can forget about coming back tomorrow. You understand?"

Matt put his hands on his hips and shook his head in disgust, as his uncle climbed back down the ladder.

Paul was right, Mike thought. *You don't stand a chance.*

Sheryl and Kate decided on Chinese, and now sat in a booth of the Sunshine Garden sharing a plate of pot stickers.

Kate dipped one of the dumplings into the garlicky brown sauce and bit into it. "I could eat these for the rest of my life."

"Maybe we should just get another order of these and forget the moo shu pork," Sheryl said, trying to get her chopsticks around the slippery dough. She finally gave up and picked up the pot sticker with her fingers. "I could lose a lot of weight if I ate with those damned things."

"Like you need to lose weight."

Sheryl eyed Kate. "Looks to me like you could gain a few pounds. What the hell do you eat at home?"

Kate shrugged, dismissing the topic, and eyed the last pot sticker.

"It's yours," Sheryl said.

"I really like Matt. He seems like a nice kid."

"Yeah, I've pretty much decided to keep him. So, he's doing a good job?"

Kate nodded, sipping her tea. "He and Mike are working their tails off."

"Mike's really enjoying it. He loves that kid."

Kate leaned back and let Beth, their decidedly non-Chinese waitress, remove the plates from the table. "He looks a lot like you."

Sheryl grinned. "I'll take that as a compliment."

Beth was back with their lunch. Kate waited impatiently as the college student meticulously spread the thin Chinese pancakes with duck sauce, piled the moo shu in the center, added a few wisps of green onion, and then proceeded to attempt the intricate folding process. Afraid they'd never get to eat, Kate said, "It's okay, Beth. We'll take it from here." A look of relief crossed the girl's face. "Where was I?" Kate asked.

"You were telling me how much my gorgeous son looks like me."

"Oh, right." Kate chewed, swallowed, then said, "Don't take this the wrong way, but where did he get those eyes?"

Sheryl's own eyes flickered away from Kate's for an instant, then returned. "Who knows. Some latent gene, I guess."

"Does he miss his dad much?"

"No, I think he's doing okay. Don't get me wrong, Dan is a great father. And Matt loved spending the summer with him, but he's always been pretty self-sufficient, and Mike's always been there for him when Dan couldn't be."

"Has it been hard for you?"

"The divorce?" Sheryl shook her head. "No, it needed to happen. Dan and I really grew apart. We were married so young . . ."

The two women ate in silence for a few minutes, then Sheryl said, "Kate? Can I ask you something?"

"Sure." Kate concentrated on scooping up the last bit of moo shu pork.

"I mean, I know we've never been bosom buddies or anything..."

"Well, I've known you for over twenty years, but I've just gotten to *know* you since you moved back. I think that qualifies you as some kind of buddy." Kate smiled slyly. "Although I happen to know you didn't like me much in high school. I could never figure out why."

Sheryl waved away Kate's observation, not wanting to get off course. "It was a long time ago. What I want to know is, how do you feel about Mike?"

Kate's fork stopped in midair and she stared at Sheryl. "I think I just figured it out. You knew all along how Mike felt about me."

"Yeah. How come *you* didn't?"

"Is that what this lunch is about?" Kate put her fork down and it clattered against the plate. "What a dirty trick."

Sheryl's face reddened, and she rushed to get the words out before Kate could stop her or, worse, get up and leave. "Kate, you're all he cares about. He's crazy about you. I don't think a day goes by that he doesn't think or worry about you. I think you both deserve a little happiness at this point. Can't you give him a chance?"

"I'm happy," Kate said with false conviction.

"You're happy? Kate, you've cut off all your friends, you sleep on the couch when you sleep at all, you've lost interest in everything that ever meant anything to you, and you drink too much ... do I need go on?"

"Don't tell me how to live my life."

Sheryl sat back in the booth. "What life?" Then, softening her tone, she asked, "Don't you miss the closeness of someone? Don't you want to love anyone again?"

Kate's chin began to quiver and she clamped her jaw tightly to stop it. Her hand nervously kneaded the napkin she was holding.

Sheryl reached across the table and covered her

friend's hand with her own. "I know you do, Kate. Why won't you admit it?"

Kate found her voice, and said, "You don't know anything about me or how I feel." Fumbling in her purse, she extracted a ten-dollar bill from her wallet and slapped it on the table. "Leave me alone." She slid out of the booth and stiffly walked out of the restaurant.

Sheryl sighed deeply, put her face in her hands, and whispered, "I tried, Mike."

Mike looked at his watch for the third time in twenty minutes. It was five o'clock. He had sent Matt home half an hour ago. Where was Kate? He was putting his tools on the back porch when he heard Kate's phone ringing, and he stepped into the kitchen to answer it.

"Mike?"

Hearing his sister's voice, Mike said, "Where did you guys go for lunch? Richmond?"

"She's not home yet?"

"No, and I was just getting ready to leave. Is Kate on her way?"

"The last time I saw her she was throwing money at me and walking out of the restaurant. She didn't even eat her fortune cookie. You know what it said? 'Fortunes come and go, but friendships last forever.'" She chuckled mirthlessly.

"What happened?"

"Let's just say it didn't go well, and leave it at that."

"Let's not."

After Sheryl's summary of her luncheon fiasco, Mike said, "I think I know where to find her."

"Don't do it, Mike. She definitely wants to be left alone. She'll come home after you leave. Count on it." She paused. "I'm sorry, Mike. I thought I could help, but she's impossible to talk to."

"She needs time."

"She's *had* time," Sheryl said harshly. "She doesn't care about anyone but herself."

Mike's sarcastic "Thanks for your insights" ended the phone call.

Kate let herself into the back entrance of the shop and stood in the small kitchen, waiting for her eyes to adjust. She didn't want to turn on any lights. Didn't want to lose the blanket of protection the dark provided. There was no moon, but she began to see faint outlines of shapes with the help of a streetlamp in the back parking lot. Feeling her way along the counter, she found a mug and filled it with tap water. She wished for a glass of wine.

She'd spent the afternoon meandering along the Skyline Drive on the Blue Ridge Parkway. But it had been a gray day, and the heavy fog brought her back into the valley sooner than she wanted. Her mood hadn't improved, and at four-thirty she'd stopped at the Blue Bottle, a small cocktail lounge in Waynesboro, and ordered a glass of rosé. An hour later, she'd had three glasses. She then drove to the shop, knowing Cindy had closed it up at six. She didn't see any point in going home.

The slow-motion, what-the-hell feeling from the wine had worn off, leaving her cold and dry-mouthed. Finishing off the water, Kate made her way out of the kitchen and into the small back room she and Cindy used as a lounge. Kate curled up on the old plaid sofa, pulled a quilt over her, and using her coat as a pillow, tried to close her eyes. But it was early, and sleep wouldn't come. Kate lay in the dark, eyes open, listening to the night sounds of the old building. Fifteen minutes passed. An eternity. A cold eternity. The automatic thermostat had obviously downshifted to its nighttime setting of 55 degrees.

A high-pitched chirping echoed through the shop, startling Kate. The phone was ringing and she knew who was calling. It stopped after nine rings. She turned to face the back of the couch, pulling herself into a tighter ball. The hum of the refrigerator in the kitchen stopped with a mechanical clack and silence enveloped her. A sharp, scrabbling sound reached her ears. A mouse—a rat?—in one of the kitchen cupboards. She closed her eyes tightly, wishing she could start this day again.

Don't you want to love anyone again?

Her brain screamed *"No!"*

Trying to clear her mind, she scrunched her eyes shut and silently repeated the words, *"Don't think . . . don't think."* It was a trick she'd used since her teens, but it didn't seem to work anymore.

"You promised . . . you promised we'd be together always."

Kate knew how childish the words sounded. How naïve they were. When would this pain go away? What was wrong with her, that she couldn't leave it behind?

"Don't you miss the closeness?"

The voice in her head shouted, *"Yes, damn it!"*

"Stop it!" she said aloud. "Don't think!"

She wanted to talk to someone who'd listen to her problems. She wanted to talk to the friend who'd always been her touchstone. But how could she? Mike had become the problem. How could he possibly listen now?

Now that she knew how he felt about her, how could she talk about Paul without hurting Mike? Oh, God, she was lost without his down-to-earth advice; his knowing just when to make a joke. She already missed the way he rode her when her stubbornness threatened to cease being a good thing. Kate wanted to go home. She wanted the warm cocoon that a drink provided; the dreamless sleep it gave her.

The phone was ringing again, and she let it. He knew her so well. Damn it! Mike knew everything about her.

And she wanted . . . *"Why don't you admit it?"* . . . him.

Her eyes flew open.

Locking the shop door behind her, she turned to the near empty parking lot. A frost had settled, making the pavement sparkle under the streetlamp. The leather soles of her boots fought to get a grip on the slick asphalt as she made her way to her car. The wipers and the car heater made quick work of the feathery ice on the wind-shield, and she drove home through the deserted streets of Staunton.

The kitchen light was on when she let herself in. A note was propped up against a mug in the middle of the table.

I fed Homer. You know where I am if you need me. Mike

She quickly dialed his number, before she could change her mind. After the fifth ring she gave up.

Mike gave up waiting for Kate around seven and called Susan Lake. She'd already eaten, but had leftovers if he wanted them. They both knew what he wanted, but they played the game anyway, and Mike drove to her house with anticipation.

Susan, her two divorces leaving her with a healthy respect for noncommitment, was uncomplicated, fun, easy on the eyes, and a very inventive lover: a winning combination for Mike these days. "I love men," she'd said many times. "But shoot me before I marry another one." Susan could make him forget his day. No mean feat.

The music was soft, the wine was good, and the candles were, like Susan, warmly seductive. But a strange thing happened once Mike was comfortably ensconced on her sofa. His mind kept wandering.

He was staring into the glass he held, when Susan playfully poked him, and said, "So, what do you think? I'll call up my two exes, and we'll have a little contest . . ."

Mike looked up and smiled vaguely. "Sure, whatever you want."

Susan chuckled. "Mike. Where are you tonight?"

He sighed and set the wine glass on the coffee table. Turning to Susan, he said, "I'm sorry. What did you say?"

"Wasn't important." She kissed his hand.

"I'm sorry," he repeated. "Guess I'm tired."

"Do you want to leave?"

He shook his head.

"Well, then, we could just kick back and watch TV."

"Sounds good."

Not much later, he was asleep. When he awoke, Mike folded the afghan she'd covered him with. He went into her bedroom waking her to kiss her good-bye—to thank her.

"For what?" she sleepily asked.

"For putting up with me. For being here."

"Don't give it a second thought." She smiled. "It's been fun."

"That it has," he said.

"I think it's time for you to find someone who can give you what you need, Mike."

He nodded. "How about you?"

"What I need is to go back to sleep. That," she said, closing her eyes, "and occasional great sex."

Mike smiled and pulled the blankets up over her shoulder. He left her Victorian cottage as the sun's rays crept over the Blue Ridge.

CHAPTER

SEVENTEEN

Mike let himself in through Kate's front door as he had for the past three days. As he walked _____ down the hallway to the kitchen, he glanced into the den.

Kate, fully dressed, was asleep on the couch. He reached in to close the door. When he saw the empty wine bottle and glass on the coffee table, he silently swore. It was getting worse. Matt's voice reached him from the front of the house and he quickly shut the door. Putting his finger to his lips, he ushered Matt back outside. "She's still sleeping. Why don't you take the day off?"

Matt happily agreed.

By half past ten Mike had fed and walked the dog, read the morning paper, and made a pot of coffee. Kate slept on. Pouring her a cup of coffee, adding the two tea-spoons of sugar she liked, he walked back into the den and set the cup down. He gently nudged her with his knee. She buried her face deeper into the pillow.

He shook her shoulder. "Kate? Time to get up." She moaned, but didn't move. "Kate!" Louder this time, with a harder shake.

Earthquake, Kate thought. *An earthquake in Virginia. How strange.*

Mike walked to the window and pulled up the blind. It didn't catch and made a loud, flapping noise as it spun into a tight roll.

"Katie. Damn it, wake up!"

His angry voice reached through her sleepy brain and latched onto a functioning lobe. She groaned and mumbled something into the pillow. *There's that shaking again.* It was hard to ignore, and she slowly lifted her head. Blinking, barely able to open her eyes, she gazed at the flowered print of the pillowcase until it came into focus. She sluggishly turned over and squinted up at Mike's unsmiling face.

She started to speak, but instead of words a croaking sound emerged. Clearing her throat, Kate finally said, "Go away."

Mike looked at the bags under her eyes, and her mouth, puffy with sleep and wine. A crease ran across her right cheek like an old scar. A streak of mascara formed a shadow under her eye.

"You look like shit."

"You say the nicest things," she responded.

"Drink the coffee while it's hot." He stalked out of the room.

Kate sat up and her head pounded. She slammed her eyes shut and the pain turned to a dull thudding. When she opened them again, he was standing in front of her, holding out a wet towel. Wordlessly taking it from him, she sank her face into its cool, soothing folds and sighed.

"Better?"

She nodded, lifting her face from the cloth.

Mike pushed aside several magazines and sat on the coffee table. He handed her the cup and she took a swallow.

"So, is this what it's come to? The thought of my being in love with you is so horrible that you have to get stinking drunk?"

"No." She handed back the cup and pressed the towel to her eyes again.

"What, then?"

"I couldn't sleep, okay?"

"No!" He pulled the towel away from her with a jerk. "It's not okay. Where were you all afternoon and evening?"

"Out."

"Out where?"

"Just out, y'know? And where were you? I tried to call."

He abruptly stood. "Out."

"Out where?"

"I was with a friend."

"Male or female?"

"Why do you care?"

Kate tried to pull off a nonchalant shrug. It didn't come across very well. "Is it okay if I take a shower, warden?" she asked sarcastically.

"Be my guest."

"Gee, thanks. Maybe you'd like to stand guard at the door?" Bracing herself against the arm of the sofa, she slowly stood to face him, her eyes sending out a familiar "I dare you" signal.

The two of them had sparked off each other from the beginning. She had fallen in love with Paul, and that had been a different kind of fire. But she and Mike had more in common. Their likes and dislikes and ideas ran on a parallel plane, and when one of them crossed that line, their debates lasted for hours—days. Paul would sit and listen, amazed that the two of them could go on for so long about a question like: Who deserved the Oscar that year for best actor? Was Alfred Hitchcock the greatest director of all time or was he playing a joke on everyone? Did Anastasia die or was she really poor Anna Andersen who lived in nearby Charlottesville?

Sometimes, the debate would span months. Paul and Kate would arrive home from San Francisco and Mike would show up the next weekend, plunk down a stack of books, and begin citing passages to prove a point he'd been trying to make back in February. Neither would back down. They simply called a truce and went on to another, less incendiary, topic.

Mike and Kate sparred and parried and lit small fires that could be put out with a few well-chosen words. Maybe it was the Irish in both of them. Maybe it was something more.

Paul was smart enough to stay out of the discussions. And he was smart enough to know that Kate needed them. There was a combative streak in her that was always questioning. Paul could hold his own with Kate or Mike, but it just didn't mean that much to him to do so.

Kate knew that Paul didn't see much point in discussing the use of color in a Van Gogh, or a camera angle in a Hitchcock film, or the use of light and dark space in an Edward Weston print. To Paul, the things were there and done. What was there to talk about? This attitude became stronger as the years went on and Kate turned to Mike more and more for the mental games she loved to play. Twenty years down the road, they knew each other better than any married couple.

Kate has read the same page three times before putting aside the book. Bored and depressed that Paul is back for only a three-day home stand, she sits staring out at the Bay. He has already left for the ballpark, and the only thing she has to look forward to is another cold, windy night at Candlestick Park. And then the phone rings, and it's Mike, lifting her spirits.

"Put on your red dress, mama, cause we're goin' out tonight."

"Mike!" She's surprised and pleased. "Where are you?"

"At the moment I'm in a phone stall at the San Francisco airport. Can I come over and play?"

"How soon can you get here?"

When the doorbell rings Kate runs, flinging open the door, and throws her arms around Mike, crushing the flowers he's brought her. Laughing, she pulls him inside, saying, "God, if you aren't a sight for sore eyes!"

"More likely just a sight." He hands her the flowers. "I feel like I've been on a plane all my life."

"Let me get you something to drink." She is moving toward the kitchen.

"What I'd really love is a shower."

Kate is leaning against the wall next to the bathroom door that he's left open a crack so they can talk.

"What are you doing here?" she shouts over the rush of the water.

"The Foundation for Architectural Heritage is having a fund-raiser. I was invited. And I could use a date."

"Tonight?"

"Yeah. It's at the Sir Francis Drake. Black tie. Got something tasteful, yet sexy, you've been dying to wear someplace?"

"As a matter of fact, I do."

"Is that a yes?"

"I'd love to go."

Mike smiles to himself and shuts off the water. Wrapping a bath towel around his waist, he steps out of the shower.

"I'm tired of talking to this door," Kate says. "Are you decent?"

"In the immortal words of Kate Armstrong: 'Never, come on in.' "

Kate sits on the toilet lid and talks to him as he shaves. He can see her eyes on his profile as he looks in the mirror. He's suddenly flustered.

"So, what time is this affair?" she asks.

"Cocktails at six. Dinner at seven," he answers, marveling at her choice of words.

"That only gives me an hour to get gorgeous." She is looking at his chest now. "I never realized what great shape you're in."

He shrugs, quickly rinsing the razor and wiping off his face.

"Where are you staying?"

"They booked me into the Sir Francis."

"Wrong. You're staying here." She stands, and as she walks past him, pinches a fold of the towel he is wearing. "Better watch out. One false move and all your secrets will be revealed." She grins at him. "Let me show you where the guest room is."

Mike is standing at the living room window admiring the view.

"Ta da!"

He turns at the sound of Kate's voice, and in a reverent voice, he says, "Holy Christ."

"You like?"

The floor-length royal blue dress shimmers like liquid sapphires as she slowly turns around. The thousands of beads on the figure-hugging silk catch the light and send out small flashes of light. Long-sleeved, high-necked, it reveals nothing, and everything. She steps forward and he sees the slit up the left side.

"And I was just going to comment on the view from the window," he says, getting his voice back. She is looking at him strangely. "What?" he asks.

"You could be on the cover of GQ." Kate moves closer to him. "You look gorgeous." She runs her hand down the lapel of his tux. "You are *gorgeous."*

"You just noticed?" he says lightly, trying to disguise his intense reaction to her nearness.

He takes in her auburn hair casually piled on top of her head, held there with a rhinestone clip. He breathes in her perfume, and knows he has to move, or die from wanting her.

"If you're ready. . . ?" Kate dangles the car keys in front of him.

They are seated at a circular table, Kate on Mike's left, finishing their dinner. Seated at the table with them is James

Alderson, the head of the foundation, a congressman, a representative from the California Preservation Foundation, and their wives. They are all thrilled to be introduced to the wife of Paul Armstrong, a San Francisco legend at that point, and Kate sparkles for them.

As the plates are being cleared, Mr. Alderson rises from his seat and walks to a podium that has been set up at the head of the banquet room. The string quartet that has been providing elegant background music stops playing, and the room grows quiet.

"I want to thank you all for coming and supporting the Foundation for San Francisco's Architectural Heritage. You'll be happy to know that the money you've so generously contributed over the past year, and the three hundred dollars per plate tonight, has been put to good use. By the way, dessert is coming." The two hundred-plus people in the room chuckle, as the head of the foundation goes on to report what has been accomplished. Then he pauses. "But we're not here just to raise money. Tonight, the foundation would like to honor a man whose vision, expertise, and talent has done more for San Francisco preservation this past year than we could have possibly dreamed. I'd like to introduce the man behind CraftWork Incorporated, Michael James Fitzgerald."

As the applause begins, Kate stares at Mike, dumbfounded. He winks at her and makes his way to the podium to accept the award.

"I can't believe you knew this all along and didn't tell me," Kate chides him.

They've gone up to the Starlite Roof to finish off the evening with brandy and dancing, and they now move to the haunting strains of "A Summer Place." Mike doesn't want to talk, he just wants to hold her.

He quietly says, "I didn't want to make a big deal out of it."

"Like you didn't want to make a big deal out of the fact that your picture was on the cover of Time *magazine last year? I could've killed you for not telling us."*

Time *had done a special issue on preservation in America*

in 1990. Mike's company had won many prestigious awards by then, and he had landed on the cover. A head-and-shoulders shot of Mike in a hard hat, his gray eyes intent on the crumbling façade of a once-splendid opera house.

Paul Armstrong had already made the cover of Time. *Twice.*

"How come that Hoover woman didn't come with you?"

"Regina." Mike corrects her.

"All right, Regina. I knew it had something to do with vacuum cleaners. Why didn't she come?" she asks again.

Mike stifles a laugh, then says, "Katie, hush. Let's dance."

She moves closer to him, and always one to get the last word in, whispers, "I'm very proud of you."

They let themselves into the condo a little past midnight, Kate carrying her shoes. Paul is waiting up for them in the living room, as they knew he would. It takes him a couple of hours to wind down after a game. Mike is unknotting his bow tie, unfastening the top button of his shirt, as Paul rises to greet him.

"Pretty sharp, buddy," Paul says, giving his hand a quick pump.

Paul glances at his wife, but makes no comment. Mike frowns at Kate, and she gives her head a small shake.

"How was the game tonight?' she asks.

"We won, four to two. I hit a home run, batted in a couple of runs."

"And the world goes on." Kate smiles wanly. "If you guys will excuse me, I'm beat. I'll see you in the morning, Mike. And thanks for the wonderful evening. Congratulations, again." And she is gone.

The two men sit talking for twenty minutes before Paul yawns.

"I'd better hit the sack. I'll be better company tomorrow." He pauses at the master bedroom door. "What time does your flight leave?"

"Pretty early. Nine-fifteen."

"I'll try to get up. If I don't, it was great seeing ya."

"*Same here,*" *Mike answers, with the odd feeling that neither of them really means it.*

The door closes behind Paul. Mike stays on the couch for a few more minutes, then wearily gets up and goes into the kitchen for a glass of water. Paul's angry voice can be heard clearly through the walls, rooting Mike in place.

"Why the hell weren't you at the game tonight?"

He can't hear Kate's reply.

"Yeah, I got your message. And what the hell is that? Leaving a goddamn message, for chrissakes!"

"Lower your voice." Kate's voice is suddenly clear. She must have been standing at the connecting wall. "I couldn't reach you. You were on the field."

"You're supposed to be at the game, Kate."

"It was an important night for Mike. I'm glad I went."

"Fuck Mike! You belong at the games."

"I go to every game, Paul. Every game! Missing one isn't the end of the world."

"I need you there!"

"I'll be there tomorrow night. And the night after that. And then you'll be on the road again. Why don't you need me there?"

Paul doesn't answer. There is a thudding noise and a sudden, ominous silence. Mike has reached the kitchen door in a split second, but he hears Kate's voice again.

"Are you happy now?" She's crying. "That was my favorite piece."

Mike breathes deeply, as he realizes the sound was some object knocked over—broken. Not Kate.

"I'm sorry."

She makes an unintelligible sound.

Not wanting to listen anymore, yet unable to stop himself, Mike leans against the doorjamb and closes his eyes. Was this how it always was with them? God, he hoped not. Couldn't be. Why the hell did she put up with it?

"Kate, I'm sorry," Paul says again. "I haven't seen you in nine days. I thought we'd be alone." There is a pause. "Come on, baby . . . I love you. You know that."

Mike strains to hear Kate's words, but none come. It's quiet for a very long time and Mike understands the silence when it's broken by a small moan. His question has been answered.

He takes off his shoes and creeps to the guest room to spend a lonely, restless night.

Mike is up very early, and is surprised to find Kate in the kitchen, drinking coffee. "Morning." Mike kisses her cheek. "What are you doing up?"

"I didn't want to miss you."

He doesn't fail to catch the wistful tone of her voice.

"We're friends, Katie, so I have to tell you . . . I heard the fight last night. Are you okay?"

"I'm fine." She meets his eyes. "Really. Hey, we're married. We argue."

"I'm sorry if I was the cause of this."

"Don't be." She gives him a small smile. "I had a great time. It was very special."

They talk quietly through breakfast and then it's time for him to leave. As they wait for his cab, he says, "I guess I'm not gonna get to say good-bye to Paul."

"He usually sleeps till about eleven."

Mike nods.

"I miss the old days, Mike."

"We had a lot of fun. But we still do, Katie."

She doesn't say anything.

"You'll be home in a couple of months. We'll get together for a marathon weekend of Trivial Pursuit."

Her eyes fill with tears. "I love you, Mike."

He takes her in his arms and rocks her. "I love you, too, darlin'. Don't get lost in all this." The buzzer rings, signaling his ride. "Have a little faith. Lots of good things to come. I know it."

Hidden scars. Hidden betrayals. Hidden pain. They'd all been concealing something. The damage had been done. But at least his love was out in the open at last. It was a start.

Mike went into the kitchen to wait. When the sound of running water stopped, and he knew Kate was done showering, Mike poured her another cup of coffee.

CHAPTER

EIGHTEEN

Kate shuffled barefoot into the kitchen, tightening the belt on her terry-cloth bathrobe. "Still here, _____ huh?" she said wearily, eyeing Mike.

"Still here," he answered. "What do you want for breakfast?"

"Aspirin. Lots of aspirin."

"Think you can handle some toast?"

"No." As she sat in the nearest chair, the towel she'd wrapped around her head began slipping. She tried to catch it, and the sudden movement made her groan. The towel landed on the floor. "Would you get that for me? I don't think I can bend over and live."

Mike obliged and then went to pop two pieces of bread in the toaster.

"Where's Matt?" she asked.

"I sent him home. I didn't think his youthful eyes could take the sight of you today."

"And the hits just keep on comin'." Kate reached for the aspirin bottle and began struggling with the safety cap.

Mike's fingers closed around her hand. "Here, let me." With minimal effort, he opened the bottle. "How many?"

She cupped her hand and said, "Just pour. I'll say when."

In minutes, a plate of buttered toast appeared in front of her, along with a cup of coffee.

"You're a man of many talents," she said, just a touch of sarcasm in her voice.

"More than you know." He straddled the chair across from her, and watched as she gazed at the toast as if it were a small alien that had somehow landed in her kitchen. "Oh, you *are* in bad shape when you let a line like that get past you."

"Do you want snappy repartee or do you want me to eat this toast?"

"Eat."

Kate choked down most of one piece before speaking again. "Y'know, that was a fairly high school thing, Sheryl talking to me like that."

"Used to work in high school."

"Did it really?" Kate asked in disbelief.

"Oh, yeah. You wouldn't believe the perks of having an older sister, especially when you're a sophomore and your sister is a senior."

"Well! This is a side to you I know nothing about. Mike Fitzgerald, teenage gigolo."

His smile spoke volumes.

She was intrigued. "Who was your first?"

"You don't know her. She was in Sheryl's class."

"Ah, an older woman," Kate stated. "Where?"

"Why are you so interested?"

"Keeps my mind off the pounding in my head. Come on. Where?"

Teasing her, he looked up at the ceiling as if deliberating whether or not to tell. He finally said, "The supply closet in the journalism room."

"What? Oh, that's disgusting!"

"Hey, it was carpeted!"

"I don't believe you."

"You never saw that little commemorative plaque in there? It's right next to the filing cabinet."

"What, the one that says Michael J. Fitzgerald is full of shit?"

His eyes widened in mock indignation. "Have I ever lied to you?"

Kate looked into his kind, gray eyes. They smiled at her and she suddenly understood how that unnamed girl felt all those years ago. It was not the reaction she'd expected, and Kate struggled to halt the flush that was coming over her. Grabbing the coffee cup with both hands, she brought it to her lips and hid there.

"Well," Mike said, standing. "I think you can get through the rest of the day without me. They're calling for rain the next few days, so I think Matt and I are going to move indoors."

"Fine," she said from behind the cup. "Thanks, Mike. I mean it."

"I know you do." He had started for the hallway, and Kate put the cup down in its saucer with hands that trembled. "Oh—and Kate?" His voice was close—just behind her. "Don't let it get this bad again. If you can't sleep, or want to talk, just call me." He picked up her damp, heavy hair and held it.

"I tried last night. You weren't there."

He wouldn't let her make him feel guilty. "I waited as long as I could, Kate." He still held her hair and brought his head even with hers. "There are some things I can't do without."

His words, almost a challenge, were a whisper on her neck and she shivered. Her eyes closed. He let her hair fall back into place and walked out.

Kate drifted through the day, unable to shake off her hangover. She couldn't read. Her eyes hurt too much. Watching TV made her head ache. In the end, she put a couple of classical CD's on and simply sat. But that brought on thoughts of Mike and what he couldn't do without, and she wondered who he was doing it with. It was only three o'clock, but the combined forces of lust and envy told her it was time to go to bed. She was asleep in minutes and didn't wake until she heard the doorbell ring.

The room was dark and she honestly didn't know what day it was, or whether it was early morning or late night. The doorbell chimed again as she snapped on the hall light and went downstairs.

"Oh, man. I'm sorry. Did I wake you up?" Matt stood on the porch, holding a short rope that was attached to Homer.

"It's okay. What time is it?"

"About seven, I guess." He shifted his weight from one foot to the other, uncomfortable that he'd interrupted her. "I just drove by to see if Mike wanted to go to a movie, and I found Homer down the street." He held out the makeshift leash to Kate.

She took it from Matt. Thanking him, she turned to close the door, when Matt's hand shot out, holding it open.

"Uh, would you like to go? To the movies?"

"I don't think so, but thanks for asking."

He moved in closer, leaning an arm on the doorframe. "Come on. My treat. I'll even spring for some popcorn."

"Really, Matt. No." His persistence flattered her. There was something vaguely familiar about it. "This just isn't the best time." Kate looked up at him, and he smiled slowly. It was a knowing smile that crinkled the corners of his eyes, transforming him from the nineteen-year-old boy he was, to an adult male.

"So, there'll be a better time?"

She was mesmerized by his eyes, and he knew it. This realization moved her to action and she stepped back. "Yes, some other time. Thanks for bringing Homer back."

Kate closed the door and breathed in deeply. She quickly decided it was the hangover that left her susceptible to his obvious charm. This was Sheryl's little boy?

Turning her attention to the dog, she said, "I've got to get that fence fixed."

Getting up at ten in the morning, followed by a four-hour "nap," was not conducive to sleeping. Kate finally succumbed to the lure of a Johannisberg Riesling that had been cooling in the refrigerator.

Lately, the first glass left her languid—wanting. It had become the hardest time of the night for her. As she tipped back the glass, her hair brushed the nape of her neck, and she remembered Mike's hands on her hair earlier that day. She also remembered willing him to touch her, but his fingers hadn't strayed to her skin.

The second glass dulled her senses enough to forget, and the third finally put her back to sleep.

She'd set the alarm for eight, and when it went off, the first thing she did was pick up the glass and bottle and carry them into the kitchen. The glass went in the dishwasher, the bottle back in the refrigerator. He wouldn't know. She'd keep it out of sight from now on.

CHAPTER

NINETEEN

The rain continued into Sunday. The house seemed very empty without Mike's and Matt's heavy footsteps and masculine voices. She'd always hated Sundays. It was a holdover from her childhood. Sunday had meant dresses, and church, and a quiet lunch, and an afternoon that stretched out endlessly to a quiet dinner, and early to bed for school the next day. Even though none of these little rituals followed Kate into adulthood, the feeling had never left her.

A phone call from Donna Estes had further darkened her mood, and not even the weekly call to her mother helped Kate's spirits. She'd gone to the front window to see if Mike's truck was parked in its usual spot. It wasn't, and she frowned, watching the rain come down.

She still stood there when a car pulled up behind hers, and Matt jumped out and ran to the porch. Kate stepped behind the curtain as he knocked on the door. She wanted to hide, but knew her car gave away the fact she was home.

Kate reluctantly opened the door.

"I'm here to kidnap you," Matt stated.

"Excuse me?"

"We were about to start a game of Trivial Pursuit, and Uncle Mike sent me to get you." She began to beg off, when Matt interrupted her. "I was told not to take no for an answer. Sorry." He grinned.

Mike groaned theatrically, then read the question off the card. "What group backed up Wayne Fontana?" He ignored his nephew, knowing he wouldn't have a clue, and looked at Kate, Matt's partner.

"The Mindbenders," Kate announced smugly, placing a pink wedge in their game piece.

Mike shoved the card back into the box. "Why do you always get questions like, 'What's your middle name?' and we get 'What was the date and hour Einstein developed his theory of relativity?' "

"Karma," she answered, rising from the armchair she'd been sitting in for the past half hour. She stepped over Mike's legs and walked around the big, square coffee table the game board rested on, making her way to the fireplace. Kate held her hands out to the coal fire. Matt, who had been sitting on the hearth, made room for her to join him.

Kate hadn't called Mike's sister since their lunch, but, then Sheryl hadn't called, either. If there was one thing they had in common, it was a willful obstinance.

She knew that Mike's bullying her into coming had been a ploy, and it had worked. Kate had walked through Sheryl's front door, thrown off her coat, and said, "Two women against two men hardly seems fair. I think we should share the wealth. That way at least one of the guys has a chance of winning."

Sheryl laughed and Kate then said, "I'll take Matt."

The warmth of the fire reflected the way she felt in this room, with these people. Cozy, safe, loved. She was very glad she'd come.

"Come on, Matt. Roll the dice," Sheryl was saying.

Their game piece landed on a Sports square and

Mike said, "I give up," then read the question, which Matt aced.

The team of Kate and Matt finally missed one. Matt pulled the card for the next question, and laughed. "Here's one I *know* you'll get," he said, looking at his uncle. "What lunch meat did British comedy group Monty Python immortalize in song?"

Sheryl snorted, as Mike gave Matt a deadly look.

"Is that really a question?" Mike asked.

"Yeah! Right here. Wanna see?"

"Well? What's your answer?" Kate said, curious at the reaction the question was getting.

"Spam," Mike said, chagrined.

"What's so funny?" Kate asked, as Sheryl and Matt burst into laughter.

"It's one of those family skeletons we try to keep hidden. Spam"—Sheryl made a gagging noise—"is one of Mike's favorite—and I use the term loosely—lunch meats."

"Spam?" Kate looked at Mike for confirmation. "Since when?"

"Since he was a kid," Sheryl answered for him.

"And I thought I knew you," Kate teased. "I'm devastated." The expression on Mike's face told her he'd been through this many times before.

"Can we get on with this game, please?" Mike snapped.

Another hour sped by, and the two teams were tied.

"Matt, throw some more coal on the fire. I'm going to order the pizza," Sheryl said.

"Be sure to order the Spam Surprise," Kate said on her way to get another Coke.

Mike grabbed her ankle as she walked by, pulling her down to the carpet next to him. In a low voice, he asked, "You won't hold this against me, will ya?"

Matt looked over his shoulder at the two of them.

Mike's fingers still clung to her, and she leaned toward

him. "Gosh, I don't know, Mike. Spam? That's pretty scary. How did this happen?"

Picking up her cue, he said seriously, "It started small. You know ... first it's a can of Vienna sausage. Then that's not enough. You move to corned-beef hash. Pretty soon you're hooked on the really hard stuff. You just have to have that rectangular blue can. I remember one day my mom's supply ran out and I had to go out on the streets to score eight ounces. That's when I knew I was an addict, and I'd do anything to hold that little key in my hand."

Kate looked at him sympathetically. "Was it the actual taste? Or was it the slurping sound it makes when it slides out of the can?"

"It was everything."

Placing her hand on his cheek, she solemnly said, "Surely there must be groups that help with this sort of thing. Spam-eaters Anonymous?'

He looked at her with sorrowful eyes. "I've tried, Kate. But I couldn't make it past the second step to a Spam-free life."

"Well, I'm here for you, Mike."

"It's good to know." He released her ankle, but instead of getting up, she settled in next to him.

"The pizza should be here in about half an hour." Sheryl's voice preceded her. When she saw Kate and Mike sitting side by side, their backs against the couch, she asked, "Did we change partners while I was gone?"

Matt looked up from the fire, which he'd been assiduously tending since the verbal exchange between Mike and Kate had begun.

Mike draped his arm over Kate's shoulders. "I say we start a new game. This time the Silver Screen version."

"We don't stand a chance against you two," Sheryl complained.

"Exactly."

• • •

"Anyone want this last piece?" Matt asked, his hand already reaching for the slice of pizza.

Sheryl, Mike, and Kate simultaneously said, "It's yours."

Mike had moved up to the couch, and now Kate leaned back against his legs.

"I meant to ask you . . ." She directed her question to Mike. "How was the movie?"

"What movie?" he asked.

Kate peered at Matt. He gave her a pleading look, and she quickly said, "I thought I heard you mention something about going to see a movie. Guess I was wrong."

Sheryl began clearing the debris from the coffee table. "So, I hear you got a call from Donna today."

Kate made a face. "Yeah, she *just knew* how *busy* I was, so she took it on herself to call me. I was thrilled," she deadpanned. "How did you know?"

"Donna feels the need to report any dealings with you to me. God knows why."

"Who's Donna?" Matt asked.

"The head of our reunion committee," Mike answered.

"And a general pain in the ass," Kate added.

"Well, she was ecstatic that you agreed to be there for the dedication."

"That's *all* I agreed to."

"What dedication?" Matt asked.

"You ask a lot of questions," Mike stated.

"It's okay, Mike." Kate's eyes focused on a lamp across the room. "The high school is dedicating the new gym to Paul. On the date he died."

"That must be hard for you," Matt said, watching her.

Her eyes found his. "Yes. Very hard."

The change in Kate was felt by everyone in the room. Mike's hands stole to her shoulders and began a gentle, reassuring massage.

"I hope you don't mind me telling you this," Matt began before anyone could stop him. "But I met Paul a couple of times when I was a kid. He was great."

Mike and Sheryl exchanged glances, but didn't say anything.

"Really? Isn't that funny that Paul knew you before I did?" Kate said softly. "When was it?"

Mike stepped in. "I took him to a game in Philadelphia once. What were you, Matt? Eight?"

"Nine. It was incredible! But I'll never forget him showing up at my Little League game on my thirteenth birthday. Remember, Mom?"

Kate looked at Sheryl. "You never told me."

"Really? It was so long ago, I guess it didn't seem important."

"Paul never told me, either," Kate said, almost to herself.

"Well, I think you were in San Francisco, and the season had just opened in New York . . ."

Sheryl was floundering and Mike jumped in to save her. "Yeah, and I got in touch with him for Sheryl."

"I can't believe no one ever told me," Kate said thoughtfully. Then she gathered herself together, and gave Matt a small smile. "I'm glad he could do that for you. He loved kids."

Sheryl saw the tears in Kate's eyes, and she heard the unspoken words. *He always wanted kids.* She flashed a warning look at Mike, but it was too late.

Kate pulled away from Mike's hands and struggled to get up. "Excuse me." She was leaving the room. "I'll be right back."

When they heard the bathroom door close and lock, Mike spoke to Matt in a low voice filled with anger. "I told you not to mention him. Didn't I?"

"I'm sorry," Matt said, his apology heartfelt. "I didn't mean to upset her."

Mike turned to Sheryl, his eyes burning into hers, his lie hanging over them.

Finally, Sheryl spoke. "I'm sorry I put you on the spot, Mike. Paul's visit was my idea. I thought it would be a terrific gift for Matt." Then, almost defensively, she said, "He was my friend, too."

Kate stared at her reflection in the mirror. Bitterness welled up in her and her mouth twisted in anger. Why couldn't he tell her he'd gone to see Mike's nephew? Had he been afraid of hurting her? And, in all honesty, how could he have hurt her any more than he already had?

Kate is staring at the twinkling lights of the Christmas tree. Holidays are the worst for her, when she aches for a child the most. She can picture the two of them, shopping, wrapping, putting together bikes and swing sets on Christmas Eve. Playing Santa to the delighted eyes of a child. But her thirty-first birthday has just passed, and they have given up.

The initial tests have proved that it is Kate's body that is the traitor. She's had irregular periods since puberty. Her doctor started her on birth control pills at the age of nineteen and she has taken them for three years. She waited a year after she and Paul were married. When it was obvious he had a career in baseball, she threw them in the garbage, and tried to get pregnant. A year went by. The late periods always turned out to be just that. Late.

The first doctor told them to relax and it would happen. It didn't. The second tried hormone therapy with no results. And another year of frustration had passed. The fertility clinic put them through more tests and then tried drugs. Again, nothing. They had high hopes for artificial insemination, but after two attempts, Paul had finally said, "Enough."

He's told her it's all right. Not to blame herself. They don't need children to be happy. But he has begun pulling away from her. Not physically. Never physically. But she can sense the distance, nevertheless. She remembers overhearing a conversation

*between her father and mother, when they had understood some-
thing was wrong in Kate's marriage. Her mother had said, "I
just think Paul would seem more married if they had a child."*

It is only in the past couple of years that Kate has thought
about adoption. She has brought the subject up only once, but at
the time Paul didn't seem interested.

"Kate?" Paul's voice brings her out of her reverie. "What
are you doing in here? I thought we were going out for
dinner."

"Can we talk for a few minutes?"

"Sure, but I'm starving, so make it quick."

"Please, Paul. This is important. Can you sit down?"

He catches the seriousness in her tone, and quickly sits on the
chair facing her. "What is it, Katie?"

She looks into his concerned hazel eyes and thinks she has a
chance. She begins speaking before she loses her nerve. "Paul,
you know how hard Christmas is for me. I know we can't do
anything about it this year, but I'd like to adopt a baby. I'm
thirty-one years old. I want a child to love, and I don't care if I
didn't give birth to it. I need this—"

"I don't want to adopt, Kate. You know that."

"But why?" She tries to keep her voice steady. "If we can't
have our own—"

"If we can't have our own," he interrupts, "we won't have
any. End of discussion."

"No! You have to give me a good reason why, Paul!"

"I would never feel like it was mine. I couldn't love it." He
reaches for her hands and takes them in his, trying to placate
her. "I'm just being honest with you, Kate."

Her eyes drop to the floor, and she whispers, "I need someone
to take care of, Paul. Right now I don't feel like I can live
without it."

"Don't be silly, Kate. You've got me."

"It's not enough." A tear slips down her cheek. "Why can't
you understand that? Can't you at least think about it?"

He sighs, exasperated. "Okay. I'll think about it."

But they both know he won't, and the subject is never men-

tioned again. And this Christmas he does one of the stupidest things he's ever done. He gives her Homer.

Paul is as excited as a child. When she opens the large box and sees the squirming black puppy, her eyes narrow and in a barely controlled voice says, "How could you?"

She runs from the room and doesn't speak to him again that day. He goes to his mother's in Charlottesville alone, and when he returns that night finds their bed empty. She is asleep in the guest room.

Paul lifts the covers and lies down next to her. The movement brings her awake. He runs a finger down her spine. Moving his hand to her hip, he pulls her close to him. "Katie, I'm sorry," he whispers. "Please forgive me. I know it was a really dumb thing to do, but I just wanted to give you something that you could take care of, and maybe just love a little."

"I know what you meant, Paul," she says, the hurt in her voice undisguised.

"I'll take him back tomorrow. Just tell me you forgive me." Gently turning her toward him, he finds her mouth and kisses her deeply. "Katie, I need you. Please. Forgive me?"

He kisses her eyelids, lovingly caresses her stomach, and against her will, she finds herself responding. This makes her sadder than anything that has passed till now, and through her tears, she says, "I forgive you."

Kate lies awake afterward, remembering Mike's words of only a few months ago. "Have a little faith. Lots of good things to come." But she has no faith left, and she can see that things won't get better.

The puppy stayed on. She cared for it, learned to love it just a little, but in the end, it was just another one of Paul's possessions. Wanted so badly in the beginning, taken for granted in the long run.

Wiping her eyes one last time, Kate left Sheryl's bathroom and went back into the living room. She quietly asked Mike to take her home.

"Mike, talk to me about the good times." Kate's voice had an hysterical edge to it he'd never heard before. "I know there were a lot of really good times. Help me remember them, please!"

He took his eyes off the road to look at her face and didn't like what he saw. In an instant, he'd pulled the truck over and cut the engine. He reached for her, holding her against him, as dry sobs shook her body. "Katie, don't do this. Please, darlin'," he murmured.

"Tell me he loved me . . ."

Mike winced at her demand. "You know he did, Katie. He just didn't know how to handle what life gave him. But he always loved you." He stroked her hair, wondering when they'd ever be close without the shadow of Paul between them.

"I loved him so much . . . Was it too much, Mike?"

"How can you love someone too much, Katie?"

"I don't know!" she wailed. "I don't know what I did wrong!"

"Nothing. You did nothing wrong. Why can't you see that?"

"He wanted a son. Next to his career, it was the one thing he wanted the most."

"The thing he wanted the most was you. But you know how Paul was. He was used to getting everything, and didn't know how to deal with disappointment. He had a huge ego. It got in the way and he knew it." Mike heard the words coming out of his mouth, and hated saying them. "He tried to be the best husband he could." Mike could feel her warm breath on his chest and thought he couldn't do this anymore. Then she moved her head slightly, until it rested in the hollow between his neck and shoulder, and he *knew* he couldn't do it anymore. His voice husky, he said, "But you've got to know how hard this is for me, Katie. Because, as much as Paul loved you, I love you more." He kissed her hair. "Please. If you remember anything, remember how I've loved you."

So slowly the movement was almost imperceptible, she turned her head and Mike felt her lips on his neck. His breath caught in his throat. He couldn't move, sure that if he did he'd find he was dreaming.

But she was moving away from him. *No, please* . . . Her arms, which had clutched his waist, were sliding away. *Oh, Katie, don't go* . . . He shut his eyes, praying for the pain to stop.

And then her hands were holding his face, and she brushed his mouth with a tentative, questioning kiss. He answered it softly. He tasted her lips, the corner of her mouth. Small, lingering kisses. He couldn't stop himself. The tip of his tongue traced the line of her lips till they parted, allowing him entry. He groaned and grasped her shoulders, covering her mouth with his, silently begging for her response. When it didn't come, he whispered, "Katie, please . . . please." But it was too late.

She was pushing him away. "I shouldn't have, Mike. I'm sorry."

He shut his eyes tightly, trying to regain his equilibrium. "No, I'm sorry," he said through clenched teeth. "I'll take you home now."

What he wanted to do was shake her, shout at her. *Did you feel anything?* But the short drive home was silent. Mike saw her to her door, then, leaving his truck parked outside her house, made the short walk across the street to his dark house.

The rain slapped at his face. He didn't notice.

CHAPTER

TWENTY

Slamming the glass down on the counter, he poured himself three fingers of scotch. He took a _____ long swallow and felt the liquor set fire to his stomach. He wanted to get blind, stinking drunk. He wanted to forget that Kate and Paul Armstrong ever existed, if only for a few hours. Pouring the rest of the amber liquid down his throat, he began to refill his glass when it hit him. If *he* felt this way, what was Kate's reaction going to be?

You're doing it again, Mike. Leave it alone.

But his hand was already on the phone, dialing her number. He let it ring eleven times before smashing the receiver against the cabinet.

"Damn it, Kate! What did I ever do to deserve this?"

He was out the door, running across the road, and pounding on her front door. He could see her silhouetted behind the curtain in the glass of the door, unmoving. Rattling the knob, he shouted, "God damn it, open up! I mean it, Kate! If you don't, I swear I'll break the glass!"

She reached for the dead bolt, and when he heard the *snick* of it sliding open, he turned the knob. Before she had a chance to say a word, he pushed past her and headed for the kitchen.

Kate ran after him, grabbing his arm. "What the hell do you think you're doing?"

Shaking her off, Mike strode into the kitchen. When he didn't find what he was looking for, he turned back toward the den and flung open the door. It banged against the wall, leaving a dent in the plaster.

"Mike, for God's sake!"

The bottle and glass were on the coffee table. He could see she'd already started. Picking them up, he said, "You're not going to hide behind this shit anymore," and he went back into the kitchen.

"How dare you!" she shouted, as he emptied the bottle into the sink.

"This has got to stop, Kate. Understand? All of it! If you and I aren't meant to be, so be it. I can't fight a ghost. And I can't compete with a saint, which is what Paul's become to you. But, for Christ's sake, open up your eyes and grab on to a piece of reality!"

She turned her back to him, angrier than she ever remembered being. "I want you to get out of my house."

"Not until you tell me where the rest of the wine is."

"No!" She spun around, her face livid. "What's this all about really, Mike? Is it because you couldn't get poor, vulnerable Kate to put out?"

Mike's anger matched hers. "As I recall, you started that. Not me! So *you* tell *me*. What's this all about?" She didn't answer him, and he continued. "Is it because maybe you felt something and you don't know how to deal with it? Tell me the truth, Kate!"

"Get out!" she spat.

In a voice filled with wonder, he stated, "I'm right, aren't I?"

She was blushing furiously, a combination of guilt and rage.

Mike leaned back against the counter, not sure what the appropriate emotion should be. Elation won out, and a slow smile spread across his face.

"I asked you to get out," Kate said with less conviction.

"Okay, I'm getting." He pushed away from the counter. "I can't help you unless you want it. I won't do anything, unless you want it. Understand? It's all up to you from now on." He walked past her. "See you tomorrow." He suddenly felt lighter than air.

Kate waited for the front door to close, and then defiantly walked to the pantry and took out another bottle of wine. As she sat on the sofa, glass in one hand, TV remote in the other, Homer slunk in from wherever he'd been hiding since the shouting had begun.

Kate held up a glass in toast, and wryly said, "Here's to us, Homer. Alone, and loving it."

Homer wagged his tail.

"Hey, old boy. You need something to toast with. How about a Reese's cup?" She opened the old biscuit tin she kept the candy in.

He seemed to smile, and Kate smiled back at him. Mike's words echoed in her head. Unwanted. She reached for one of the photo albums on the shelf under the coffee table. This would help her remember something good.

The pages were filled with small moments in their lives. She looked very happy. In those small moments she *had* been very happy. Kate snorkeling in Hawaii. Paul holding up a live crab on Fisherman's Wharf, a look of horror on his face. Kate holding out a handful of hay to one of the wild ponies on the Eastern Shore. Homer, lying with his face between his paws, surrounded by gold foil candy wrappers. He'd eaten nearly a whole bag of Reese's cups before they'd discovered him. Paul teetering on a stool, trying to place the star on top of the Christmas tree.

The years flashed by in frozen images. She tried to see the changes in Paul, but they weren't external. The camera hadn't caught them, and she sighed in relief. The Paul Armstrong she wanted to remember was right there in front of her—laughing, handsome, loving. It *had* been good. Had to have been. If it hadn't, what was the point of being Paul's wife all those years? Kate lay back on the couch. *Paul's wife*. It was as if she'd never been anything else. *Paul's career*. There hadn't been anything else.

She flipped to the front of the album again. *What happened to me? Where's Kate Moran?* Two photos caught her eye. Both were taken in their senior year in high school. The first was at the high school championship series. The game had just ended, with Paul hitting a mammoth home run to win the game and series. Kate had run out onto the field, along with all the other spectators and Paul's teammates. Mike snapped the shutter just as Kate reached Paul's side. She and Paul were surrounded by people. Kate's hand clutched Paul's arm and she was gazing up at him with a combination of adoration and expectation. But Paul's face looked back over her shoulder and he was accepting a kiss on the cheek from another girl.

Kate peered closely at the photograph, unable to make out who it was. She was shorter than Kate. Blond. Familiar. But her face was hidden by Paul's head. It didn't matter. Immediately after the picture was taken, he had turned back to Kate and kissed her on the mouth, accepting her congratulations. She remembered that clearly.

The other photo, just beneath the first, was of Kate and Mike. It had been taken by a photographer on the annual staff, on their school's Earth Day celebration. Kate and Mike had headed the recyling committee, and on this day they were in the old gym, sitting at a long table along with all the other committee heads. The local press was there for the event, and Staunton, Waynesboro, and Harrisonburg reporters took turns asking questions and snapping photos of the students. Kate was standing in front of an easel that held a graph, and as she turned to explain the chart using her pencil as a pointer, the shutter clicked. Kate looked earnest—in control. Mike was sitting, leaning against one elbow on the table, gazing up at her with a closemouthed smile of pride. Before giving it to her, the photographer had written *"The future as seen by Kate Moran"* across the bottom.

Her eyes drifted back to the other photo and, without thinking, she pried it loose from the little flaps that held it in place. She stared at what she'd written on the back. In block letters, she had printed "PAUL'S GIRL."

A nightmare plagued her sleep. She was standing at the head of a classroom. Her parents, Mike, Sheryl, Paul, and even Matt, sat at the small desks. Suddenly her mother raised her hand and asked, "Where is Kate Moran?" Puzzled, Kate answered, "I'm here, Mom." They were all talking at once, but the question they all repeated was, "Where is Kate?" Kate was shouting at them—"I'm here! Can't you see me? I'm right here!" But no one heard her.

"Kate? Where are you?" Mike's voice was raised above the rest.

Terrified now—unable to make them see her, she screamed "I'm still here!" over and over again.

"Is she okay?" She recognized Matt's voice.

"She's dreaming. Get out before she wakes up."

Kate came awake with a start, her eyes flew open, and with great clarity asked, "Where did I go?"

Mike was kneeling in front of her. He smoothed her hair back from her forehead with a cool hand, and said, "You're right here, Kate. You were dreaming, darlin'."

Her hand reached out for his, gripping it tightly. "I was dreaming," she repeated.

"Yes. You're all right."

She nodded, and slowly sat up.

Mike hadn't failed to see the remnants of last night's binge littering the coffee table, but he didn't say anything. Instead, he told her, "The rain's quit. We're going to work outside today."

Again she nodded, not willing to look him in the eye.

"Can I get you anything before we start?"

She shook her head, saying, "No. I'm fine," finally relinquishing his hand.

For the next few days Mike watched as Kate pretended nothing had happened between them. Her studied politeness toward him was in stark contrast with her treatment of Matt. She went out of her way to provide any comfort the young man might need. And Matt, who didn't have any idea why Kate was treating him like visiting royalty, basked in the attention.

Whenever they were alone, Matt would step up his flirting a notch or two. And Kate, who had always enjoyed the wordplay between the male and female of the species, went along with it. It was harmless, it was fun, and it helped take her mind off the truths that Mike was baring. Besides, it wasn't hard to take from someone who looked like Matt Keller. Not hard at all.

One morning, Kate was putting groceries away in the pantry. She sang along with Linda Ronstadt on the radio, oblivious to everything else. She was bending over, picking up the forty-pound bag of dog food, trying to get it on the top shelf out of Homer's reach, when it was suddenly taken out of her hands.

"Let me do that for you," came Matt's voice from behind her, and he lifted the bag to the shelf, deliberately brushing up against her.

The whole process seemed to be taking longer than it should, and Kate found herself trapped between Matt and the shelves. She smiled at this obvious attempt at intimacy, and as Matt brought his arms down and his hands "accidentally" swept over her shoulders, she said with a swoon in her voice, "Oh, Matt. You're so big and strong." She slowly turned around to face him. "What would I do without you?"

He looked down at her and playfully asked, "What would you do *with* me?"

Kate leaned back against the shelves, and Matt's body followed. She abruptly craned her neck to look over his shoulder, and exclaimed, "Mike! I thought you were outside."

Under his breath, Matt said, "Oh, shit," and quickly turned to see an empty kitchen.

Kate scooted past him, laughing. "You're dealing with a seasoned pro, Matt. I've been doing this longer than you've been alive." She watched him grin, and said, "Now quit reminding me how old I am and get back to work."

"Yes, ma'am," he said respectfully. "Oh, and ma'am? Anytime you're ready to give me an answer to my question, I'll be ready."

"I have no doubt about that, Matt," she said matter-of-factly.

Mike's voice reached them from the back porch. "How much time do you need to take a leak?" He entered the kitchen. "If you're done, run down to Lowe's and pick up that paint I ordered."

"Yes, sir," Matt said, passing his uncle on the way out.

"Yes, sir?" Mike repeated. "What brought that on?" Kate shrugged, and went back to emptying the grocery bags. "Hey, Kate?" She looked at him over her shoulder. "Sheryl wanted to know what you had planned for Thanksgiving."

Turning back to the groceries, she said, "Unfortunately, I promised Paul's family I'd spend the day with them. But tell Sheryl thanks anyway."

"Sure," he said, knowing Kate would rather cut off her thumbs than visit Paul's mother and sister. It was an interesting lie. "I'll let her know. Oh, and Kate? The Cobble Hill inventory . . . They stepped it up a couple of days. We need to start work on that on the twenty-ninth. Is that okay with you?"

Folding up the last brown bag, she nodded. "Yes, that's fine."

"Great. I'll pick you up on Monday, then. Around nine?"

She finally turned around, and he was glad. He was tired of talking to her back.

"Pick me up? What for?"

"I'll need to show you around. Introduce you. Don't worry ... after that you're on your own. I'll still be working over here. I'd really like to get this house done before Christmas."

"Whatever you say, Mike."

A beat passed and then he said, "Yeah. *Right*."

CHAPTER

TWENTY-ONE

"So, how's the Armstrong clan these days?" Mike asked, waiting for Kate to buckle her seat belt. "Fine. Paul's mother asked about you."

Mike put the truck in gear and pulled away from the curb. "And how was the dinner?" He glanced over at Kate, who was busily rummaging through her purse.

"The turkey was dry and she made oyster stuffing, which I hate."

Mike nodded to himself. "Did Patty make her famous Jell-O mold?"

"You mean *Patricia*," Kate stated, referring to Paul's sister who had always been Patty growing up, but after marrying Gordon the lawyer, became Patricia at all times. "Yes. It was disgusting, as usual."

Mike kept on, knowing he was annoying her. "Did Gordon make it in time for dinner this year?"

"Yes, but the kids didn't. They were on a ski weekend." Kate pulled a small mirror and a tube of lipstick out of her purse.

As she began applying a second, unnecessary, coat, he finally said, "Come off it, Kate. I know you weren't there."

She calmly replied, "Well, if you know that, why the third degree?"

"I just wanted to see how far you'd take it."

"Now you know," she said, staring straight ahead. "And how was your Thanksgiving?"

"Not nearly as inventive as yours," he answered.

Kate had missed Mike, but wasn't ready to admit that to him. The four days he wasn't in her house had seemed like forever, and those days seemed to blur together. She'd wandered from room to room, looking for something to distract her. Out of desperation she'd actually finished her To Do list. She read three books—all mysteries. Rented two movies—psychological thrillers. Love stories were out of the question. She'd managed to keep her drinking confined to a glass or two of wine after what passed for dinner. Thanksgiving Day she'd called her parents and then eaten a turkey sandwich. And all the while, she had to keep telling herself to stop thinking about Mike, which only served to make her think of him more.

She continued, as if he hadn't spoken. "Did Sheryl have to cook a second turkey just for Matt?"

Kate in denial was more stubborn than any mule. "No, but my mom sent us a five-pound box of chocolate-chip cookies. I think I got to eat one," Mike replied.

They sat in silence, waiting for the light to change. Mike searched for something to say. "Speaking of Matt, you've made quite an impression on him. One could even say he was smitten."

"He's a walking hormone. What does he know?" Kate said sharply, but she secretly smiled.

"More than you or I think." Mike turned the truck into the long, curving driveway of a stucco and stone mansion. The front door opened and a slim, elegant woman smiled and gave Mike a small wave as he stepped out of the truck. "The owner," Mike said under his breath, ushering Kate up the stone path.

Taking his hand in hers, the woman said, "Well,

hello, you handsome thing," in a husky voice laced with
generations of Virginians. "And this must be Kate Armstrong?"

"Kate, I'd like you to meet Julia Parrish."

Kate took the perfectly manicured hand of the stunning blonde. A thick gold bracelet circled a wrist covered
in cashmere. The rock of a diamond perched on Julia
Parrish's ring finger cut into Kate's skin. "A pleasure to
meet you, Mrs. Parrish."

"Oh, please!" The woman smiled warmly, revealing
beautiful pearly white teeth. "I haven't been Mrs. Parrish in several years. Call me Julia." She took Kate's arm,
leading her inside. "You are a gorgeous thing." Her voice
dropped a notch. "Nothing like the ladies from the Hysterical Society."

"You're exaggerating, Julia." Mike chuckled, following them into the foyer.

Julia Parrish looked over her shoulder. "Well, maybe.
But not by much."

"You have a lovely home," Kate said, realizing the
word "lovely" didn't begin to cover it.

"Well, thank you, sugar. Let me give you the ten-
cent tour. Michael, there's coffee in the kitchen. You
make yourself at home while I get to know your pretty
young aide."

Young? Kate thought. Julia Parrish couldn't be a day
over forty herself.

"Why don't we start upstairs?" The word came out of
Julia's mouth *up-stay-uhs*, and Kate hid a smile. She'd
always loved hearing the various accents that Virginia
spawned and Julia Parrish had one of the most charming.

Kate followed Julia up the sweeping staircase,
detecting a subtle hint of a flowery-spicy perfume. She
couldn't name it, but knew it was something very French
and very expensive.

When the two women reached the landing on the
second floor, Julia turned her silvery-blue eyes on Kate,

and they sparkled as she said, "So, tell me the truth, sugar. Is he as good as he looks?"

Kate was so startled by the question that came out of this refined beauty's mouth, that she was momentarily struck dumb. But Julia was peering at her with eager curiosity, and Kate finally stuttered, "Excuse me?", thinking maybe she'd misunderstood her.

"Come on, honey. What's he like in the sack? I've been dying to know."

Oh, God. She'd heard right. The woman's eyes were actually twinkling. Kate was searching for something to say, when a look of concern came over Julia's face.

"Oh, Lordy! You mean to tell me you haven't bedded that gorgeous man?" Then, to herself, "Ole Julia's put her foot in it again." She took Kate's hand. "I'm so sorry."

Kate wondered if she was sorry for what she'd said, or sorry that Kate hadn't slept with Mike. A little of both, she suspected, and smiled. "It's all right. You couldn't know."

"I am *constantly* opening my mouth without thinking."

"I've been accused of the same thing. Don't apologize."

Kate liked this woman who reminded her of a Southern Lauren Bacall. It struck her that she hadn't met anyone new in a very long time, and that she'd been missing out. This was someone she wanted to get to know.

Mike could hear the easy conversation between the two women as they made their way to the back of the house, and he smiled. He stood as they entered through the batwing doors. "Well, I guess it's safe to leave now?" He spoke to Kate.

Julia watched the two interact with great interest.

"I think so," Kate answered, taking her briefcase from him.

"What time do you want me to pick you up?"

Kate looked at Julia, then back at Mike. "I'm not sure. Why don't I call you?"

"Good enough. Julia? Neil Shafer from the foundation said he'll be dropping by this afternoon to see how the inventory is progressing."

"That's fine, Michael. Thank you," she said, pouring herself a cup of coffee. "Oh, Michael? Did you remember to bring me that article?"

"It's in the truck. I'll get it."

"I'll save you a trip." Julia took his arm as they walked out of the kitchen. Over her shoulder she said, "Be right back, sugar."

As Mike handed Julia the July issue of *Historic Preservation*, she said, "I'm disappointed, Michael."

"What about?"

"You didn't tell me you were in love with her. Now all my hopes are dashed."

Mike smiled. "I think you and I took it as far as either one of us was willing to go at the time."

Julia studied his face, then said, "Yes, I suppose the gazebo at Neil's house wouldn't have been the best choice."

Mike chuckled. "It was fun. Right up till the moment his son found someone else in his own personal make-out spot."

Julia laughed. "The look on his little girlfriend's face really told the tale, didn't it? Well, honey, thanks for Kate. It must be hard to part with her."

One corner of his mouth turned up in a wry smile. "Oh, that it is." Leaning closer, he gave her a kiss on the cheek. "Sorry it didn't work out."

"Me, too, sugar. Hope everything else does." She winked and turned up the walkway.

Julia was more than a little disappointed. Michael Fitzgerald would have been a pleasant diversion. Okay. Truth be told, he would have been much more than that. But she could see the situation was hopeless. He had that look of a man helplessly in love. What she hadn't realized until she'd met Kate was that he was suffering with it. A man like that shouldn't have to suffer.

Kate was eating her way through a mouthwatering crab omelet that Julia had prepared for lunch, the spinach salad that accompanied it long gone. The inventory had progressed only through the living and dining rooms. There were so many treasures in Julia's collection—and so many fascinating stories behind them—that Kate found herself doing more listening than cataloging.

"Julia, do you mind if I ask you a personal question?"

"Not at all. My life is an open book."

"How long have you been divorced?"

Julia arched an eyebrow. "What makes you think I'm divorced?"

"I don't know. I guess I just assumed . . ."

"I lost Jeffrey five years ago. Heart attack. No warning. He was only forty-six years old. Which, by incredible coincidence, is my age now."

She'd said it all so matter-of-factly that Kate didn't know how to react. Everything about this woman was surprising. Kate recovered, and quickly said, "I'm so sorry, Julia."

"Well, I'd rather be forty-six than not," she teased.

"Jesus, Julia. You know what I mean."

"Of course I do, sugar. And thank you."

Kate hesitated, then asked, "Were you happy? You and your husband?"

"Very. We had our disagreements, but look who he had to live with." Julia grinned mischievously. "And we went through a few rough periods. Listen, sugar, do you mind if I smoke? Eating takes away all my resolve." Kate shook her head and Julia got up to retrieve a pack of cigarettes from a drawer. Lighting one, inhaling deeply, she went on. "But all in all, it was a wonderful ride. Short, but wonderful."

"How short?"

"Jeffrey died a few months before our sixth anniversary."

"Only six years . . ." Kate breathed.

"Took me a long time to find him. And, no, we didn't have any children." She watched Kate shut down. Wondered how long it would be before she confided in kind.

Julia Parrish already knew Kate's story. Not many people in Staunton didn't. But she wanted to hear it from her own lips. When Mike told Julia it was Kate Armstrong who would be helping out with the inventory, he told her the subject of Paul was very touchy.

Kate was beginning to sense a setup. "Tell me something, Julia. How long have you known Mike?"

Julia's mouth formed an O and she blew a perfect smoke ring. Then, as if reading Kate's mind, said, "Don't worry, honey. He didn't ask me to talk to you. Staunton's a small town. Everyone knows everybody else's business. I just wanted to let you know I've been through it. And if you ever want to talk, well, I'll listen." Crushing the cigarette into a Wedgwood ashtray, she pushed her chair back. "Think we should get back to work? Wouldn't want Mr. Shafer to get here and find us with idle hands."

Mike picked Kate up at four.

"How was it?" he asked.

"Good. It was fun. We didn't get very far, though."

"Yeah, Julia's a talker. What do you think of her?"

"She's fascinating. I really like her. She's a beautiful woman."

"She surely is that," Mike said, reaching over to adjust the heater.

A small prick of jealousy stung Kate, and she glanced at Mike. But his face was unreadable and on the ride home she asked about the work he'd done on the house instead of the question she really wanted him to answer.

CHAPTER
TWENTY-TWO

"Looks like snow, sugar. Better pack it in for the day."

Julia Parrish stood at the library window, the smoke from her cigarette hovering over her head like a miniature wraith. Kate didn't look up from the Rozenburg vase she was examining, too wrapped up in her work to hear Julia's statement.

"Where and when?" Kate asked, holding up the delicate piece of porcelain.

"Here and today."

Kate finally raised her head. "Huh?"

Julia smiled. "Snow. Today. We'd better quit now, or you'll get caught in it."

Kate joined Julia at the window just in time to see the first fat flakes drift down.

"Any plans for the weekend?" Julia asked as they walked to the front door.

"Nothing special. With this snow I'll be stuck inside anyway. You?"

"An old friend of the family is driving down from DC to keep me company." She peered outside. "I hope he got away before it started coming down."

"What did you have planned?" Kate asked, envisioning

a white-haired gentleman arriving with his Lincoln Town Car and walker.

"Why, nonstop sex, honey. And I'll be an absolute *bear* if he doesn't show up." She grinned wickedly. "I've been looking forward to this all week."

Kate recovered from the initial shock and then, in her usual fashion, bluntly asked, "How do you do it?"

Julia lifted her eyes to the ceiling in thought, then answered, "In my experience, about thirty-six different ways."

"Come on, Julia. You know what I mean. Don't you think about Jeffrey?"

"Of course I do, sweetie. But I'm alive and he's dead. Can't fuck a ghost." Julia smiled into Kate's sad eyes. "Now, you scoot. And say hello to that handsome neighbor of yours."

Everyone else in town had decided to leave work early due to the impending storm, and it took Kate much longer than usual to get home. She impatiently sat in the long line of cars waiting to get through the last traffic light on her route. What was the holdup? Rolling down the window, she stuck her head out to see, but was blinded by the blowing snow. A group of young women from Mary Baldwin College walked by, laughing, holding their faces up to the snow. Now she understood. It was Friday and the students were leaving town for the weekend. She was truly out of touch with the real world.

Kate, and the rest of the commuters, inched along. Sitting through three red lights gave her too much time to think. The week had gone by quickly, and at the rate she and Julia were going, they wouldn't be done for at least another five days. But Kate was enjoying the work so much, she hated for it to end. Maybe it was time to ease her way back into the shop. A couple of days a week, just to spell Cindy. Maybe.

And there was Mike. She had seen him only once after

that Monday that he drove her to Julia's because she always arrived home after he and Matt had finished for the day. The progress they were making was astounding. Soon they'd be finished, too. This fact unsettled her more than she wanted to admit.

Green light at last. She nosed her car into the left turn and was soon making the right up the steep hill that was High Street. The tires lost traction halfway up the street that was now completely white with snow, and Kate gave up in frustration. She let the car roll back to the curb, got out, and walked the remaining two hundred feet to her house.

The fresh snow squeaked under her shoes, the only sound in the neighborhood. It was colder than she thought, and Kate was glad she didn't have far to go. The wind buffeted her, and she leaned into it. The flakes of snow had turned hard and dry, a sure sign of major accumulation, and they stung her face as she turned up her walkway.

Matt's car was gone, even though it was only two-thirty, and she guessed that Mike had sent him home. She assumed Mike had finished for the day as well. A gust of wind caught the door, slamming it behind her. Kate winced as the glass rattled, and she shrugged out of her coat.

"Well, hello there. I was just thinking about coming after you." Mike stood at the head of the stairs, resting his weight on the banister.

"Well, hello there, yourself." She smiled up at him, genuinely pleased to see that he was still there.

"Where's your car?" he asked, coming down to stand in front of her. Snow glistened in her hair and eyelashes, her cheeks were flushed from the cold. As she answered him, he brushed away a few flakes from her forehead. It was an uncalculated gesture. He couldn't help himself. She looked lovely. His hand dropped back to his side and he said, "I'll get out of your way. I was just leaving anyway."

Mike reached around her to pull his jacket off the hall tree. He was inches from her. Kate tried to think of something to say to keep him there a few moments longer. She lamely said, "Julia says hello."

He was putting the jacket on now. "Give her my regards."

Come on, Kate. He's practically out the door.

"Any dinner plans?" she asked his back.

Mike hesitated, then turned. "Not really. Why?"

He wasn't making this easy.

"I don't know. I thought maybe between the two of us, we could come up with something. I could make a salad. Fry up a little Spam. Or whatever it is you do with that stuff . . ."

There it was. A small Fitzgerald smile.

"In other words, you want me to cook dinner for you," Mike said.

"Well, thanks! Now that you mention it, I would."

Mike rubbed his forehead and squinted at her. "I know I'm gonna be sorry I asked, but, how about my place?"

"Now why would you be sorry?" she asked innocently. "So. It's settled? I'll bring the salad, and you work your magic in the kitchen. I'll even try to dig up the Scrabble board. It's a good night for it, don't you think?" She was positively beaming.

Mike peered at her. "Who are you? And what have you done with the real Kate Armstrong?"

She ignored him, and asked, "What time do you want me?"

A chuckle escaped his throat, and he shook his head, amused at her choice of words. "Anytime, Kate. Whenever you're ready."

"Okay, I'll get out my cross-country skis and see you in a couple of hours."

• • •

Mike had just peeled and diced the last potato when he heard Kate banging on his back door.

"Open up! I'm freezing my ass off out here."

She trundled in, her arms loaded with a salad bowl and the promised Scrabble game. Rescuing the glass bowl as it began to slide off the box, he glanced outside and saw that a good two inches of snow had accumulated, and it was still coming down.

"You always did know how to make an entrance. Make yourself at home."

She sniffed as she started peeling off layers of clothing, saying, "Smells good. What is it?"

"Beef stew. It'll be ready in about half an hour." He slid the potatoes into the pot, then began cutting the carrots.

Kate perched on a stool and pulled off her boots, watching him work. "Is there anything you can't do?"

"Can't program my VCR." The carrots went into the stew, and he turned to her, still holding the wooden spoon.

Kate grinned. Was it just her? Or was there something incredibly endearing about a man who could clean the carburetor in his car, put a new roof on a house, *and* throw together a great dinner? She heard a buzzing noise. "What's that?"

"The dryer."

"You do your own laundry?"

"Well, hell, Kate. Who do you think's gonna do it? The laundry fairy?"

She followed him down the basement stairs and watched as he pulled a load of jeans out of the dryer and began folding them. "Paul never did anything around the house."

"He didn't have to, did he?" Mike remarked.

"No, I guess not . . . Do you do everything?"

"Sheryl helps me out sometimes, but yeah. Basically, I do it all. I used to have someone come in a couple of times a month, but I'm gone so much it didn't work out." He gathered up the stack of jeans in his arms. "Make yourself useful. Turn out the light on the way up." He paused at the top of the basement stairs. "And why are you acting like you didn't know all this already?"

"I guess I never thought about it." She trailed after him as he passed through the kitchen and entered the hallway.

"I learned how to survive on my own a long time ago, Kate." He paused at the foot of the staircase that led to the second floor. "I'll be back down in a minute. Why don't you wait in the living room?"

Kate entered the room and was transported back in time. The strategically placed lamps gave off warm amber pools of light, reflecting off the oak and maple and walnut. She was drawn to the inglenook, where a fire crackled in the hearth, sending flickers of light across the tiles that surrounded the fireplace. A book lay facedown on the bench, and she sat and picked it up. It was a well-read volume of poetry by John Donne. As Kate paged through the book, she stopped to read the notations Mike had made in his precise hand.

She heard him walk into the room. "I'm impressed," she said without turning. "Donne was an astonishing man."

He sat on the step that led up to the inglenook and leaned against the bench, his back to her.

"Do you have a favorite?" she asked.

"A sonnet called 'The Broken Heart.' Do you know it?"

She thought for a moment. "Is there a line in it that goes something like, 'what a trifle is a heart, if once it comes into love's hands'?"

"Yes, that's it."

They sat in silence. Then Mike softly began the third verse. Kate closed her eyes and listened.

" 'What did become of my heart, when I first saw thee? I brought a heart into the room, but from the room, I carried none with me. If it had gone to thee, I know mine would have taught thine heart to show more pity unto me: but Love, alas, at one first blow did shiver it as glass.' "

The intimacy in his voice and the words he spoke were lovemaking in its purest form. A tiny spark in Kate's belly was kindled into a flame that spread to her groin, taking her breath away. Unfair. It had been so long since she'd felt anything like this. Layers of emotion were piling up, one on top of the other, like the snow outside. Footprints that had been visible a few moments ago were now being blanketed with a soft cocoon. And Paul's memory would soon be covered.

Mike heard the small gasp that escaped her lips. He felt himself grow hard and he stifled the moan that threatened to lay bare his feelings. He squeezed his eyes shut and let his head fall back against the pad on the bench.

Kate's eyes opened and she gazed at the back of his head. She reached out. Her warm fingers traced the furrow that appeared in his forehead, then stroked his thick hair.

His voice was a strained whisper. "Kate, for God's sake ... This is torture for me. If this isn't going anywhere, stop it now and give me back my heart."

But she didn't stop. Instead, she moved closer, her fingers lightly moving across the bridge of his nose, his eyebrows, down his jawline, until he couldn't take it anymore. He reached up to end it. To push her hand away. But he opened his eyes and saw her looking down at him. Sad, smoky blue eyes.

His hand closed around hers, pulling her down to him.

Their lips met and butterflies swooped and whirled in his stomach. Had he ever felt like this before? Her hands held his face, the tip of her tongue tentatively fluttered between his lips—investigating, testing—before slipping inside him. God, this was sweet. Years of waiting for this. Years of telling himself it would never happen. He didn't dare move, knowing it all had to come from her.

Kate felt herself falling headlong into a deep pit, unable to stop. This familiar ache, too strong to control anymore, made her whimper his name. She was terrified to go on, but afraid to stop. Her hands slid down his chest, resting momentarily on his belly, and then slipped down further, pressing against the denim bulge of his sex.

The fuse was lit. How could he hold off the explosion? It would be like trying to run away from a tornado. Impossible. Hot tears were dripping from her eyes onto his cheeks. They mingled with her fervent kisses as she drew him in deeper. He was barely aware of what he was doing, when he finally turned and grasped her wrists, pulling her off the bench, pulling her onto his lap. Her arms went around his neck, and her mouth found his again with a sob. He heard it somewhere in the furthest reaches of his brain, and it left its mark.

Cradling her head between his hands, he drew her away from him, kissing her closed eyes. "Kate, listen to me." Her lashes parted, and he was staring at Fear. A fresh tear trickled down her cheek and he brushed it away with his thumb. "I've never had to force myself on a woman. I'm not going to start with you." She was ashamed of her tears. Ashamed at what she'd done to him. He could see it in the cast of her eyes, and he said, "Dinner's probably ready. Why don't we eat."

Kate contemplated him from across the kitchen table. She watched his lips as he talked; his eyes, now laughing, as he related a story Sheryl had told him about one of their former classmates; his hands—calm—only moving to punctuate a comment. They were strong, capable hands. Work-hardened. The veins stood out prominently through the dark hair.

Had she not noticed the confident maleness of him in all these years? Had she simply been blinded by her adoration of Paul? Or had she just not wanted to acknowledge the fact that Mike was a sexual being? He had always been so much a part of her landscape. Always there—always loyal—no matter what she said or did to him. She remembered her teasing through the years and felt a blush rising to her cheeks.

"Why did you put up with it?"

The question came out of thin air, and Mike was non-plussed. He looked over his shoulder, then back at her. "You talking to me?" She nodded. "What exactly is the 'it' we're talking about?"

"My flirting."

"You mean, your prick-teasing," he said dryly.

Kate gave him a dirty look. "Well, I guess that's another way of putting it, if you want to be crude."

"It's the only way of putting it . . . and it was crude. You were shameless. The worst part about it was you never knew what you were doing to me." Mike toyed with his fork. "I guess I was shameless, too. I put up with it because it was the only time I really felt alive." The fork's tines made four tiny dents in his napkin. "Your sass and Paul's arrogance . . . I don't know why, but I loved you both." He leaned back in his chair, contemplating her. "Y'know, Paul once told me I didn't stand a chance with you." He grimaced. "It wasn't one of our better moments."

"When was that?" she asked.

"Doesn't matter. Sometimes I still believe he was right. And I wonder if you'll ever be able to look at me and not see Paul." His eyes held hers. "If you'll ever remember the good times and maybe see me."

He searched her face for an answer, saw a wistful smile flicker across her lips, and sadly thought that her response would be a resounding no.

They sat in silence, until Kate said, "Let's go for a walk."

"It's still snowing."

"I know."

They bundled themselves against the elements and went out into the cold night. The street was deserted— pristine. The last car had left its tracks an hour ago, and the ruts had all but filled with sparkling white powder. They set off up the road, toward Gypsy Hill Park, in companionable silence. The wind had stopped, and the snow fell softly, deadening all sounds. When they came to the corner, and the streetlamp, Kate stopped and watched the flakes tumbling through the amber light. Mike watched her.

His voice broke the stillness. "Are you warm enough? Do you want to go on?"

"Yes," she whispered.

The park gate was closed, but they simply ducked under the steel bars and made their way to the bandstand and shelter. The ornate lampposts, with their flickering replicas of gaslights, transported them to the turn of the century.

"I've never seen anything more beautiful," Kate said in wonder, leaning against the trunk of a maple tree.

Mike turned to Kate. Her heart-shaped face was framed by the knit scarf she wore. A few errant strands of hair, wet from the snow, curled around her forehead.

A beat passed, and then he said, "Neither have I." Leaning his body close, but not touching her, he bent to kiss her lips. To his astonishment, she lifted her mouth to accept him, as if she'd been waiting. As if this were the most natural thing in the world. "Katie—I'm going away for a few days. I have a consultation in Williamsburg." He ran a gloved finger across her cheekbone.

"I thought you were staying home till the new year." The slight accusatory tone in her voice betrayed her. She didn't want him going anywhere. Not now.

"It just came up. I can't say no. Do you want to come along?"

His thoughts had been on the trip all evening. He'd tossed the idea of asking her back and forth in his mind, but after her small acceptance of him, he'd made the decision, hoping she would say yes. Hoping that getting away from Staunton, and the house, and Paul's ghost, she could truly see him apart from the threesome they'd once been.

"Maybe we'd better go back," she said tonelessly.

"Katie—I didn't mean to offend you." She was already starting for the park's exit. "I just thought you might like to get away for a few days. Have you ever seen Williamsburg in December?" He ran to catch up to her. Taking her arm, he pulled her to a stop. "The offer didn't include one room and one bed. I told you before—it's your decision."

"Stop it, Mike. Please." She continued walking.

His response was suicidal, and he knew it. "What is it really, Kate? Is Saint Paul standing here between us again?"

Another snowy night had come back to Kate. Another walk to the park and the bandstand. And another kiss under a leafless maple tree. Why had she wanted to do this? It had been masochistic, thinking she could come here and not have to deal with the memory of Paul's kiss, Paul's arms.

Paul. He had walked with her to the dark, sheltered side of the Victorian bandstand and leaned her against the white boards. He had opened her coat and his. He'd pushed up the wool skirt she wore, and undone his zipper. His fingers pulled her panties aside and stayed there until he'd found her warmth. And, wrapped in each other's coats, he had fitted himself against her and taken her.

Mike now followed her, shouting, "Doesn't your back ache from carrying his weight around all the time? Don't your knees ever get weak from such a heavy load?" He went on—relentless. "Don't your arms shake from holding that halo over his head? Christ, Kate! You must be exhausted after all this time. Why don't you give it a rest?"

How could she tell him the truth? That Paul was everywhere—and nowhere. That was the problem. She felt a spurt of anger with herself, and with Paul. Paul, who had desired her, won her, made her his. So much so that if he'd physically branded her with his initials it couldn't have been more binding. *Paul's girl*. Paul, with his own particular physicality and charisma that when she was with him, it was as if there was no one else living in the world. It had never occurred to her that he used others in the same way, because somehow, she never felt used. Just as others hadn't. It was one of Paul's many gifts . . . He got what he wanted, but the people on the receiving end never knew they were sacrificing themselves on the altar of Paul. It was always a privilege to do for him. Always an honor.

A sadness—heavier than any she'd felt up till now—overwhelmed her. Kate had come to an understanding with herself. She was mourning the years she'd wasted on her faulty memories of Paul. And she needed time to grieve. There was no way to explain this to Mike.

He watched her disappear into the darkness of the street beyond the park. God, she was infuriating. And, oh God, that kiss just wasn't enough. Her mouth had tasted of bay leaf and promise. Her breath had been hot in the frigid air. It warmed his entire body. This was not the way he wanted the night to end. He'd had a hint of her and now wanted to savor it all.

She had come to *him*. He hadn't imagined that. Trudging homeward, he realized she hadn't had a drink that night. There had been no outside influences. She'd received no false courage. So why this pulling away now?

The blackness of the night surrounded him. The snow, just a few moments ago so soft and sensual, choked him. It stuck to his eyelashes, stung his eyes, filled his nose.

Kate slipped and fell just before she reached her front door. The pain was tremendous and she could already feel her ankle swelling inside the nylon snow boot. Fifteen more feet and she'd have been inside and safe. Swearing in pain and frustration, she picked herself up and limped up the last of the steps. Kate didn't look back as she let herself inside.

CHAPTER

TWENTY-THREE

K ate sat propped up on the couch, her ankle wrapped in an ice pack. Pulling off her boot had _____ been a test of fortitude, but she'd yanked it off and was proud she'd only screamed once. The ankle seemed to work, and was only a little purple and a lot swollen.

She'd downed a Percocet left over from a dental visit, with half a glass of wine, and waited for the drug to take effect. Homer, who had watched curiously as she hopped from point to point, now lay on the hearth rug halfheartedly gnawing on a rawhide bone. The only sounds in the house were the steady ticking of the banjo clock on the wall and Homer's squeaky chewing.

Finishing off the glass of wine, her eyes began to feel lazy, and she let her head fall back into the pillow. Something was pinching her back, and she stuck her hand behind her. It was her bra and she unhooked it. Pulling her arms out of the sweater she wore, she took off the bra and let it fall to the floor. Kate was back in the sweater in seconds, and she sighed in relief. And then she sleepily smiled, surrendering to the pull of a memory long forgotten.

• • •

He passes her on the two-lane road doing about fifty. Mike holds his arm up and out the window of his old Mustang, and she sees him twirling something above the roof. It's his tie. Kate grins and waits for his car to pull back in front of her rented Buick.

Mike's graduation from the University of Virginia earlier that day had been a splendidly pompous affair. Paul, his career always in control of his life, managed the ceremony but had to fly back to Cincinnati for a night game. But Kate had decided to stay on a few days to help Mike with his move to Richmond and his new job with the architectural firm of Rodes, Thompson.

It takes Kate but a second to decide on a plan, and she lifts her rear off the seat and pulls her panty hose down to her knees with one hand, steering with the other. Kicking off first her left shoe, and then her right, she pulls the nylons off. Putting her bare foot down on the gas pedal, Kate signals to pass him, and as she does, lets the panty hose flutter from her fingertips in the warm, June breeze—a beige flag of challenge.

Slowing down to a more sedate forty-five, she glances in the rearview mirror and sees Mike's head duck down. She waits.

A few minutes later he passes her again, his socks flying from his fingers. She can't see his eyes—they're hidden by the sunglasses he wears—but she sees his broad smile. Suddenly, one of the socks is torn from his hand by the fifty-five-mile-per-hour wind he's generating. Kate watches it whiz by and begins to laugh.

It takes some doing, but she slips out of her pale green lace panties, and with a wicked grin on her face, she floors it. The expression on Mike's face is priceless, as he does a double take and leans out the car window to get a better look.

Kate laughs harder. She feels carefree and alive on this beautiful summer day. No worries, no pain, no obligations but to have fun. "Thank you, Mike!" she shouts at the canopy of newly leafed trees and blue sky that floods her windshield.

He's passing her again, naked from the waist up, his pale blue shirt bobbing and weaving above the Mustang's roof. The look he gives her through the passenger window says, "Let's see you top this."

So she does. The sleeveless white, nubby silk dress she wears buttons up the front and Kate quickly undoes a few buttons near her waist, slips her hand behind her, and unsnaps her bra. Pulling her arm out of one hole, she drops a bra strap and wiggles out of it. The other, she simply pulls through the dress's remaining armhole. Refastening buttons, she makes the final pass by Mike. She can tell he's stunned to see the wispy undergarment, and when she loses it to fumbling fingers and the wind, and it lands across his windscreen, he is laughing so hard he can barely keep the car under control.

Kate completely falls apart with laughter, tears running down her cheeks. She slows the car and pulls off the back road they've been driving. She sits in the dappled shade of an old sycamore tree, wiping her eyes. Mike pulls up in front of her and stops, a small cloud of dust flying into the air behind them.

She's still giggling as she steps, barefoot, out of the car. Mike's door opens and she sees his foot, and then a bare ankle and calf. And as he stands, she can see the white band of his Jockey shorts.

Kate doubles over with laughter as Mike grins at her and then winks. "Ready for that picnic, darlin'?"

"Oh, Christ, Mike," she gasps. "Tell me you didn't!"

She holds her breath as he steps out from the screen the door provides. A fresh spate of giggles overtakes her as he says, "I didn't."

Mike is leaning against the car, pant legs rolled up, waistband rolled down.

Despite the Percocet and the alcohol, Kate felt a laugh welling up from deep inside. With a hand that seemed to be moving at half-speed, she picked up the old-fashioned telephone, stuck her index finger in the appropriate hole, and slowly dialed his number.

• • •

He had not gone home angry; just dismayed that the promise of Kate in his arms had vanished so quickly. Mike knew that sometime soon—if not tonight, then maybe tomorrow—his phone would ring and it would be Kate apologizing in her own way. And they would go on. But where were they going?

He was sitting up in bed when his prediction came true. He picked up on the second ring. Kate's voice—a little slurred, a lot dreamy—sent his blood pressure up.

"Mikey? . . . I remembered one of the good times."

"I'm glad, Kate," he said, not wanting to hear another "Paul was perfect" story.

"You don't understand . . ."

Her voice faded away for a moment, and he asked, "Kate? You there?"

"I'm here." She paused. "Remember your graduation day?"

"Yeah—I do," he said, his voice almost sad.

"When I remembered, all I saw was you . . ."

She fumbled the receiver. He could hear the hard plastic thudding against something. And then she found the cradle, and was gone.

Mike wearily rubbed his eyes, disheartened to hear the evidence of her drinking—afraid he was the cause. Her words didn't penetrate till a few minutes later. The phrase "all I saw was you" suddenly became his mantra.

Graduation day. God, they had been so young. Twenty-two? Twenty-three? Kate, still fiery. Still Kate Moran in his eyes, although she and Paul had been married for a little over a year. Oh, yes. He remembered.

At that moment, he doesn't think there can be anything in the world more entrancing than Kate Moran Armstrong standing barefoot in the red dust of Virginia, wearing a white raw silk

dress, the sun playing hide-and-seek in her auburn hair. She is
still laughing gleefully, and as she turns to close the car door, the
breeze blows the skirt of her dress against the back of her legs,
vividly emphasizing the fact that she is wearing nothing but
that dress.

Mike bends to ostensibly roll down his trouser legs, when
actually, he is trying to hide his erection. He quickly puts on his
shirt, letting the tail hang out. When he looks up from his hands
doing up the buttons, she is walking toward him, shoes in hand.
Her hips sway in that sensual motion that seems to come naturally to women when they walk barefoot. This doesn't feel safe
and he wishes Paul were there with them.

"Well?" she is saying, still smiling.

Mike doesn't know what she's referring to, and he cocks his
head, glad he is still wearing the sunglasses that hide his gaze.

"The picnic. Where are we going to have it?"

"Maybe we should just go on to Richmond," he says, not at
all sure that's what he really wants.

"Oh, no . . . you promised me a picnic. We have a cooler full
of chicken and potato salad and beer. I'm not letting you off
the hook."

How can he say no? But as he watches her walk back to the
rental car, he wonders how he can't.

They drive until Mike spots a neglected baseball diamond,
the backstop made up of weathered boards, the field overgrown
with dandelions. There is one double-tiered wooden bleacher,
the wood gray with exposure to the elements.

Signaling with his arm, he pulls on to the dirt road and
comes to a stop near what was once first base. Kate is already
out of her car, and he notes with relief that she has at some point
slipped on her panties.

"I can't seem to get away from this damned game," she says.

And although her words are light, her voice isn't. It's the first
time he's heard a note of dissatisfaction from Kate.

They spread the moth-eaten wool blanket somewhere between
the pitcher's mound and second base. They eat and talk. The

subjects innocuous, and always about him. His new job. His new home. His family.

Tired of it, he finally asks, "Are you happy?"

"The food is good, the weather's beautiful, the company is you ... Sure. I'm happy."

"That's not what I meant."

She smiles at him. Says, "I know." And goes back to listing the virtues of living in one of Richmond's historic districts.

Mike looks at Kate, who is now stretched out on her stomach, head cradled in her arms, eyes closed. He lets his vision drift down the length of her, finishing with her pale, shapely calves and dusty feet. Her heels have just a hint of roughness to them. She doesn't like wearing shoes once the temperature reaches the seventies.

He wants to kiss the back of her knee, run his fingers down the muscle of her calf, take her toes into his mouth one by one. He wonders what she'd say if he told her that. Wonders if Paul truly appreciates what he has in Kate.

Mike realizes she is speaking to him.

"You're awfully quiet. Penny for your thoughts."

Feeling like a voyeur who's been caught, he answers, "I was just thinking maybe we'd better get going. You're getting a little pink."

"Am I?"

She lifts herself onto an elbow and cranes her neck to see the back of her legs, giving him a breathtaking view of shadowy cleavage.

He abruptly stands. "Let's go, Kate."

She looks up at him, obviously puzzled by his change in attitude. "What's wrong?"

He wants to tell her there and then. Get it over with. But he is so afraid of losing her friendship, that he can't bring himself to do it. The thought of never having Kate to look at or talk with is worse than the ache he constantly feels when he is near her.

"Nothing's wrong. It's been a long day and I'm a little tired." He holds his hand out to her. "Come on, darlin'. Time's a-wastin'."

• • •

He stared at his reflection in the mirror of the armoire across the room and saw a desperate, lonely man who didn't look anything like Mike Fitzgerald. Time was, indeed, a-wastin'.

Everything he'd done in his life—all the awards, the buildings he'd saved, the good he felt he'd done— suddenly meant nothing. He'd been holding his breath for twenty-one years, waiting for someone to tell him it was all right to let it go. They had all tried—Allison the hardest. But he was still alone.

He wanted to finally give it away. He wanted to breathe into Kate the full extent of himself. He knew that she was the only woman who could take it from him. With Kate he was himself. Or the "self" he used to be. Who was this man in the mirror?

There was no one else for him except Kate. But it was becoming obvious that even the few small steps it would take for Kate to come to him was too long and too arduous a journey for her.

Mike closed his eyes and tried to picture his life without her, because he knew that's the way it would have to be. No more phone calls. No more I love you's; want you's. No more. He didn't want to be her savior. Their relationship had to be real; equal. Adult. Or it couldn't be anything at all.

Somewhere, somehow, he had to find the strength to pull himself out of her orbit and get on with his life, no matter how much it hurt them both. It would be better that way. The big question was how?

How do you leave behind a lifetime of memories? How easy would it be to forget she lived across the street, for Christ's sake?

Sleep didn't come that night, and Mike was up at sunrise, throwing necessary items into a small suitcase. If nothing else, he wouldn't have to see her for a few days. Maybe the drive would help him think more clearly.

The portable phone squeezed in the crook of his shoulder, Mike barked orders to Matt as he finished packing.

"She's still working at Cobble Hill," he was saying. "But I want you to check up on her a couple of times while I'm gone. The furnace is iffy at the best of times, and it's supposed to snow again by the weekend."

"No problem," Matt said, keeping the grin out of his voice.

"I'll be at the Williamsburg Ramada. Tell your mom."

"Yeah, I will."

"I should be back Friday at the latest. If things go smoothly, maybe Thursday. But don't count on it."

Turning off the phone, clutching it in his hand, Mike stared at the suitcase and sighed deeply. He resisted the temptation to call Kate to say good-bye. And he realized that the first step toward detaching himself from her would be to finish the work on the house as quickly as possible.

Decisively shutting the bag, he zipped it up, took one more look around the room, and walked out.

Heading down Highway 64, he heard her words: *All I saw was you . . .*

Yes, Kate, he thought. *All I've ever seen was you, too. It's time to take off the blinders.*

He'd missed her call by ten minutes.

CHAPTER

TWENTY-FOUR

K ate sat in Julia's living room absently rubbing her ankle. The swelling was down but it still ached, a _____ reminder of her last evening with Mike.

She and Julia had been discussing where to go for lunch the next day, when Julia stopped mid-sentence, let out a low whistle, and said, "Whoa, sugar! Is that him?"

Kate's eyes followed Julia's, watching Matt come up the walkway. "Yes, that's Matt," she answered, rising from the couch.

"Michael's nephew. Lordy! Does it run in the family?"

"Down, girl. He's not even twenty years old."

"Who the hell cares?" The doorbell rang and Julia stood, smoothing nonexistent wrinkles from her skirt. "This is one gorgeous piece of male flesh."

Kate smiled, especially thankful for Julia's humor the past two days. With Mike gone, all the really bad feelings came back to haunt her. She suddenly felt *more* alone. He had been stealthily filling up a place in her, and what empty space remained seemed to echo without him. Late at night, unable to sleep even with the wine, she'd get off the couch and go to the front window. The sight of Mike's dark house frustrated her. It never had before.

Introductions out of the way, Kate watched with

amusement as Matt turned his charm on Julia Parrish, and Julia—not to be outdone—poured another layer on top of his.

"If you two don't mind, I'd like to get home in time for Letterman." As she spoke, Matt's eyes lazily settled on her, and she shivered slightly. Where had that come from?

"Jumper cables are in the car. Be ready to go in a sec," he said. Matt strolled back down the driveway, highly aware of the two pairs of eyes on him.

"How do you stand it, Kate? This Adonis *and* Michael in your house at the same time? I'd be like a cat in heat."

"Julia, is that all you ever think about?"

Julia grinned her wicked grin, and answered, "Why sure, honey. Doesn't everybody?"

Kate rolled her eyes. "I'll put in a good word for you. See you tomorrow."

Kate turned on the ignition and the engine turned over and caught. She gave Matt the thumbs-up sign. He disconnected the cables and closed the hoods before walking to Kate's car.

"Thanks, Matt. You're a lifesaver."

"No problem." He leaned the heels of his hands against the roof of the car, and ducked his head down to talk to her. "Are you doing anything tonight?"

"Getting a new battery."

"After that."

She found it disconcerting looking at his waistline. Even more disconcerting looking at his face. She finally turned her eyes to his left ear. "No plans. Why?"

"How about that movie you promised me?"

There was no way to get out of this, and she said, "Only if we go dutch."

His face lit up. "Great! I'll pick you up around seven."

"Great," Kate muttered under her breath.

•　　•　　•

Kate discovered her cinematic choices were limited to either the latest Sly Stallone or Steven Seagal movie.

Matt looked up at the marquee, then at Kate. "Do you have a preference?" he asked.

"No. All overinflated testosterone glands look the same to me."

"We don't have to stay."

"Well, truth be told, these aren't my idea of great film-making." She could see disappointment flooding through him. "Tell you what. Why don't we go somewhere for coffee and dessert? That way we can talk."

"Great!"

He opened the passenger door for her with a flourish. She folded herself into the tiny front seat of the old MG he drove, wondering why someone six feet two and probably growing would buy such a small car. The roof cleared the top of his head by only half an inch.

"Where to?" he asked, shifting into first.

Seated at a linen-covered table in McCormick's, Matt ordered apple pie à la mode and a Coke, while Kate opted for tiramisu and coffee with brandy. She stared into the flames of the massive fireplace and wondered what in the world she was doing there with him. And what on earth would they talk about?

Kate had noted that he'd gotten "dressed up" for their date. He still wore jeans, but his white band-collared shirt was tucked in, although the top button was undone. Over that he'd put on a loose-fitting gray wool blazer. His cowboy boots matched the jacket. He looked very cool and very masculine and much older than his years. *Great*, her ironic inner voice muttered.

He was sitting back in the heavy antique armchair, looking at her. "Did I tell you you look great?"

Kate, trying to play down the date aspect of the evening, had simply put on a pair of forest-green denim pants and an oversized gray and green turtleneck sweater. She wondered what he'd say if she'd really made an effort to look "great."

"Thanks, Matt." She refrained from returning the compliment. Searching for a topic of conversation, she said, "So, tell me about Savannah. What did you do there all summer?"

"Not much."

Kate could see the question had made him uncomfortable but, for the life of her, couldn't understand why. "Oh, come on, Matt. You must've done *something*."

He shifted in his chair.

"Did you enjoy being with your dad?"

"Oh, yeah. That was great." He nodded.

Why was everything "great"? And who did he remind her of? It was driving her crazy.

"Well, what else did you do?"

His face colored slightly, and she thought she understood now. Teasing him, she said, "I get it. You found yourself a girlfriend, or twelve, down there. Is that it?"

The waiter arrived with their order. As soon as he was out of earshot, Matt answered, "Well, as a matter of fact, I did meet a couple of girls."

"Broke a few hearts, did you?" Kate smiled, sipping her brandy-laced coffee.

"Nothing to write home about." He paused to take a bite of the warm pie. "I prefer women."

Change the subject, Kate.

"Your mom said you were working down there. What kind of work did you do?"

Her fork sank into the delectable rum-soaked sponge cake and cheese.

"I'm not supposed to tell you."

She still held on to the fork, but it stayed on her plate, the first bite ready and waiting for her. "What do you mean, you're not supposed to tell me?"

He shrugged, attacking his pie once more. Her mind

raced. What wouldn't they want her to know? Did he work in a funeral parlor? No, he wouldn't have that tan. Insurance salesman? Short-order cook? Male stripper? No, it had to be something outdoors. What could be so awful that Mike and Sheryl didn't want her to know? Oil rigs? Maybe. They knew how Kate felt about offshore drilling.

She put the fork in her mouth, watching him eat like there was no tomorrow. Pushing the plate away, Matt sat back once again and combed the fingers of his left hand through his hair, not once, but three times. And then she knew. Kate had seen that gesture all her life. Comb—comb—comb—slap on the cap.

"You play baseball, don't you?" she said, her voice a mixture of accusation, wonder, and horror.

She'd said the words loudly enough for several heads in the restaurant to turn, and Matt sank down in his chair. He had been spared the sight of Kate's anger up till now. She had always saved her outbursts for Mike and Sheryl. But now he received her wrath full force, and Matt didn't know how to deal with it.

"I don't believe this! How long were you going to keep up this little charade?" He tried to answer, but she wouldn't let him. Matt flinched as she slammed her fork down on the table. "The thought of the three of you conspiring not to tell me something like this!" Kate's hands were shaking, and Matt reached out to calm her, but she snatched her hand away from him. "Don't touch me!"

The diners who hadn't already been curious enough to see what the commotion was, now turned their way. Their waiter was making his way to the table. Matt could see the look of distress on his face, and he quickly shook his head at him. The man stopped mid-stride and dubiously withdrew.

"Why would you do this to me?" she asked.

Matt's voice was just above a whisper. "I shouldn't have said anything, Kate. I'm really sorry."

"Sorry?" She picked up her coffee cup with trembling hands, drained it, and signaled the hovering waiter. He reached their table in two strides. "Bring me a double brandy. Now!" she spat at him. Then she turned back to Matt. "Baseball took my husband away from me! I never wanted to think about it again. I have enough reminders in my life without *you*." The brandy snifter magically appeared in front of her, and she took a deep swallow. "Your mother and Mike should have kept you a deep, dark secret. Christ, I wish I'd never met you."

Her words were like a slap across the face, and Matt reacted accordingly. "Look, I can't help it if baseball is what I'm good at. It's what I do, okay? Besides, you're not the only one who was affected by your husband's death. Paul Armstrong was my idol. He's the reason I'm in the game."

"Excuse me, but don't tell me about what a big *fan* you were! I lost my husband, for Christ's sake! I'm sick to death of people telling me how much they loved him. They didn't even know him! I was the one who lived with him . . . *I* loved him." Another quarter of the brandy disappeared.

Matt leaned forward. "Did you know he sent me something of his every Christmas?"

"What?"

Matt nodded. "Yeah. Every Christmas since I was nine years old. Uncle Mike always delivered whatever it was, and it always came with a letter." Kate reluctantly looked into his eyes and saw unshed tears. "Christmas was always more special for me because of those letters. He encouraged me and made me feel like I could do anything. Paul Armstrong was like an angel sitting on my shoulder. So don't tell me about missing him."

"Why didn't anyone ever tell me?" Kate said, almost to herself. "Why all these secrets?"

"I don't know," Matt said. "I wish someone *had* told you. I hate to be the cause of any hurt for you."

The sincerity of his words brought Kate out of herself. "I'm sorry, Matt. I can be very selfish." Now she was the one reaching across the table, taking his hand in hers. She attempted a smile, but it wavered. "All this time, you've reminded me of someone, and now I know who it is and why."

His fingers interlaced with hers. "Please don't be mad anymore, Kate. My mom and Uncle Mike . . . they were only trying to save you some pain. Their intentions were good."

"I'm trying to see it that way." Kate withdrew her hand from his. "I think you'd better take me home, Matt."

They had driven home in silence. Now that the secret had been let out, Matt wanted nothing more than to talk with Kate about Paul, but he held back. He was wise enough to know that it had to come from her first. And there was something more he wanted from Kate.

Her touch in the restaurant had shocked him with its intensity. As he gripped the steering wheel, he could still feel her fingers in his. A chance at a woman like this was a once-in-a-lifetime opportunity. Matt wasn't thinking about the difference in their ages. He wasn't sure what he was thinking at the moment. All he knew was that he was sitting beside Paul Armstrong's wife—widow—and he wanted her. He didn't examine the reasons why. Matt Keller never dealt in introspection. He knew what he wanted, and went after it. It was this single-mindedness that had gotten him where he was at such a young age. Matt Keller never doubted Matt Keller.

Helping her out of the car, Matt walked Kate to her door and waited for the invitation that never came.

●　　●　　●

Kate spent another restless night. Her ankle ached. Her mind wouldn't let her sleep. Questions ran around and around inside her head, never finding a way to stop, like a hamster on a wheel. With the help of another glass of wine and a Percocet her ankle didn't hurt anymore and her eyes closed sometime after two A.M.

CHAPTER

TWENTY-FIVE

"I can't believe it, sugar, but we're almost done."

Julia and Kate were eating a late lunch in Julia's kitchen Friday afternoon. Kate had been unusually quiet, and Julia wanted to pull her friend out of her introspective mood. Kate nodded, continuing to push her shrimp salad around her plate. "I'll miss having you here. We'll have to get together at least once a week so you can catch me up on the latest news." The corners of Kate's mouth lifted to approximate a smile, and she nodded again. "What is it, sweetie? You're not yourself today."

Kate shrugged. "I didn't get much sleep last night."

"I hope it's because you miss Michael."

"Maybe. I don't know." Her pensive eyes met Julia's. "I keep wondering why people can't just tell each other the truth."

"What happened last night?"

"Nothing, really. Nothing important. Just a small secret that got away from Matt." Kate pushed her chair away from the table and stood. "I don't like surprises, that's all."

"Sometimes surprises are the jolt we need to get back on track. Make us remember we're alive."

Kate thought of Mike quoting John Donne, and her

face softened. "Yes, I guess some of them can do just that."

Kate and Julia hadn't quite finished the inventory, and Monday would be their last working day. As sorry as she was to see it end, a chilling rain had begun in the late afternoon and Kate looked forward to getting home, lighting a fire, and finishing the mystery she'd started a few days ago. She didn't want to think about anything except how Inspector Morse was going to find the killer.

She ran from her car to the front porch with a magazine over her head. As usual, her umbrella was in the house and not where it was needed. Kate quickly changed into a pair of jeans and a sweatshirt, tucked her feet into her slippers, and headed for the kitchen. She turned on the oven to preheat it for the frozen pizza that she called dinner, and filled Homer's food bowl.

Expecting Homer to be under the cover of the back porch, she didn't bother calling him. Instead, she left the back door open and went into the den to start the fire. When she returned, the oven was ready and she began unwrapping the pizza. But something was missing. She looked around and wondered why she wasn't hearing the sounds of Homer's crunching noises as he ate.

She sighed and went to the back door. "Homer? Where are you?"

There was no sign of him. Kate peered through the rain and the gathering dark, then flipped on the floodlights. "Homer!" she called, waiting to see the familiar black streak come across the yard. Again, nothing. "Shit, Homer . . . where are you?" she whined, knowing full well he'd gone through the hole in the fence again.

Resigning herself to it, she put on her shoes. Grabbing the umbrella out of the hall tree, she went out the front door and headed for Mike's house, Homer's favorite hangout.

"Homer," she muttered to herself. "You are ruining my evening and there will be hell to pay." She was surprised to find Mike's front porch empty, and she traipsed around to the back of the house. "Homer? Damn it, will you come *on*!" Nothing. Kate stood still, the rain drumming on the umbrella, and grew frightened. He had never run away before. Surely he was somewhere in the neighborhood. She called for him again.

"Damn it, Homer," she said again in a whisper, walking across Mike's yard and up the street to the next house.

She had rung every doorbell on the street, but no one could help her. It was totally dark now, and she ran back to her house in a panic. She made a quick pass through the house, in case she'd missed him, or closed him in a room by mistake, but he wasn't there. The backyard, still lit up like a midnight-madness sale, yielded nothing. She checked the garage, but the scurrying sounds she heard were only mice running for cover.

Testing the flashlight, she discovered it needed batteries, and Kate wasted precious minutes searching for a fresh pack. Once they were installed, she went out in the street again, and, starting at the bottom, began slowly working her way through the neighborhood, shining the light in corners, calling his name.

Paul will never forgive me. Never in a million years.

As she stood in the middle of the street, tears of frustration welled up in her eyes and spilled over her cheeks. The oncoming headlights didn't register with her.

Matt jammed his foot on the brakes and swerved to miss her. His heart pounding, he quickly clambered out of the car and ran to her. "Kate! What's going on? Shit, I could've killed you!"

She let the umbrella drop to her side. "Homer's missing. I've looked everywhere for him! Everywhere!" she sobbed.

"Come on, Kate. You're getting soaked. Get in the

house." He grasped her elbow and pushed her toward the steps and walkway.

"No! I have to find him. What if he's been hurt?"

"Okay, then get in the car and we'll look for him." He didn't want to say that it would be a near impossibility trying to find a black dog on a night like this.

Matt slowly drove down street after street, while Kate, clutching the edge of the door, peered out into the darkness, silently crying. Once in a while she'd whisper, "He'll never forgive me. Never."

An hour went by, and Matt finally said, "Kate, I don't think we're gonna find him tonight. We'll try first thing in the morning, again. Okay?"

She didn't answer, and he took it upon himself to drive her home.

As they passed the park, she put her hand on his arm. "Please . . . can we check here?"

"But Kate, the park is closed. We'll have to do it on foot."

"I don't care."

She jumped out of the car before he'd stopped completely, and ran toward the gate, shouting the dog's name. Squinting against the rain, she scanned the lighted areas, and then thought she saw something move in the shadow of the bandstand. Ducking under the gate, she began jogging toward it. Her foot found an indentation in the grass, and her weak ankle twisted under her weight, bringing Kate to her knees with a cry. The large raccoon that had been scavenging through the trash bin scurried away, and Kate cursed in pain and frustration.

Matt's fingers closed around her upper arm, lifting her to her feet. "Let's get out of here. I promise I'll look for him tomorrow, Kate."

Back at her house, he settled her in the armchair next to the fireplace in the den and threw a blanket over her shoulders. "What can I get you?"

"Brandy," she said, through chattering teeth. "It's in the pantry. And bring my purse."

He poured a generous three fingers into a glass and brought the bottle into the den with him. She took the glass and felt the first swallow burn its way down her throat. He left the room for a moment and she swiftly pawed through her purse until she found the bottle of Percocet. When he returned holding a towel, she had already finished what he'd given her, along with two pills, and was pouring herself a second helping.

"Hey, aren't you supposed to sip that stuff?"

She obliged him by taking a small amount into her mouth and letting it trickle down her throat. He knelt in front of her and began untying her shoelaces. The leather court shoes she wore were soaked through, and he pulled them off, while Kate allowed the brandy's warmth to seep through her body.

Kate felt his fingers on her ankle as he found the cuff of her socks and rolled them off, one foot at a time. He took her right foot between his hands and slowly began rubbing it. She pulled her foot away at the intimacy of the gesture.

"I think the brandy is doing the trick, Matt," she said. "I'll go get a dry pair of socks."

Before she could move, he was on his feet. "I'll get them for you. Just tell me where."

She was so tired. Really didn't want to move. "Upstairs. The second door on the right. They're in the top drawer of the long dresser."

Matt bounded up the stairs, two at a time. Switching on the light in her bedroom, his eyes swept the room until they found the dresser. She'd said the socks were in the top drawer, but there were three top drawers, and he opened the one on the left. He was confronted with silk, satin, and lace—her underthings. His hand involuntarily reached in and fondled a black lace panty. A matching

camisole nestled nearby and he picked it up and brought
it to his cheek, letting the smooth fabric caress his skin
before placing it back in the drawer. Taking a deep
breath, he shut the drawer and moved on to the next
one. Pulling out a pair of thick wool socks, he quickly left
the room.

Kate was sitting back in the chair, her eyes closed, the
nearly empty glass in her hands. She heard him come in,
and mournfully said, "I can't stop thinking about Homer.
I know he's out there somewhere, hurt. And it's all my
fault."

"You need to get your mind off him. We did all we
could do tonight." Matt took the glass from her fingers,
and she began to protest, but he stopped her. "I just want
to towel off your hair. It's still really wet." He walked
behind her and draped the towel over her head. He gently
used the towel as a blotter to remove the excess moisture
from her heavy hair. "Lucky I came by," he said.

"Yes," she murmured. "Lucky . . ."

Kate didn't stop to think why he had come by in the
first place. It didn't seem to matter, now that she was
warm and tired. Her neck seemed to have turned to
rubber. She could barely hold her head up.

"Mmm, that feels so good," she said, as he let the
towel drop to the floor and began massaging her temples.
His fingers moved through her hair and found the nape
of her neck, where they continued their soothing pressure. She felt herself floating on a warm sea, and didn't
immediately notice that he'd stopped.

Lazily opening her eyes, she watched him as he knelt
in front of the fire, worrying it with the poker. He had
pushed up the sleeves of his sweater, and the play in the
muscles of his forearms hypnotized her.

"I could use another drink," she said softly.

He turned to look at her. "I thought you were asleep."
He stood and picked up her glass and the bottle. Pouring

the last few drops, he held up the bottle and waggled it. "Empty."

Her voice thick, she found herself speaking carefully, slowly. "There's another. In the pantry. Bring the key, too."

"Key?"

"Hanging there . . . The key . . ."

When he was gone, she upended the glass and swallowed the last of the liquor. "Where are you, Homer?" she whispered. "Paul is gonna be so mad when he finds out I've lost you."

She could hear Matt's returning footsteps, and then he was standing above her, backlit by the greens and purples of the Tiffany lamp. The only other light in the room came from the fireplace, and with unfocused eyes she gazed at him. She felt her heart skip a beat and struggled to stand, wanting to take him in her arms, but her knees wouldn't let her.

"Kate? Are you sure you really need this?" he asked, as he put down the bottle.

"I'm so sorry, baby . . ."

Her voice was so low, it didn't reach him.

Kneeling, he held out the key. "What's this for?" he asked.

Straining to concentrate on his hand, she then returned her eyes to his shadowed face, puzzled. "You know what it's for."

"The tower room?"

Kate slowly reached out and cradled his face with her hands. "Can you forgive me, baby?"

"For what, Kate?"

"Please tell me you forgive me," she whispered.

"Kate. It's me. It's . . ."

But for Kate it was too late for understanding. She brought her lips to his, cutting off his words. He responded with their first touch, and it was too late for Matt. Kate's lips parted, and his tongue mingled with hers. Her breath was hot and sweet from the brandy, and instinct took over.

Matt pulled her out of the chair and onto the carpet. Using the blanket as a pillow for her head, he lowered himself next to her and found her mouth again. His hand swept down her shoulder and worked its way under her sweatshirt, covering her breast. Rubbing his thumb across her nipple, he felt the sensitive skin begin to pucker and she arched her back.

He released her mouth, and she cried out, "Don't leave me!"

"I'm not leaving, Kate." He straddled her, pushing the shirt above her breasts.

He bent to take first one, then the other, nipple between his lips. Then his hands were on her waist, unbuttoning her jeans, unfastening the zipper. He looked up for a moment and saw her gazing at him through heavy-lidded eyes.

"Hurry," she urged him.

He couldn't do anything but hurry. He was so hard it hurt.

Pulling her pants down, he freed one of her legs, but didn't bother with the other. Her panties, barely there, met the same fate. Staring down at her for a split second, he groaned, "Shit, you are so beautiful." Matt hastily stood, his fingers already working the buttons on his jeans.

She reached her arms out to him. "Please . . . I've missed you so much."

Kate's words stilled him and he realized he'd lost her to another time and place. As much as he wanted her here and now, Matt didn't want her like this.

Kneeling down, running his fingers across the smooth skin of her stomach, Matt leaned close and softly said, "Kate? Say my name."

Her lips parted as her eyes closed. "Paul . . ."

CHAPTER

TWENTY-SIX

S he was climbing up out of a deep hole. As she scrabbled to get to the faint light at the top, her _____ hands kept slipping and she'd fall back a few feet. The light would dim, nearly going out, and then the struggle began again. At last, she pulled herself up and out.

Kate's eyes came open slowly, and she blinked foggily. It took her a long moment to fully understand where she was. The floor felt hard and unyielding. Her back hurt. With great effort, she turned her head to stare at the fireplace. A few embers still glowed in the hearth. Despite the blanket that covered her, she was chilled, and tugged her sweatshirt back in place. It was then she realized she was naked from the waist down.

Bewildered, she sat up and had to smother a groan. The top of her head throbbed and the room dimmed for a second. Groping for the edge of the blanket, she pulled it aside and gazed at her bare legs with incomprehension. Her jeans and panties lay in a crumpled ball near her feet.

She closed her eyes and tried to remember, but all she saw was the deep, red pulse behind her eyelids. Forcing her eyes open again, she found herself looking at something white. It looked like a piece of clothing. She reached for it, but even before her fingers had grasped it, Kate recognized the white fabric for what it was. Underwear. A man's underwear.

Her mouth filled with saliva, as nausea overtook her. "Oh, God . . ." she whispered. "Oh, God, what happened?" Swallowing hard, she tried to keep the sick feeling under control. Taking deep breaths, she was on her knees when it all came back to her. "Oh, Lord," she moaned, knowing she was going to vomit.

On her feet, Kate stumbled out of the den and down the hall to the bathroom, her hand covering her mouth. Planting both hands on the rim of the sink, she emptied her stomach. Kate retched again and again, tears running down her cheeks. Deep, gasping, shuddering breaths wracked her body, and it was over.

She sobbed out loud as she ran water to clean the sink. Pushing her hands under the frigid water, she splashed her face, and then finally looked at herself in the mirror. An unrecognizable woman looked back at her—her face filled with horror.

Christ, Kate, what have you done?

Matt sat on a rickety chair in the middle of the small room, wearing one of Paul Armstrong's gloves. His eyes moved over every object the tower room held. He had been there for nearly an hour. Had touched everything. Opened every drawer. Breathed in the aura of his hero.

He had left Kate sleeping—passed out?—he didn't know. He only knew he couldn't stay there with her. God, he'd come so close. Even knowing she had no idea he was Matt, his fingers had stroked her—entered her. She was so wet. So ready. And then she'd moaned, saying, "Paul . . . I can't take it anymore."

Matt didn't know what that meant. But he couldn't forget the way she'd said Paul's name. And what he *did* know was that she'd never really wanted *him*. She'd gone so still that he'd become frightened. But she was breathing. That was when he'd pulled on his pants and come up to the tower room. She'd given him the key, hadn't she? Immersed in the silence of the house and the tangible memories of Paul Armstrong, Matt tried to understand what had just happened. He didn't like what he learned about himself. Because the more he thought about it, the more he realized he had wanted Kate because she'd been Paul's. As if, by taking her, he could take in some part of Paul. As if she were the secret to Paul's success.

Shit, Matt. Shit!

And now what? How were they going to face each other? They'd have to see each other day in and day out, and remember.

Pulling the glove off, he put it back on the shelf.

"What are you doing in here?"

Startled, Matt turned to face a pale, tight-lipped Kate. He started to speak, but couldn't find his voice right away and had to clear his throat. "Are you okay?" he finally asked.

Ignoring his question, she repeated hers.

"I—uh . . . You gave me the key. I didn't think you'd mind . . ." His voice trailed off, as he got a good look at her reddened eyes. She clung to the doorframe, as if it were the only thing holding her up. "Kate, I'm sorry. It shouldn't have happened the way it did."

Kate stared at him bleakly. "What are you saying, Matt? That at some other place in time it would've been all right?" She watched him blush. "It was wrong, plain and simple. And it's my fault."

His eyes on the floor, Matt said, "You didn't want *me*. I figured that out." Then he lifted his eyes to meet hers. "We didn't go that far, Kate."

"We didn't? Who are you kidding? I woke up naked! Your underwear was on the floor." She choked on a sob. "We went far enough!"

"I can't apologize for wanting you, Kate."

"Matt, you're *nineteen years old*! You could be my son, for Christ's sake!" She groaned. "You *are* my friend's son," she said, and another wave of nausea engulfed her.

"Mom'll never know. She'll never find out. I promise!"

Almost to herself, she said, "And then there's Mike ..." Kate clutched her stomach. "Oh, sweet Jesus, Mike."

As if on cue, the telephone began to ring. They both stood still, listening. It seemed to go on forever, and when it finally stopped their guilt became a palpable thing binding them together.

What time was it? Why was he calling now? Kate had no doubt that the caller had been Mike. Propelled by fear, she stepped to the window and looked across the street. His house was dark. There was no sign of his truck. Kate let out a ragged breath.

"Kate?"

She turned.

"What about Mike? What's he got to do with anything?"

There it was. The million-dollar question. What did Mike have to do with anything? A faint voice in the back of her mind said, *Everything*.

"Mike and I ..."

What, Kate? Why can't you say it?

But she couldn't bring herself to speak the words out loud. If she did—if Kate admitted she wanted Mike as much as he wanted her—then what had happened earlier was treason.

Puzzled, Matt asked, "You're not going to tell him, are you?"

"I have to tell him, Matt. I've always been honest with Mike. He ... his friendship means the world to me."

And then understanding flooded Matt's face. All the talk about Kate, the protective actions, the innuendos that his mother made. They suddenly made sense when placed in context with Mike.

"Don't tell him, Kate. He'll hate us both."

Kate stared into Matt's hazel eyes, and knew he was right. The phone rang again, jarring her into action. "I have to answer that. It's him."

She ran from the room, leaving Matt standing alone. He felt a thin trickle of cold sweat run down the back of his neck at the thought of what his uncle's reaction would be if he found out.

When Kate walked back into the tower room, Matt was gone. She moved to the window and saw the tail-lights of his MG disappear up the street.

The caller hadn't been Mike, but Sheryl. And that made Kate feel even more afraid, because she'd come to count on Mike's devotion. Which was why, after she'd told Sheryl Matt was on his way, Kate asked where Mike was staying.

CHAPTER

TWENTY-SEVEN

Mike lay on the left side of the king-sized canopy bed, idly running his fingers across the rice _____ design of one of the posts. The bed seemed to stretch out forever, mocking the fact that he was alone.

A late call from Kate, aside from surprising him, left him feeling dissatisfied and edgy. A portion of their conversation kept running through his mind.

She'd told him about Homer, and then said, "I really wish you were here. Maybe—" But she'd cut herself off.

"Maybe what?" he'd asked.

"Nothing. It's been hard for me. That's all."

He knew what that meant, and he'd asked, "How much did you have to drink?"

"A couple of brandies."

"Is that all?"

She had hesitated. "And I took a Percocet."

"God damn it, Kate. When is this gonna stop? When I come over someday and find you dead?"

"I'll never do it again." A small catch in her voice made him believe that maybe she meant it this time. She'd sounded afraid, almost cowed, and he'd reacted before he could stop himself. "What happened? Are you all right?" The line had been so quiet he couldn't even hear her breath.

"When are you coming home?" she asked.

"Tomorrow night or Sunday. We ran into a few snags. Why?"

"I need to talk to you."

Again, that little hitch in her voice, making him wonder what she wasn't telling him. His voice hardened. "So, talk."

"I can't . . . not on the phone."

"Then I'll see you when I get back," he'd replied firmly. "And don't worry about Homer. He'll turn up."

She'd hung on the line, and he'd finally said, "Good night, Kate," and severed the connection himself.

Mike closed his eyes, needing to leave now, knowing he couldn't. The client was insisting on a complete run-down of expenditures, and the foundation was bending over backward to accommodate him. James Savage owned a good portion of Williamsburg's commercial property, and they needed his funding.

This had been a hard trip for him. Williamsburg, dressed up for Christmas, was meant to be shared. Earlier in the day, while he had been holed up in a conference room at the College of William and Mary, a light dusting of snow had fallen. Coming out of the five-hour meeting, seeing the grounds transformed into a veritable winter wonderland, he was sorry he'd turned down the dinner invitation from one of the foundation's members. It would've been better than being alone on a night like this.

Setting off on foot, he walked the short distance to the end of the campus. Passing the Wren Building, he ended up on Duke of Gloucester Street, the heart of Colonial Williamsburg. The wide, brick-lined street, bordered by expensive shops and restaurants, gave way to the Disney-perfect re-creation of a colonial town.

Leafless trees lined the broad street, their bare

branches outlined in glittering snow. Mike stepped up onto the brick sidewalk and stopped to look around. It was dusk, and the streetlights were just being lit by a young man. The oily yellow light reflected off the pristine buildings. Electric lights, made to look like candles, began to come on in the windows of houses. Cedar boughs, like cake decorations sprinkled with powdered sugar, were draped over railings and doorways. The street hadn't been opened to traffic yet, and it was quiet.

The dinner hour loomed, and Mike walked on. It seemed that the only people on the street were couples. Arms linked, or hand in hand, they moved along, caught up in their own world. He'd never felt so lonely. The bells from the church chimed six times, and he picked up his pace.

A woman's laughter, familiar, tumbled out across the empty street, and he quickly looked up to see where it was coming from. The door of the King's Arms Tavern was just closing behind a man and woman. Feeling the first pangs of hunger, Mike crossed the street and followed the couple's footsteps into the warmth of the building.

He waited only ten minutes before he was shown to a small table near a window. The room was dim. Only candlelight glimmered off the silver and pewter. A fire blazed in the hearth and the smell of bayberry filled the air.

Mike sat at the linen-covered table, sipping a glass of wine, knowing he should have eaten in his room at the hotel. This was definitely a night for romance. He felt out of place—left out. To pass the time until his dinner arrived, he took some papers out of his briefcase and began reading, but he couldn't keep his mind on the words. He wanted to look across the table and see Kate.

"You work too hard."

The woman's voice came from behind, and he swung around in his chair and looked up. "My God. Allison!"

She smiled. "I wasn't sure it was you, until you opened that briefcase. Who else would come to the King's Arms and work?"

Losing some of his despondency, he smiled back and gestured toward the other chair. "Have a seat." Allison came around to face him and he saw she hadn't changed.

"I can't, Mike. I'm not alone." It was then he saw the diamond ring on her left hand. "I just wanted to say hello."

"You look wonderful, Alli."

She blushed at his use of her nickname.

"I see best wishes are in order," he said, indicating the ring.

"Oh, yes. Thanks." She lowered her voice. "I wanted to tell you how sorry I am about Paul Armstrong. I liked him."

"Everybody did. Thanks."

"I'm sorry it's taken me this long to tell you, but at the time I still felt like the walking wounded." She smiled. "You were hard to get over, Mike Fitzgerald. But I finally did it." Looking into his gray eyes, Allison saw the past, and wondered if he knew she was lying.

"I understand, Alli. It was a tough few years for me, too."

"How's his wife doing? It must've been very hard for her."

He nodded. "You're a good person, Alli. I know it's not much, but I'm sorry for the way things worked out."

She looked away for a moment, then said, "Did I hear that you moved back to Staunton?"

"Yeah. It suits me."

Summoning up her courage, she casually asked, "Still dreaming the impossible dream?" His face didn't change, but his eyes narrowed slightly. "I'm sorry, Mike. That was uncalled for." She took a breath. "I'd better get back to Brian."

"It was good seeing you, Allison. My best to you both." He put out his hand and she took it.

Softly squeezing his fingers, she said, "I want to wish you all the luck in the world. I know what it's like loving someone that much." Her fingers trailed across his palm. "Merry Christmas, Mike."

His dinner arrived, but his appetite had fled. *The impossible dream*. Yes, and it was time to wake up.

He'd gone back to his room and, with the television on, worked until the phone had rung. And now, replaying the conversation over and over again, he finally fell asleep. But instead of dreaming of Kate, he had a nightmare that had him locked in the suffocating tower room, surrounded by images of Paul, with a grinning Matt peering at him through the window. Mike struggled to get the window open, to get out, to breathe fresh air. When he finally picked up one of Paul's trophies and shattered the window, Matt's face disappeared in a shower of glass.

The image woke him. His heart pounding, his body drenched in sweat, he sat up in the huge bed and attempted to breathe normally. Rubbing a hand across his face, he tried to make sense of the dream. He told himself it was just a dream and wasn't supposed to make sense, but he stole a look at the clock on the nightstand, just in case it wasn't too late to call Sheryl. To make sure Matt was okay. The digital display read 1:45, and he picked up the phone.

Sheryl answered his call with a frantic, "What's wrong?" When she heard his voice, and he assured her that nothing was wrong, that he just wanted to make sure everything was all right there, she said, "Are you nuts, calling at this time of night? God, Mike, I *hate* it when you do this."

"Is Matt there?"

"Of course he's here. Where else would he be?"

"You're sure?"

She took a deep breath, trying to curb her annoyance. "Yes, Mike. He put on his jammies and I tucked him in myself. What's this all about?"

"Nothing."

"You wake me up at two in the morning for nothing?"

"Kate sounded a little funny when I talked to her. I was just wondering if Matt happened to say anything."

"Kate again? I'm hanging up, Mike."

"No, really, Sherry . . . did he say anything?"

"No, really, Mike . . . he didn't. And if you know what's good for you, you won't say anything else and go to sleep."

Matt was startled when he heard the phone ringing in the middle of the night, but it quit and he assumed everything was okay. He listened, but didn't hear his mother coming down the hall to tell him any bad news, so it must have been a wrong number. Just in case, he got up from his bed and checked to be sure his door was locked. Then he went back to poring over the scrapbook he'd "borrowed" from the tower room. Kate didn't know he had it. It had been easy to sneak it out to his car while she'd gone to answer the phone.

There had been a scrapbook for every year that Paul had played baseball, all of them carefully, lovingly, pieced together. Matt chose 1984, the year his uncle had taken him to his first major league game. The year he'd first met Paul Armstrong.

Matt read every article, every clipping. He found the *San Francisco Chronicle's* report on the game he'd attended in Philadelphia and read through it twice. He remembered the game like it was yesterday. The three-run homer, the single that scored the winning run, the amazing double play that got the team out of a one-out, bases-loaded situation. It was all there.

Matt moved on to a short magazine piece on baseball

card collecting. He couldn't figure out what it was doing in the scrapbook, until he turned the page and saw Paul's name highlighted in yellow. The article focused on rookie cards, and a small photo showed Paul holding his own card. The caption under the photograph read: *Giants great Paul Armstrong won't give up his rookie card to just anyone. "I'm saving this for someone special."*

Matt smiled. The card, signed and framed, hung on his bedroom wall. It had been in one of his Christmas packages from Paul. His smile faded to puzzlement. The article had been published in the April edition. The season had just started, and Matt hadn't met Paul yet. Mystified, Matt read the article through. He continued looking at the picture, as if it would give him some clue as to who Paul meant by "someone special."

Getting off the bed, he went to his desk and opened the bottom drawer. Lifting out the small box that held the six precious letters from Paul, he picked out the one from Christmas of 1988 and unfolded it. He knew them all by heart, and he found the line he was looking for immediately. Paul had written: *"I've heard my rookie card is worth a lot of money, so don't trade it! I've been saving it for you for a long time and I think you're old enough to appreciate it now."*

Matt's eyes strayed to the framed card and squinted in concentration, and he became even more confused. He went back to the scrapbook and didn't turn off his light till well past three.

Matt stood at the kitchen sink eating his second bowl of cereal.

"You're up early. What's the occasion?" his mother asked, smothering a yawn.

"I promised Kate I'd help her look for Homer," he answered, rinsing out the dish.

"Oh. Kate. How could I forget?"

Her sarcastic tone wasn't lost on Matt. "How come you never told me about Uncle Mike and Kate?"

Sheryl hid her surprise at his question, and simply said, "There was nothing to tell."

"But he's in love with her. Right?"

Sheryl nodded as she made herself a cup of instant coffee. "That's old news, Matt. He's been in love with her for a hundred years. And speaking of Kate—and God, when aren't we?—was she okay when you left her last night?"

Matt's defenses came up. "What d'you mean?" He could feel gooseflesh prickling his arms.

"I don't know what I mean," Sheryl said, her irritation at Mike's late-night phone call still festering. "Your uncle called me in the wee hours and asked me if she was okay." She plopped into a chair. "How the hell am I supposed to know?" she said to herself.

Matt didn't think an answer was called for. He was wrong.

"Well?"

"Well, what?"

His mother raised an eyebrow and speared him with her "don't get smart with me" look.

Matt quickly answered, "Yeah. She was okay. Just upset about Homer, that's all." And not one to be swayed, Matt returned to the original subject. "So, does Kate feel the same way about Uncle Mike?"

"Why are you so interested?"

Matt shrugged. "I just can't believe no one ever told me."

Sheryl grinned at him. "And I can't believe you never noticed. Mike can be about as subtle as a jackhammer when it comes to Kate."

"Well, *I* never knew." Ruffling his mother's hair, he jokingly asked, "What else are you hiding from me?"

Sheryl elbowed him. "I thought you were going someplace."

"Okay, I'm outta here." He planted a kiss on the top of her head and took his jacket from the back of the chair. The phone began ringing, and he asked, "Want me to get that?"

"No. Get going," she said, standing. "Hello?"

"Sheryl? Has Matt left yet?"

Speak of the devil, Sheryl thought. "He's on his way out the door."

"Well, stop him. Tell him I found Homer and he doesn't need to come over."

Sheryl peered out the kitchen window. Matt was just unlocking his car door. Covering the receiver with her hand, she shouted for him. He looked up and then trotted back to the house.

"The search and rescue party is off. Kate found the dog."

CHAPTER

TWENTY-EIGHT

The knock on the door came at eight o'clock in the morning. Kate had just fallen asleep an hour _____ before. It had been one of the worst nights of her life. She could remember only one other that had been as bad, and that was the never-ending night after Paul's death.

The knock came again and the doorbell rang as Kate, practically sleepwalking, shuffled to the front door. She confronted a man in his early thirties and a young boy she assumed was his son. The boy, his eyes downcast, was holding a leash that was attached to Homer, who wagged his tail when he saw Kate.

"Homer!" she cried out, kneeling down to take the dog's huge jaw in her hand. "Where have you been?"

"Mrs. Armstrong?"

"Where did you find him?" Kate asked, still petting the dog.

"We didn't exactly find him, Mrs. Armstrong." Kate looked up and the man was taken aback at the look of pain on her face. "I'm really sorry about this. You see, my son, Mark, was a big fan of your husband's . . ." His voice trailed off as Kate closed her eyes for a moment. "Are you all right?" She nodded. "Anyway, we live on the next street. By the way, I'm Jim Hunter."

What was she expected to do? Invite him in for a cup of coffee? Kate remained silent, and the man went on, obviously flustered.

"Like I was saying, we live over on Hancock, and Mark here saw your dog yesterday afternoon ..." Despite the cold, the man was starting to sweat, as Kate vacantly stared at him. "Mark, tell her."

The boy couldn't have been more than ten years old and his eyes grew large with fright. Kate—despite being tired, hungover, and still in shock over the night's events—sat down cross-legged in front of him and tried to smile. "Did Homer behave while he was visiting you?"

The boy nodded and then blurted out, "I'm really sorry, Mrs. Armstrong. I just wanted to play with him for a while. He wanted to play. I could tell."

"Y'see," the father continued. "Mark knew he was your dog. We didn't know he had him until last night. Late."

"Homer slept with me . . ."

"Mark hid him in his room and we discovered him when he started barking. But by that time it was too late to bring him over. We're really sorry for any trouble we may have caused you."

Trouble? Kate thought. *Mister, you don't know trouble.*

She held her hand out to the boy. "Thanks for taking such good care of Homer, Mark. You didn't do anything wrong. It's my fault for not getting the hole in my fence fixed, but believe me, I'll have that taken care of this weekend." Kate let go of his warm hand and struggled to stand. "If you'll wait here, please."

Kate returned a few minutes later holding a baseball cap. Handing it to the little boy, she said, "This was Paul's. See? It's got his name stitched on the inside. I think he'd want you to have it for helping Homer."

The look of awe on the boy's face made her turn away, her eyes suddenly hot with tears. "Come on, Homer."

She bent to unsnap the leash. "Time for breakfast." She thrust the leash out to the man and quickly went inside and closed the door.

Giving in to the anger she felt at the senselessness of what had happened, Kate leaned against the door, put her face in her hands, and began crying. Homer sat in front of her, head cocked to one side, watching.

Kate sat in the den Sunday morning, reddened eyes on the clock, watching the hands slowly push Mike home. Unknowingly, she picked at a ragged cuticle on her thumb until the pain filtered through and she looked down to see blood smeared on her hands, her jeans.

She sprang out of the armchair and tried to think what to do with herself. Nervous, unable to sleep the night before, Kate knew she couldn't wait in the empty house any longer. She needed to think but the walls were closing in on her, and the right words that would explain her fall from grace to Mike were elusive.

He'll hate us both.

She didn't know when he'd arrive. She only knew it would be too soon, because what could she possibly say to make him understand what had happened? Nothing. There were absolutely no words that would make the truth sound anything but repulsive.

God, she wanted a drink so badly. Pain gripped her stomach and the clock struck ten.

He'll hate us . . .

She had to talk to someone. Tell the story out loud, as if that would make it seem a little less hideous. A little more justifiable.

"I am in *so* much trouble," Kate said. And then, voice shaking, she told Julia everything. But she'd been wrong. It didn't sound any less disgusting.

Julia, to her credit, remained silent during Kate's admission. But when Kate finished with, "I need to tell him," Julia succinctly said, "Sugar, if you do, you'll break his heart."

"If I don't, I'll have to live with it for the rest of my life. I can't do that, either."

"You're Catholic. Go to confession, Kate. God will understand, but Michael is human, and he won't."

She knew Julia was right.

You'll break his heart.

Kate walked out of the house. She spent the day driving through the valley, and out of habit ended up at the cemetery. She sat under the giant beech tree, bundled up against the cold, staring at Paul's gravestone while the word "betrayal" lodged itself in a corner of her brain. And, like a cancer, it began to grow until it was all she heard or felt. She had betrayed everyone—herself most of all.

The sky was nearly dark when she got home. Mike's truck was parked across the street, and the familiar sight made her heart stutter. But not with fear. Taking a deep breath, she pushed open her front door and stepped inside the silent house.

Without a thought, Kate climbed the stairs. The sound of water filling the tub echoed against the tiles. The scent of lavender clouded the bathroom.

Kate stripped off her clothes and found herself staring into the full-length mirror that hung on the door. Unhooking her bra, she let it fall to the floor, then pushed her panties down over her hips and stepped out of them. It had been a long time since she'd really looked at her body.

She supposed she was lucky. Her breasts were still fairly firm, but then she barely filled a B cup. No stretch marks marred her belly and this always made her sad. She would listen to women with children complain about them, and envied them their scars that actually meant something. Her hip bones jutted out—more than before—and her thighs had lost some of their muscle tone. She didn't turn to look at her backside. Didn't want to look at the scar. Her eyes traveled up her pale body and she noticed her collarbone was more prominent. How much weight had she lost? The scale told her. Eight pounds since ... when? She couldn't remember the last time she'd weighed herself. The loss didn't look good on her.

It should've been Mike. The only other man to see me this way should've been the one who loves me ... The one I love.

She felt as if she'd lost a part of her soul.

Kate turned off the water, stepped into the steaming tub, and gingerly let herself down. As she lay back, eyes closed, and let the water lap over her body her last thought came back to her, and aloud she said, "The one I love." She stopped breathing. Her eyes flew open. Wondrously, she repeated the words.

Mike gazed out the study window at the rectangle of blue light coming from her TV room, the mechanical pencil he held forgotten, along with the report he was trying to finish. He couldn't concentrate.

Over an hour ago he had seen Kate pull up to the curb in front of her house. Seen her get out of the car and slowly walk to her front door. Seen her turn, look at his house for a second, and then enter her own. It was then he'd resolutely decided to stay put. If there was something she needed to say to him, she'd have to come across the street. And he'd gone back to the report he was working up for James Savage in Williamsburg.

How had he missed Kate exiting her house and traversing Frazier Street? The knock on his back door had come as a complete surprise. She'd looked up at him, and asked, "Can I come in for a minute?"

As he stepped aside to let her by, he was enveloped by the clean fragrance of lavender. And after closing the door and turning to face her, he saw her thick hair piled on her head, a few damp strands trailing down the nape of her neck.

Kate saw his eyes go to her hair and she put her hand up to it.

"Oh," she said, by way of explanation. "I forgot to take it down. I was in the bath."

Mike was inexplicably—unwillingly—aroused by the thought. He gestured impatiently, saying, "I'm a little busy . . ."

"Oh. Right." Kate tried to smile. "How was Williamsburg?"

He'd nodded. "It's still there. Never changes. What did you want, Kate?" He watched her smile fade, and her eyes dart away from his. Crap. He couldn't seem to find that middle ground. "Sorry. I'm tried. Was there something you wanted to tell me?"

Kate swallowed and looked at him again. "I—uh. I just wanted to let you know I found Homer."

"Good. Great. Where was he?"

Kate waved her hand. "Long story."

"Is that it?"

Kate shook her head, and then the words burst out of her. "I really missed you, Mike." She pushed past him. "That's all. I'd better go . . ."

He'd smiled in spite of himself and followed her to the door. "Your call sounded a lot more urgent than you missed me. You could've said that on the phone."

"Hey, you're tired. We'll talk later." She stepped outside.

He held the screen door open with one hand and placed the other on the doorjamb. "Hey." She turned around to face him. "I missed you, too."

The next thing he knew, her arms were around his waist, her head on his chest, and although he tried to restrain himself, his arms reflexively took her in. But her hands moved up to his head. She'd pulled him down to meet her mouth and kissed him—he could think of no other word for it—desperately.

He'd managed to break it off. And when he did, she'd said, "I'm sorry. Forgive me," and then she'd run back across the street, pursued by a demon he couldn't even begin to imagine.

Now, sitting at his desk staring at the flickering light of Kate's television that penetrated the darkness of Frazier Street, Mike wondered why she wanted forgiveness. He knew it wasn't for the kiss. He could still feel its heat. Could still taste her tongue assaulting his.

As he bent his head to the desk again, the faint odor of lavender wafted up from his sweater, and he finally put the pencil down, unable to continue his work. His heart pounded as his mind said, *There's hope, after all.*

CHAPTER
TWENTY-NINE

Julia skimmed page after page of inventory, while Kate looked over her shoulder. "Here it is." Her plum fingernail tapped on the paper. "I told you we'd already inventoried it."

"I guess I'm just looking for an excuse to stay," Kate said, straightening up.

It was only eleven-thirty on this final Monday of work, and Kate had hoped to avoid her house for the better part of the day.

"You'll have to face them both eventually," Julia stated, reading her thoughts.

"I know."

"No confrontations, sugar. Remember what I told you."

"I remember, Julia," Kate said without conviction. "But I really don't feel good about lying to Mike."

"Honey, you're not lying if the subject doesn't come up." Julia looked at Kate thoughtfully for a moment before deciding to go on. "Tell me, Kate. How much longer are you going to hold him at arm's length? He's been patient for a very long time and he's only human. A wet kiss only goes so far."

Kate turned on Julia. "I'm not ready! Look what happened with Matt."

"Then the other women don't bother you."

"Did Mike say something to you?" Kate asked, trying desperately to hide the hint of jealousy she suddenly felt.

Pleased with herself, Julia said, "Well, now, sugar, I'm not sure. I asked him how his trip to Williamsburg went and he happened to mention running into his ex."

"Really?" Kate feigned indifference. "I wonder what Allison was doing there?"

Julia shrugged her elegant shoulders, lit a cigarette, and casually exhaled. "Listen, honey, if it were me I'd want to know what all the fuss was about. And if it weren't for you, I'd be trying to get him into *my* bed."

Kate couldn't hide her shock at Julia's words. "You and Mike?"

"If not me, then someone else. The man's not a monk. Surely you realize that, sugar." Julia's wicked grin appeared. "But the man absolutely worships you. Whatever that nineteen-year-old boy did can't even begin to compare to a thirtysomething man. Talk about sexual healing. I'm very envious." She could see Kate silently struggling with herself. But Kate wasn't the only one. Julia's conversation with Mike that morning had taken an unforeseen turn when he'd said he was considering a project that would take him out of town for three or four months. That he felt the need to distance himself from Kate for a while. This was especially surprising to Julia now that she knew Kate had made a small move in his direction.

Julia's head won the battle. Mike needed to tell Kate himself. It was too important to be treated like gossip. Kate's voice broke into her thoughts.

"I love him, Julia. I've loved him for a long time." Kate's eyes pleaded with Julia to understand. "He kisses me and I want more. And then I remember Paul, and I . . ." *You what, Kate?* She couldn't say it. Couldn't tell even Julia, who had now put her arms around Kate.

Julia hugged her tightly. "Paul was your whole life for

so long, sweetie. Surely you can understand that it's time for you to move on now."

Kate pulled away. "I can't start a relationship with a lie, Julia."

"You made a mistake. You know that. Forgive yourself. If you don't, you're going to alienate Michael entirely."

Kate was shaking her head. "You don't understand." Her hands covered her mouth and her eyes closed, as she tried to find a way to tell Julia the truth. She finally said, "My marriage to Paul—"

Julia interrupted, saying, "You can't compare every man to Paul. It's a no-win situation. You're so busy holding Michael up next to Paul, you can't see what's real."

"That's what I'm trying to tell you, Julia. I've known the reality of my marriage to Paul for years." Julia's forehead wrinkled in puzzlement. Kate, frustrated, sank into the sofa. She looked down at her hands clasped tightly in her lap, and then met Julia's eyes. "Let me ask you something. What was it really like between you and Jeffrey?"

Julia, baffled by this change of subject, sat on the arm of an overstuffed chair and stared at Kate. "Whew, sugar! You've lost me."

"Come on, Julia. Just tell me."

Julia reached for another cigarette, lit it, and after a moment's thought, began speaking. "I thought I was the luckiest woman on earth when I found Jeffrey. He wasn't what most women would call handsome. He wasn't much taller than me, and he had a lot more forehead than most men his age, but he was in terrific shape. He had beautiful eyes. I loved the way they looked at me . . ."

Her voice trailed off, and Kate waited for Julia to continue.

"We met at a New Year's Eve party. He flirted with

me outrageously. Well—you know that's my forte, and I matched him innuendo for innuendo. He was witty, bright, intelligent, and he had a wonderful laugh. He called me every night for a week, and our conversations would last for hours." Julia smiled, remembering. "We had wonderful debates. By the end of the week I knew I was in love with him, and we hadn't even slept together. Imagine that!"

For a few seconds Julia stopped talking, and Kate listened to the years that had passed—wasted.

"A week after that we were sitting in a restaurant and he told me he loved me. I begged him to take me to bed right then. I'd had my share of men up to that point, but Lord, how he made me feel! That's when I told him I loved him. We were married three weeks later." Julia's eyes shone. "I guess if you wanted to reduce our relationship to one word, it would be 'respect.' Decisions were made mutually, but we each had our own life and interests. We weren't exactly young and we already knew what our lives were all about. We loved being together, but we weren't joined at the hip. We didn't *need* each other to be happy. We were just lucky enough that being together made life better." Julia stood to stub out the cigarette.

"I've had that same relationship, Julia," Kate said, as she gazed at a small figurine on the coffee table. She decided to finally say it out loud. "Not with my husband, though." Kate breathed in deeply and looked up at Julia. "With Mike. My marriage—most of it, anyway—was a joke. I can't even begin to guess how many women Paul slept with while we were married. He didn't understand me and I certainly didn't understand him. I couldn't have children and he never let me forget it. And he wouldn't let me adopt."

Julia's eyes filled with tears. "Oh, sugar," she said softly. "I'm so sorry. I didn't know . . ."

Kate shrugged. "The crazy part is I still cared about

him. He was my world. But every so often, when Mike would come into our lives again, I saw another world. The one you just told me about. And that scared me, Julia, because I wanted to live in that other world and I didn't know how that was possible. I learned to live with Paul's lies because I had my own little secret." Kate's voice had become a whisper. "I've never said this out loud. But Julia, there were so many times in all those years that I wished Paul away because I wanted his best friend." Kate dropped her head in her hands. "His *best friend*, Julia!"

"And Michael wanted his best friend's wife." Julia knelt in front of Kate. "I'm amazed that the guilt didn't eat you both alive."

Kate sobbed. "But I think it has. There are parts of me that can't feel anything anymore. I let it happen with Matt because, for a few minutes, I believed he *was* Paul. And that's the only way I know." Tears ran down her cheeks and into the corners of her mouth. "Paul's way."

Julia took Kate's hands in her own. "It's time to learn a new way."

CHAPTER

THIRTY

M att waited until he heard the squeal of the attic ladder coming down, and then he quickly _____ entered the kitchen. The pantry door stood open, and he replaced the key to the tower room. The duplicate he'd found at a locksmith who specialized in antique keys hung on his key ring.

Mike's faint footsteps two floors above, and the sound of Kate's shower, told him it was safe to retrieve the scrapbook from his car. He wanted to exchange it for another year, and he did so easily, stashing the new one under his jacket before joining his uncle in the attic.

Matt looked up at Mike, who stood on a ladder wiring in a new light fixture. "You need me up here? Or do you want me to start working on the windows?"

"Hand me the pliers," Mike said, holding splayed wires in one hand while reaching back with the other. His fingers closed around the tool Matt slapped into his open palm, and he quickly stripped the insulation, inserted the plastic nipples, and stuffed the finished product into the fixture's base. As he began screwing the base back into the attic beam, Mike casually asked, "So, what's going on with you and Kate?"

Matt's heart sped up. As coolly as he could, he said, "What do you mean?"

"I mean . . . Hand me the bulb, will ya?" Mike turned the bulb in the socket. "I mean, why is she avoiding you? Hit the switch."

Matt did as he was told. White light flooded his uncle's face. Mike gestured for him to cut it off and climbed down the ladder.

"Well?" Mike said, dusting off his hands on his jeans. "What's up?" He looked at Matt expectantly.

Matt replied with the words he'd been reciting to himself for the past few days. "She's pissed off 'cause she found out I play ball." They seemed to flow from his mouth smoothly enough, and he waited to see his uncle's reaction.

Mike's eyebrows went up. "When did this happen?"

"Over the weekend."

"Don't make me drag it out of you, Matt. Tell me how it happened that the subject even came up."

Matt stopped to gather up a handful of sawdust—a substance that now seemed to fill his mouth. "Actually, she guessed."

"She guessed?" Mike repeated, confounded.

Matt shrugged, straightening. "Yeah. Don't ask me how."

Mike regarded Matt for a moment, his face unreadable. "Start on the living room windows."

Kate sat on the edge of the tub in her bathrobe. The towel she'd been using to dry her hair dangled from her hand, forgotten, as she listened to Mike and Matt. Negligible attic insulation, and the fact that the two men were directly above her, broadcast their conversation loud and clear.

She marveled at Matt's fluid use of the half-truth. No one could accuse him of lying and Kate realized that was Matt's intention. But she'd known Mike too long to miss the hint of skepticism that crept into his voice, despite his seemingly innocuous words. It filled her with a cowardly dread.

The kitchen was unbelievably quiet considering the three people that occupied it. Matt sat at one end of the table eating a sandwich and poring over a garden catalog as if it were the latest issue of *Baseball Weekly*. Kate stood next to the door, looking for all the world as if she were poised for flight.

And Mike sat at the other end of the table, his back to the pantry, drinking his second cup of coffee, watching. Tired of the remote silence, he put his mug down on his plate. The sound of porcelain striking porcelain was like a shot, and Matt's head jerked up. Kate took a step toward the hallway.

"Matt. Why don't you go pick up that light for the bathroom." Mike could feel Matt's eyes on him, but kept his on Kate.

"But I thought . . ."

Mike quickly turned to his nephew. "Never mind what you thought. Just do it."

The wave of relief that came over Matt's features was almost comical, as he speedily stood. He obviously wanted to be out of the house, and Mike was more than happy to oblige him. Matt was out of the door so quickly he practically left a vapor trail.

Mike turned back to Kate, who he imagined would've joined Matt if she could have. "He's gone. You can sit down now."

"I've been sitting all morning," she said, a stubborn tone creeping into her voice. "I'll stand."

Mike shrugged, rising from the chair and moving toward her. "Suit yourself. Now, why don't you tell me what you wanted to talk to me about?"

Kate resembled a very pale deer caught in the headlights of an extremely large truck, and she went on the offensive, as he knew she would.

"I suppose the three of you thought you were very clever hiding the fact that Matt plays baseball?"

"That's it? That's the urgent topic you wanted to discuss?"

He noticed she hesitated ever so slightly. "It was a shock, that's all."

"Well, now that you know, why don't you forgive us, and we'll go on."

Indignant to the end, Kate said, "I'd just like to know why you felt you had to lie to me."

"We weren't lying. We just didn't tell you. Seemed like a good idea at the time."

"The sin of omission," Kate said.

"Something like that," Mike replied, perplexed by the faraway tone of her voice. "Anything else you want to tell me?"

"Like what?" she asked defensively.

Mike's smile was genuine, if puzzled. "I don't know. You're the only one who can tell me what to forgive you for." It was Kate's turn to look confused. "Why did you kiss me and then ask me to forgive you?"

He could see he'd flustered her. And a flustered Kate— so rare—was an aphrodisiac to him. It took an enormous amount of willpower for him to step away from her. Even more courage to state, "Nothing's changed, has it, Kate."

"You're wrong." She turned from him. "Everything's changed."

"Tell me how."

"It's complicated."

"I have all day."

"I love you, Mike."

Her voice was strong. It sounded like she meant it. And those words coming from Kate's lips should have brought him joy. Why had she pronounced them like a death sentence? Mike silently took another step back, too stunned to speak.

The phone rang at that moment, startling them both. Kate ignored it, and it stopped after six rings.

Mike finally said, "Explain how loving me is complicated."

Kate turned to face him. Her lips parted to answer just as the telephone invaded their privacy again. Mike swore, as she impatiently snatched up the receiver.

"Yes? What is it?" Her voice shook with anger at the interruption until she realized it was her mother. "Mom. Sorry. Hang on just a second." Holding the receiver against her chest, Kate whispered, "I really do want to talk to you. Can we go somewhere for dinner?"

"I'll come get you at seven," Mike said, and walked past her on his way back to the attic.

CHAPTER

THIRTY-ONE

Mike's eyes scanned the wine list. "What do you think? A bottle of merlot?" He looked up and _____ their eyes met. His heart did a slow *ka-thump* at the thought of sitting across a table from her for the next couple of hours. He was a teenager again, and he wished he still had that old Mustang. Parked up at Inspiration Point, steaming up the windows in the backseat would have been fun, and he smiled to himself.

"What was that smirk for?" Kate asked.

"If you're a good girl I'll tell you later."

No biting rejoinder came from Kate. Not even a dirty look. Nothing but an uncomfortable silence.

She'd fought coming to McCormick's for dinner, but he wanted prime rib and theirs was the best in town. Kate had argued for someplace called The Wharf. And Mike had countered that anyone who ate in a place called The Wharf in a landlocked town deserved what-ever he or she got. He'd finally won on a coin toss.

"So?" he said. "Merlot? Yes or no? Or do I have to flip that quarter again?"

"None for me. I'll have iced tea. But you go ahead."

His left eyebrow went up, but he didn't comment on her abstinence.

The waiter glided to the table and looked at Kate.

"Lovely to see you again. We have a very nice selection of desserts tonight."

"I think we'll have dinner first," Mike said.

The young man finally noticed Mike, and turned to him, a thin smile on his lips. "Oh, yes. Of course. Have we decided?"

Mike looked straight at the man. "I don't know about you, but *I* have." After the waiter left, Mike said, "What the hell's happened to this place? And are you a regular here, or what?"

"I was here with Matt while you were in Williamsburg. We had dessert. Okay?"

"You went out with Matt?"

Kate picked up her water glass and took a drink. "He'd been bugging me about going to a movie. They were playing *Rocky Twelve,* or something, and I didn't want to see it. So we came here."

"Why are you getting upset?"

"I'm not. I just think there are subjects we can talk about other than Matt." Her eyes wandered the room.

"Okay. Cindy wants you to call her. Something about the days you're planning on working."

"She called you?"

"Said she couldn't reach you at home, and when are you going to get an answering machine." Mike went silent as the waiter decanted the bottle of wine, poured a thimbleful, and waited for his approval, which Mike took his time giving. When they were alone again, he laughed and leaned forward. "I was tempted to tell him it wasn't fit for cooking just to see his face." The corners of Kate's mouth lifted slightly. "Why didn't you tell me you were going to start working again?"

"I guess I forgot."

Mike leaned back in his armchair, gazing at her. The fingers of her right hand restlessly traced the cutwork pattern of the tablecloth as she intently studied a painting that hung on the wall behind him. Her mouth opened and her tongue appeared, wetting her lips. Mike, recalling those lips and that tongue on his mouth, was mesmerized. Then he remembered one of the reasons they were here, but just as he was about to speak, the waiter returned with their Caesar salad.

In the latest tiresome trend, he wheeled a cart to the table, asked if they wanted anchovies, freshly ground pepper, tossed the salad in a large wooden bowl, and then meticulously portioned it out. By the time all this was finally over, Kate had begun eating and Mike decided the time wasn't right to tell her his latest plans.

They talked about the groundbreaking for the museum; the newest exhibit at the Woodrow Wilson Birthplace; the latest round of the battle at VMI as to whether or not they should allow women to enroll. Their entrees arrived and Mike ate with relish, while Kate's plate went nearly untouched. And still they talked about unimportant things.

As he dug into his rare prime rib, he said, "I think we've exhausted local current events. Want to move on to statewide?"

Kate flaked off a small morsel of salmon, which eventually found its way to her mouth. Either she didn't hear, or she chose to ignore him. Reaching across the table, he covered her hand with his, and she jumped as if stung. "Where'd you go, Kate?"

"Sorry. My mind hasn't been exactly razor sharp lately."

Now that he was touching her, he couldn't seem to stop himself, and he slowly ran his thumb over her smooth knuckles. "I've noticed." Circling her wrist, he turned her hand over and his feathery touch continued over the delicate skin. Dark blue eyes the color of smoked sea glass looked at him helplessly, and Mike felt the skin on his arms turn to gooseflesh. Quickly releasing her, he picked up his fork again and pointed it at her plate. "Eat your fish. It's brain food."

"Sometimes I don't think I have a brain left," she said, enviously watching him finish the wine in his glass.

Mike saw her thirsty stare and decided it was time to find out what had scared her straight. He waggled the glass between his fingers. "Why?" he asked.

"I wanted to see what life was like sober."

"And?"

"And it doesn't look any better."

Mike set the glass down. "Come on, Kate. You can't mean that."

"I can't help the way I feel."

"Christ, Kate. What *do* you feel? I can't tell anymore." When she didn't answer he leaned into the table, its edge cutting into his rib cage. His voice was a hard whisper. "I thought we were getting past all the garbage."

"Don't push me, Mike. Please."

His mouth opened to tell her his decision to leave. But he heard the words through her ears and knew she'd see it as an escape—an act of cowardice. Or a way of forcing the issue. And maybe in some small way it was all those things. But he knew what the big picture was; it was a means of learning to live without her.

Kate watched Mike struggling with his temper and she detested herself even more. He was pouring the last of the wine into his glass, downing it in three quick gulps, and she knew she had to tell him now.

Her voice shook as she said, "I want you to believe I'd never hurt you on purpose. I need you to remember that no matter what."

"Go on."

Kate reached across the table, begging for his hand. "I do love you, you know."

"But?" he asked, sliding his hand out from under hers.

"No but. You mean the world to me. Without your

friendship all these years ..." He made an angry noise.
"No ... listen! You're my friend, yes. You're also the
man I want to be with." *God, this isn't working.* "Mike,
when you've been with other women, did you still want
me?"

He sat back and looked at her. When he spoke, his
words took her breath away.

"When I'm with someone else, it's almost impossible
not to say your name."

She shut her eyes for a moment. "And when Paul was
still alive? Did you want me then?"

"You know the answer to that."

Kate took a shallow breath. "I can only say this to you
once, because it makes me very ashamed. But I want you
to hear it, so you'll understand that I'm telling you the
truth." Her eyes fixed on his. "I wanted you, too."

It was Mike's turn to be overwhelmed. "What's going
on, Kate? Tell me now."

"Not here."

The ride home had been quick and silent. Kate
had stared out the windshield, more afraid than she'd
ever been.

Now, they stood on her porch. She tried to form the
right words, but none came.

"Talk to me, Kate. Don't shut me out."

"You deserve better than me, Mike."

He grasped her arm, forcing her to turn to him. "There
isn't anyone better for me." His hands moved to her face
and his lips met hers with fevered desperation. "You said
you loved me." Her breath was hot on his face.

"I do," she whispered.

"Then show me. I'm running out of time, Kate. Invite
me in."

His words, so raw, shook her with their implicit need.

"There's something you need to know."

"It can wait," he said hoarsely, pushing her against the door, molding his body to hers.

"It can't!"

At her words, desire turned to frustration. He slammed his fist against the wooden frame of the door. "God damn it, Kate! Why are you doing this to me?"

"Mike! Please," she sobbed. "Something happened . . ."

He released her and fixed stone-colored eyes on hers. "What?" he asked harshly. "Did Paul rise from his grave?"

Mike was already on the walkway.

She screamed at him. "This isn't about Paul!"

"The fuck it isn't!" Slamming the truck door, he pulled away from the curb and disappeared into the cold night.

It took him some time, but he finally heard what she'd actually said.

CHAPTER

THIRTY-TWO

Mike parked the truck and wearily stepped out. Inside his house, the dark surrounded him; the _____ loneliness smothered him. His footsteps echoed on the polished oak floors as he made his way to the living room. He sank into the worn leather of a morris chair and closed his eyes. The house was so quiet that it unnerved him and he finally reached over and switched on the table lamp, just to hear the creak of the chair and the crackle of the bulb.

Warm light spilled across his legs and, slowly, the room came out of the shadows. It was a perfect room. It was a perfect house. Just as Kate had said. But to Mike, it was the most desolate place in the world. His eyes moved from object to object. He had done it all for her, he realized. As much as he had loved the labor he'd put into it, and all the time he'd spent finding just the right pieces, somewhere in the back of his mind, he had been trying to please Kate.

The whole thing worked only if Kate was willing to be the final piece that made it whole. Did she or didn't she? Loves me, loves me not? He may as well have been plucking petals off a daisy. It made just about as much sense as anything else he'd done.

After leaving Kate, he'd driven across town and back.

The time he'd had to think left him with no choice but to find Matt.

"He's at the movies," Sheryl had said. "What wrong?"

"I think something happened between Kate and Matt."

Sheryl had been stunned at his accusation, and shouted, "What are you saying? He's nineteen years old, for God's sake!"

"I know. I remember what it's like to be nineteen."

Sheryl's words had been sharp—clipped. "Kate is thirty-eight years old!"

"Kate is a beautiful woman, who Matt happens to have the hots for, in case you hadn't noticed."

"I can't believe you'd even consider something like this. Your own nephew!"

But Mike wouldn't let up. "What other explanation is there, Sheryl?"

"You know what I think? I think you can't be objective about her anymore. She's turned your brain to mush. Get a life, Mike. And while you're at it, tell her to get one, too."

"Kate *is* my life."

"Listen to yourself," Sheryl had said. "You're pathetic."

"Thanks, *sis*." He'd spit the words out. "Like you're the queen of great relationships."

Mike turned off the lamp and reclined the chair. His mind wouldn't let him alone. Much as he tried, he couldn't shake the feeling that sometime between Friday morning and Homer's disappearance that night, something devastating had happened. And it was causing Kate to disengage from him—from life—again.

Like a detective who hates the sight of blood, but knows he has to see it to get his job done, Mike went over all the clues. What he came up with was pretty gory.

So much so, that he couldn't bring himself to accept it. And so he'd start all over again, until an hour had passed, and he was exhausted and unstrung and out of his mind with fear and longing.

The newspaper slammed against the front door, waking him. The morris chair, comfortable for sitting, wasn't made for sleeping.

Mike came awake on his side. His left arm was folded under his head and completely useless. It took a full minute to get the circulation moving. His right leg dangled over the chair's wooden arm.

He could still taste the scotch that had finally put him to sleep, and his head felt too heavy for his neck. When he tried to get up, a sharp pain in his shoulder blade caused him to wince, and pushing himself out of the chair became an event.

The very long, hot shower he took was good for his body, but did nothing for his soul. He was on his third cup of coffee when he heard a car start in the neighborhood. It was early enough for him to wonder who it could be, and as he looked out the kitchen window he saw Kate drive away.

"You have to come back sometime, Kate," he whispered against the mug he held to his lips. "And then we're gonna have this out."

Mike let himself in her back gate. Homer greeted him at the porch and waited for a moment to see if any playtime was forthcoming. When it wasn't, he slowly walked back to his cedar bed, and with a loud, snorting sigh, lay back down.

There wasn't much left to do on the house. Mike's plan was to work in the basement most of the day, but first he wanted to install the new bathroom light fixture. He was just connecting the wires when he heard the phone ring. He had no choice but to ignore it, and he continued working until the light was mounted and secure. As he flicked on the wall switch to test it, the phone rang again. This time he ran to catch it.

"Hello?"

"Hello?" came the confused female voice. "Is Kate there, please?"

"No, she's not." The voice had a familiar cadence to it, and Mike asked, "Is this her mother?"

"Yes, it is."

"Hi, Mrs. Moran. This is Mike Fitzgerald. Did you try to call earlier?"

"No, I didn't, but what a nice surprise! My goodness, it's been a long time." She seemed genuinely pleased to hear his voice. "Kate told me you were working on the house for her. It's a very nice thing you're doing."

He had to bite his tongue to keep from saying, "Aw, shucks, ma'am." Instead, he said, "Always glad to help out where Kate is concerned."

"Yes. I remember." Her voice had a smile in it. "And where is my daughter?"

"I'm not sure."

"Is she still running away from life?"

"You might say that. Did I hear you're coming out for Christmas?"

"That's why I'm phoning. We haven't been able to get a flight out. All the airlines are booked solid. She called on very short notice."

"*She* called?"

"Uh-hm. Her father and I asked her to come out here for the holidays. Even offered to pay for her ticket. But since Paul's accident, she won't even consider it." She paused, as if unsure she should go on. "I'm very concerned about her, Mike, but I don't think anyone can help her. I believe she has to do it herself."

"I'm finally beginning to believe that myself."

"Kate can be very black and white in her thinking.

Maybe she'll eventually learn to see the shades of gray in life."

"I'll tell her you called, Mrs. Moran." He thoughtfully returned the receiver to its cradle.

Julia put down the coffeepot to answer the phone.

"Hi, Julia. Mike Fitzgerald."

"Michael! It's been too long."

"So, how've you been?"

"Fine—fine. But I surely do miss seeing you now and again, especially now that Kate's finished her job."

"Is she there?"

"Now you've disappointed me, sweetie," Julia pouted. "I thought this was a social call."

"Is she?"

"My, but you are persistent."

"Julia . . ." he warned.

"Sorry, sugar. Haven't seen her lately."

There was a pause, then Mike said, "Just tell her her mother called."

"Well, I will if I see her, honey. Anything else?"

"Nothing I'm willing to use a messenger for."

"Damn, honey. Ol' Julia could use a thrill, even if it is a vicarious one."

"That Southern belle routine isn't fooling anyone," Mike said before hanging up.

Julia turned and said, "He knows you're here."

Kate put her face in her hands. "What did he say?"

"Your mother called."

Mike played the flashlight along the solid wooden beams above his head until he found the area directly below the kitchen sink. A water stain about the size of a dinner plate caught his eye and he wanted to make sure it wasn't recent, but the ceiling of the basement was just high enough for him to need a stepladder.

He switched off the light and rubbed the back of his neck. It was still stiff from his night in the chair. He remembered when he could sleep sitting up in the backseat of a car with three other people, and still get up and hike fifteen miles without a twinge. Those days were long gone. Climbing the basement steps, Mike went out the back door and headed for the garage.

Matt drove around the block, didn't see Kate's car, and parked his MG directly in front of the house. There didn't seem to be anyone stirring at his uncle's house and he unfolded himself from the small car. He carried a plastic bag.

He felt along the edge of the front porch eave and his fingers found the spare key that Kate left in case of emergencies. He quietly let himself in and stood in the entry. Matt listened for the telltale sounds of work being done, but heard nothing.

He climbed the twelve steps to the upper hallway and then up the final four to the little landing in front of the tower room's door. He waited. Still no sound. Slipping the key into the hole, he entered the room.

As always, the atmosphere engulfed him in nostalgia, and he took it in, before placing the scrapbook back in its place. An intricately carved box that he'd only superficially looked into was his next goal. Opening the hinged lid, Matt lifted out the divided shelf to see what was underneath. He was rewarded by the sight of one of Paul's World Series rings, and he reached inside. Hefting the massive piece of jewelry in his palm, he then reverently slipped it on his finger. It was a perfect fit. God, did he want one of these for himself.

Reluctantly, he took it off and replaced it on the suede lining of the box. A heavy gold chain, over a quarter inch in width, lay coiled like a gilt snake in one of the corners. Plucking it up, he let it dangle from his fingers before putting it back.

Matt examined every piece of Paul's life in that box, not realizing how much time had gone by. When he'd finally memorized the box's contents, he looked at his watch, and was stunned. He'd been standing there for nearly half an hour. Shutting the box with a sharp snap, Matt reached for the next scrapbook, but his fingers slipped on the slick cover and the scrapbook crashed to the floor. "Shit!" Matt grasped the spine, and as he brought it up, a brown five-by-seven envelope fell out. He was just bending down to pick it up when Mike's voice froze him.

"How the hell did you get in here?"

His heart in his throat, Matt slowly straightened up to face his uncle. Trying to keep his voice steady, Matt said, "With a key."

"Don't be a smart-ass. You know what I mean."

Matt bravely went on, even though he knew the shit had truly hit the fan. "It's okay. Kate lets me come in."

"Since when?"

"Since the night I helped her try to find Homer. She wanted to thank me, so she told me where the key was."

Mike's eyes narrowed. "I don't believe you."

Matt cockily shrugged. "It's the truth."

"Then you won't mind me asking Kate about it, will you?"

The muscles in Matt's legs began to tremble, but he shrugged again. Not able to bear Mike's silent stare, Matt turned to put the scrapbook back.

Mike finally said, "I don't think I'll need your help anymore. I can finish by myself." He started down the steps.

Matt felt the unaccustomed sting of tears at his uncle's rebuke. In all his nineteen years, Mike hadn't been anything but loving and kind to him. The only sharp words he'd ever aimed at him had been during the summer Matt was seven years old and had climbed to the top of the roof. He'd wanted to emulate his uncle, who had been helping his parents with a leak, and had followed him up the ladder. Matt had slipped, nearly sliding off the steep slope of the slate roof, and Mike had caught him by the cotton shirt he wore and let him have it. He'd cried then—from the angry words and from fear. He felt the same way now.

Matt squatted to pick up the envelope he'd dropped, was about to put it back into the scrapbook, when he realized this was probably the last thing of Paul's he'd get to examine. Holding it by the short edge, he didn't take long to decide what to do. He slipped it inside his jacket, and left the tower room and Kate's house. Where was Kate? He wanted to warn her, but wasn't sure what good it would do now.

CHAPTER

THIRTY-THREE

Mike sat in Kate's den. He didn't bother to turn on a light and let dusk overtake the room. _____ Once in a while he'd bring his arm up and sip the scotch rocks he'd made for himself, but he didn't taste it or feel it.

He'd stopped work at four o'clock. Had begun drinking at four-fifteen. The banjo clock struck five, then the half hour. And still, he waited. Every car that drove by was Kate's. Every crunching footstep on the sidewalk was Kate coming home. So that when her car engine stopped, her car door slammed shut, and her boots clicked on the cement walk, he was prepared.

The front door opened and closed. She went into the kitchen and opened the pantry. Dog food rang in Homer's stainless steel bowl, and the back door opened and closed. He could hear her talking to the dog as she fed him.

She came out of the kitchen and went upstairs. The third step still creaked, and somewhere in his tortured mind, he filed that away. She was above him now, in her bedroom. Her boots dropped to the floor. Drawers that presumably had been opened, slid closed.

Except for the squeak of the step, she had soundlessly come back downstairs. The door opened and she entered the den. She switched on the Tiffany lamp, making him blink. And then she saw him.

Kate jumped and her hand came up to cover her heart. When her brain registered it was Mike, she sighed. "You scared the hell out of me." She took a step toward him and her eyes took in the drink in his hand and the look on his face. Alarmed, she asked, "What is it? Has something happened?"

"You tell me," he said in an oddly emotionless voice.

"Is it Dad? Is something wrong with him? Julia told me Mom called . . ."

"Your parents are fine. This isn't about them."

Mike still hadn't moved a muscle and Kate stood rooted to her spot.

"What, then?" she asked.

"I want to know what happened the night Homer ran away." He watched her face. "I want to know what happened between you and Matt."

Her body seemed to sag. A pounding began in her temple. Kate tried to pull her eyes away from his, but the pain in them held her. "Do you believe that everything in life happens for a reason?" she asked, forcing herself to remain standing despite liquid knees.

"Tell me, Kate."

"I can't," she whispered.

"Your vocabulary has become pretty limited."

She shook her head. "Don't make me . . ."

"What I'm imagining is pretty ugly. Please. Tell me I'm wrong," he implored. "Tell me that I'm way out of line."

"I can't," she said dully.

His face collapsed as her words confirmed his worst fears. "Is this some kind of bad joke?" he said in disbelief.

"I was drunk—drugged."

But Mike had stood now and anger erupted out of

him, sulfurous and hot. "Let me get this straight. You fucked my nephew?"

She stared at him, horrified at his words. "No! That's not what happened!"

"Then what *did* happen, Kate?"

How could she tell him? The truth was bad enough. How in the world could she say the words, when even she wasn't sure.

"Mike, I was half out of my mind!"

"But with the other half you fucked Matt?"

"Please," she entreated him. "Please stop saying that! It's not true!"

"I can't think of any other way to put it."

Wringing her hands, she tearfully said, "You don't understand how it was, Mike."

He came toward her. "You're right. I don't understand. After all these years of wanting you. Loving you. I don't understand. And I don't think I want to." Her face was bathed in tears, and as she reached a hand up to wipe them away, he caught her wrist. "Don't. This is the first time in a long time that tears look good on you."

Bowing her head, she quietly said, "I didn't mean to hurt you."

"You told me you loved me. I've waited all my life to hear you say that." He flung her arm away. "And now it doesn't mean shit."

But she went on. "I never wanted to hurt you, Mike. You said you'd remember. You said you'd believe me . . ." She couldn't bring herself to tell him the reality of that night.

"Tell me something, Kate," he said harshly. "Was it his youth you wanted? Or did he remind you of Paul?" He silence told him all he needed to know. "I could've given you so much more. My love was yours for the taking. But you told me you weren't ready for it. Have you ever told me the truth, Kate?"

"I'm telling you the truth now! I've never lied to you,

Mike. Never! I told you I love you and that's the truth, too."

"You don't know the meaning of the word 'love.' When you figure it out, come and tell me, because I think I just forgot what it means myself."

He walked out of the room.

CHAPTER

THIRTY-FOUR

K ate's first impulse was to run after him, throw her arms around him, tell him it would be all right if _____ he could just understand.

What stopped her was a memory so strong that nine years faded away, and she instinctively knew that the last thing Mike wanted was a show of affection from her, however real it may be. Betrayal, and the almost irreversible loss of trust it caused, called for a shutdown. A time to lie quietly and lick wounds. A time to think and regain hope. A time to forgive, because you never forgot.

"A little more to the left . . ."

"Didn't I just do that twenty minutes ago?" Paul says from underneath the eight-foot Fraser fir. "C'mon, Kate. I don't care if it's straight anymore. I'm growing moss down here!"

"Mom, what do you think?"

Kate's mother looks up from the string of lights she is trying to untangle. "It looks fine to me. What do you think, Jim?" There is no answer, and Mary Moran glances behind her. "Jim! Are you asleep?"

Kate's father comes awake with a snort. The box of ornaments he's been holding falls to the floor and lands with an unhealthy tinkling sound.

Kate swallows a giggle, as her father says, "What now?"

"The tree. Does it look straight?"

"Since when do we do Christmas by committee?"

Mary Moran rolls her eyes at her daughter, and Kate says, "You can come up for air, Paul. It'll do."

She is brushing fir needles out of his hair when the phone rings.

Kate's mother moves to get up. "I'll get it."

"No—let me," Kate says, rushing to the kitchen. "It might be Mike."

Mary Moran looks at her son-in-law. "Mike Fitzgerald?"

Paul nods, concentrating on stringing the first set of lights around the plump tree.

"Will he be coming home for Christmas?"

"Yeah. He usually stays with us a couple of days if his mom is visiting Sheryl in Maryland. Then he spends Christmas with them."

"That's a lot of driving," she comments.

"Kate wouldn't have it any other way." Paul looks up as Kate enters the living room. "When's he coming?"

"It wasn't Mike."

Paul turns his attention to the tree once more. "Well, don't keep me in suspense. Who was it?"

"Wrong number, I guess. There wasn't anybody on the line."

"Probably the phone company taking a bathroom break," Paul comments.

What Kate has left unsaid is that since they've returned from San Francisco—since October—these hang-up calls have increased in frequency from once or twice a month to almost daily. And they never seem to happen to Paul. She's chosen to ignore their implications for the sake of harmony, but with Christmas just a week away it's becoming more and more difficult.

Kate turns to her father and teasingly says, "Daddy? Do you want some coffee?"

"No. You can keep me awake with your sparkling wit, Katie."

Her smile turns to a slight frown when the phone rings again. "Paul, you get it this time." She takes the lights from him. "Dad can help me with this."

As Paul leaves the room, her mother says, "I didn't know Mike Fitzgerald was coming."

"Well, I hope he's coming. We're still waiting to hear."

"Is he married yet?"

"No. He's too busy proving that there are still a lot of fish in the sea." Kate steps back from the tree to check her work. "Why?"

Just then Paul comes back. "That was Mike. He'll be here day after tomorrow."

Kate's face lights up. "Good!" Walking past Paul, she gives him a peck on the cheek. "This calls for some music."

A Christmas tape comes on and Kate's throaty voice fills the room as she sings along with "Winter Wonderland."

It's early but her parents have gone to bed, saying they were tired. Kate suspects they want to leave the three friends alone in the den.

She and Mike are working their way through their first bottle of wine, and an endless argument about who was the better writer, Steinbeck (Kate) or Faulkner (Mike). Paul, who had suffered through both in high school, simply sits back drinking his rum and Coke and keeping score. Mike has just pulled ahead with his last point when the telephone rings. Paul raises himself out of the comfortable wing chair. No one notices that he opts to pick it up in the kitchen.

Kate is busy saying, "You can't possibly compare The Grapes of Wrath to any of Faulkner's stuff! Steinbeck spoke to a whole nation. If you're not from the South, Faulkner's almost unreadable."

"In your opinion," Mike answers, holding out his wine glass.

Kate upends the bottle and pours Mike the last of the wine. "I have a right to my opinion."

"The rules say I do, too."

"Not when your opinion is wrong." She grins, standing. "I'll go get another bottle."

It surprises her to hear Paul's voice. It surprises her even more to realize she hadn't noticed him leave the room.

His tone is annoyed. His voice is low. But she hears his words clearly.

"Look, you can't keep calling me here."

Kate stands still.

"God damn it, it's Christmas! I've got family and friends here."

She has stopped breathing.

"No. You listen. I don't want you calling me again."

Kate tries to slow her heartbeat.

"No. I fucking well mean it, Liz. Not now—not ever." He hangs up.

Stifling a sob, Kate takes a few steps back down the hall. There is nowhere to hide but the bathroom, and she quickly takes refuge there. A few minutes pass before she hears Paul's footsteps pass the door and go back into the den.

Kate follows him moments later, a fresh bottle in her hand, a smile on her face. Paul excuses himself twenty minutes later. Kate allows him to kiss her good-night. She gives him a five-minute head start, and then tells Mike to keep the wine flowing; that she'll be right back.

She quietly closes the bedroom door and leans back against it. Paul, wearing only his Jockey shorts, has just gone into his nighty push-up routine.

"Who was on the phone, Paul?"

He doesn't slow down, answering, "My mom."

"When did she change her name to Liz?"

That makes him stop mid-push and he slowly gets to his knees.

"Don't even think about lying to me again, Paul."

With absolutely no sense of shame, he says, "She's a fan who got the wrong idea when I said hi to her at a game."

Kate stares at him in disbelief. "And how did she happen to get our unlisted telephone number?"

Paul's jaw tightens. He stands, but he has no easy answer for her, and the something inside Kate that wants to be wrong shrivels.

"Let me get this straight, Paul. You gave one of your sluts our phone number, somehow expecting her not to call, and me not to find out?" *God, he was so handsome, standing there half-naked. The thought of Paul pounding his hard body into another woman sends a shiver of pain through Kate, and her agony comes out in her words.* "You promised me, Paul. You said you'd never do this to me again."

His eyes, so soft, reflect her anguish.

Pleading with him, she quietly asks, "What am I doing wrong? Just tell me and I'll fix it. I want you to love me again."

"Kate, I do love you. It's just . . . I get lonely on the road."

"Then why won't you let me go with you? We can afford it! Why?" *Her voice hardens.* "Answer me, damn it!"

But he continues gazing at her.

Enraged, she says, "Is it because I'd cramp your style?" *A sudden realization hits her.* "God, Paul! How many have there been?" *Her stomach convulses. Bile rises in her throat and she has to stop herself from being sick.* "You—are—disgusting."

"Kate, I'm sorry."

"You don't know sorry yet." *Her voice lowers to a hiss.* "While my parents are here you can sleep in this room, but not in our bed. After they leave, you can move into the guest room. I'll act like nothing's wrong. Don't take that to mean all's well. By the end of this winter you'll wish you'd kept your pants zipped, 'cause the only time you'll get to take your cock out is to piss."

Shocked at her words, he says, "Come on, Kate! You don't mean that."

A small snort of mirthless laughter escapes her lips. "I have to get back downstairs. Mike's waiting."

When she comes to bed, Kate can just make out the outline of Paul's form on the oversized armchair near the window. He seems to be asleep.

She wearily crawls into her side of the bed, exhausted from keeping up the pretense of happiness; anesthetized by the wine. It's going to be a very long week.

She closes her eyes and tries to banish the images of Paul's unfaithfulness that keep scrolling past her vision. But his measured breathing is a constant reminder, and she resorts to her childhood trick. Stop it, her mind repeats over and over. Don't think. Stop it . . .

Kate dozes on and off for most of the night. At one point, when she thinks she feels Paul move next to her, her inner voice says, I'm dreaming, and she goes back to sleep. It is a while later that his hand touches the curve of her waist. Not fully asleep, she flinches away from him. He becomes more persistent—his hand making slow circles down the small of her back, possessively cupping her buttocks. She moves again.

"Let me just hold you, Katie. I can make it better."

That's when she sits up. "Get away from me, Paul. Nothing you can do is going to make it better. Not for a long time." Scooting up against the headboard, she pulls the covers up around her. "I want you to get out of the bed."

He gets up without another word.

Paul's exile lasts nearly two weeks. Christmas has been a farce played out for the benefit of her parents. Once they are safely on the plane that will take them back to Tempe, Kate reenters their home, goes directly to their bedroom, and removes his pillow, underwear, and bathrobe to the guest room.

Paul never does understand her need for distance from him. His advances would have been sweet, playful sexual forays had Paul and Kate been living in happier times. But, as things stand, Kate sees them only as prurient reminders of what he's done.

Kate doesn't know how she'll get through the New Year's party she's planned, and on December 27, she cancels it, to the very vocal dismay of all their friends. Kate is also disappointed. It has always been her night to shine.

Mike is probably the most surprised at the change in the natural order of the universe, and he says so. "Wait a sec, Kate.

Do you mean to tell me I have to come up with my own form of entertainment on December thirty-first? I won't know how to act."

"Things change, Mike," she tells him, and she wonders if he knows, when he says, "Not really, darlin'."

Kate is already dressed for bed when Paul knocks on the door. She sits up a little taller and puts the book she's been trying to read across her lap.

"Come in."

It takes a moment for the door to open. What she sees makes her smile shyly, and causes her heart to melt.

Paul is standing in the doorway, barefoot, dressed in his tuxedo, a boyish grin on his face. He holds a bottle of Perrier-Jouet champagne in one hand, two glasses in the other.

"I know things aren't good between us right now, but I couldn't stand the thought of New Year's Eve without you, baby." He takes a step inside. "Let's at least drink a toast to the good times."

As he walks to the bed, she can feel herself giving in to his appeal. And as he sits down in front of her, she reaches for his bow tie, saying, "You never could tie this thing straight."

She had forgiven him that night, but she would never lose the small corner in her heart reserved for the significant pain he'd brought into her life.

Kate knew exactly how Mike felt. The only difference—and it was a major difference—was that she truly regretted what had happened. Paul never had.

CHAPTER
THIRTY-FIVE

After Mike had made it clear he wanted nothing more to do with his nephew, Matt stayed away from home the rest of the afternoon. When he finally pulled into the driveway, and his mother greeted him as she had any other day, he knew his uncle hadn't said anything to her, and for that he was grateful. Matt was eating his dinner when he remembered the envelope he'd taken from the tower room. It lay on the passenger seat of his car, and as soon as he'd finished his second helping of meat loaf, he excused himself from the table and retrieved it.

Sitting on the edge of the bed, Matt studied the nondescript envelope. It was addressed to Paul Armstrong care of the San Francisco Giants. The address was printed in black felt pen. There was no return address. The postmark—faded and partially gone where the stamps had given up their hold—gave no clue from where it had come.

He folded up the metal tabs that held it closed and one of them broke off in his fingers. Matt shook the contents out onto his bed. Five photographs of various sizes fluttered to the blanket.

Matt flipped the top photo over. He didn't know what to expect, but this wasn't it, and he quickly turned over

the rest and spread them out. Completely baffled—
totally engrossed—he was startled by the knock on
his door.

"Matt?"

Swiftly collecting the pictures, he shoved them back
into the envelope, saying, "Yeah?"

"Mike's on the phone for you."

"Oh, man!" he whispered to himself. Standing, he ran
a hand through his hair, wishing he could somehow disappear.

"Matt? Come on, he's waiting."

"Yeah—okay. I'm coming." He took a deep breath
and slowly expelled it. There was no denying it. He was
scared shitless.

Matt followed his mother downstairs and cautiously
brought the receiver to his ear.

Without preliminaries, Mike said, "Meet me at Gypsy
Hill Park right now. I don't want to have to wait for you."

His uncle hung up, but Matt kept talking, pretending
Mike was still on the line. When he hung up, he turned
away from his mother's gaze and, with a mouth gone
dry with fear, said, "He needs some help. I won't
be long."

Mike's truck was easy to spot. It was the only vehicle
in the park on this frigid December evening. Matt pulled
in next to it, but didn't see his uncle. He climbed out of
the MG on shaky legs. The muscles in his arms contracted in adrenaline shock when he heard Mike's voice.

"Over here."

Mike stood in the shelter of the bandstand, nearly
invisible. Walking as confidently as he could, Matt trod
along the path that circled the duck pond and then
crossed the tiny stream that meandered through the
park. The grass, brittle from the cold, crunched under his
shoes.

When he was a few feet from Mike, he said, "It's cold.
Why did you want to meet here?"

In a voice as chilled as the air, Mike answered, "Because I didn't want you in my home."

Matt didn't know how to respond to the frosty words. Mike pulled himself out of the shadows, and Matt got a good look at his grim face.

"Once I was out of the way it didn't take you long, did it?" Mike said.

"It wasn't like that."

"You little shit," Mike growled.

Matt looked away, then at the ground. "I didn't know how you felt about her. I'm sorry, Uncle Mike."

"Don't call me that. If you're old enough to fuck the woman I love, you're old enough to call me Mike."

"That's not what happened! I swear!"

"So she said. How come I don't believe it?"

"She's telling you the *truth*!" Matt was shivering and he stuck his hands in his coat pockets. "Y'know . . . what happened . . . it wasn't her fault."

"Excuse me, but it takes two."

"Look—she was really drunk . . ."

"*I don't care.* You both knew what you were doing."

Matt faced Mike. "I'm trying to tell you! She didn't know."

"Bullshit!" The words exploded around Matt's ears. "You got into her pants and into her precious room. Was she worth it?"

Matt rocked back at the force of Mike's wrath.

"Tell me, Matt! I've been waiting a very long time to find out." Mike grabbed a handful of Matt's jacket and brought him close. Matt could smell the leather of Mike's jacket and the scotch on his breath. "How did she sound? What did she feel like under you?"

"She thought I was Paul," Matt said in a strangled voice.

But Mike was beyond reason. "Where did it happen, you shit? Did she take you into her bed? Did she scream out your name when she came?"

"She thought I was Paul!" Matt repeated, shouting this time. "Listen to me, Mike, please! She didn't know who I was, okay?"

Mike suddenly let him go, and Matt staggered backward.

"Get out of my sight," Mike said.

Pleading with him, Matt said, "You've got to forgive me, Mike. If I'd known—if you'd said something about the way you felt about Kate—I would've stayed away. I didn't know!"

"Get out of here!" Mike said with more force. "I mean it, Matt!"

From the sound of his voice, Matt may as well have been on his knees when he said, "Please don't say anything to Mom . . ."

"You selfish little prick."

"It's not for me. I don't care about me!" He held out his hands in supplication. "I just don't want Kate to be hurt anymore. I didn't realize how things were with her."

"How noble of you." Mike sneered. "The next Prince Charming of baseball."

"It was a mistake! Haven't you ever made a mistake, Mike?"

"The biggest mistake I ever made was trusting the two of you." He swept past Matt and headed for his truck.

Matt's voice battled with the wind that had kicked up, scattering desiccated leaves along the ground. "You've loved her for all these years, Mike! Don't cut her loose now."

Mike sat in the bay window of his dark bedroom, staring out across the street at Kate's house. It was long past midnight. The wind that gusted around the house made it come alive with low moaning sounds. The maple tree's bare branches whipped back and forth, casting moon shadows on his tired face.

No one . . . no one to talk to.

The upper hallway light came on in her house, and then, a few seconds later the window of the tower room lit up. He could just make out her figure moving through the room, and his face became grim as he remembered Matt standing there.

She thought I was Paul . . .

Mike closed his eyes for a moment, and when he opened them she was standing at the window, looking out at his house. He knew she couldn't see him, but he sat perfectly still, holding his breath. She finally turned away, and he slowly exhaled, trying to force the longing out of his body. She could hurt him like no one else, and that was his fault. He'd let himself in for it.

It was a mistake . . .

Three days now since he'd talked to her. Three long days had gone by, and he'd gone over their last words a hundred times. He had come to the inevitable conclusion that he couldn't live without her, but didn't know if he could live with what she'd done. Out of nowhere, his mind would show him clips of Matt and Kate that made him cry out in anger and frustration, and he'd think, *I can't forgive this.* And then he'd remember the Kate he'd grown up with, and he'd want her all the more.

God, he needed to talk with someone. He perversely wanted to know every detail of what had happened that night. But he didn't trust himself to be able to rationally listen to the two people who could tell him. That night in the park, Mike had barely been able to control himself. He'd wanted to beat Matt senseless. That kind of anger had scared him with its force. He'd never felt anything like it, and it took every ounce of restraint to rein himself in. If *he* could contain himself, why the hell couldn't Kate?

The light went out in the tower room, followed by the

hall light, and her house sank into the night. Too weary to move to his bed, Mike let sleep overtake him on the padded bench of the window seat.

The slamming of a car door woke him. Blinking against the light of day, he watched as Matt strode up Kate's walkway and onto her front porch. The door opened and, after a few seconds, he slipped inside the house.

A rage so strong—so uncontrollable—welled up inside Mike, that he brought his fist up against a windowpane. It shattered under the force. A thin trickle of blood ran into the crevices of his hand as he opened his fingers to stare at what he'd done.

He had to get out of town.

CHAPTER

THIRTY-SIX

Bad enough that the doorbell was ringing at—Kate looked at the clock—eight-fifteen. She'd had _____ only four hours of sleep. Actually, she hadn't really slept in days. But a deep, depressive sleep had finally caught up with her early this morning, and she would've ignored the person at her door, except she hoped it was Mike.

Kate struggled to get off the couch and didn't give a second thought to her appearance. She still had on the leggings and oversized sweatshirt she had worn the day before. Her thick socks made a whispering sound against the hardwood floor as she shuffled to the front door. *Please let it be Mike.* She wanted to talk to him. Tell him, again, how sorry she was. Tell him—show him—that she wanted him. Only him.

She wasn't prepared for Matt, though. Disappointment, and then anger, flooded through her.

"What do you want?"

Matt flushed at her harsh greeting. "I just wanted to see how you were doing." It wasn't what he wanted at all, but it was obvious now was not the time to talk to Kate about anything.

"Have you lost your mind, coming over here?" She

pushed open the screen door. "Get inside. God! What if Mike sees you? What's he going to think?"

Matt stepped past her and waited uneasily. He had no idea what to say to her now.

Slamming the door, Kate turned and said, "Get this straight, you little shit. I don't want to see you right now. We have nothing to say to each other."

"I'm sorry."

"Sorry doesn't do me any good."

"Look, I know how pissed off Mike is . . . was . . . but I'm sure—"

The color in Kate's cheeks deepened. "Pissed off? Are you kidding? Our little interlude may have cost me the only chance I had at happiness. Worse than that, I gave Mike a reason never to trust me again."

Matt edged toward the door. "I guess I'd better go."

Kate's hand shot out and gripped his forearm. "Not until I tell you something. That was a really lousy thing you did to me. You took advantage of me when I was at my weakest and that really stinks." She let go of his arm and opened the door. "When and if Mike forgives me, *then* I'll forgive *you*. In the meantime, stay away from me."

Matt could feel the envelope in his back pocket, reminding him why he'd come. He couldn't make her any madder, and decided to give it a shot. "But I really need to ask you something. It's important."

Kate looked at him in disbelief. "Have you suddenly gone simple? Get out!"

"Look, Kate, you're the only person—"

She was enraged. "What part of 'get out' don't you understand?" She was pushing him out the door.

"But it's about Paul."

Kate's mouth opened, then closed. She was stupefied at his gall. Her finger stabbed him in the chest, as she said, "Look, you imbecile. I don't give a shit what this is about. This obsession you have with Paul has got to stop!

Not only is it a colossal pain in the ass, it's not important. Right now, what's important is Mike." She gave him another push. "Now, get the hell out of my house."

Kate's hands shook as she spooned coffee into the filter. The phone was tucked in the crook of her shoulder. She had called Julia the moment Matt left. Three days of being alone were enough, and she needed to talk to someone.

Kate had drifted through the past few days, unable to do much of anything. When sleep came, it was fickle. She would wake at odd hours, craving the alcohol she'd gone without since that night with Matt. Sometimes she would actually pour the brandy and sit staring at the glass, thinking the act would somehow calm her. But there was nothing like the real thing. Then she'd pick up the glass and see reflected in it Mike's look of pain at what she'd done, and the golden liquid would go down the drain. She didn't know how much longer this could go on. The small amount of strength she'd gained was deserting her, and there had been Matt at the door, reminding her of all her weaknesses.

Kate swiped at the spilled grounds, but only managed to make a bigger mess. "I've never been so angry at anyone, Julia."

"Let me get this straight. He came over to see how you were?"

"That's what he said." Kate sat at the table. She couldn't remember anything but her rage at Matt. "Why?"

"Because most eighteen-year-olds don't know how to *spell* 'empathy,' let alone practice it."

"Forget Matt! I miss Mike, Julia. I miss him so much." There were those damned tears again. "And I'm so sick of crying."

"Then talk to him."

"He won't listen to me. I've called and left messages, but he doesn't call me back."

"Then go over there. He can't ignore your beautiful face."

Kate grabbed a tissue. "God, Julia. It doesn't get any worse than this."

"Sugar, you're inviting trouble when you say things like that."

Kate tried Mike's number once more, but his machine answered. She slammed down the receiver. Pulling on a coat, shoving her feet into a pair of old moccasins, she ran across the street and pounded on his door in a fruitless attempt to bring him out. When she turned away in frustration, Kate saw his truck was gone, and fresh tears ran down her cheeks.

This was as alone as it got.

Mike was already heading down Highway 64 by then. He had thrown enough clothes in a suitcase to last him a week, locked up the house, tossed the bag into the cab of the truck, and with one last angry glance at Matt's car, roared away. Somewhere around Norfolk he'd called Sheryl from his mobile phone to tell her he wouldn't be around for Christmas. Her stunned "Why?" didn't faze him. He gave her no explanation, simply repeating he wouldn't be there, and he hung up.

He'd been on the road for nearly seven hours and stopped in the town of Aden, North Carolina, population 5,655 according to the road sign. His dinner consisted of a greasy burger and fries. The first motel he came to turned out to be the only one in the drab little burg.

The room probably hadn't changed since the fifties, when the place had been built. Scarred maple furniture and drapes faded to an unrecognizable shade that might have been green at one time exuded a musty odor. The tub and sink had matching rust stains. But the sheets were clean and the TV worked.

He thought about checking his messages, but when he looked over at the phone he knew he'd have to wait. It had no buttons. It didn't even have a dial. Strictly an in-house telephone, they might as well have strung two tin cans together. His cell phone was in the truck, but he was too weary to pull his clothes back on to retrieve it.

Mike stretched out on the bed after switching on the television. The last thing he saw before falling asleep wasn't on any network. It was the shadow of Kate standing in the tower room, looking out at him through the window.

He drove through the outskirts of Charleston, South Carolina, with just one thought in mind. He wanted to be pampered. He wanted luxury and great food and expensive wine. He wanted to feel cared for. And he knew the Church Street Inn, and Eleanor, could do all those things for him.

Plunking down his American Express Platinum card, he asked for their best room for the next four nights. Despite the season, the concierge was happy to accommodate him, and once the bellhop had left the room, Mike pulled a Beck's out of the bar hidden in an antique armoire and picked up the phone.

He tried to stop the thought before it was fully formed, but it was too late. *Kate would love this.* Predawn, and everything outside the hotel, from the Market to Waterfront Park, was bathed in a pale rose light. Mike always called Charleston the Pink City in his mind. Pink brick buildings, salmon houses with wide piazzas, and carnation-colored plaster trimmed in black ironwork.

He turned away from the window and his eyes fell on a wisp of fuchsia satin that covered Eleanor's hips as she slept. He watched her for a few seconds, sighed deeply, then quietly went into the bathroom and shut the door.

The tile floor was cold and he quickly started the shower. As he turned to the marble counter to pick up his shampoo, he caught a glimpse of himself in the mirror. He wasn't thrilled with the man he saw. He'd never run away from anything in his life, yet here he was, hundreds of miles from his family at Christmastime. And why? Because he couldn't deal with real life when it smacked him in the face. Because some fairy-tale vision he had of rescuing the fair Kate had gone awry. Because still, after all these years, he wanted Kate to be his, and his alone.

His image began to blur as the mirror clouded over. Mike stepped into the hot shower.

"Is there room for two in there?"

Eleanor's voice penetrated the dense fog that surrounded him. Her sleep-warm body pressed against his back as her arms circled his chest, yet he shivered. Still holding the bar of soap he'd been using, he said, "I'm sorry about last night, El."

"I noticed your heart wasn't in it."

"It had nothing to do with you."

"I know that," she answered. "You said her name when you came."

Mike winced. "God. Can you ever forgive me?" He turned to face her.

"We've been all through this, Mike. I knew the score coming in. You sounded like you needed someone and I was happy to be there."

He kissed her forehead, her pale blond hair.

"We're not going to do this again, though, are we," she said.

He shook his head. "I'm afraid not."

Taking the soap from his hand, Eleanor placed it on the ledge. "Then give me a proper good-bye kiss."

Mike sat at the desk in his room, phone in hand. Although the anger he felt was so insidious it exhausted him, and although he didn't know where to put it except at Kate's and Matt's feet, he realized this was no time for doubts. Not after all this time. Kate had said the words. He had to believe her. About everything. Or it had all been pointless.

He punched in the numbers that would allow him to retrieve his messages. They were all from Kate, pleading with him to answer the phone. Her voice was desperate.

In her final message, though, her voice grew subtly stronger.

"I physically lost Paul three years ago. But I lost the Paul I loved years before that. I've barely lived through both losses," she said. "I know for a fact that I won't be able to live through losing you."

Mike began packing.

As if the sudden snow flurries along the coast hadn't been bad enough, and the traffic through Norfolk at rush hour hadn't been excruciatingly slow enough, the broken fan belt on the outskirts of Richmond made him lose all self-control, and Mike got out of his truck and kicked the fender.

He just wanted to get home. And now, calling Triple A from his mobile phone, he cursed his luck. It would take them at least forty minutes to get to him. Seems he wasn't the only road casualty on this crappy night. Everyone was in a hurry to get somewhere four days before Christmas.

Mike pulled on his parka and settled down for the long wait. He tried reading, but it was too dark. The nearest highway light was a good three hundred yards ahead of him. His stomach gurgled, reminding him he hadn't eaten since leaving the hotel that morning. Rummaging through the glove compartment, he came up with an opened pack of breath mints and some stale crackers that had probably been there since the last administration. Sucking on a mint, Mike unzipped his suitcase, pulled out his Walkman, and tuned into a radio station that did a nightly blues program.

"That fits," he said, leaning back and closing his eyes, letting Muddy Waters tell him how minutes seem like hours, and hours seem like days.

His headlights didn't pick out his dark house until nearly eleven o'clock that night. Wearily climbing out of the truck, Mike dragged his suitcase across the seat and let it drop to the ground. Slamming the door shut, house key in hand, he glanced across the street. What he saw made his pulse quicken.

Kate stood in her living room window. It was the only light on in her house and he saw her clearly for only a moment, and then she was gone. And just as he thought he'd imagined her, the front door opened and she was coming toward him. His suitcase forgotten, fatigue only a memory, Mike quickly skirted the truck.

They met in the street and as they faced each other, they both recognized a change had taken place. Kate, afraid it was too late for them, searched his face for a sign that he still felt something for her. She reached up to his face with both hands and brought her lips to his. He seemed to pull back at her touch, and she let him go.

"Please forgive me," she said.

"Give me a reason," he said.

"I love you, Mike. I don't have any other reason."

He moved away. She was too close, and he was too vulnerable. "I'm tired, Kate. I need some sleep ... I need some time."

She nodded, looked away. "I understand."

The sadness in her voice shook him a little. There was

...y about her that was new. He
... I bet you do," he replied.

... round his again, and she said, "I'm glad
... back."

I'm glad you're glad," he answered with a small
smile. "Why don't we talk more tomorrow."

CHAPTER

THIRTY-SEVEN

Matt's hand shook as it hovered over the phone. Each time he attempted to dial Kate's number, he remembered her angry words. There was no one else to turn to, though.

Mike was gone. And besides, Matt figured he'd pretty much screwed up that relationship. How could he talk to his uncle about Paul now?

The thought of asking his mother was too weird. What if he was wrong? What would she think of him, then?

That left Kate. Did it matter if she hated him for the rest of her life? Better her than his family.

His fingers finally punched in her number and he waited. When she answered, Matt's bowels contracted in fear, and he almost hung up. But this was too important to let himself be intimidated by whatever Kate could say or do.

"It's Matt. Don't hang up!" he said quickly. But he was suddenly, and not surprisingly, listening to a dial tone. He hit the redial button before he could chicken out.

She said, "Stop bothering me," and hung up.

His third try was met by a busy signal.

• • •

Matt sat in his mother's car. She'd bought his story of a bad battery and he was supposedly on his way to a friend's to borrow a charger. Instead, he waited with uncharacteristic patience two houses up from Kate's. He figured—hoped—she'd have to go somewhere eventually, and he was willing to wait all day if necessary. In case it *did* take hours, he'd brought along a sandwich and his portable CD player.

Just as he was settling into his third hour, and Pearl Jam's latest, Matt was rewarded.

He followed Kate to the parking lot on Market Street, where she got out of her car and entered a shop from the back door. Puzzled, Matt walked around the block. The sign in front of the building read Remember the Time. And another, smaller, sign hanging below it told him it was an antique store. According to the small plastic clock held to the door by suction cups, the shop was due to open in fifteen minutes. But just as he put his right foot on the first porch step, the front door swung open and Kate backed out, holding a rocking chair.

Out of the corner of her eye she could see there was already a customer coming up the stairs. Setting the chair down, she turned to greet him, and was horrified to come face-to-face with Matt.

"Can't you leave me alone?" she hissed.

"Well, you wouldn't talk to me at your house, so I figured I'd try and meet you somewhere else. What is this place?"

"Don't be dim, Matt. This is my shop."

"I didn't know you had an antique store . . ."

"If you didn't know, how did you find me? . . . You followed me here?"

"It looks like a nice place," he said, stalling.

"Don't change the subject. Did you, or did you not, follow me here?"

"I guess I kinda did. But Kate, I really need to talk to you!" She started to close the door in his face. "Please."

He took hold of the doorknob, his body taking up most of the frame. "This is so incredibly important. Just give me ten minutes, and I won't bother you again. I promise."

Peggy James, the owner of the flower shop next door, walked by at that moment, a curious look on her face. "Everything all right in there?" she called.

Kate peered around Matt. "Yes. Thanks, Peggy."

"Kate? Well, I'll be! It's been an absolute age."

Kate could tell from Peggy's voice that she was about to be treated to a visit. "Yes, it has, Peg. And I'd love to chat, but I'm trying to get a delivery straightened out. Will you excuse me?" And with that she grabbed Matt's arm and pulled him into the shop. Once the door was closed, she said, "You've got five minutes."

Now that he had her undivided attention, he could feel himself beginning to falter. Everything he wanted to say suddenly seemed stupid. All the questions seemed childish.

"You said it was important, Matt," Kate said impatiently.

"Yeah." He finally reached into his jacket pocket and pulled out the envelope. Taking out the photographs, he handed them to her. Kate's eyes questioned him, and he said, "Just look at them." Kate quickly flipped through them, and Matt asked, "Do you know who that is?"

"Of course I do. They're Paul when he was a baby." She looked up at him. "How did you get these?"

Matt ignored her question. "Look at them again."

Any patience she may have had now eroded dangerously. "I don't need to look at them again. These are Paul's baby pictures. What else do you want me to say?"

"Where did they come from?"

"This is ridiculous. Why don't you tell me where you got them? Did you take them from the tower?"

"They're not Paul."

Kate snorted. "What are you talking about? Of course they're Paul."

"They're *not* Paul," he repeated. "I know. Because these are photos of me."

"This is outrageous. You take these out of my house and then try to tell me I don't know my own husband?"

"I'm telling you the truth." Matt pulled a photograph out of the back pocket of his jeans and handed it to her. She snatched it from him. It was identical to the second picture she'd looked at. "Turn it over," he said.

She read the words written in blue ink. *Matt—age 1½ — Clinton, MD*

"I don't get it," she said almost to herself. "Why would Paul have photos of you?"

"That's what I'd like to know."

Kate stared up into his hazel eyes, forcing her mind to work logically. "Let me see the envelope." Matt silently passed it over to her. It told her nothing, and she gave it back to him. "Mike must've sent them," Kate finally stated.

"Why?"

"I don't know why," she said angrily. "And your time is up."

Kate walked away from him, her thoughts turning back to Mike. By the time Matt let himself out of the shop, she'd already forgotten he'd been there.

It had been so long since she'd been in the store that the inventory seemed to have completely changed. Kate wandered through the rooms and found new pleasure in the old pieces. Three customers, all men, came in before noon, and all three found the perfect last-minute Christmas gifts for their wives.

Kate made her way upstairs with a box of linens with the intention of exchanging dusty for clean. Each room in the shop represented a room in a real house, and each was decorated in a different style. She entered the "library," with its mission oak furniture, leather-bound books, and Persian rugs, and saw it immediately.

It had to be the most elegant lamp ever made by Handel. A perfect dome of cream-colored glass reverse-painted in shades of taupe floated above the slender deep-copper base. Where on earth had Cindy found it? As Kate walked toward the table it sat on, she realized she'd been holding her breath. The closer she got, the more flawless it appeared. Reaching out, she ran a finger over the cool glass. It was perfect. And when she found the switch and turned it on, she gasped. "You are a beauty," she whispered.

"Kate?"

She whirled around. "Cindy. You scared me."

"I've been yelling for you since I came in." Her partner pointed at the lamp. "Isn't that something?"

"Where did it come from?"

"Didn't you see my note?" Cindy said. "It arrived a few days ago. No return address on the label. There was an envelope in the crate addressed to you. I left it under the tray in the register."

Kate turned to look at the lamp once more and, for the first time, noticed the "For Display Only" card.

"You think it's a gift?" she asked.

Cindy shrugged. "I just figured I'd better wait before I put a price on it."

Kate followed Cindy down the staircase to the old-fashioned brass and wood cash register in the entry. The note in the envelope, on rose-colored heavy stock, was typewritten: *My gift to you is your gift to him, which I hope will become my gift to both of you someday. Be happy.*

"Julia," Kate said softly. "Oh, Julia, you shouldn't have." Then she laughed out loud as she remembered the day she'd told her friend about the Tiffany lamp that sat in her own study. The memory had been brought on by the same Handel lamp that now sat in her shop.

Julia's husband had given it to her as a Christmas gift, and Julia had said the same thing that Kate had said to Paul. "Either I've been very, very good, or you've been very, very bad." Only she'd added her own Julia-ism. "Oh, but what am I saying? I'm always very, very good . . ."

Kate hadn't recognized it because the lamp had been crated, and she'd only had Julia's description to go by when they inventoried it.

Cindy was smiling at her. "It's good to see you here, Kate. Good to have you back."

Kate looked up from the note and reached for Cindy's hand. "I'm sorry for not being here. For making you deal with everything on your own."

"What's going on with you, Kate? Some kind of good news that you've been keeping from me?" Cindy paused. "Have you met a new man?"

Kate smiled distractedly, and answered, "No, not a new one." She quickly hugged Cindy. "Well, my shift is over. I'm going to pack up the lamp and go."

"Merry Christmas, Kate."

"Same to you, Cindy."

CHAPTER

THIRTY-EIGHT

The doorbell rang, scattering his thoughts. Mike opened the door to find the object of his daydream standing on the porch.

"Since when do you use the front door?" he asked.

"I wasn't sure if I was still welcome at the back." When he didn't respond, Kate said, "I guess that answers my question."

He stood aside to let her in, but she bent down, and it was then he noticed the large box at her feet.

They silently walked into the kitchen and Kate placed the box on the table. "It's for you. Open it."

"We need to talk."

"We will. But first I want you to open this."

Mike pulled back the flaps. It was wrapped in an old sheet and he lifted it out. As he unwound the cloth, she said, "Lamps seem to be the way to forgiveness in these parts."

Gently setting the beautiful combination of glass and metal on the table, he said, "I wish you hadn't."

"I didn't. Not really." He looked at her across the table. "Julia sent it to the shop."

"I don't know how to deal with what you and Matt did."

"I know," she said. "I can't make it go away. But I can try to make you understand what happened."

"And I guess I can listen."

"Do you believe that everything happens for a reason?" she asked.

"I'm not sure what I believe anymore."

Kate looked away, trying to erase the look of resignation in his eyes. But it didn't work, and she had to face it anyway.

"I'm sorry and ashamed for what I did, Mike. I'm not trying to make excuses, but I'd hit rock bottom that night. Homer was missing, I was drunk. I was scared. And then I took some painkillers." She moved around the table to stand closer to him. "There's a reason they tell you not to mix those with alcohol. They turn you into the stupidest person alive. By then I truly didn't know what I was doing."

"Why didn't you just tell me?"

"What difference would it have made? Would you have been any less hurt?"

She waited, and he finally said, "No."

"Mike, I just don't know what to say here. For what it's worth, I think I lost my mind for a while that night. It wasn't Matt there with me."

"But it wasn't me, either."

Completely frustrated, she said, "No. It wasn't. And I can't help that, Mike. But I wasn't the only one to blame for that. Matt's become totally obsessed with Paul. It was so damned convenient for him."

Mike stepped away from her. He didn't want to hear any more. What he suddenly wanted was to take her right there—to fuck her until she screamed out his name. Because then he'd know she was really his, and his alone.

"Mike, the only reason he did what he did was because I'd been Paul's. He's been taking things out of the tower room. He's been hounding me about Paul."

She turned her head and ran a hand through her hair. When she looked at Mike again, something in his eyes made her quickly go on. "He followed me to the shop today. Even after I told him to leave me alone . . ." At the end of her rope, she began scrambling for something to save her. Her hand went to his forearm. "We didn't have sex." She could feel the muscle tighten, and she gripped him harder, forcing him to acknowledge her. "*We didn't*. If I can't make you believe that—"

Without warning she was backed up against the counter, his thigh between her legs. His hands gripped her face, and his mouth—his tongue—stopped any other thoughts she had. Shock turned to desire. Like the inescapable pull of a magnet, Kate's body met his.

When he was finally able to draw away from her, he said, "I believe you. The subject is closed."

The only sound in the room was their ragged breathing. Kate wiped unsteady fingers across her lips, her eyes never leaving Mike's.

"The perfect place for that lamp is my bedroom," he said.

"Yes," she answered. "Let's try it there."

They both knew what they were talking about, and it had nothing to do with the lamp. It remained on the kitchen table, a forgotten prop.

The faint strains of Robert Cray drifted into the bedroom from his study, where he'd been working when she'd come to the door.

Kate stood in the center of the room, the late afternoon sunlight turning her hair to molten lava. She held out her hand.

"Dance with me."

Meshing his fingers with hers, he drew her close. "I didn't come up here to dance."

Her arm came up to surround his neck. "Just for a minute," she whispered.

The music was unadorned in its sensuality. The loneliness of the lyrics wasn't lost on them, and they gravitated closer. Thigh to thigh, pelvis to pelvis, they slowly moved. Time came to a standstill as they became lost in the mournful sounds. As naturally as breathing, his lips found hers. They unwittingly teased each other—holding back. Holding back. Their mouths touched, fluttered away, touched again, nibbled, until the tip of her tongue touched his. It was what he imagined liquid fire must feel like. Suddenly they were standing still, his hand grasping the back of her neck. She tasted of the coffee she'd had earlier, hot and sweet, and he drank deeply.

The sounds in the room telescoped down to a melancholy saxophone and their hard breathing. Her fingers traveled up the muscles of his back until they found his neck, where they began a mindless caress. Finding the music's measure again, she swayed against him and felt him—solid. She moaned when his hands moved down to pull her into him. The male scent of him overwhelmed her. How had she stood it this long?

They both sensed a new plateau and stepped away from each other, dazed.

Her eyes, dark with desire, held his as she bent to remove her boots. Her hands disappeared behind her, and then her skirt slid to the floor with a swishing sound. The black tights she wore inched down over her hips, revealing smooth thighs that looked so creamy he dropped to his knees to taste them. His work-roughened hands moved up the back of her legs and she shuddered, rocking forward.

He was lost in the reality of her. The dreams and fantasies were nothing compared to this. He wanted it all and here she was in front of him. And he didn't want to wait anymore. He buried his face in her stomach, and his tongue found her navel and rimmed it slowly. She gasped and clutched at his hair. Pulling away from her, he undid her blouse.

Mike stood and pushed the silky green fabric off her shoulders. His hand cupped her breast as he bent to place a deep kiss in the hollow of her neck. She had to hold on to him. Her knees had gone weak.

"Katie, darlin'," he whispered. "I can't believe you're really here."

She took his hand and guided it to her belly. "Feel," she said. His fingers slipped beneath the waistband of her panties and into the wet of her. She groaned. "I'm here and I want you."

"I've dreamed about this."

"Was I any good? In those dreams?"

He let his breath out. Without a word he laid her on the bed.

Kate watched as he undressed and realized she was trembling. As he slowly pulled off her panties, and she lay naked next to him, she said, "It's been a long time for me, Mike."

"I know." And as he said the words, he was suddenly flooded with apprehension at what he thought would be the inevitable comparison to Paul.

Kate saw the look of doubt flicker through his eyes, and her heart went out to him. She could tell him over and over again that Paul didn't matter anymore, but would he believe it?

"I don't want to wait anymore," she said.

Unable to restrain himself any longer, he pulled her on top of him. Her cool, bare skin on his own—already feverish—sent a chill through him. When she brought her lips to his, her nipples grazed his chest. Like two small bullets, they seared him, and he shut his eyes.

Her thighs had closed around him and he could feel her, slick, as she pushed against his erection. Her hips rolled to the music. Her mouth was relentless as she devoured his lips, his tongue, his neck. He was murmuring her name over and over again in counterpoint to her small moaning sounds. He was lost and never wanted to find his way back. He had never felt like this before.

When his fingers skimmed the inner cleft of her buttocks, she gave a little cry and tucked herself in closer to him. His need for her ferocious now, he swiftly rolled over, taking her with him. Her legs opened to him and she whispered, "Please, Mike, please . . ."

Her throaty voice saying his name brought him to the edge, and he plunged into her without another thought.

Mike waited in the bathroom while she dressed. He had already pulled on his jeans, and now sat on the toilet, head in hands.

They'd lain there in devastating silence when it was over. God, it had been awkward. She had done a good job of faking her orgasm. A lot of practice had gone into that performance, but he hadn't been fooled. And he'd come fast and hard after that.

Her desire had been genuine. Of that he was sure. It had been a tangible thing he'd reached out and taken hold of and run with. And he'd held back, letting her dictate the terms. When she'd cried out, shuddered, and gripped the back of his neck he had been too far gone. He couldn't stop and question her at that time any more than he could stop the sun from rising.

But even his climax hadn't felt right. It had been nothing more than a quick release. He might as well have been jerking off.

Mike knew what the problem was, and he walked back into the bedroom. Kate looked up from pulling on her boots, and then quickly looked away.

"Wasn't quite what we expected, was it," Mike said.

"Not quite." She stood and adjusted her skirt. "I—I don't know what happened."

"I can't speak for you, but there's still too much of Matt between us."

"What does *that* mean?"

"It means this isn't about you and me and Matt. It's about just me and Matt. And I need to deal with that."

She nodded, then said, "So what does *that* mean?"

He ran a hand through his hair and sighed. "It means I need to be here for Sheryl. For Christmas. And I need to hash this out with Matt. And you and I need to take a break from each other until I can come to terms with everything."

"You're scaring me, Mike. It'll get better."

The corner of his mouth lifted, and he reached out to cup her face. "I know that, darlin'. But I think you need a little time, too."

"How long?"

"I don't know. Let me get through Christmas."

Kate took the hand that caressed her cheek in her own. The tip of her tongue followed the lifeline, sending a wave of heat through Mike's groin.

"I have such a great gift for you," she said.

Kate let the warm bathwater soothe her. She hadn't wanted to wash off Mike's scent, but she was keyed up and confused. Yes, she'd wanted him. Wanted him even now. No, she didn't know what had caused her to shut down. Mike was everything she'd hoped for.

The differences between Mike and Paul were striking. How could two men so dissimilar—physically and spiritually—have been such good friends? Despite what she knew now, of Mike's feelings for her and of Paul's lack thereof, she knew there had been genuine affection between the two. In youth they'd been inseparable. And in the advance of adulthood, which tended to drive people apart with different careers and interests and friends, they'd managed to keep their friendship alive. She'd always remember the look on Paul's face when he knew he'd be seeing Mike: boyish, mischievous, playful. The two of them could come up with the most hideous practical jokes, the most disgusting foods, the most torturous puns, and the best stories she'd ever heard.

She could remember Paul's anticipation when he knew that not only was Mike coming for a visit, but that he was bringing his latest girlfriend. He'd delighted in giving Mike a complete appraisal that always ended with, "But she's no Kate, huh, bud?"

This sudden memory startled Kate. She'd always taken the words as a compliment from her husband, but now saw them for what they were. A dig at Mike. So, Paul had known all along how Mike felt about her.

Pain stabbed at her at this small revelation. Pain for her. Pain for Mike. Funny how we remember what we want.

And now, in the quiet of her bathroom with only the occasional drip of the faucet to punctuate her thoughts, Kate realized it wasn't hard to figure out when she'd stopped responding to Paul. The knowledge of what she assumed was his first affair, and the later unraveling of all the lies he'd woven together, brought about a slow loss of trust. Her inability to conceive, his reaction to that, proved the center couldn't hold. She'd wanted the old Paul back, and the harder she'd tried, the worse it had gotten. They began making love—if that's what it could be called—in the dark. It had become anonymous, with Kate trying to recapture the old days, and Paul simply using her available body. Her own pleasure had gone by the wayside.

She remembered too many nights of Paul taking her with no preliminaries, his body then rolling off her, his falling asleep while she lay in the dark, hurt and scared. Sometimes she would cry. Most of the time she'd get up, go to the kitchen, and lose herself in a bottle of wine.

The worst part was they never talked about it. Their friends wouldn't have guessed they had no marriage; that they were playing their roles to perfection. Only Mike had known some of the truth. He had always been there for her, but she chose not to burden him with it. They were all friends. The rift it would have caused between them would have been too traumatic. Besides, it'd been too shameful—too embarrassing—to even bring up.

Kate brought the washcloth to her face and cried for the death of her marriage, for the loss of all those years that should have been sweet. And then she cried out of fear. Afraid she'd never be able to respond to Mike's love the way she wanted.

CHAPTER

THIRTY-NINE

S he'd always read it in mystery novels, but never really believed it until just now. Something woke _____ her out of a deep sleep. Her eyes simply opened, as if she'd only just closed them moments before.

Kate lay very still on the couch and listened. Homer softly snored in his cedar bed. The TV screen emitted a blue glow, but no sound thanks to the mute button. As her eyes adjusted to the unnatural light, she could see nothing was unusual in the den.

Sleep started to overtake her again when she heard it: a faint clicking noise. Kate frowned and sat up. She tried to place the familiar sound, but it had stopped. She sat motionless, waiting. And just as she thought she'd imagined it, there it was once more.

Kate was off the couch and at the door in a second. She peered into the hallway. A faint light from the kitchen made her heart pound, and she grabbed the first weapon she came across. Hugging the wall and the heavy crystal vase, she made her way down the hall, and when the clicking began again, she realized it was the electric starter on her gas stove.

Kate's mouth fell open in disbelief when she reached the kitchen doorway.

"What the hell do you think you're doing?"

The spoon Matt had been stirring a cup of cocoa with flew across the room and landed in the sink with a tinny clatter as he spun around.

Kate advanced into the kitchen, slammed the crystal vase onto the table, and shouted, "You scared the shit out of me!" At that point Homer started barking, and she turned on the hapless dog and screamed, "Shut up! Where were you when I needed you, you stupid animal?"

"Kate, I'm sorry. I didn't mean to—What are you doing?"

"Calling the police," she replied as she began dialing.

Matt was in front of her in three quick strides, and he yanked the receiver out of her hand. "Don't do it. Please."

"You break into my home, I call the cops."

"Kate, be reasonable. I need to talk to you." Her intractable face told him he'd better make it good. "Look, would I do this if it wasn't really important?"

"Matt, you're driving me crazy," Kate said, and she sank into a chair. "What do you want from me?"

"I want you to answer a question for me."

"One question?"

"Yeah. And if the answer doesn't convince you to listen to everything else I need to say, then I'll leave."

"Fine." Kate crossed her arms over her chest and waited.

Matt sat across from her, and said, "Remember those baby pictures I showed you?" She sighed and nodded. "Remember what you said when I asked who would've sent them to Paul?"

"Yes, Matt," she replied wearily. "I said Mike sent them."

"Because?"

"Because . . . Paul was Mike's best friend. He'd want him to see photos of you."

"That's what my mom said when I asked her."

An odd sense of relief flooded through Kate, and she angrily asked, "Then why are you bothering me with this?"

"There's something I still don't get," Matt said, afraid to ask the question. Knowing he had to. "Who told you the photos are of Paul?"

"He did." And as Kate said the words, she paled.

"He lied to you," Matt said quietly. "And my mom lied to me, Kate. What does that mean?"

Hundreds of thoughts crowded into her head, all vying for attention. And then Matt voiced one of them.

"What if Paul's my father, Kate."

"No . . ." She quickly stood and turned away from him. But he was in front of her, and took her arm, forcing her to look at him. His eyes were bright with unshed tears. "Could I be Paul Armstrong's son?"

"NO!" She put her hands over her ears, trying to shut out his voice, but all that did was let the words echo through her brain. And then someone mercifully pulled the shades down, and her vision went from gray to black.

Kate had to beg Matt to leave. He'd wanted to stay with her. He'd wanted to talk. She wanted someone to tell her it was all a bad dream. She wanted to scream at Paul until the pain she felt in her heart was transferred to some other, less vulnerable, organ. She needed Mike to hold her and tell her she'd live through this. And, oh Christ, she needed a drink.

When she finally convinced Matt to go, Kate was crying. She felt as if she'd never be able to stop. The hours before dawn went by, and still Kate sat on the couch, tears stopping and starting like a drip system on a timer. She fell asleep and when she woke it was just becoming light outside. And when she remembered what the night had brought, she began sobbing again.

Kate reached for the phone. Mike would know what to say. He'd know what to do. She wanted him to talk to her and hold her in his arms. She needed to hear him call her "Katie, darlin' " in his leprechaun voice. And then she remembered Mike's words.

It's about me and Matt . . . I need to deal with that.

God, how would he deal with this? Me and Paul's son.

"Can't call him," she whispered.

By that afternoon Kate was past anger and well into denial. Dan Keller was Matt's father. Of course he was. Sheryl had married Dan—when was it?—in the fall of 1974. October. She always remembered because they'd been married on her birthday. And Matt had been born in April of the next year.

Dan had been there for Matt's birth. Sheryl never tired of telling the tale of being in labor for thirty-eight hours. How could Paul be his father? It was a crazy idea and she couldn't believe she'd let herself get caught up in it.

But what about the photos, Kate?

Well, there had to be a reasonable explanation. Maybe she was remembering it all wrong. Maybe Paul never told her they were of him. Possibly she was thinking of some other photos. She seemed to recall his mother sending some once. Those must be the ones she was thinking of. So Mike must've sent the photos of Matt to Paul. Just as she'd suspected all along. She'd have to ask him.

Paul and Sheryl? It was unthinkable. Sheryl was already engaged to Dan. And Kate to Paul. It wasn't only unthinkable. It was laughable. She and Sheryl hadn't exactly been close back then, but they were friends now. And Matt was getting too wrapped up in the Paul Armstrong mystique.

In the end, Kate chose to trust Paul one more time. And when Matt called and asked to meet with her again, she said yes. She'd set him straight.

With Matt sitting across from her at the kitchen table, Kate patiently explained why it was impossible for Paul to be his father.

"It's not impossible, Kate."

"Look, Matt. I know every kid goes through the 'maybe I'm adopted' phase, but you're wrong about this."

"What about my birthday?"

"What about it?"

"I was born eight months after my mom and dad were married."

"So you were a little early."

"I don't look anything like my dad."

Kate was nodding. "That doesn't mean anything. Look at your mother and Mike. They have completely different coloring. You happen to look like Sheryl."

The next words out of his mouth came hard. "I know you don't want to believe this, Kate. But I think it's very possible." And then he told her about the interview.

She listened with growing annoyance. When he finished, she said, "I'm going to tell you something that really isn't any of your business, but I want to clear this up once and for all. I was a virgin when I married Paul. Back then I asked Mike if Paul had ever been with anyone else. And he said, 'No, he's never slept with anyone.' Mike would never lie to me."

Matt couldn't believe how naïve a thirty-eight-year-old woman could be, and his voice expressed that as he said, "Those were his exact words? 'He's never slept with anyone'? Well, I hate to tell you this, Kate, but I've had sex with a lot of girls I never slept with."

Kate's tight-lipped response was, "No, you're wrong. If you don't believe me, then you need to talk to your mother."

"I'm planning on it. But I wanted to talk to you one more time. I thought you needed to know." He pushed a plastic bag he'd brought in with him across the table. "Look at this, then call me. I won't say anything to Mom until I hear from you."

Her hands began to shake and she placed them palm-down on the table to steady them. In a frightened voice, she said, "Don't you understand? I don't *want* to know."

"But I need to know, Kate."

"Why?" she whispered. "What difference could it possibly make now, after all these years?"

In a voice much older than his years, he said, "Because, as overrated as it seems to be around here, I think I deserve to know the truth." And then he left.

Kate sat looking at the bag, afraid of what it contained. It lay on the table where he'd left it—a small white time bomb waiting to detonate.

Minutes passed and then she carefully pulled it toward her and opened it. The label on the videotape confirmed what she'd already guessed. It was a baseball game, and for more reasons than one, she didn't want to watch it. Kate hadn't seen a game since Paul had died. Why should she start now?

She held the box in trembling hands until morbid curiosity forced her to her feet and into the den. She slipped the tape into the VCR and touched the play button, and sat down to watch.

Silent, unnoticed tears leaked from her eyes as she saw Matt playing ball in a style she'd always considered inimitable. Like father, like son. Isn't that what they always said? Was a batting average in the genes? Was a swing inherited? Did he play second base because he worshiped Paul, or was it in his DNA?

Kate hit the rewind button and watched the video for the third time, fast-forwarding only through the innings Matt wasn't up to bat. The game had been aired by one of Savannah's local stations and Dan Keller had taped it.

The proud father, she thought grimly, and then this act of stunning betrayal hit her with tornadic force. Was God really that capricious that Paul would be given a son after all she'd been through?

Sheryl's son. Sheryl and Paul's son. Paul's son!

"WHY?" she screamed, ripping the tape out of the machine and throwing it across the room. "Why did you do this to me?"

Was she talking to God or Paul? Did it matter anymore?

"What possible reason could you have for putting me through this?" she railed at the four walls. "This is too much! I can't handle this . . ." Sinking to her knees, she pounded her fists against the coffee table. "Oh, God! I can't take any more!"

Her sobs became deeper. Her breathing became ragged as she fought for control.

"It's—too—much . . ."

CHAPTER

FORTY

M att had walked out of Kate's house hoping she
would call him back. He couldn't wait much
_____ longer. The anger and hurt he felt had reached
critical mass and was about to explode out of him.

And then, just as he'd gotten to his car, he'd heard
Mike's voice calling. His uncle stood at the corner of his
house.

"Matt! I need to talk to you," he'd shouted.

But Matt hadn't responded. Instead, he'd panicked.
He was in the MG and driving away as Mike ran to the
sidewalk. When he'd looked in the rearview mirror his
uncle was in the middle of the street, staring at Matt's
retreat.

Matt held open the refrigerator door and searched for the
makings of a sandwich. His mother was with a late
appointment which meant dinner wouldn't be for
another hour at least. Anticipating Kate's call made him
nervous and antsy. He'd stayed close to the house the
rest of the afternoon. He'd wanted to be able to pick up
the phone. Didn't want the answering machine taking
any messages from Kate.

He needn't have worried.

The first inkling he had of something wrong was the sound of the front door opening, but not closing. Before he could put the jar of mayonnaise down on the counter, he heard something that made his blood freeze.

Sheryl had just oiled up her hands and was passing them along Judy Stewart's shoulders when Kate burst through the door. Her hair fell wildly around her tear-streaked face. Reddened eyes glowing with venom rooted Sheryl to the floor. Sheryl's first thought was, *She's drunk. Over the edge.*

But then Kate's hoarse voice pierced her. "I thought you were my friend. How could you do this to me?"

Sheryl moved quickly, walking around the table. She tried to take Kate's arm—to lead her out of the room—but Kate wrenched her arm away and screamed, "I know about Matt! I know about you and Paul!"

The day Sheryl had dreaded—the day she prayed would never come—had arrived and she steeled herself. Voice low, as if soothing a hurt child, she said, "Kate? Come on with me. We can talk somewhere else."

Kate seemed to notice the woman lying on the massage table for the first time, and Sheryl took the opportunity to look over her shoulder at her shocked client. "Judy, I'm sorry. I have an emergency here. We'll have to reschedule." Then she turned back to Kate. "Please, Kate. Let's go. Let me get you something."

Kate looked her square in the eyes and said, "I don't want anything from you again."

Sheryl could feel the pain radiating from Kate, and she drew her friend to her in a tight hug, whispering, "I'm sorry, I'm sorry . . . Please let me talk to you."

But Kate pulled away from her. "No! I'm through being shit on. Stupid, naïve Kate is *through*." She pushed past Matt, who had come to the doorway.

Sheryl flinched at the slamming of the front door. She looked up into her son's somber eyes and her heart contracted. "You know," she quietly stated.

"Yeah. What I don't know is why I had to wait so long to find out."

She reached up and tentatively touched Matt's cheek. "Then we have a lot to talk about."

Matt stonily listened to his mother. Time seemed to stand still. In the end, after everything she'd told him, he only seemed to remember one thing, and he said, "He didn't want me. He was my father and he didn't give a shit about me."

His mother put her arms around him. "Oh, honey, don't you understand? Dan is your father. He raised you and took care of you. He loves you."

Matt pulled away from her. "Paul Armstrong was my father. He knew he was my father and he didn't care!" His voice grew thick with emotion and irony. "My idol was my father and he never did anything for me except send me six lousy letters. And you all lied to me."

Sheryl's composure deserted her when she saw her son's tears. "Sweetie, we just did the best we knew how. Think how much Dan loves you. He knew you were Paul's, but he couldn't have cared for you any more if you'd been his own."

Matt's voice rose, and he sobbed, "But Paul didn't care about me!"

"He *did* care, Matt. But so many people would've been hurt if the truth came out. We thought we were doing the right thing. We were all very young. And very stupid. Paul didn't love me and I didn't love him." She reached for his hand and held it to her cheek. "But I wanted you and loved you from the second I knew you were growing inside me. Everyone did. Dan and Mike and even Paul, after he knew. But there were too many things to consider. Paul loved Kate. His career was taking off. I was in love with Dan. It just seemed like the right thing to do, Matt." Sheryl took his other hand and looked up at her tall, handsome son. "I'm going to let you go in a minute, but I want you to think about everything I've told you. People make mistakes when they're scared. Try to remember that. And remember how much you're loved. Your dad and I. Your grandparents. Mike. We all love you so much."

"Mike doesn't know?"

"He'll know soon enough. And it won't make any difference to him." Sheryl released his hands and stepped back. "I love you with all my heart, Matt. That's all you need to remember. Now go. I know you want to be alone."

Matt started for the door, then stopped and turned. He saw the tears on his mother's cheeks—the look of pain and fear on her face—and realized he'd never seen her cry before. The sight disconcerted him, and yet he said, "What do you think would have happened if you'd told the truth back then?"

Sheryl lifted her chin a little higher. "I think you would've spent your life trying to live up to being Paul Armstrong's son, and you wouldn't be half the man you are today."

It wasn't the answer he expected. In a voice that quavered only slightly, he said, "I love you, Mom."

The tenuous hold she had on her emotions drifted away like a piece of flotsam as soon as Matt left the room. Sheryl collapsed into a nearby chair and put her face in her hands. She wept with such force that her body shook.

Only three people had known the circumstances of Matt's birth, and one of those people was dead. She had held the secret for nineteen years. Now the world of three other people would fall apart because of it. She thought of Kate, and pulling her head up, wiped her wet cheeks. She'd never be able to make her understand. Kate had always been insufferably stubborn.

•   •   •

As parties go, this one is unexpectedly good. Sheryl has been enlisted to buy the beer and she fully understands why she has been invited in the first place. She's the only twenty-one-year-old around. But she doesn't let that bother her. A party is a party, and she is lonely without Dan.

He'd begun his job as a sales rep for a tire company that was headquartered in Vienna, Virginia, six months before. They'd both managed to save enough money so that when they were married next month, they could move to Vienna with the first and last month's rent on a small apartment and still live on his salary.

Sheryl has been waitressing since she graduated from high school—nearly three years now. All her tips have gone into a special savings account that has grown weekly to the sum of almost five thousand dollars. She plans to keep working after they're married and envisions the money as the down payment on a house someday.

Her father was laid off seven months earlier, and even though it looks as if he'll be rehired soon, there just isn't much money coming in. Because of the situation, Sheryl has insisted on a small wedding and has even paid for the wedding dress herself. She has brought up the subject of a civil ceremony, but her mother won't hear of it. Sheryl knows it'll be nothing like the wedding Kate's been planning. And she doesn't care.

Sheryl sits back a little deeper in the wing chair and downs her third rum and Coke, the rum unknowingly provided by Mr. and Mrs. Armstrong. Paul's parents are out of town for the weekend. They have given the okay for a party, but Sheryl's pretty sure they don't have a clue that their baby boy has sprung for a kegger.

The festivities to celebrate Paul's being drafted by the Giants started at eight o'clock. By eight-thirty approximately thirty teenagers had converged on the house on Frazier Street and the party is now in its third hour, louder than ever. The second keg has been tapped, the music has shifted gears from the Stones and Led Zeppelin to Eric Clapton and Pink Floyd. The air in the living room hangs heavy with cigarette smoke and if you're *looking for a cheap high, all you have to do is walk into the small bathroom downstairs and inhale deeply. Somebody's been growing their own.*

The only room in the house that's off-limits is the master bedroom. Every other available space is being put to good use, as couples press themselves into corners and improbable angles on pieces of furniture that were never meant for such activity. If Paul's mother knew what was going on in her dining room, she'd never eat there again.

Sheryl has danced with a couple of the guys that have come stag, but has had enough when the last one—Larry? Lonnie?—sticks his tongue in her ear. The only male worth looking at is Paul Armstrong, and not only does he know it, but he has Kate there as a reinforcement in case he somehow forgets. He may be only eighteen years old, but Sheryl doesn't remember any boy that remotely resembled him when she was that age.

She stares at her empty glass and decides it's time for another drink, and since it doesn't look as if anyone is going to offer to fix it for her, she stands unsteadily and makes her way to the kitchen. Sheryl passes Mike in the hallway. He's been cornered by Rosemary Donovan who seems to be whispering sweet nothings in his ear. The pained expression on his face tells the whole story, and Sheryl winks at him as she walks by.

She'll never understand why he tortures himself at these parties. The only girl he has eyes for is Kate, and her eyes are always glued to Paul. Sheryl secretly thinks Kate is either a fool or very naïve about Paul, but the one time she's voiced her opinion to Mike he's cut her off. She remembers ending that conversation with, "She doesn't know what she's missing, passing you up for him."

The kitchen is, unbelievably, empty and Sheryl opens the refrigerator and pulls out a can of Coke. The ice trays have recently been filled, so she bends to open the ice chest. She hears voices raised above the slide guitar Clapton is playing, and she stops to listen. Sheryl recognizes Paul and Kate arguing on the back porch. The window is open and it's hard to ignore them.

She seems to have come in on the tail end of their discussion, but Sheryl gets the gist of it when Kate says, "You're the one who wanted to wait to get married. And you knew that meant waiting to have sex."

"Shit, Kate, you can't expect me to wait another two years!"

"If I can wait, so can you."

Paul's answer is muffled by the starting riff of "Layla," but Kate's reply comes through loud and clear. "You're pretty disgusting when you're drunk. I'm going home."

"What are you gonna do? Walk?"

"If I have to."

"You're not gonna walk," Paul relents. "I'll ask Mike to drive you."

When she realizes they're coming into the kitchen, Sheryl quickly pours three fingers of rum into her glass, gives it a quick stir, and hurriedly leaves the room. From her vantage point on the staircase, Sheryl listens to the dating woes of Frank Trumbull with one ear, while she watches the minidrama unfolding in the hallway below.

A defiant Kate and a sullen Paul have approached Mike, who is still in the clutches of Rosemary Donovan. Paul says something to Mike and Kate turns away. Rosemary steps aside. Mike nods, says something in return, then steals a glance at Kate's intractable face. Shoving a hand in his jeans pocket, Mike comes up with his car keys, and together, he and Kate leave the house. Another notch on the torture rack, *Sheryl thinks.*

Frank is asking her something she doesn't quite hear. It sounds like, "Do you think I should mask the fairy?"

Sheryl turns to him and her head swims. "Huh?"

"Do you think I should ask Rosemary?"

Sheryl's words come out at half-speed. "Ask her what?" Then, not really caring "what," she slowly stands and grabs the newel post for support. "Excuse me, Frank. I need some air."

She is sitting on the glider on the front porch, but the swaying movement makes her dizzy and she moves to a wicker armchair around the corner. She sighs deeply and lets the darkness surround her. The sweet smell of pot drifts on the cool night air and she thinks that it's probably a good thing Paul's parents aren't coming home till Sunday night. It will take that long to deodorize the house.

"Want a hit?"

Paul's voice gives her a start and she turns in the chair. He is sitting on the porch railing, but she doesn't see him until he takes a drag from the joint and the ragged tip glows orange-red. He extends his arm.

Pulling the chair around, she takes it from him. "Thanks. Don't mind if I do . . ."

Inhaling deeply, she hands the joint back to him. They pass it back and forth a few more times, not speaking. The stuff is good and it's making her incredibly horny. She can only guess what it's doing to Paul's eighteen-year-old libido. When he stands up to pull a clip out of his pocket, her eyes have adjusted to the dim moonlight enough for her to admire the way his jeans fit his body. He catches her looking and slowly smiles. An understanding passes between them and Sheryl smiles back.

He has been her brother's friend forever and is a permanent fixture at their house. She recalls the night of her sixteenth birthday. Sheryl had caught Paul peeking in her bedroom window as she and four of her friends danced around the room to Creedence Clearwater Revival. The screams could be heard down the block as the girls raced to put on robes to cover their nighties. All the girls but Sheryl, that is. She had pulled up the window shade and confronted Paul's wide-eyed stare. Hands on hips, she'd said, "Take a picture. It lasts longer, you little weasel."

Now, too much liquor and a little dope loosens her tongue. "Don't need to look in windows anymore, do ya, Paul."

"Not for a long time." He moves closer to her and hands her the roach.

"When the hell did you grow up?" she says with grudging admiration.

Sitting back down on the porch rail, he brings one foot up against the wicker table in front of her and watches her finish the joint. "Where's Dan these days?"

"Working," she answers, trying to keep her eyes above his waist.

"Lonely?" he asks.

She leans back in the chair and it creaks softly. Looking him square in the eyes, she says, "I feel like a cat in heat."

He doesn't even have the decency to hesitate when he says, "Can I be of assistance?"

She can't believe she is actually considering this. "What about Kate?"

His calf brushes her knee and he grins. "What about Dan?"

He has a point.

Paul now leans over her and traces the scoop of her neckline with his fingers. His touch electrifies her nerve endings, and she knows she wants to see this through to the end. One final fling before she gets married. What could it hurt?

"Could be fun," he says. "Nobody needs to know."

"You're a very bad boy," she says, letting him run a finger along her collarbone.

"Actually," he chuckles. "I've been told I'm a very good boy."

That does it. "Where?"

"I'll meet you in my parents' bedroom in five minutes."

Sheryl looked up and saw the clock. She'd been sitting there for nearly an hour, which meant that Matt had been gone that long, too. *Jesus,* she thought. *Matt is the same age as Paul was when I told him he was going to be a father.*

Sheryl got to her feet and went to the phone. She didn't want Mike hearing this from his nephew. But there was no answer at her brother's house.

CHAPTER

FORTY-ONE

"Dan, it's me," Sheryl said.

"I already know. I just got off the phone with Matt."

Sheryl squeezed her eyes shut, fending off tears. "How did he sound?" she asked.

"Hurt," Dan answered curtly.

"What did you tell him?"

"The truth. Just like you told it to me nineteen years ago."

Sheryl looks at the doctor in disbelief. "How can I be pregnant? I've used my diaphragm every time!" And even as the words come out of her mouth, she remembers the one time she hadn't inserted the damned piece of rubber. Her eyes shift away from her doctor's face and she wonders if he can see the word "guilty" burning across her forehead.

"It happens. I know you've only been married a couple of months and this could be a hardship for the two of you. You have choices."

But there's never really been any choice for Sheryl. A baby is growing inside her now, and that is the only choice she has. She listens numbly as the nurse talks to her about prenatal care.

Sheryl takes the pamphlets and gazes at them blindly. The only thing she can think about is telling Dan.

That night in bed, after a very long evening with her parents, Sheryl lies on her back in the dark. She holds her hands together so tightly she can feel her fingernails biting into her palms.

"Dan?" she finally says. "Are you asleep?"

His weight shifts in the bed. "Almost. Why?"

"I need to tell you something."

"Tell me."

"I'm pregnant."

The springs of the mattress squeal as he sits up. "You're pregnant?" The light comes on and they blink at each other like owls. "How?"

Sheryl pushes herself up and takes his hand as she settles in front of him. "I'm afraid to tell you."

"Sherry, I promise I won't get mad. But we've been so careful . . ."

She holds his hand tighter, not speaking. Dan exhales slowly, guessing what she is trying to tell him.

Sheryl finally says, "Dan, I want to keep this baby. I'll understand if you want to leave."

"But I love you, Sherry. You told me it was only that one time . . ."

"It was. The only stupider thing I've ever done was forgetting to use my diaphragm. The whole thing meant nothing. I already told you that, and I meant it. And I love you for understanding. I know how hard it was for you."

"But now you're pregnant with Paul Armstrong's baby." For some blessed reason, she can tell he isn't angry. Just confused. "Does he know?"

"No! Of course not! Dan, I just found out today."

"Sherry? Do you really love me?"

"Sure I do, Danny."

"Will you let me be the baby's father?"

She looks at him and smiles for the first time that day.

Putting her arms around him, she says, "Of course you'll be his father. Who else?"

"What about Paul? Aren't you going to tell him?"

"No."

Dan is silent for a moment. "If it were me, I'd want to know."

"Thank God you're not."

"But don't you think he'd want to know?"

Frightened, she says, "But Danny. What if he wants the baby?"

Dan pulls away from her and she can tell he hasn't thought of that. There isn't a deceptive bone in his body, so Sheryl is surprised when he answers, "Don't tell him till after he's married."

He's right. Paul doesn't have the scruples of a toad, and he'll never be able to bring himself to tell Kate the truth. And so, that night, Sheryl and Dan enter into their own conspiracy.

Matt, born the following April, is beautiful—perfect. Eight pounds, eight ounces, of fair-haired sweetness. Grandparents, uncle, and parents are thrilled. A baby couldn't be more loved.

And when Kate and Paul are married, Matt is nearly two years old. Paul is entering his first season in the major leagues. Sheryl will never forget the way making this phone call makes her feel. Her heart pounds so hard she's afraid she'll pass out. Her palms are so wet, she can barely hold the telephone.

It's ten o'clock in the morning and he's still asleep. The phone has been answered by his roommate, who has to be convinced she is Paul's wife and it's an emergency. When a very fuzzy-voiced Paul comes on the line, Sheryl says the lines she's rehearsed for months.

"Paul. This is Sheryl. Mike's sister. I have something really important to tell you. You need to call me back from a private phone right now."

She's said it all in one breath, so her courage won't give out. He mumbles something about giving him fifteen minutes and what's her number? And she waits as fifteen minutes grow into twenty, and then thirty.

When her phone finally rings, she pounces on the receiver. "You said fifteen minutes!"

"Hey, I'm sorry. It took me a while to find a phone. What's up, Sheryl?"

She takes a deep breath. "Remember that party you had a few years ago? You were celebrating your new career."

Paul's swagger can be heard through the phone line. "You mean the one where I fucked my babysitter?"

"I knew I could count on you to be sensitive about it."

"What about it?"

"I got pregnant that night."

There is a pause and Sheryl wonders if he's even heard her. But then he says, "So what?"

"So, you know I have a son named Matt?"

"Yeah, I know."

"You aren't getting this, are you. Matt is your son. You're the father."

His voice drops to a whisper. "Shit, Sheryl! What are you talking about?"

"We didn't use anything that night. You fucked your babysitter unprotected."

His voice turns suspicious. "Why are you telling me now?"

"Because Dan thought you deserved to know. I didn't want to tell you. I was afraid you'd try to take him from me. I should've known better."

"Dan knows?"

"Yes, he knows. And he loves Matt like his own. And if you try anything to take Matt away from us, we'll fight you with everything we've got."

"Christ, Sheryl! You can't tell anyone else. You got that? If Kate found out . . ."

"Don't worry. Mike doesn't even know."

"Look, Sheryl. I want a son. But not now. It's not . . ." He searches for a word.

"Convenient?" Sheryl finishes for him. "I have no intention of ever telling Matt about you."

"Never?"

"No. Why should I?"

"So, you just called to tell me I have a son and that's it?"

"Yeah, I guess so."

"By the way, Paul, you have a son, how's the weather?"

"Yes. And now only you and Dan and I know. That's where I want it to end."

"Does he look like me?"

Sheryl hesitates, not wanting to give up any part of her son to this man who has nothing to do with loving him and raising him. "A little."

"Tell me." She doesn't answer, and he says, "Come on, Sheryl. I need to know."

"He has your eyes. But he's not going to be anything like you."

"I'd really like a photo of him."

"I'll think about it."

"Send it to me through the team."

"I said I'll think about it, Paul."

She hears a knocking sound, and he says, "I've gotta go."

"Before I hang up, I have something else I want to say. All your dreams have come true. You're playing ball with the Giants. You married Kate. You're gonna be a star. Please don't ever try to take Matt from me."

Paul lowers his voice to a whisper. "I just got married, Sheryl. You really think this is something I can tell Kate now?"

When she finally sends the photos, it isn't because Paul has asked for them. It's because Mike tells her that Paul and Kate can't have children.

Sheryl never hated Paul. Didn't even dislike him. Her feelings for him were neutral. After all, he had nothing to do with her life. But over the years she'd heard the stories that Mike felt he could tell about Kate and Paul. Kate, who'd gone into marriage with all the pomp and circumstance befitting royalty. Who was now married to the man dubbed the Prince Charming of baseball. Who was being treated like something less than a doormat since he'd discovered she couldn't bear him a son.

And Sheryl suddenly found herself thinking of Kate. She could feel Kate's pain across the miles. The only mistake Kate had made in her life was loving the wrong man. But no one knows that until it's too late. Sheryl's heart went out to Kate Armstrong, and the child she could never have, and the life she'd dreamed of that had turned into a nightmare.

Sheryl's position changed the day Mike told her the way Paul was pushing Kate away, castigating her for a fault that wasn't in her control. She found Paul Armstrong not worthy of an emotion as deep as hatred. Sheryl found his behavior offensive, and an offense deserved punishment. She wanted to hurt him because she knew Kate was defenseless.

The baby photos of Matt had gone out in the mail the day after she learned of Kate's condition. It took Paul nearly a year to respond, but when he did, he truly surprised her.

CHAPTER

FORTY-TWO

K ate sat on the chair and stared at the phone, a blanket wrapped around her shoulders. Her body _____ slowly rocked in rhythm with the banjo clock.

It was late. Why hadn't Mike called? Surely he knew by now. Surely Sheryl had told her own brother. And surely he would call once he found out.

But there was nothing truly sure in life. Why hadn't she learned that lesson long ago?

She had to talk to him. *Had* to. When he'd said they needed to spend some time apart, he hadn't factored in a seismic event of this magnitude. This involved them both. She needed his love now more than ever. They would need each other to get through this . . . to make sense of it.

The clock struck eleven and Kate made up her mind.

"I know you don't want to see me right now," she began, as Mike's back door opened. "But I have to talk to you."

"What's wrong?" He took her arm and pulled her through the doorway. She looked like hell and Mike was afraid that their sorry attempt at intimacy was to blame. Maybe it *had* been too soon.

"You haven't talked to Matt yet, have you." He shook

his head. "I didn't think so." She took his hand and led him to a chair. "You'd better sit down."

"Katie, your hand is frozen. Are you all right?"

She turned her back to him and leaned into the counter. "You know how they always say, if you don't like the weather wait fifteen minutes, it'll change? But they never tell you it can change from bad to worse." Shaking her head slightly, her voice resigned, she said, "They never tell you that."

Mike remained silent. He was aware that every muscle in his body was tensed, and he made a conscious effort to relax. But nothing could have prepared him for what Kate said next.

She sat down across from him. "In the past forty-eight hours an earthquake measuring about seven on the Richter scale hit, and they're still adding up the damage." Her eyes met his. "Mike, there's no other way to tell you this. And I wish to God I didn't have to be the one to tell you . . ."

"Jesus, Kate. What the hell happened?"

"Matt is Paul's son."

His first thought was, *She's drinking again, and this is the result. She's lost her mind.* And he almost said it out loud, but the steadiness of her hands and the new wisdom in her eyes stopped him.

She went on. She had obviously rehearsed everything she was saying. Her composure—her calm—this too was new. He never once interrupted her as she told it all from beginning to end. He listened, his disbelief ebbing away and replaced by a deep, burning fury for the heartbreak she had gone through thanks, once again, to Paul.

And then he thought of Sheryl, his own sister, whom he would have sworn he knew forward and backward, voluntarily taking part in this deceit. The rage at this new pain brought him up out of the chair. It tipped over backward, falling onto the floor with a loud clatter. Kate flinched, and quickly stood.

"He was supposed to be my friend," he said in a harsh voice. "He desecrated the word, and he contaminated everything I've ever loved. And my own sister let it happen."

Kate knew what he wanted to do next, and she put her hand on his arm to stop him. "Don't go over there feeling like this, Mike," she said. "It won't help."

Like a skittish horse calmed by his owner's touch, Mike went still. "How are you dealing with this, Kate?" he asked in a low, tight voice. "Why aren't you mad?"

"I was. I still am."

She told him of the two hellish days and nights she'd spent. Of the night she *did* open that bottle and take a drink. Of the anger she felt at even that being caused by Paul's betrayal, and the subsequent deep cut she'd received in her knee as she knelt to clean up the shards of broken glass after she'd thrown the bottle against the sink. That episode brought her a brief moment of clarity, and she realized she needed help. His help.

She'd fallen into an uneasy sleep only to wake an hour later, sweating and scared, from dreams that seemed too real to speak of. This went on and on, until she finally fought off sleep and had now been awake for over thirty-six hours.

But Kate couldn't tell him of the phone's continuous ringing. Either Sheryl or Matt. She hadn't wanted to know. Hadn't wanted to hear Sheryl's excuses.

No more blaming herself. Paul's duplicity was the reason they all found themselves in this incredible morass, and Kate's days of protecting his image were over. The doorbell had rung at one point and she could see Matt's car outside, but she couldn't make a move to answer it, so she'd hidden away in the den, away from his anguish.

She'd had too much time to think. And she began wondering what Matt was going through. Then she'd think of Sheryl, and her anger would reach new heights, only to be topped by her anger at Paul. He'd fouled off enough balls, but Kate knew this had been the final strike. He was irrevocably, inevitably, out.

But most of all she thought about Mike. What they had was so fragile. What would this do to them? But she'd gaze at his house and think, *No, Kate. Hold on. It's Mike you're talking about—the one person in the world you can trust to still love you.* So she'd waited and waited. Hoping that Sheryl had the decency to tell Mike. But apparently she hadn't, and it became physically impossible for Kate to wait any longer.

She looked up at Mike now and continued. "I'll never understand the things Paul did. Why he hurt me over and over again. Why I let him."

Kate moved closer to Mike and he put his arms around her. She was rigid. Trying so hard to pretend this was something she could deal with by simply saying she'd dealt with it.

"Katie. Darlin'," he whispered into her hair.

And she broke. Her body shook with sobs. "I'm so furious with them, Mike. What am I going to do? She's your sister . . . How can you and I have a life?"

"We will. We'll get through it and everything else will fall into place."

She raised her wet face to look at him. Her hand came up to caress his cheek. "I love you so much." He kissed her palm as she said, "I want to start living again. And I want you."

He pulled her head to his chest and she couldn't see the unexpected tears fill his eyes. He closed them, but couldn't trust his voice.

The house was so quiet that for a few minutes it felt like they were the only two living beings in the world.

"Please let me stay here tonight," she said.

His breath clouded the glass pane as he turned to gaze out the window at the thin blanket of snow. It must have started and stopped suddenly, while he and Kate had made love. Now, the clouds had formed thin wisps across the face of the waning full moon. The wind gusted around the eaves of the house and he shivered slightly, pulling the woven cotton blanket across his bare legs.

Too many people crowded into Mike's head. A secretive Sheryl, who had fucked his best friend for some unfathomable reason. A manipulative Paul who always got what he wanted when he wanted it. A devastated Kate who had somehow managed to live through it all, and had retained enough of herself that she could fall in love again. And then there was Matt. Mike couldn't even begin to imagine what his nephew was feeling. Hurt? Anger? Disgust? What could he say to Matt now, except he still loved him?

Kate moved on the bed and he shifted his body on the window seat so he could watch her as she slept. The icy light from the moon fell across her back, raising the scar into relief. She'd tried to hide it from him. He'd told her he knew it was there. That Paul had told him. She'd said it was supposed to be a secret. And Mike had said Paul wasn't very good at keeping secrets. They'd both smiled ruefully at that, both thinking there was one he did manage to keep to himself.

Mike thought of getting up—of running his fingers down her spine, of tracing his tongue back up the seam the doctors had left that was paler than her own pale skin. But he didn't want to disturb her. Looking at her was enough for now.

The clock on the mantel downstairs chimed twice. She had fallen asleep soon after they'd finished, and now she lay sprawled across the bed, an arm tucked under the pillow, one knee bent. Hair a wild, auburn aura swirling around her head, she looked like every man's fantasy. A Vargas girl right here in his own bedroom. But the scar made her real—a slightly skewed vision of a pinup.

He had voiced her name with each thrust until he was
spent. Mike had called out her name, and realized that
was what had been missing all these years, and women,
past. His dreams of making love to Kate, while he lay
with Allison or Eleanor or the woman of the moment,
had been what held him back from giving them all of
himself. His mind would give him a sharply etched picture of Kate that erased anything else. And he could
never bring himself to let go completely, because what
he wanted—needed—more than anything in the world,
was to intone Kate's name.

The absolute release he felt at the moment he climaxed
with Kate had brought tears to his eyes. This time it had
been all he'd hoped. He was in awe of the power she had
over him, but he wasn't threatened by it. On the contrary.
It made him feel stronger. And he wanted to show her
that. Show her that she didn't have to pretend any longer.
He suddenly didn't care what kind of relationship she
and Paul had had in the bedroom. It didn't matter anymore. The only thing that mattered now was how Kate
responded to him.

A muffled sound reached his ears and he peered at her.
She was talking in her sleep. Nothing intelligible, but he
could tell she was struggling with something. She raised
her head for a moment.

"What is it, Katie?" he whispered.

But she didn't answer, and he realized she was still
asleep.

A blast of wind hit the window he'd leaned his face
against. It found its way through the glazing, sending a
chill through him. Kate pulled her legs up and hugged
the pillow a little closer.

Mike pushed the coverlet aside and quietly made his
way to the fireplace. The blue flannel shirt he'd been
wearing earlier lay on the floor and he stopped to pick it
up and slip it on. The logs were already placed on the
grate and newspaper crumpled underneath them. The

first match he struck hissed and went out. The second caught and he hunkered down and touched it to the paper. It burned brightly for a moment. He could hear the small sticks of fatwood begin to sizzle, then flare up.

Mike sat cross-legged and held his hands out to the fire. The crackling and hissing soothed him, and he stared into the flames, forgetting everything else except what had gone on between the two of them. A log shifted and he reached for the poker.

An unfamiliar bed, coupled with a nightmare and a thudding noise, brought Kate awake. A warm light suffused the room and her eyes sought its source. She focused on Mike's shoulders. Backlit by the fire, a soft glow outlined his body. She could see he'd put his shirt back on, but he wore nothing else. A chill went through her, whether from the cold or the memory of his body on hers, she couldn't tell.

Kate watched this man—her friend—sitting a few feet away, and thought of all the years that had slipped by. Would it have worked all those years ago? If she hadn't been so dazzled by Paul? So taken in? She mentally shook her head to rid herself of the past. It was gone and it didn't make any difference anymore. She sat up and reached for the quilt.

The rustle of the bedclothes caught his attention, and he turned. When he saw she was awake, he slowly smiled. "Hello, darlin'. You okay?"

"I'm a little cold," she replied cautiously.

"Fire's warm." She didn't move. "Want to bring the quilt and join me?" She gave a little nod. He watched, amused, as she pulled the cover around her tightly and carefully planted her feet on the floor. The quilt slipped slightly and she gave it a quick tug to secure it around her shoulders. "Don't you think it's a little late for modesty?" he asked as she made her way to the hearth.

Lowering herself to the carpet, she replied, "This feels—I don't know—funny, Mike."

"Well, why don't you sit on the quilt?"

"You know what I mean."

He set down the poker. "I know what *you* mean. But it feels very right to me."

Kate looked into the flames. "You've thought about this—us—for a long time. I haven't had that luxury."

"Katie, look at me."

She turned her head, careful to keep her eyes on his face. To see the rest of him would summon up the things they'd said and done earlier. His sweet eyes waited for hers, and her breathing turned shallow.

"I'm not new at this. But I need to tell you that making love to you was the best it's ever been for me," he said.

"Yes. It was nice."

Nice? Mike inwardly cringed.

She realized how that sounded, and amended it with, "Very nice."

Very nice? Mike tried to keep the disappointment off his face.

God, it still sounded bad, and she grew frustrated. "Damn it, Mike. What do you want me to say?"

"Nothing." He held up his hand. "Don't say anything else, please. My head is already too swollen from all the compliments." They were both quiet for a moment, and then he said, "I hope this doesn't mean you won't try again."

She had been studying the pattern of the quilt, and her head came up sharply. "You knew?"

His smile was melancholy. "Of course I knew. I'm a nineties kind of guy."

She could feel her face flushing, but couldn't come up with any explanation for him.

He hadn't meant to disconcert her. He felt behind him until his fingers circled the leg of the armchair, and he pulled it closer. Mike's hand closed over her shoulder and he gave a gentle tug. "Come here, Katie." He could feel her resistance, but he persisted. He leaned against the chair, taking her with him, opening his legs to make room for her. Mike wrapped his arms around her as her back sank against his chest. "I just want to hold you."

He wanted to hold her—yes. But he also wanted to touch her, caress her, lick her. He wanted to see her come. He wanted to hear her shout his name. This last thought came to him with such force that he had to suppress a groan, and he felt his cock begin to stiffen.

Placing his chin on top of her head, he closed his eyes and tried to breathe normally, but all that did was pull her scent into his nostrils till it reached the doorway in his brain marked *Sexual Fantasies: Kate Moran Armstrong, M.D.*, and the doorway swung fully open.

Kate too felt an unaccustomed sense of desire the moment his arms enveloped her. He smelled of aftershave, woodsmoke, and sex, and she held her breath, knowing that if they made love, it would just end up the same way, and he'd be hurt again.

"I lied, Kate." He lifted his chin, and then her hair. His mouth pressed against the nape of her neck. She felt his breath—hot—as he whispered, "I want to see you by firelight."

"Mike, it's not going to happen for me." Her voice was kind and matter-of-fact. "It hasn't for a long time."

"Shush, Katie." He was nibbling her earlobe. "Why don't we see?"

But the thought of going through it again—the humiliation of hoping, and then having her body betray her—was too much. "Please stop, Mike." She could feel the soft exhalation of his warm breath on her cheek. His arms tightened around her before letting her go, and she began to move away when he stopped her.

Gently taking Kate's chin, he turned her to face him. "You've been hurt, and I wish to God I could take away the past. But I can't. All I can do is try to make you believe that I'll never intentionally do anything to cause you pain." Her eyes filled with tears, and she closed them. "I'm counting on you to tell me when the time is right, Kate. You'll do that, won't you."

She nodded, and he brought his lips to hers to seal the bargain.

CHAPTER

FORTY-THREE

There. The front door opened and closed. Matt was home. Sheryl waited in the kitchen, but his footsteps faded up the stairs. As tired as she was, she decided it was better to get it all out in the open now. There was no sense in waiting anymore.

Pushing herself out of the chair, she went into her office. The middle drawer of her desk held the usual supplies needed to run a small business, but underneath the ledgers and business cards was a small, flat box. Sheryl pulled it out and opened it. The contents hadn't changed in nearly sixteen years. The only thing it held was an envelope. Written on the outside were the words "Safe-Deposit Key." The bank and key had changed only once, when she'd moved back to Staunton.

Sheryl drove to the bank. Signing for her box was strictly a formality. She had gone to school with the bank manager. In the tomblike quiet of the vault, Sheryl pulled out the medium-sized metal box. Under the deed to her house, her insurance policy, and Matt's birth certificate was the envelope she'd come for.

She never thought this was something she'd have to do. Mike had the other key. He was executor of her will. Had she expected him to live forever? To take care of this task when he didn't even know the truth? Sheryl stood still, the envelope in her hand, trying to imagine what Mike's reaction would have been to the melodramatic words she'd written on the outside: "For Michael Fitzgerald's Eyes Only."

Well, it wouldn't happen now. The son she'd tried to protect would be the first to see what the envelope held. She hoped he'd be able to handle it.

Closing the hinged lid, Sheryl returned the box to its slot and left the bank.

Matt had heard his mother leave the house. He had stood at his bedroom window watching her drive away, and he stood there still when she returned half an hour later. Walking to his door, he opened it and waited for his mother as she climbed the steps.

"There's more," she said, holding out the white envelope.

He took it from her, but his eyes never left hers. "What is it?"

Sheryl shook her head slightly. "Just read it."

"Mom?" His voice betrayed his fear. "Can I have a hug?"

"Oh, honey!" Sheryl stepped into her son's embrace and wrapped her arms around his waist. Her head barely reached his chin, but she held him as if he were eight years old again, swaying to and fro, loving the feel of his need for her. "I'm so proud you're my son," she said softly.

Pride wasn't something he was feeling right now, as he reviewed his performance with Kate, and his confrontation with Mike. He never wanted to feel like this again. He made a vow to himself to never again do anything that would erase the pride his mother felt for him. He couldn't bring himself to tell her the truth. Not now. It would be more than she could take after all that had come down this day. The concept of hiding the truth to prevent pain was suddenly made crystal clear to him, and Matt grew up a little more just then.

His mother was downstairs in the kitchen. He could hear her pulling pots out of the cupboard, getting ready for dinner. He sat at his desk, staring at the unopened envelope in front of him. What new hurt was this going to inflict, that it had been meant for his uncle only?

Matt put his fingers on it, as if he could get some sense of what it would tell him. Finally, he opened his pocket knife, slit the envelope, and read the letter written in Paul Armstrong's familiar, spiky handwriting.

April 21, 1981

Sheryl,

I'm not good at this kind of thing. I can't remember the last time I wrote a letter.

I got the photos you sent of Matt and I wanted to thank you for that. He's a good-looking kid. You didn't tell me anything about him, but Mike talks about him once in a while, so I hear about him that way. Sounds like he's pretty bright. And Mike says he's got a pretty good arm for a six-year-old. If he's got some kind of talent for the game, I hope you won't hold him back from it just because he's my son.

Those last two words are pretty special to me. I guess Mike probably told you that Kate can't have kids. I'm sure you think that's some kind of judgment on me. I noticed you didn't send me any photos of Matt until after we'd gotten the bad news. If you did it to make me feel like shit, it worked. I shouldn't be telling you this, it just gives you more ammunition against me, but after my career got going I wanted a son more than anything in the world.

I want to be part of Matt's life, but I know you won't let me, so I want to make a deal with you. The only thing I can do now is help out financially. The five hundred is for Matt—however you want to spend it. I'll send it every month, always cash. Please don't send it back. I want him to have what he needs. It's not charity. The only thing I

want in return is a photo once a year and a letter from you
telling me how he's doing . . . in school, with sports, what he
likes to do. Whatever you want to tell me. He's got my blood
in him, Sheryl, and I really need this. No one else will ever
know. Send them to PO Box 143, Charlottesville, 22901,
anytime between October and February. I have a safe-
deposit box there and that's where everything will stay. My
lawyer has the other key with instructions.

I'm really hoping you'll do this for me, and I'm really
hoping I get to meet him someday, just so I can see him in
the flesh. I promise I'll never say a word. I'm sorry things
happened the way they did. Write me c/o the team to
confirm. Even if I don't hear from you, I'm still going to
assume it's okay to send the money.

                                                            Paul

Matt held the letter with one hand, the open passbook
in the other, and he gazed at both in disbelief. A little
over 65,000 dollars sat in an account in his name. A final
deposit of four hundred dollars had been made March 6,
1994, just a few days before Paul had died.

Everything had grown very quiet. The blood rushed in
his ears. It was the only sound he heard for some time.
Then his face scrunched up like a little child's and he
began to cry.

Sheryl had been calling him down for dinner. When he
didn't answer, she ran upstairs and pushed open his bedroom door to find him there, sobbing, his face hidden in
the crook of his arm. He still held Paul's letter and the
passbook.

"Matt? Sweetheart?" Her fingers touched his hair, the
back of his neck. He turned and buried his face in her
stomach. "Do you understand a little better now? He did
care. This was the best he could do." Matt shook his
head back and forth, but she went on. "I always kept out
a hundred dollars. Remember the time you wanted that

new glove and shoes, and I told you I'd help pay for half if you saved the rest? And you mowed lawns and did yardwork for two weeks? It was really Paul who paid the half. It was always Paul's money that got you those extra things you wanted. That hundred helped pay for your clothes, and books for school, and camp.

"The rest of the money went into that savings account. It was going to be for college, but you got that scholarship. It's yours now. You'll be making good money in a few years, if things go the way you hope, but you'll always have it to fall back on."

Pulling away from her, he said, "I don't want it! It's guilt money."

Sheryl looked at him in dismay. "But he really wanted you to have it, Matt. He didn't have to send anything."

Flinging the little book across the room, he shouted, "Fuck him! I can live my life without it. He's nothing like I thought he was! He's fucking nothing!" Matt stood and strode across the room to the framed baseball card. He ripped it off the wall and threw it on the floor.

Sheryl flinched as the glass shattered, but she raised her voice above his. "Matt, he was human. He wasn't perfect. No one is!"

"How come you're on his side all of a sudden?"

"I'm not. Believe me, I'm not! But I know those photos of you and the letters I sent meant the world to him. You were the good part of him, no matter what else he did."

Matt whirled around to face her. "He treated Kate like shit, *didn't he*?" When she didn't answer, he yelled, "*Didn't he?*"

She couldn't meet his eyes.

"I knew it! He had Kate, but I bet she wasn't enough for him." Fists clenched at his sides, he said, "I don't want to be like him. Tell me I'm not like him!"

"You're not, Matt."

But he was so afraid that he was. In a tight voice, he said, "I don't want the money. I want you to have it. You're the one who deserves it."

"God, I wish Mike were here. Maybe he could help you more than I can."

Matt thought about what he might have done to Mike and Kate and their love for each other. He thought of Christmas without his uncle. And he suddenly blurted out, "I'm sorry. I'm sorry for everything!"

"What are you talking about, Matt? You haven't done anything wrong. None of this is your fault."

"I don't think Mike feels that way."

"It's not going to make any difference to Mike. He'll always love you. I already told you that."

"Yeah, we're gonna have a really merry Christmas this year, aren't we, Mom," he said sarcastically.

Sheryl checked the anger she suddenly felt. "Please come down and have dinner with me, Matt. We can talk some more."

"Sorry, Mom. I don't feel much like eating. And I don't want to talk about it anymore."

"All right, Matt. If you get hungry, there's chicken and dumplings." She started toward the door. "I was going to decorate the tree tonight. I'd like your company."

Two hours later, as Sheryl strung the garlands around the tree she and Matt had cut down two days earlier, he quietly entered the living room. Without a word, he took one end of the string of silver beads from his mother.

She looked up at him and a tentative smile played across her lips. "Make sure it's straight."

He smiled a little himself. "You say that every year, Mom."

RECONSTRUCTION

CHAPTER
FORTY-FOUR

They had finished trimming the tree to the sounds of Christmas carols and occasional _____ teasing, but Matt knew something was missing. It was his third Christmas since his mother and father had divorced and he still had a hard time with it. He tended to imagine his father alone in his town house in Savannah, putting up some pathetic artificial tree, no one to open presents with on Christmas Day. Actually, nothing was further from the truth, and Matt knew this, but the drama of it seemed to alleviate his own feelings of loneliness.

But not this year. This year there was no Mike to join in the good-natured baiting of his mother. This year he'd met Kate, and had wished for a holiday that might include her. This year there was the specter of Paul hanging over them all. And as Matt hung his favorite ornament, a blown glass baseball, he felt a sudden wave of hatred for Paul Armstrong so strong that he knew he had to get out. Had to think. Had to try to make some sense of it all.

He told his mother he was going out to meet a friend, and left the house before she could question him. The MG was balky in the subfreezing temperature, but it finally started with the choke pulled out fully, and it roared away into the night.

There was no friend to meet. Nowhere to go, really. He drove through the deserted streets of downtown Staunton. Streetlamps were trimmed in silver tinsel. Plastic golden bells hung from the traffic lights. The heads of the parking meters were covered with candy-cane striped bags, wishing the citizens a merry Christmas. The city's gift to its inhabitants was free parking for the holidays. Passing the lighted revolving sign on the bank, Matt was informed that the time was 10:33 and the temperature was 28 degrees.

He ended up on Kate's street. Matt slowly drove past her dark house, then around the block and coasted to a stop. He killed the engine at the far corner of her lot, on the street that intersected Frazier, and was just getting the courage up to get out of the car—to knock on her door and see if she'd talk to him—when a car's head-lights penetrated the darkness.

Matt sank down, and the car continued up the street. Matt had been holding his breath and now let it out in a rush. Time seemed to pass slowly—"erosion" was the word that came to mind. Twenty-five minutes had ticked by on the MG's clock while he battled with him-self. But he was cold, his feet felt numb, and Matt finally got out of the car.

His knock brought nothing but Homer to the door. The doorbell made the dog whimper. He was truly freezing now, yet unwilling to go home. As angry as he was at what Paul Armstrong had done to his memories, Matt still harbored a morbid fascination for him.

He let himself into Kate's house with the spare key. When the dog saw who it was, he wagged his tail so hard his entire body undulated with delight. "Hey, boy." Matt rubbed the dog's head, then went into the kitchen for the flashlight.

Homer followed him up the stairs and into the tower

room. With the flashlight pointed at the floor, Matt tried to decide what his next move should be. He was still searching for some clue as to why Paul had acted the way he did. Still looking for something to give him hope that Paul Armstrong had some good points.

He crossed in front of the window and the light in Mike's bedroom caught his eye. Matt was irresistibly drawn to the scene he beheld.

Mike and Kate as one. Like a scene from a movie, their love unfolded before him, and Matt found it hard to equate this man and woman, and their passion, with his uncle and Kate. Mike's head dipped down to take Kate's mouth in a lingering kiss, and the film Matt watched flickered into slow motion and then freeze-frame as they broke apart. Kate moved first. Matt watched as she disappeared. Mike followed, and Matt knew they had found the bed.

He turned away, feeling like an intruder. Feeling a pang of jealousy. Feeling very alone. He knew how this movie ended, and he was ashamed he'd watched this long.

They had somehow managed to forgive each other. Matt couldn't help wondering what Kate had told his uncle. If Mike had granted Kate a pardon, would he do the same for him?

Matt sank to the floor and felt Homer's damp nose nuzzle his hand. He pushed the dog away, also trying to push away the image of what Mike and Kate were doing, but it wouldn't leave him. And then a superimposed picture materialized in his mind and he saw his mother and Paul Armstrong together. A painful sob erupted from deep inside him and he wished out loud that he'd never learned the truth. Everything in his life was now tainted by one insignificant moment in Paul Armstrong's life.

Matt raised his head as bitter tears flowed freely down his cheeks, and he cried, "I hate you! I hate what you've done. You hurt everyone you touched, you son of a bitch!" Standing, Matt picked up the first thing his hands encountered. The carved box flew across the small room, spewing its contents in a deafening clatter. "I don't want to be your son!" he sobbed. "There was *nothing* good about you! Nothing!" Matt slumped to the floor overcome by exhaustion and anguish, and fell into an unrestful sleep.

The tower room was cold. Cold enough for him to see his breath, frosty and white, in the shaft of moonlight through the window. Cold enough for him to wish he'd snagged a blanket on the way up all those hours ago.

Matt shivered uncontrollably and sat up. He huddled in a corner and listened to the wind buffeting around the house. The flashlight sat upended beside him. He'd needed it earlier, but now the sky had cleared and he could make shadow puppets in the moon's bright rays. Sitting there, surrounded by gloves and trophies and the musty smell of old paper, he was reminded of childhood games of hide-and-seek in the attic of their old house in Clinton. A tear threatened to leak from his eye. Breathing deeply, he carefully stood and stretched his legs.

Matt turned to the window. A dim, warm light emanated from his uncle's bedroom window across the street. He had to wait only a few minutes and then he saw a figure move across the room. Kate. She disappeared from view, leaving only the flickering light to play on Mike's bed.

Matt tried to imagine the fire, cozy and comforting, but he just felt cold. Lonely and cold. The tear fell. It would be daylight soon and he had to get out, that much he knew. What he didn't know was where he would go.

Matt picked up the flashlight and stepped toward the door. His foot came down on something hard and round. He flicked the light on and the beam picked out a small white plastic bag, slightly torn where he'd stepped on it. There was no doubt that it had come from the box he'd thrown. What puzzled him was that he'd never seen it before. He played the beam over the floor until it came to the carved box, upended and shattered. There had been another compartment hidden in the bottom, and the blow the box received had revealed the secret.

Matt pocketed the bag without hesitation. Not looking back and not bothering to clean up the rest of the box's contents, he called Homer and together they left the tower room.

CHAPTER

FORTY-FIVE

Kate lay on her side looking at Mike's utterly peaceful face as he slept beside her. A lock of hair had strayed across his forehead and she reached out to smooth it back. His eyelids fluttered open, he saw her, sleepily smiled, then fell back asleep, his thick dark eyelashes a shadowy smudge in the dim room. She couldn't take her eyes from his face. It was a beautiful face, with its fine web of smile lines around his eyes and shapely mouth. The well-defined jawline, the slightly off-center dimple in his chin, the straight nose. With age, his features had all come together to make him extremely sexy—extremely sweet.

Paul hadn't deserved a friend like Mike. He'd taunted him, used him, walked all over him. She gazed at Mike and whispered, "Why did you let him do it?" Then she amended her question. "Why did *we* let him do it?"

Mike's eyes opened and his drowsy smile warmed her. "Can't sleep?" She nodded. "It's too early to get up, Katie."

"Could you hold me? Until I fall asleep?"

"Nothing I'd like better." She turned and he pulled her against him. "Actually, that's probably a lie, but this'll do."

Nestling in deeper, she tucked his arm under her own.

Their breathing became a syncopated rhythm of his one long breath to her two shallower ones.

His voice, although sleepy, was deep and reassuring. "We let him do it because he was Paul and we loved him, and we knew he'd never change."

Somehow, she wasn't surprised he'd heard her earlier musings.

"We weren't being fooled," he continued. "Not really. He never pretended to be anything he wasn't."

Kate was silent for a moment. "He pretended he loved me."

Mike's arms tightened around her. "I think you know better, but I can't convince you of that. Right now, I don't want to. I only want to convince you that I love you."

She brought his hand to her lips. "Thank you," she said softly. "You're doing a good job."

The room grew quiet and he thought she'd fallen asleep. He was well on his way himself, when she said, "Mike?"

"Hmm?"

"I was right . . ."

" 'Bout what?"

"You really do have a very nice ass."

He grinned, nuzzled her hair until he found her ear, then whispered, "I'll take that as the opinion of an expert."

He had been awake for about twenty minutes. He'd forgotten to pull the shades and a blinding winter sun spilled into the room through the windows, but Kate slept on in his arms. A car door slammed and moments later the doorbell rang. He contemplated ignoring it, but then it rang again and an impatient knocking echoed through the house.

As carefully as a new father places his baby in a crib,

Mike eased his arm out from under Kate's head and let the pillow take her weight. He kissed her shoulder as he pulled the covers aside and rose from the bed. Slipping into his jeans, he closed the door behind him.

The knocking, which had stopped, began again at the back door. He was pretty sure it was Sheryl, and he ran down the stairs, wanting the noise to stop.

As he passed the oven clock, he mumbled, "Christ, Sheryl. Seven-thirty?", and he flung open the door. A blast of frigid air hit him just before the sound of his sister's voice.

"You *are* home!" She had started back around the side of the house, and now stood at the corner looking at him.

"Do you know what time it is?" But his question didn't invite an answer, and he went on. "God, it's about twelve degrees out here! What are you standing there for?"

Glaring at him as she strode into the kitchen, she sarcastically said, "*So* sorry."

Pushing the door closed, it all came back to him. Matt. Paul. Sheryl. He wasn't ready for this. Not now. Not with Kate sleeping upstairs. But he couldn't think of any way to sidestep it.

Sheryl, her eyes narrowed, her voice shrill, said, "You couldn't call to let me know you were back? And where the hell were you?"

Mike sighed deeply and walked toward the counter. "Want some coffee?"

Sheryl was pulling off gloves, her muffler, her coat, with vicious tugging motions. She didn't hear his question. "Matt didn't come home last night."

Scooping coffee into the filter, Mike said, "He's a big boy, Sheryl. I'm sure he'll find his way home." The moment the words left his mouth, he regretted them. Turning to apologize, he watched his sister dissolve into tears.

"You don't understand, Mike. There's something I have to tell you."

His voice softened just a little. "I already know."

It took her a moment to realize what he'd said. She'd been using a paper napkin to wipe her eyes and now she stared at him. "You can't know. How could you? Nobody knows except Dan." She took a step forward. "Is Matt here? Have you seen him?"

Shaking his head, he answered. "I haven't seen him, Sherry. Honest." He didn't want to have to explain how he knew, but Mike could see an explanation wouldn't be necessary. Looking over Sheryl's head, he saw Kate coming down the hallway, wearing his shirt and nothing else, and he winced. There was no way to warn her to go back upstairs.

Sheryl had seen the pained expression on his face and, in an accusatory tone, asked, "Are you lying to me?"

Kate heard Sheryl's voice at the same moment Sheryl heard the floorboards creak behind her. She whirled around, expecting her son, and was startled into silence. Her face, pinched white with worry, suddenly flushed pink. A quiet descended over the room as both women recalled words spoken and deeds done.

Kate could feel herself becoming hot with anger as she stared at Sheryl's surprised face. Quickly, before any ugly words could escape her lips, she moved her eyes to Mike's for an instant. Her guileless face told him what was happening to her, and he helplessly watched as she turned away from them both and rigidly walked back down the hallway.

When the sound of the bedroom door closing reached them, Sheryl turned to Mike. "You should've told me she was here."

"What difference does it make, Sheryl?" he said, his voice hard again.

"She's the one who told you, then."

"Yeah. Imagine my delight," he said sarcastically. "What, exactly, were you thinking all those years ago? I don't get it, Sheryl."

Defensive, embarrassed, she stated, "It wasn't just me. Paul was there, too. Nobody was married yet."

"Christ! Listen to yourself! What about Dan! Didn't he matter?"

"It just happened. Choices were made, okay? Maybe they were wrong—"

"Maybe?"

"All right! They *were* wrong." Sheryl's hand came up in a sweeping gesture. "But she made a choice, too. She chose not to sleep with him until after they were married. And everyone knew it."

"So, that makes it okay?" He was enraged and he could feel himself slipping out of control.

Sheryl took a step back. "No! I'm just telling you there were—reasons—it happened. Too much booze. Too much grass. They'd had another argument. *You* were the one who took her home that night."

"So what? Now it's *my* fault?" He snorted, shaking his head.

"No! You're turning this all around."

They stood in the middle of the kitchen. Two equally stubborn prizefighters who knew their blows were ineffective, but were trained to keep going until only one was left standing.

"No, I think you are. What you did was wrong. From the minute you said yes to Paul, you were wrong!" Mike shouted.

"We didn't think we were hurting anyone. I didn't expect to get pregnant. I didn't know she wouldn't be able to have kids."

Mike's voice lowered with suppressed fury. "Say her name, God damn it!"

Sheryl looked away.

"Say it! Say 'I didn't think *Kate* wouldn't be able to have kids.' She's not some abstract object that happened to be in the way. She was—is—your friend! Kate was the girl Paul loved. Kate is the woman I love."

"*Stop it!*" Kate's shout, unexpected, brought Sheryl and Mike up short. "Stop it, both of you! *Enough!*" She stood in the doorway, wearing her own clothes, her face white with anger. "Aren't you both forgetting someone else in all this?"

CHAPTER

FORTY-SIX

Kate swept past Sheryl and Mike, leaving a wake of hurt and anger that was palpable. She grabbed her coat on the way out the back door. It slammed behind her with resounding finality. She took deep breaths as she strode across the street. The icy air burned her nostrils and stung her eyes. She could hear Mike shouting for her, but she didn't look back.

The house felt cold when she entered. Chilly and silent. So different from Mike's warm bedroom. She had hated to leave its sanctuary, but after the scene with Sheryl she had to get out.

Kate dropped her coat on a kitchen chair and opened the back door to let Homer out. It was then she saw the footsteps in the snow. They led across the backyard to the gate, and Kate knew Matt had been in the house. She turned to the telephone and had actually dialed Mike's first three numbers when she slowly replaced the receiver. Matt didn't want to be found yet. That was obvious. And she understood completely how he felt.

The mess in the tower room was further evidence of Matt's pain. It hit her hard, seeing Paul's things strewn across the room. Kate knelt to pick up the pieces of the carved box when her eyes caught the glint of a gold chain that had slithered into a crack in the floorboards. She picked it out with a paper clip and held it a moment, hesitated, then slipped it over her head. The box was a lost cause. She tried to fit it back together. Impossible. It would never be the same.

Their rehearsal dinner has ended an hour earlier. Paul and Kate sit across the table from one another holding hands, sipping wine. The restaurant is empty. Occasionally the maitre'd or a waiter passes through the small room, but they leave the couple alone.

"I've got to leave soon," Kate says. "It's almost midnight."

"Gonna turn into a pumpkin?" Paul grins.

"The groom isn't supposed to see the bride on their wedding day. Not until she walks down the aisle."

"Why?"

Kate shrugs. "Bad luck, I guess."

Paul moves his chair closer and leans into her. "Fifteen more hours, Katie," he whispers.

In a perplexed voice, she says, "What do you mean? The wedding's at eleven."

He grins slowly—seductively. "And four hours after that you'll be naked and in my arms."

A wave of heat passes through her body. He brings her hand to his lips, then traces a slow circle around her palm with his tongue. Kate's eyes flutter closed at his touch and it takes all her willpower to open them again. "I—I have to go, Paul." She hastily stands and her foot kicks a box under the table. She's forgotten it and bends to retrieve it. She holds it out to Paul.

"What's this?" he asks.

"Your wedding present from me." He takes it from her. He seems embarrassed. "Go ahead. Open it."

"Katie, I don't have anything for you. I didn't know . . ."

"It's okay," she says, smiling. The truth is, it isn't okay. She is the tiniest bit disappointed that he hasn't thought to give her something. It didn't have to be something big. Just a little

remembrance. But she repeats, "It's all right, Paul. Come on. Open it."

He lifts the intricately carved walnut box out of its wrapping. "It's beautiful, Kate." He stands and takes her in his arms, kissing her deeply.

She forgets her disappointment and they walk out of the restaurant together. Paul waits for her to get settled in her car before going to his own. When the dashboard lights come on Kate's mind registers the time automatically. It is twelve-thirty.

Had there been a wedding? She can't even remember. The morning had gone by in an instant. The feel of her father's sturdy arm and the look on Paul's face as she walked down the aisle are the only recollections she has. The photographs have been taken, the reception is behind them, and now Paul waits in her parents' living room while she changes out of her wedding dress.

Kate's mother stands behind her, undoing the first of forty buttons on the dress. As Kate steps out of the yardage and turns to pick up the skirt on her bed, her mother comments, "That may have been a present from Paul, but I think a little selfishness was involved."

Kate blushes. Not because of the white lace merry widow she wears, but because of the lie she has told her mother—that Paul had given it to her as a wedding gift. Now she answers, "Well, he does get to unwrap it, doesn't he?"

Her mother chuckles and leaves the room to answer the phone.

Kate is about to step into the skirt when she discovers a run in one of her stockings. She has just snapped the garter into place when a voice outside her bedroom door asks, "Are you decent?"

She smiles at Paul's choice of words, and answers, "Never. Come on in."

The door opens and there is a moment of stunned silence. Then Mike swiftly turns around, saying, "Christ, Kate! Is that your idea of decent?" And Kate grabs for her robe, saying, "God, Mike! I thought you were Paul!"

As Kate belts the robe into place, she giggles. "From the look on your face, I guess this has the desired effect."

Mike makes a strangled noise.

"You can turn around now." She grins as his reddened face comes into view. "I'm sorry, Mike. I really did think you were Paul. What the hell are you doing here, anyway?"

"Excuse me while I catch my breath."

"Oh, come on, Mike. It isn't anything you haven't already seen in those Playboys you and Paul keep hidden in that tower room."

"How did you know about those?"

She laughs. "Good guess, huh? Now, why are you here?"

"I just wanted to say good-bye."

Her smile softens. "You look so sad."

"I'll miss you. And Paul."

"We'll come back here in the winter. Maybe you can come out to see us in San Francisco. That'd be fun, having you as my architectural tour guide." Kate puts her arms around his waist and hugs him closely. "Who do I feel like there's something else you want to say?" She can feel his chest expand as he takes a deep breath.

"Ever wonder what 'best man' really means, Kate?"

"Nope, but I know you were a gorgeous one."

He pushes her away and she smiles at him. Mike reaches out to stroke her cheek. "I can't believe you're a married lady now. I hope you'll be happy."

Before she can thank him, Paul's shout from downstairs interrupts her.

"Hey! You're holding up the honeymoon!"

Kate cocks her head and gives him a little shrug. "Gotta go, Mike. My husband awaits."

He nods and turns toward the door, but he is suddenly holding her again, and he says, "I just feel like nothing will ever be the same again."

"Mike. Sweetheart. You're scaring me. Of course things'll be the same. You'll always be my best friend." Now she is pushing him away. "Go on. Tell Paul I'll be down in a few minutes."

"Take care of yourself, darlin'."

Kate watches his retreating back for a moment. Smiling to herself, she thinks, Things won't be the same . . . they'll be better.

Kate stood and moved to the tower window. Sheryl's car was gone. She absently fingered the chain and watched as Mike came out his back door. He stopped to look at her house then raised his head. Shading his eyes with one hand, he peered up at the place where she stood. Kate smiled wistfully. He knew her so well. Had they really made love last night? Would *they* ever be the same?

Mike let his hand drop and headed for his truck. Kate took one last look around the room—at her past—before walking out. She didn't bother to lock the door. It didn't matter anymore. The past, locked away in her heart, stood at the cage's open door waiting to take wing. She knew what she had to do to set it free.

CHAPTER

FORTY-SEVEN

Matt counted the last of his money as he ate breakfast in the dingy coffee shop on the outskirts of town. Three dollars and seventy-eight cents. Sixty cents of that had come from under the car seat. He'd have to go home for the cash he kept in an old cigar box, but he didn't want to risk being seen by his mother. He wanted to see Kate, but knew he couldn't go to her house. Someone was bound to recognize his car. Downing his third cup of coffee, he finally stood.

Leaving the MG parked nearby, Matt walked the two blocks to the bus stop. He waited an interminable twenty minutes on the cold bench. The seventy-five cents he dropped into the driver's box would take him to the end of the line, wherever that was. The brightly lit interior of the bus contrasted with its stuffy warmth and, with no plan, he soon nodded off in the rear seat he'd taken.

A voice saying, "This is it, son," woke him from a dream that left him foggily wondering where he was. Matt looked up into the face of the driver and blinked. "End of the line. You'll have to get off," the driver said impatiently as he strode to the front of the bus.

Matt found himself at the entrance to Gypsy Hill Park. Indecision plagued him. He was close enough to Kate's to go there, but that also meant he was close enough to Mike's. He had to get moving, though. It was too cold to just stand around.

The back streets took him to the rear of Kate's house. He was relieved to see Mike's truck gone, but so was Kate's car and he kept going, disappointed. The sun glinting off the snow blinded him as he slowly wandered back to the park. He was making his way along Thornrose when he saw a car that looked like Kate's turn into the cemetery gates. Matt picked up his pace and followed, but when he got to the entrance the car had disappeared. He stood quietly for a moment, then entered the hushed grounds. He knew where Paul's grave was.

The groundskeeper was running the snowblower near Paul's headstone. When he saw Kate park across the narrow road, he knew it was time to move on.

It had become an unwritten rule in the cemetery that Kate Armstrong was given complete privacy when she came to visit her husband's grave. He remembered the first time she had come, her beauty somehow enhanced by her sorrow. She had moved slowly across the lawn to the beech tree that hung over the Armstrong plot. He was sure she'd seen him standing a few yards away, but she began speaking anyway. Her voice had been low—a mere murmur across the windy, hilly cemetery—and he couldn't understand what she was saying, but he'd quickly left her alone. He'd seen a lot of loneliness and grief in his fifteen years at Thornrose, but Kate Armstrong's was too much even for him to bear. He'd related the incident to the rest of the crew the next day. That had been nearly three years ago and when any one of them saw her they moved their work to some other part of the cemetery.

Now, Kate stepped out of her car, seemingly oblivious to the cold wind that gusted around her. The groundskeeper watched her walk toward her husband's marker. As he stowed the snowblower into the back of his electric cart, he noticed something different about her. There was a determined strength to her stride that had never been there before. He wasn't sure why, but it made him happy.

Matt had just crested the small hill when the cart drove away. Kate stood in front of Paul's headstone, and as Matt drew closer he could hear her voice. He stepped behind a tree. She was talking loudly and the wind blew her words his way.

"I've wanted you back—alive—for so many reasons, but right now I wish to God you were alive so I could tell you this to your face. I put up with your cheating and your lying. I told myself it was all right as long as we were still together. When you died, I let part of me die, too. I wouldn't let myself see the people who really loved me. I was a fool." She clenched her fists. "I was afraid to tell you about what happened between me and Matt. I was even more afraid to tell you about Mike. He loves me . . . but you already knew that. *You knew that!* The things you did to me closed me up to the point that I can't even trust anymore." She paced back and forth, her voice growing louder. "But now I've found out your secret. How cruel! To have a son and to hide it from everyone! I almost slept with *your son*, you bastard! Can you imagine how I felt when I found out? God! You've hurt so many people. Matt most of all."

She stopped for a moment, drawing in her breath, trying to hold back her tears. "But you are not going to hurt anyone anymore. I am not going to cry over you anymore. I'm finally going to live my life. I just hope you haven't destroyed any chance I might have at that. And I hope you haven't destroyed an entire family with your lies."

Kate suddenly dropped to her knees, her voice a plea. "Did you ever really love me? Did you ever love anyone but yourself?"

Matt couldn't take it anymore, and he moved away from the shelter of the tree. "Kate?"

Her head whipped around, a look of pure fright on her face. Seeing Matt there was like seeing a ghost.

"I'm sorry," Matt said as he walked toward her. "I didn't really mean to listen in."

She closed her eyes, willing her heart to slow down. When he knelt beside her and took her hand, her eyes opened and she quietly asked, "Are you okay?"

"I don't know."

"I know you were in my house last night."

"I'm sorry. I didn't have anyplace else to go. I wanted to talk to you, but you were with Mike, and I didn't think he wanted to see me."

Kate took his other hand. "Everyone's worried about you."

Matt looked at the ground. "I've caused a lot of trouble."

"What are you talking about, Matt? None of this is your fault."

"Then why do I feel like it is?"

The hurt in his voice made her heart contract, and she pulled him close and put her arms around him. "Oh, Matt . . . what is it about Paul that makes people think that way?"

He tried to stifle the tears that stung his eyes, but they came anyway.

Kate held him tighter. "Don't let him do this to you. A week ago you didn't know, and you had everything in your life to look forward to. Don't let this make a difference. I've spent too many years under his spell. I've let him hurt me for too long. That was my own fault. I was the one who wasn't willing to see the truth. We can't let him hurt us anymore. He's dead now."

Matt's body shook as he sobbed, "That's what makes this so hard. I'm totally confused . . ." He wanted to go on, but couldn't catch his breath.

Kate gently pushed him away. "Come on, Matt. I think you know that Dan is your father, despite the fact that Paul gave you life." She squeezed his hand. "Matt? Am I right?"

Embarrassed by his tears, Matt turned his head and stood. He walked a few feet away from her. "That's not it."

"Then what?" Kate's eyes followed him as he moved toward the beech tree.

"I idolized him. I guess I loved him. I know how much he hurt you. I think I hate him now." His fist came up and sharply hit the tree trunk. "But, shit, Kate! A part of me still wants to love him. He was my *father*! And he was a piece of scum! And I still want him to have *loved me*."

Kate stayed silent for a few seconds, then said, "Let's get out of here, Matt." She stood, brushing off her jeans. "Come to my house." She put her hand on his shoulder and pulled him away from the tree. "Let's go, Matt. Where's your car?"

"I came on the bus." He turned to look at her, his hazel eyes filled with fear at all these emotions. "I don't want to see anyone else."

"You don't have to. I promise." Their eyes locked and his likeness to Paul took her back in time.

"What?" he asked.

Kate wordlessly shook her head.

"Kate?"

"Come on, Matt. It's cold," she interrupted, going toward the car.

"Kate," Matt said, catching up with her. "He must've loved you. He would've been crazy not to."

"Thanks, Matt," she said in a clipped tone, afraid of where his words were leading. "Get in the car, please."

He complied, and as she settled in behind the wheel, he quietly stated, "I love you, Kate."

"Oh, Matt!" She pressed her forehead against the

steering wheel and whispered, "Please find someone to love who loves you back."

"I saw you with Mike last night. I know you don't care about me . . ."

Her head shot up. "I *do* care!"

"I know you don't care about me *that way*," he continued. "I'm not stupid, Kate. I saw how you were with Mike. I just wanted to tell you. That's all. And I'll never regret what happened between us."

Her face flushed with embarrassment. "Please, Matt. I can't talk about this anymore. Don't bring it up again." She turned the key in the ignition and they drove away.

A heavy silence hung between them, which Matt finally broke. "I don't know if I can face Mike." Kate sighed deeply. "I'm sorry, Kate. I know you don't want to talk about it, but I need to know how he feels about me."

"I explained what happened. He seemed to understand. The two of you are going to have to deal with this now."

"You and Mike are okay, then?"

Kate glanced over at him, wondering what he wanted her to say. She finally answered, "Yes. I think we're okay." But as she spoke the words, she began to wonder if she'd be "okay" with anyone ever again.

CHAPTER

FORTY-EIGHT

M att, wrung out emotionally, was asleep in the guest room. It wasn't late, but a sudden urge to take a drink had sent Kate upstairs to the safety of her room. The den, the living room, the kitchen—all were too tightly linked to long lonely nights and alcohol-induced sleep. Kate sat on the bed, back against the headboard, a book open on her lap. She had read the same sentence three times, her thoughts erasing any memory of what the words were. The sentences blurred together, forming a gray mist that floated on the paper.

She hated to admit it, but it had been a relief to look out the front window and not see Mike's truck. Their night together, and the closeness it had brought, was still too new to her. It was overwhelming. Her life had become so structured that she was like an inmate who had served twenty years and was suddenly free. She didn't know how to deal with real life anymore. And the small amount of freedom she had felt after the visit to the cemetery was elusive. It had shown her what could be, and that was intimidating. What if she began to step out of the cage that had held her all these years and the door slammed shut in her face, leaving her to gaze out at the world alone again?

The doorbell brought her back and she looked at the clock. Nearly ten o'clock. She knew it was Mike and her heart beat a little faster, a paradoxical combination of apprehension and pleasure. High school all over again. She remembered the feeling well.

She opened the front door to a very weary Mike.

"Hey, darlin'." His hands were in her hair as he kissed her. "Where've you been all day?"

"I had some business to take care of," she answered, loving the feel of his fingers on her neck.

"Hope it went better than my day."

His hands dropped away from her, but Kate caught one and tugged him inside. Moving close to him, she slid her hands up his back and pressed her lips in the vulnerable underside of his chin. His pulse sped up. The smell of winter air clung to him, and she forgot all her anxieties for a few moments as she closed her eyes and breathed him in.

"I could get used to this." His voice brought her around.

"So could I." The words came out of her mouth without hesitation, making them both smile.

"I hate to break this spell, but if you've got coffee, I'll take it."

A day that should have begun with Kate waking in his arms quickly degenerated into a day of arguments and tears with his sister. Mike and Sheryl spent the rest of the morning shouting at each other until they tired of the endless circle the words took them around. Mike's anger fed off the promise of the morning and Sheryl's fed off the fear for her son's well-being. It was a no-win situation and Sheryl had finally put an end to it by walking out the back door. "I'm going to look for Matt."

Mike followed, hurriedly shrugging into his jacket. "I'm coming."

They'd driven all over town, intermittently squabbling and apologizing halfheartedly, as the tension of their fruitless search caught up with them. Several times, Mike passed through his own neighborhood hoping to catch Matt trying to get to Kate. It was then he'd noticed Kate's car was gone for a good portion of the day.

As the afternoon wore on, Sheryl told him bits and pieces of the whole story. Mike remembered the time he'd taken Matt to that game in Philadelphia. He played the whole day back in his mind. It amazed him that even then, Paul had known Matt was his son and he hadn't departed from his script. Mike hadn't spotted anything different about him, and even with what he knew now, Mike still couldn't find a flaw in Paul's performance.

And while he was digesting that, Mike realized his own sister deserved an Academy Award for Best Actress. They had stopped at the Shoney's on the east side of town for lunch. Mike had looked across the table at her and harshly asked, "How did you do it, Sheryl? How in hell did you live with that lie every day of your life?"

"I had to," she'd retorted. "I just did what I had to do, Mike. What? You're so perfect you've never done anything you're ashamed of?"

He'd snorted. "Nothing like this!"

She'd pursed her lips and her eyes narrowed slightly. "How about lusting after your best friend's wife?" He'd turned away from her then, and Sheryl had continued to push it. "I've watched you throw away relationships with women because they somehow didn't measure up to the Kate Armstrong standard. I've listened to you piss and moan about the way Paul treated her, but you know what? That was her choice. I told you before. We all made choices."

"You're right, Sheryl," he'd snapped. "We all had something to hide. But a lot more people are hurting now. Maybe if you had come clean with this all those years ago, she would've finally left Paul. Maybe all our lives would've been a lot less lonely. Maybe Kate and I would've had a chance back then, and Allison would've never happened!"

"That's bullshit, Mike, and you know it. You're not thinking with your head right now." She threw her napkin on the table. "Let's get out of here. I've got more important things to worry about."

They'd gone on with their search in weighted silence.

Kate handed Mike a mug of reheated coffee, then joined him at the table. He gazed at her thoughtfully over the rim of the cup, but didn't ask the question that had been running through his mind since that conversation with Sheryl. *Could it have worked back then? Would you have let him go easier, Kate? Would we be lovers now? Husband and wife?* Maybe it was better not to know the answers. Instead, he said, "We found Matt's car out on Route 613. No sign of him, though. Sheryl's terrified."

"And you?"

"There's a bus stop a couple of blocks from where he left the MG. I figure he hopped on the bus and he's been wandering around all day. He'll find his way home eventually."

"Are you still angry with him?" Kate asked.

"For running away?" Mike shook his head. "It's been a long day, but I don't blame him."

Kate shifted in her chair. "What about the other ... thing? Are you still angry about what happened between us?"

The room grew quiet. Homer's soft snoring reached them from the den. Mike finally spoke. "I was going to say no. But I guess I'd be lying."

"Have you forgiven me?"

"Didn't I prove that last night? I love you, Kate."

"And you don't love Matt?"

He put down the coffee cup and looked at her.

"Touché." She gave him a slow smile, but her eyes held just a hint of sorrow. "Is there something you're not telling me?" Mike asked.

"He's very hurt, y'know."

"I know. But how do you know?"

"If I tell you something, will you promise not to get mad?"

"No." But he smiled at her.

Kate took a deep breath. "Matt's here. He's upstairs sleeping. He was here last night, too. And he doesn't want to go home right now."

"Let me at least tell Sheryl he's all right. She won't get any sleep tonight unless I do."

Kate abruptly stood and turned to the sink. She picked up a sponge and began wiping the counter. "I'd think that sleepless nights wouldn't be something new to her . . . if she had any kind of conscience."

"Touché, again," he whispered to himself. Then, aloud, Mike said, "Christmas is day after tomorrow. How the hell do we do that?"

Christmas. She'd completely forgotten. "I don't know."

She still had her back to him. He rose, circling her body with his arms, placing his hands on hers to still them. "Whatever you decide is okay with me." Molding his body into Kate's, he said, "Your place or mine?"

"Not tonight, Mike."

He stiffened slightly and asked, "Why?"

"It's been a long day for both of us."

"That's not good enough, Kate." He turned her to face him. "I need you very much."

She didn't answer and he let her go. "I don't know what to say or do to make your fear go away." He paused. "I'll leave the door unlocked."

A vision of another night alone—of an unopened bottle of wine in the pantry—came to her. "Will you stay here with me? Talk to me until I fall asleep?"

"As much as I love talking with you, Kate, I need more right now."

"I know that."

Their eyes locked for an instant, and Mike finally broke the bond. "You know where I'll be." Walking away from her was the hardest thing he'd ever done.

CHAPTER

FORTY-NINE

There was a soft tapping noise in the hall. Kate looked up from her book. Thinking it was _____ Homer scratching an itch, she went back to reading. But it came again.

"Kate?"

"What is it, Matt?"

"Can I come in?"

Sighing inwardly, she reached for her robe. "Just a sec." Kate turned the key and opened the door.

Matt stood before her, sleepy-eyed and rumpled. He held a small plastic bag in one hand. "You lock the door?"

"Under certain circumstances. What are you doing up?" she asked.

"The doorbell woke me up. Thanks for covering for me."

"I didn't. He knows you're here."

"I know, but I heard what you said."

Her lips thinned. "Did you hear everything?"

Matt nodded and looked down for a moment before holding out the bag.

She didn't take it, and in a tight voice, asked, "What's that?"

"I took it from the tower room the other night. I swear

I haven't looked inside. Please. Take it back." He reached for her hand and placed the bag in her palm. "I forgot I had it. I shouldn't have taken it. I'm sorry."

Her fingers curled around the plastic, conforming to the objects inside. She remembered the bag well. Remembered the weight of it in her lap and the brittle state of her emotions when she'd held it for the first time. With a sudden clarity, Kate's mind conjured up the image of the man who'd given it to her nearly three years ago, and she paled.

These are some of Paul's things. They forgot to give them to you at the hospital.

The bag slipped out of her hand and fell to the floor with a dull thud. She had hidden it away—this final reminder of Paul's death—in the secret compartment of the carved box, along with the memory of Mitchell Browder.

He saved my life, Kate. He saved me and then he died . . .

Matt was crouched, picking up the bag. Something had rolled a few inches out of the sack, and he reached for it. His hand collided with Kate's. She picked up the rock and studied it with a baffled expression on her face. "It's a desert rose," Matt said, standing.

"A desert rose . . ." Kate repeated, still staring at the translucent pink stone.

The rose was for you. He wanted you to have it.

Kate slowly turned away and went back into her bedroom, closing the door on a puzzled Matt.

As she sat on the bed, a thought came to her that gradually relaxed her clenched jaw. Something that almost resembled a smile came to her lips. *He thought about me that last day.* If he'd spared a moment in his self-centered life to want to give her this desert rose, what else—who else—had he thought about?

Kate hadn't kept in touch with Mitchell Browder. She hadn't wanted to. He was too vivid a reminder of that nightmarish day in March. He had called her several times in the months after Paul's death, but the calls had been too hard for her. Her own sorrow was enough. But his guilt at being alive made him call repeatedly. He was sure she'd blamed him for Paul's death, and his apologies were terrible and pain-filled. She had been polite. Distant. He finally gave up.

Mitch played baseball that year, but his heart had gone out of the game, and he gave that up, too. The rumor of his nervous breakdown had reached her, but by then she was too busy trying to get through her own fragmented life.

Where was he from? Some little town in Oklahoma. Kate thought hard, but couldn't come up with it. It was a person's name. What was it? Enid? Norman? She got up from the bed. The only place to look would be a Giants' program, and that would be in the tower room. Her hand was on the knob of her bedroom door when it came to her. Guthrie.

Information had two Browders listed, neither of which was Mitchell. Kate dialed the first number, hoping to find his parents. She got lucky.

And as Kate waited for someone to pick up the phone at Mitch Browder's Tulsa home, she wondered just what it was she wanted to ask him. She only knew she had to talk to him about that last day. A drowsy male voice answered. "Mitch?"

"Yeah?"

"Mitch, this is Kate Armstrong. I'm sorry if I woke you." There was silence, and for a moment she thought he'd gone back to sleep.

"I wasn't sleeping," he finally said.

Kate hesitated now. His words were a little slurred, and she realized that what she thought was sleepiness was actually the effects of alcohol. She also realized something else. He might not want to talk to her. "Is this a bad time, Mitch?"

He snorted. "One time's as bad as another. Wha'd'you want, Kate?"

The words she'd intended to say were forgotten. "I wanted to say I'm sorry for the way I treated you after the accident." She could hear the clink of ice on a glass as he took a drink.

"S'okay. Don't give it another thought," he said with polite sarcasm. "So, how've ya been, Kate? How's your life going?" Another pause. Another sip.

She knew this rhythm all too well. "It's been hard, Mitch, but I think I'm finally getting over losing Paul."

"Well, thas just great, Kate. Jus' great . . ." The liquor accentuated his low drawl. "Ya wanna know how I'm doin'? Wanna know how mah life's been?"

"Mitch, I can call back tomorrow . . ."

"Wha' for? Naw, Kate . . . I wanna talk to you now." The hostile tone collapsed into self-pity. "My life is shit, Kate. Pam left me. Jus' took Kristy and left. Army died an' I couldn't play ball anymore, an' now I don't have nothin'." A sob bubbled out of his throat.

Muted by shock, Kate clutched the receiver and squeezed her eyes shut. But Mitch was still talking and she couldn't shut out the suffering in his voice.

"I miss mah little girl, an' I still love Pam. An' she tole me she loves me, but cain't live with me like this no more . . ."

"Mitch, how long has Pam been gone?" she asked gently.

"Nine months . . . nine months!" He paused. "Wanna hear somethin' funny? She left me on April Fools' day. Ain't that a hoot?" He was crying again.

"It gets worse for you in the spring, doesn't it, Mitch," Kate said. "I know. It was the same for me. But Mitch, it wasn't your fault. Paul made the choice. You could've both died out there, and what good would that have been? It was *an accident*, Mitch."

"But he didn't have to die, Kate," he nearly wailed. "It was like, one minute he was holdin' on to the front of the Jeep, and the next, he was climbin' into it. Like there was somethin' he wanted in there. If he'd just stayed on the hood, he would've been okay. But he pulled himself in through the door. I yelled at him, but I guess he couldn't hear me."

Kate evenly asked, "What do you think he went back for?"

"I doan know. He'd put that rose in his pocket for you . . ."

"The desert rose."

"Yeah, that was all they found on him. That, and his wallet." He stopped suddenly and Kate felt herself grow still. "Wait a minute! The wallet wasn't on him. Thas right . . . thas right!" He was talking to himself now. She no longer existed. "They found it under his arm. Funny, after all this time to remember that. Yeah. It was under his arm and they took it along to the hospital. I guess that's what he wanted."

Kate turned her eyes to the small plastic bag. "And that's what you brought me from the hospital? The desert rose and his wallet?"

"Why're ya askin' me like you don't know?"

"I never looked in the bag, Mitch. I couldn't bear it."

"What coulda been so important in his wallet? What in the hell was in it worth dyin' for?"

They were both silent for a moment, then Kate hesitantly asked, "Mitch, did you and Paul ever talk about anything—personal?"

"Like what?"

"Like—did he ever tell you anything that he wanted kept secret? Something maybe he didn't want me to know?" She realized his silence meant he was struggling with something, and she added, "I already know about the other women, Mitch. It hurt me then, and it hurts me now, but I mean something else."

"No," he quickly said, his voice nearly sober. "If Army had any secrets, he never told them to me."

She couldn't bring herself to tell him about Matt. "If I find out anything important, I promise I'll let you know."

"Thanks."

"I'm sorry if I disturbed you, Mitch. I didn't mean to cause you any more pain."

"S'okay, Kate. I'm kinda glad you called."

"Get some help, Mitch," she said gently. "If you and Pam still love each other, it's worth doing." He started to protest, and in a calm, chiding voice she stated, "And don't give me any of that macho bullshit, Mitchell Browder. Everyone needs help once in a while."

"I tried. It was too hard."

"Listen to me, Mitch. I know all about it. I've been drinking, too. It's been a real easy way to hide from life. There was a lot I just wasn't seeing because of it."

"Have you been able to quit?" he asked.

"Yes. Recently."

"How do you feel? Without it, I mean?"

"The truth? Scared . . ."

"I already feel that way."

"I know, Mitch," she said, understanding in her voice. "But one of these days you'll be drinking, and you'll do something that'll scare the hell out of you. And you may not be able to undo it. Don't wait for that to happen. I'm sure it's not too late for you and Pam. Forgive yourself, Mitch. Do that, and I'm sure Pam will forgive you, too."

"What made you quit, Kate?"

"It's not something I can tell you. Let's just say I hurt a lot of people I care about very much."

"Are you still alone?" he asked. She didn't answer right away and he said, "Kate?"

"No, Mitch. I guess I was never alone. I just didn't realize it."

•   •   •

The longer she sat on the bed staring at the little bag, the more nervous she became, and by the time she reached for it, her palms were damp. The desert rose and Paul's wallet tumbled out onto the blanket.

She lightly placed her fingers on the water-stiffened leather and waited. No mystical revelations came to her. No messages from the past. Nothing. It was just an old wallet that somehow held the power to hurt her if she let it.

As she picked it up, her heart began a hollow thumping and the skin on her arms prickled with fear. She dropped it back onto the bed and plucked up the desert rose, closing her eyes. Kate let her thumb worry the weathered surface. She guided her fingers around the "petals." Her heart rate returned to normal after a few seconds and she inhaled deeply, opening her eyes. When she finally opened the wallet, it made a dry creaking sound and she half expected a moth to fly out, like in a cartoon.

The desert is the greenest he's ever seen it. Spring rains have been plentiful this year and the Arizona earth has been waiting for just this moment to bear fruit. Shrubs that had been skeletons a few days ago have suddenly developed miniature leaves. Golden barrels and prickly pears sport masses of nodules that look like alien pods, ready to release pink and white and yellow fingers of color. Looking up, he can see two saguaros in the distance, their arms intertwined in a stately dance of courtship. He smiles and tells himself he'll bring her out here on his next off day, even if he has to kidnap her. The only time she ever seems to leave the hotel anymore is to visit her parents. He isn't a fool. He knows she's unhappy, but Christ! It's spring! The season is beginning. It's the best time of the year for baseball. It's the best time of the year for him.

Tiny wildflowers, invisible to travelers in their cars, are little jewels scattered at his feet. He bends down to pick a blossom and then, having nowhere else to put it, takes his wallet out of the back pocket of his jeans and stuffs it between two fives. He'll give it to her later. Maybe it will make her smile—a rarity these days.

He knew she hadn't wanted to leave Staunton this time. He'd wanted nothing more. The winter had begun to grate on his nerves. His final visit with Mike had left him angry and antsy. It had been one of their worst arguments—and there had been plenty over the twenty-five years they'd known each other—but pride wouldn't let him relent. He'd left Virginia without making that final call he'd always made before. And now, as the days turned into weeks, the affront has taken on epic proportions. Like a scorned lover, he tells himself Mike can make the first move. He doesn't have to take that shit from him.

He can feel himself frowning, when a shout breaks the serene silence that hovers over the desert.

"Hey, Army! What the hell are you doing over there?" Paul Armstrong turns in the direction of Mitchell Browder's voice, but can't locate him. "Over here!" A head of thick, curly black hair pops up behind a mesquite bush a few hundred yards to Paul's left. The sun glints off the centerfielder's mirrored sunglasses and he sees him grin.

"Find something?" Paul shouts.

"Yeah. Bring the bag."

Paul Armstrong's boots crunch across the dry wash toward the Jeep they've borrowed from a fellow teammate, and permanent resident of Scottsdale. Placing his wallet on the dashboard, Paul reaches between the seats for the heavy leather satchel Mitch uses for his rock collecting.

As he walks toward the spot where Mitch has once again disappeared from view, a slow trickle of sweat runs down his neck. He's glad they've come out early. Even though it is only the eleventh of March, the temperature will probably climb into the low nineties before noon. The sun, fully up now, is relentless. The low mountains in the distance are the only things in shadow, as a few dark clouds gather around them.

"Whatcha got?"

Mitch straightens up to his full five feet, nine inches, and places something in Paul's hand. "Desert rose. Kristy'll love it."

Paul runs his index finger around the pale pink stone aptly named for its almost perfect mimicry of a rose in bloom.

"I've been coming out here for two years now. First one I've found. She can add it to her collection." Taking it back from Paul, he drops it in the bag.

"You should bring her out here," Paul comments as Mitch hunkers down again.

"Maybe next year. She's still too little." Mitchell's daughter had just turned four in November and his world, which before had revolved around baseball, had now adjusted its orbit. She is the center of his universe. "Here's another one!" Mitch's fingers dig into the soft dirt and pry out a smaller version of his original find.

Paul kneels in front of him, asking, "Can I have it?"

"Didn't know you were into rocks."

"I'm not, but Kate might like it."

"Be my guest," Mitch says, tossing it to Paul.

Paul stands, pocketing the stone. "I think it's Miller time."

Mitch looks up at his friend in amusement. "Don't you think it's a little early?"

Paul is already walking back to the Jeep. "It's never too early for a good beer buzz."

Mitchell shakes his head as he picks up the leather bag from where Paul has dropped it.

The two men sit in companionable silence. The flat rock they've found to perch on is already warm, and the frosty beer tastes good, even at ten o'clock in the morning. A small collared lizard, tempted by the sun, ventures out from under a barrel cactus and climbs onto a pile of stones.

They don't move for a few seconds and are rewarded with the comical sight of the lizard doing push-ups, the better to see a cricket that has had the misfortune of crossing into his sights.

Paul chuckles. "Reminds me of Wart."

"Only the lizard's better looking," Mitch comments, taking

another pull from the bottle he holds. The lizard darts off his roost and is devouring the hapless cricket. "Eats like Wart, too."

A rumbling sounds far away and Paul looks over his shoulder at the mountains. "Thunder?"

Mitch nods. "Speaking of Koslowski, I heard a rumor he's not gonna make it this year."

John "Wart" Koslowski had been the Giants' utility infielder until shoulder surgery had sidelined him late last season.

"Yeah, I heard. Kangaroo court won't be the same without him. We could always count on him to do something flaky."

They are both quiet again, then Paul says, "I remember when you were a hound, but you weren't hunting rocks."

"Things change." Mitch stretches out his legs and then stands, fishing a pack of cigarettes out of his shirt pocket.

Unable to get a rise out of Mitch, Paul comments, "Those'll stunt your growth, y'know. Oops, sorry . . . I guess it's too late."

Mitch gives him a dirty look, then answers defensively, "I'm cutting down . . . Besides, Kristy keeps asking me, " 'Daddy, why are you on fire?' " He takes a deep drag and expels the smoke. "I never have a good answer for her." He shakes his head and smiles. "Kids. They give you a whole new perspective on things."

"I'm sure they do."

Paul has gotten up and is making his way to the Jeep. Mitch watches him and winces. "Sorry, man," he calls after him.

But Paul chooses to ignore his apology, and tosses the two bottles into the back of the car.

"How much time have we got?" Mitch asks, coming up behind Paul.

"About two hours." Paul is stripping off his long-sleeved shirt. Dark blotches stand out on his blue T-shirt where he has sweated through the cotton fabric. "Don't worry, lover-boy. I'll have you home in time."

Mitchell's family is flying in that afternoon. He hasn't seen them in nearly three weeks, and he can't wait to see his little daughter's face when he shows her all the fascinating rocks he's found. He'll hold back the desert rose until the end. She'll be thrilled.

While Mitch contentedly scours the dry wash, Paul makes his way "downstream," picking up rocks and lobbing them across the desert as he goes. He can't stop thinking about what Mitch has said about kids. Even after all these years, it never fails to hurt him when someone inadvertently comments on the joys of children. The looks of pity that come over their faces when Kate asks to hold a new baby always angers him. They always ask—in what they think is a subtle manner—why they haven't adopted. If Kate is present, she'll fix him with a sad look that only makes him angrier. But why should he have to explain his feelings about adoption to these people? It's none of their damn business.

But Mitch's proclamation won't leave him alone. He's been thinking about this for a few months, and now, standing in the vast solitude of the desert, Paul comes to a decision. He doesn't want to live the lie anymore. He's let it go on too long already. The boy is practically grown and Paul hasn't shared in any part of Matt's life. He's tired of the empty ache. People will be hurt, but so be it. He wants to acknowledge his son. He doesn't care what the consequences will be. This suddenly seems like the only possible thing to do—to be able to say to the world, "I have a son."

Thunder sounds again, almost in punctuation to his thoughts, and he turns toward the mountains. The horizon is one long line of steel-gray clouds that have stalled over the Mazatzal Mountains. A giant thunderhead looms above one of the peaks and the soft, misty color that it's painted that part of the landscape with its rain belies the true force of the storm. While Paul stands in the sunshine, it is coming down hard up there.

He looks for Mitch, who seems to have vanished into thin air. He is about to call out, when he sees a flash of red behind a stand of ocotillo, and then the centerfielder comes into view.

Paul takes a deep breath. He is frightened in that moment and the feeling of unease won't leave him.

Sheet lightning illuminates the murk that surrounds the mountains, and Paul suddenly makes up his mind.

"Hey, Mitch!" he shouts. His friend's head comes up, and Paul makes the time-out gesture. They walk toward each other to close the five-hundred-foot gap between them. When he gets within speaking distance, Paul says, "Maybe we should wrap this up."

"The rain?" Mitch asks.

Paul nods. "I know it's not flash-flood season, but it looks pretty bad up there."

"Give me fifteen minutes. I found some rocks that look like they could be geodes."

Mitch is already walking back to the spot he's left, when Paul says, "Just remember how those rocks got there." Mitch raises his hand in acknowledgment while Paul watches his retreating back. Another reverberation of thunder pushes him into action and Paul heads for the car.

It takes him five minutes to reach the Jeep, slip the key into the ignition, and turn the engine over. In those five minutes, while he thinks only of getting the Jeep out of the dry wash, Mitch is out of his line of sight. The motor starts with its characteristic unmuffled roar. But the engine's noise can't mask another, louder noise.

Only two seconds pass between the time he hears that horrible sound and his boots hit the sandy soil. Only two heartbeats. But it still isn't enough of a head start. He can see Mitch racing across the bed of the wash. Mitch scrambling up the side. Mitch losing his foothold. Mitch tumbling into the path of the oncoming, improbable river of boulders, dirt, trees, and raging water. Nature's freight train, carrying the force of sixty thousand tons of TNT, has derailed and is barreling down on them both.

"MITCH!" Paul's scream is swallowed up by the deafening flash flood.

His legs pump hard in the crumbling dirt as he speeds

toward his friend. His fingers greedily close on the waistband of
Mitch's jeans and he hauls him upward with all the strength he
has. Mitch's boots scrabble to find a toehold as the first surge of
muddy debris bears down on them.

Paul's Virginia driver's license was the first thing she
saw. Except for the haze of dried mud, it looked much
like hers. The lamination had held together, and as she
wiped her thumb across the surface to clean it, Paul's
smiling face emerged. While her own photo looked like a
mug shot taken on her worst hair day, his was wonderful.
He always managed to look perfect, and she remembered joking with him about it more than once.

There was a Chevron credit card and his American
Express Platinum card. An almost indistinguishable
proof of insurance had glued itself into the only other
slot he'd filled. Kate removed the brittle paper money.
The bills were stuck together in places and as she peeled
them apart she placed them in a tidy row on the blanket.
A twenty, four ones, a five, another one. The last two
five-dollar bills parted company and revealed a tiny, perfectly preserved wildflower. It was a vivid purple and its
delicate petals were flattened to form a one-dimensional
representation of its species. Kate carefully slid the
flower onto her palm. Inexplicably, she knew it had been
meant for her eyes, and Kate smiled at the thought of
Paul putting it away. It was his final gift to her. A final
glimpse into the past. This had been the Paul she'd
fallen in love with. Paul, before the success and all the
lying and cheating that had seemed to come with that
success. She knew just where the little flower belonged.

Kate rose from the bed and walked to the dresser. A
Limoges box made to resemble a life-sized pansy
blossom sat next to her jewelry box, and she opened it
and placed the wildflower inside. Paul had given her the
porcelain box for her twenty-fifth birthday. It had come

from Shreve, Crump, and Low in San Francisco and he'd picked it out himself, a rarity in their years together. The present had been very special for that reason. Usually, Mike had been consulted in the gift-giving department.

Kate gently closed the lid and went back to the wallet. She spread open the cash compartment. There was nothing else in it. A small feeling of disappointment came over her. There had to be *something*. He certainly hadn't gone back for forty dollars.

She found the photograph of Matt when she pulled out the American Express card.

CHAPTER

FIFTY

Mike had gone to sleep with a desperate need for Kate pervading all his senses. His last thought, _____ as he drifted off, had been, *At least let me dream about her.*

And now he was. The dream was so real he could feel her warm fingers on his forehead, her hot breath as she bent to kiss the corner of his mouth, her weight as her body settled next to his. She was whispering his name. He spoke her name in return. When her hand slid across his chest, he moaned. He heard her say, "Make love to me." He opened his eyes. In the twilight, between sleep and waking, Mike slowly smiled and whispered, "Katie. You're real."

She responded by wrapping one bare leg around his thigh, trailing kisses along his shoulder until she reached his mouth. There was nothing tentative about her lips on his. Her tongue slipped inside, assaulting him with sensual ferocity. Mike roughly took her face in his hands and let her devour him.

Kate's leg moved, opened, to grip him tighter and he could feel her sex on his thigh, steamy and wet. He groaned and moved his hands to her buttocks, holding her there. But her hips wouldn't stay still, as she urgently strained against him. She'd slid a hand between their bodies, cupping his balls and then running a smooth palm along the underside of his erection. Another groan escaped him, and he heard himself say, "No ... don't, Katie," because he knew if he didn't stop her, he'd come.

But she was already moving her hand. Across his belly, up the side of his chest, down his arm. Her mouth held his, parted momentarily, came back. Short, breathless kisses. He instinctively knew what she wanted, even if she wasn't quite sure herself. When he clutched her arms and pushed her upright, forcing her to straddle him, she made a small, sorrowful sobbing noise at being torn from him.

And then she rose up slightly, took him in her hand once again, and guided his cock inside. She let the full length of him fill her and he heard her deep gasp of satisfaction. Right then, she owned him completely and he knew nothing would ever be the same.

She was leaning back slightly, gripping his thighs, pushing against him. He reached up to cup her breasts. Her back arched as his fingertips circled her nipples. Out of nowhere, her hand was on his, pulling it down, taking it to the edge of her pubic bone, showing him where to press. Throaty moans came from above him and, slowly, her body curled forward. Her fingers dug into his shoulders. His fingers dug into her hips.

It was the friction fires were made of. She ground into him. Her voice was a deep-toned groan as she said his name over and over again. And suddenly everything about her went quiet. Her movements became economical and deliberate. The only sound was her panting. And then it started. A slow, murmured mantra that repeated, "Oh, God ... oh, Michael ..." and built into an eruption that he felt to his core.

But she wasn't finished with him. She kissed him deeply, frantically, saying, "More ... more ..."

Still inside her, Mike could think of nothing else he

wanted but more, and he sat up, bringing her with him. He leaned back on one arm, and with his other arm, held her to him. As much as he had held back a few moments ago, that was how much he unleashed himself into her. His thrusts were deep and hard, and through the haze of his own need he could hear her gasping as another wave of orgasm hit her.

His arm began to tremble. As he swiftly rolled on top of her, he slipped out. Kate's cry, and Mike's curse echoed through the bedroom. As he found her again and drove into her, reality finally hit him. He was making love to Kate Moran Armstrong, and she had come to him with only one thought.

He came so hard that he called out her name in a strangled sob.

Mike watched her struggle not to wake up. She would turn over, snuggle into the pillow, sleep a little, then the process would start all over again. At the moment, her back was to him and he ran his middle finger down the scar until he reached the edge of the quilt that covered the rest of her. His morning erection stiffened even more and he smiled at the effect just touching her skin had on him.

They had fallen asleep tangled around each other, exhausted. The last thing he remembered was kissing her damp forehead and Kate whispering, "Thank you."

Kate shifted again, and he moved down to kiss the small rise where her back met her buttocks. Sliding his hand up the curves of her body, he pulled her into his arms and fit the length of his body against her. She nestled into him. With sleep, her voice was huskier than usual. "What time is it?"

"Time to make love again."

She smiled to herself. "That could become my favorite time of the day." Kate turned to face him.

Their lips met, and he whispered, "Mornin', darlin'."
A slit of sunlight knifed across the bed, setting her hair
on fire, and he took a strand in his fingers.

The same sun turned his gray eyes to flawed dia-
monds. "What are you waiting for?" she whispered back.

A slow grin spread over his face. "I've got to wonder
what the hell happened last night between the time I
left and the time you showed up here. Not that I'm complaining, you understand . . ."

Kate brought a hand to his face and traced the lines
around his eyes. "Later." She kissed the corner of his
mouth. "I'll tell you later."

She told him over breakfast.

"I want to talk to Matt," he said.

"He may not want to talk to you," she said.

Mike snorted impatiently. "He's my nephew. He'll
have to talk."

"What you mean is, he'll have to listen. Let me talk to
him first. I'll see what he wants to do."

"What *he* wants to do?"

Kate's eyes narrowed. "Look. He's really hurt. He's
not going to believe anything you, or Sheryl, or Dan,
have to say right now."

"And he'll believe you?" Mike asked angrily.

"Why is that so hard to understand?" Her voice grew
tight. "I wasn't the one who lied to him his whole life."

"Hey! I had nothing to do with that and you know it!"

"But in his eyes you're implicated. You're family."
She paused, trying to collect herself. "Besides, he still
thinks you're harboring a secret desire to rip him apart
for what happened between us. Let's face it, Mike. You're
never going to forget it. You may have a perpetual
hard-on for me for the rest of your life, but somewhere
deep inside you'll be thinking about the time Matt
almost fucked Kate—"

"Cut it out." He pushed away from the table. The two things he felt for Matt—anger and love—were hard to put into some kind of perspective.

"See? You get mad just thinking about it, Mike, so let me go talk with him." Mike didn't respond and she drew in a deep breath and looked away.

"Tell him I love him," Mike finally said.

When Kate entered her house, it was too quiet. She ran upstairs to the spare room. The bed had been made. She slowly walked back down to the kitchen. The only sign he'd been there was a half-drunk mug of coffee sitting on the counter and an IOU for the ten dollars he'd taken out of her purse. Matt was gone again.

CHAPTER

FIFTY-ONE

K ate trawled the streets of Staunton, hoping to catch Matt. In the early afternoon she spied his _____ lanky form ducking into a bus shelter. She pulled up to the curb, rolled down the passenger-side window, and said, "Get in."

Matt's cheeks, ruddy from the cold, turned a deeper shade of red. "Forget it, Kate. I can take care of myself."

"Is that why you took ten dollars from me? Get in, damn it."

He sat still a second and then hunched forward and stood. The warmth of the car felt good to him, but he sat up stiffly, trying to maintain some sense of pride.

Kate pulled away from the bus stop and made a U-turn into a parking lot across the street. Putting the car in neutral, she turned to Matt. "Mike wants to see you, but I won't take you to his place unless you tell me to."

Matt stared straight ahead, the muscle in his jaw working. "Kate, I know he'll never forgive me. I know he's still madder'n hell."

"Not quite," Kate stated wryly. Matt glanced at her, then turned his eyes back to the windshield. "Look, Matt. This is all tangled up with Paul now. It's about a longtime rivalry that he's only just now beginning to admit to himself. Someone's got to take the first step to clear the air. Why don't you play the adult for a while?"

The car windows had fogged up with the heat of uncertainty that emanated from Matt's every pore. Kate pushed in the defrost button and waited.

Finally, Matt cleared his throat and grimly said, "Okay. Let's go. But he has to come to your house."

Kate replaced the receiver in its cradle and looked at Matt. He sat at her kitchen table nervously twisting a mug of lukewarm coffee between his hands.

"He'll be here in a minute."

Matt nodded, his throat so dry he was afraid any sound would come out as a croak.

"I'll leave the two of you alone. Wherever you want." Again, Matt nodded, and Kate tried to hide her amusement. "And try to remember that this whole business has taken him by surprise, too. We all get a little crazy when we're confronted with a truth we don't want to hear." The doorbell rang and Kate started for the front door, saying over her shoulder, "He may be your uncle, and thirty-eight years old, but right now his brain may very well be stuck at sixteen." As Kate reached for the door handle, and she recalled the feel—the strength—of Mike the night before, she smiled and said to herself, "And that might not be such a bad thing."

"What's that incredibly lewd grin on your face for?" Mike asked, stepping inside.

"For you." She stepped close to him. Her hand slid up his thigh and paused between his legs. "For last night."

His eyes widened momentarily and then a corner of

his mouth turned up. "Shucks, darlin'. T'weren't nothin'."

"I wouldn't call this . . ."—Kate's hand cupped his erection—"nothing."

"What would you call it?" His voice lowered.

"I'd call it a great Christmas present, but I'm afraid I'm going to have to open it a little later." She began pulling away from him. "He's waiting for you in the kitchen."

But Mike wrapped his arms around her and whispered into her hair, "Shit, Kate. I don't want to deal with anything except you right now."

"I'll be here when you finish." She paused, then quietly said, "He doesn't know about the photo in Paul's wallet. Don't tell him. I want to give it to him as a Christmas gift."

Mike walked into the kitchen, while Kate followed and then leaned against the doorframe. Matt stood tall in the middle of the room, hands in the pockets of his jeans, but his eyes gave away the uncertainty he was feeling.

"Matt?" Mike said by way of greeting.

Kate broke the ensuing silence. "Mike. Take your jacket off and stay awhile."

Matt said, "Can we go into the den to talk?"

When the door closed behind Mike, Matt walked to the window and leaned against the radiator. His hands had gone cold. He gripped the warm metal and stared out at the lengthening shadows of the early winter afternoon, trying to figure out how to begin. Before he had a chance, though, Mike was talking.

"I've spent most of my adult life making old, broken buildings whole again. With all the effort I put into fixing inanimate objects, I've never really had enough energy left to deal with the people in my life."

"You were always good to me," Matt said.

"I was always good to everyone that I didn't have to deal with on a daily basis."

Matt turned. "What do you mean?"

Mike's hands came up in frustration. "I guess I mean, something was always missing from my life."

"Kate," Matt said.

Mike flopped onto the couch. "Yeah. Kate."

"How long have you been in love with her?"

Mike gazed into the fireplace. "From the first minute I saw her, I think." He blinked and turned to look at Matt. "I guess you can understand that."

Matt reddened and lowered his eyes to the floor.

"It's okay, Matt. At least you have good taste . . ." Mike went back to staring at the fireplace. He took a deep breath and then went on. "I don't think I've ever talked to anybody about this before. I know I've never had to admit it to anyone." Mike closed his eyes. "God, how do I say this?" The words that followed came out of his mouth bitten and hard. "When Paul died there was a part of me that was glad. I don't expect you to understand that. Hell, I don't understand it myself. I'm ashamed for a lot of things I've done in my life, but that thought tops the list.

"While Paul was alive, I knew there was never any chance for me and Kate. And when he died . . ." He had to stop and swallow. "When he died, one of my first thoughts was he can't hurt Kate anymore. Now I can take care of her."

Matt had silently moved to the armchair. He watched his uncle's obvious pain, a lump forming in his throat.

"I resented him for getting her, and for the way he treated her later. I told myself he didn't love her, but I know that wasn't true. Not really. I harbored this fantasy that she'd eventually get sick and tired of what he was putting her through and she'd leave him. But I knew that wasn't the truth, either. I tried to make myself forget her, but that was like trying to stop the sun from coming up every morning. Couldn't be done.

"The women I went out with didn't have a clue about what a shit I really was. They didn't deserve what I put them through. They could never figure out what they were doing wrong. But they didn't do anything wrong. They just weren't Kate.

"Allison . . ." Mike's voice dropped to a near whisper. "Bless her heart, she made the biggest mistake of them all. She had the bad luck of reminding me of Kate. And she's the only one who knew the truth. I hurt her most of all."

A quiet descended on the room. The muffled sounds of Kate moving around upstairs caught them by surprise, and they simultaneously looked toward the ceiling.

Matt broke the silence. "You should've told Kate how you felt about her."

"You don't tell a woman married to your best friend you love her."

"I wish you'd told me," Matt said.

Mike's jaw tightened and, unconsciously, his hands formed fists. "Forget it. It's done."

"It's worse now, isn't it?"

Mike looked over at Matt. "What do you mean?"

Matt's eyes met his uncle's. "Because I'm Paul's son. That makes it worse for you, doesn't it?" When Mike didn't answer, Matt stated, "I'm not Paul Armstrong."

"I know that."

"I didn't do it to hurt you."

"I don't want to get into this," Mike said.

"But if we don't, you're gonna hate me forever."

Mike sighed. "I don't hate you, Matt."

"But you don't like me anymore."

"Shit, Matt!" Mike stood and walked to the window.

"Why did ya do it? If you knew what kind of shape she was in, why would you even think about it?"

" 'Cause I thought it was the only chance I had to get closer to Paul."

Matt's honest reply was like a shot of strong liquor. It jolted Mike, and he turned to face his nephew, who was looking up at him with Paul's hazel eyes. The resemblance shocked him. The special relationship he had with Matt, could it have been because he *was* like Paul in so many ways?

"That was before I knew," Matt went on. "I can't find much to admire him for anymore."

"It's hard when our heroes fall, Matt. The circumstances in this case make it even harder. It's trite, but Paul was human. Humans fail."

"Y'know, one minute you're telling me what a piece of dogshit he was, and the next you're defending him. What's with that?"

Mike slowly walked to the fireplace, while Matt waited for some kind of answer that would end the schizophrenic roller coaster he was riding.

"I guess it's guilt," Mike finally said.

"What do you have to feel guilty about?" Matt asked.

Mike snorted. "Aside from everything else I've already told you? . . . What I'm gonna tell you doesn't leave this room, because even Kate hasn't heard this one." Mike glanced at Matt, saw him nod, then went on. "When Paul died, I hadn't spoken to him in over a month. The last time I saw him we argued. About Kate. It was pretty ugly and we both said a lot of stuff that probably shouldn't have been said. I guess there's such a thing as being too honest with a friend. Because he *was my friend.*"

"But Kate was your friend, too."

"Yeah. No matter what else I wanted her to be, Kate was my friend, too. Which made it even harder. I wanted to make her life better. Maybe I wanted that more than I wanted Paul's friendship at that point." The side of Mike's fist hit the mantel and his body seemed to sag.

Matt sat still, not knowing what to do or say to take some of his uncle's pain away. His short life hadn't prepared him for this kind of thing.

"Christ! He was my friend, and he fucking died, and I can never tell him I love him. He could be a sorry son of a bitch, but I still loved him, damn it!"

Matt was on his feet in an instant. "But why? Why did you love him? I need to know!"

Mike didn't hesitate. The words poured out of him. "Because Paul didn't love many people, but he loved me. And in some ways he understood Kate better than I ever could, back then. And I know in my heart he loved her, too. And I think if he'd ever been given the chance, he would've loved you. I loved him for saving Mitchell Browder's life. I just loved him because he was Paul Armstrong." Mike gripped the mantel with both hands and leaned into it. "Not too long ago, Kate asked me if I believed everything in life happens for a reason. At the time I was too angry to understand what she meant. I've always thought we had control over the direction our lives take. Now I'm not so sure.

"Maybe Kate and I weren't meant to be until now. Maybe we both had to live the lives we've had up to this point in order to appreciate what we've found now. And maybe you were meant to find out that Paul was your father now, because any sooner would've changed who you are right now."

"Who am I?" Matt asked quietly. "All of a sudden, I don't know anymore."

Mike turned to face his nephew, and even though Matt was physically bigger than his uncle, Mike could see he was barely grown. The older man took the younger in his arms. "You're the best of Paul, and your mom, and Dan, wrapped up in a new package called Matt Keller."

"I want to be the best of *you*."

A lump formed in Mike's throat. "Thank you, Matt . . . I love you, too."

They separated and Matt asked, "Will you take me to get my car? I wanna go home now."

CHAPTER

FIFTY-TWO

"When do you want to open your present?" Kate asked Mike, trying to contain her amusement.

They lay on their stomachs at the foot of the bed, staring into the fire.

Mike, chin on his forearm, smiled as he rubbed a bare foot along her calf. "That wasn't it?"

Kate languidly rolled onto her side to look at him. "You *know* your gift wouldn't be anything that nice," she said, grinning. Their Christmas ritual of who could find the other the tackiest gift had been going on for too many years to count. She wasn't about to end it now.

Mike lazily turned his head and regarded her naked form appreciatively before speaking. "What time does Mickey say it is?"

Kate lifted her arm to look at her watch. "Ten past midnight."

"Then I guess it's Christmas." He continued gazing at her, head on his arm, not moving.

Kate poked his shin with her toe and said, "Come on, Mike. Where's my present?"

He sighed in resignation and slowly stretched. His arms surrounded her and he pulled her close. "One more kiss, darlin'." His mouth covered hers.

He took his time, and Kate felt herself fall under the spell of this rediscovered feeling of lust. When he suddenly released her and said, "I'll go get it," Kate involuntarily groaned. "You're a cruel, cruel man, Michael Fitzgerald." He was already on his feet and Kate watched the muscles in his back and buttocks with unabashed appraisal as he walked out of the bedroom. A satisfied smile came to her lips. "You're a *gorgeous* man, Michael Fitzgerald," she said to the empty room as she reached under the bed for the box she'd put there.

When Mike returned, Kate sat up and wrapped herself in the quilt. "You first."

"No way. The rules state that last year's winner goes first." Mike shrugged into a denim workshirt. "As I recall, you won with the lovely silver-plated corncob holders in the shape of breasts."

Kate grinned and took the package from him. "I bet you never used them," she said in mock hurt.

"On the contrary . . . they made great pushpins."

She had already ripped the paper off the small box and plunged her hand inside, lifting out the tissue-wrapped object. Peeling off the outer layer, she stared at a piece of porcelain, obviously old. A look of disappointment stole over her face. "Mike, this is too nice . . ." Then she turned it around and her husky laugh hit him full force.

The prewar Japanese ashtray she held portrayed a smiling man on his hands and knees. Astride him was a redheaded woman in a polka-dot bathing suit. The caption read: *"She's As Nice a Gal As You Want t'Meet, But She Loves to Ride in the Rumble Seat."*

"God, Mike!" She was still laughing. "This is priceless!"

"It struck me as perfect."

Still holding the ashtray, Kate threw her arms around him and knocked Mike over onto the bed. Slithering up his torso, careful to feel every inch of his hard-on, she throatily chuckled. "Wanna fuck?"

Her candor took him by surprise and Mike's hands circled her waist, his eyes smiling. "Who are you?"

"Don't toy with me, Michael. You're dealing with a woman who's denied herself for a very long time. So, I repeat. Wanna fuck?"

"I wanna open my present." Kate's eyes narrowed slightly, and he quickly added, "And then I wanna fuck."

"Goody!" She sprang up and grabbed the flat box for him.

He weighed it, shook it, turned it over. It was meticulously wrapped, and he took his time with it, driving her crazy as he carefully undid the flaps of the paper so as not to tear it. She watched impatiently as he slid his finger under the final piece of tape and then began folding the gift wrap. He placed it on the bed, neatly piling the ribbon on top. This was all part of the ritual, and she knew it, but it didn't stop her from muttering, "Come on, Mike, we're getting older here!"

The lid was off the box and he peeled the tissue paper apart. Mike held up the royal blue boxer shorts covered with the SPAM logo and snorted. "You don't really expect me to wear these, do you?"

Kate giggled. "And you don't really expect to get into *my* panties without putting yours on, do you?"

"Oh, come on, Kate!" He was laughing as he set them aside and reached for her.

"Uh-uh. Put 'em on," she said.

"Now?"

"Mike," she explained patiently. "You have to put them on in order for me to take them off you."

Kate came awake reluctantly, not sure why her mind didn't want to be lucid. It was early. She knew that because she could still hear embers popping in the fireplace. Mike lay sprawled across the bed, his face buried in the crook of his arm. She rolled onto her side and watched him as he slept, a smile on her lips.

Cautiously, Kate reached out to touch his hair and she was suddenly taken with the reality of him lying in bed next to her. This was a wonderful thing. To hear his steady breathing, to be able to look at his smooth, muscled back, to know that his strong hands would always bring her pleasure, to understand that this man really loved her. Yes, this was truly a miraculous, wonderful thing.

And just as suddenly, she knew why she felt uneasy. It was Christmas. She moved closer to him and kissed his shoulder blade, willing him to wake. "Mike?" she whispered as he lifted his head.

A sleepy smile greeted her, then he mumbled, "S'early . . . go back to sleep." His face disappeared into the pillow.

"Mike?" Her fingers caressed his neck. "Please? Can you hold me?"

His arm stole around her waist as he pulled her close. She could hear the rasp of his morning beard on the pillowcase as his face came into view again. His warm breath fogged her senses as his lips touched her eyelids.

"Merry Christmas, Katie," he said quietly. "What is it?"

"I don't think I can face Sheryl."

"It'll be hard, but it'll be okay." His hand moved down to her bare hip, then came to rest cupping a smooth cheek.

She draped a leg over his thigh and nestled into his body. Kate fell asleep wishing they could stay this way forever.

"Are you sure they're coming?" Matt asked from the kitchen doorway, as Sheryl closed the oven door for the fifth time.

Both the turkey and Sheryl were doing a slow burn when the front door finally opened and Mike's voice reached her. She swept past Matt, into the hallway and, still holding the baster, pointed it at her brother. "You're over an hour late!"

"Merry Christmas to you, too," Mike said as he hung his coat in the closet.

"Where is she?"

"Don't start that 'she' stuff, Sheryl."

"Where's Kate?"

"On her way. And I'm sorry we're late."

"I suppose I have Kate to thank for that?" Sheryl asked.

"First of all, don't assume anything. As it happens, it's my fault we're late. And secondly, let's not forget how awkward this is gonna be. It was tough enough getting her to come at all."

Mike had made a very uneasy peace with his sister for Matt's sake. It was hard not to think of her as the bad guy in all this, because she was here and alive. He had to keep reminding himself that Paul deserved the blame.

Chastened for the moment, Sheryl said, "Sorry. But really, Mike, where is she?"

"Parking her car."

"What?"

"We came in separate cars, in case she wanted to leave and I didn't." Mike saw the look of disbelief on his sister's face. "Look, Sheryl. Kate's not coming here to celebrate Christmas with the family."

"What, then?"

Matt had entered the hall, and now said, "She's coming to talk to you, Mom."

Sheryl's voice wavered. "What about dinner? Can't we eat first?"

There was a soft knock on the front door and Mike opened it for Kate, who reluctantly stepped inside only after he took her hand.

The standard Christmas greeting hardly seemed appropriate, and so Sheryl simply said, "Hi, Kate."

Kate nodded at Sheryl, while Mike helped her off with her coat.

Sheryl found the silence unnerving, and inanely said, "Are you hungry? The turkey's a little dry, but—"

"I'm sorry we're late," Kate interrupted. "But Mike has a hard time with the word 'no.'" She lifted her chin and leveled a look of defiance at Sheryl, wanting her to understand which of them mattered most at the moment. "I don't want to hold up your dinner, but what I have to say won't take long. Is there someplace we can talk?"

Sheryl's office seemed even smaller as the two women faced each other in the tense silence that Kate finally broke. "I've been thinking about this a lot, as you can imagine. I've tried to understand your side of the story. I've gone through it over and over again, and no matter how I present it to myself, it always comes out that what you did was wrong. All of it was *wrong*.

"Both of you are to blame. I know that. But Paul died, and he's left me with this pile of garbage to clean up. And I can't do it. Not right now."

"What would you have done if we *had* told you? What good would it have done?" Sheryl asked.

"No!" Kate's hand slammed the desktop. "Don't you dare rationalize this to me! I don't know what I would have done with the truth, but I think I deserved to know it. Maybe we weren't best friends back then, but we were like family. And what about the past few years? When I think about everything we've talked about, everything I've told you . . . my most private feelings. God! I must've given you a few good laughs." Kate's eyes stung as she heard the beginning of Sheryl's denial. Her anger erupted along with the threatening tears. "You called me your friend, but I know you've always resented me for some reason. Don't think I didn't know the way you made fun of me behind my back when we were young. And you must've gotten quite a kick out of my so-called marriage!"

"Kate, please believe me. I *am* your friend!"

"Friends respect each other," Kate said, ignoring the tears that steadily rolled down her cheeks. "I don't think you've ever respected me."

"Oh, God, Kate ... you have no idea how much respect I had for you. I knew what you had to put up with being married to Paul, and you always held your head up. I was never going to tell Paul about Matt, but I found out what he was doing to you because you couldn't have kids. I only told him to hurt him! I never meant to hurt anyone else."

"But you did." Kate's eyes held Sheryl's. "I can't forgive this. Not yet. I don't know if I ever want to trust you again. I wanted to be a part of your family so much. I used to love spending time with you. I always felt I could be myself with you. But right now I don't want to see you for a very long time."

"But what about Mike?"

Using her sleeve to wipe her face, Kate angrily said, "That's the hardest part! I love Mike. And he loves you. I'll never stand between you and Mike, but make no mistake whose side I'm on, Sheryl. Someone has seen fit to give me a second chance at this. It's taken me a long time to take off my blinders and see the world around me. I know it's not a perfect world, but finding Mike makes it pretty damned close. I fell in love with him a long time ago. I just didn't understand that till now. But more than that, he's always been my best friend. His respect means everything to me. Everything! And *I will not let you take that away from me.*" Kate's words echoed off the walls, until only silence remained.

Sheryl knew there was nothing she could say in return. Not now.

Kate turned away from her and in a steady voice said,

"Could you please send Matt in? I have something I want to give him before I go."

"I—Kate. I wish you'd stay."

"What for?" Kate asked.

"Because it's Christmas . . ." Sheryl's voice trailed off before she gathered her strength again. "It won't be much of a Christmas if you leave. Mike won't stay. You know that."

"That's up to him. He can make his own decisions." Kate faced Sheryl. "Could you please get Matt?"

Sheryl's mouth opened, then closed tightly. Kate felt the gust of wind Sheryl generated as she left the room. A few moments later Matt's body filled the doorframe.

Sheryl waited till she heard her office door close before speaking. "She's not staying, you know."

Mike shrugged. "I don't blame her."

"What the hell could she possibly have for Matt?"

"He'll tell you if he wants you to know."

"Well, can't you give me a hint?" Sheryl asked.

"Just leave it, Sherry." Mike stood and said, "I'm hungry. You want me to carve the turkey?"

Sheryl looked at him thankfully. "You're going to eat?"

"Sure," he said as he opened the oven. "And not a moment too soon, I think."

Later that night—long after Kate's departure, after he and his mother and his uncle had eaten and opened their gifts, a few minutes after Mike left—Matt retreated to his bedroom. He lay on his bed, the wallet with Matt's baby picture hidden away in it on his chest. A calm descended over Matt so profound that he could feel every muscle—every sinew and tendon—in his body let go.

Kate's words as she gave him the wallet indelibly imprinted themselves on his brain, and now they were all he heard. All he saw as he closed his eyes.

"He did care. He cared enough to die for what was in this wallet. I'm giving it to you so you'll always remember that no matter what else he did, he went back for you, Matt."

"Thank you," Matt whispered to Paul. But in reality he was speaking to everyone he loved.

CHAPTER

FIFTY-THREE

The door slammed, shaking the house. His heavy, running footsteps thundered down the hallway _____ and up the stairs. He shook off his jacket as he ran and let it fall to the floor. Mike shoved open the bedroom door. His eyes immediately found her in the bed and he went to her. Pinning her between his arms, he brought his mouth down on hers. He was like a starved man. Nothing else mattered but the nourishment her body gave him.

Drawing a deep breath, he said, "I couldn't think of anything else but you the whole night."

"I'm here," she answered.

"Thank God," he responded before pulling the quilt down and burying his face in the silky fabric that covered her soft belly.

He couldn't remember ever being this hungry for anything in his life. Kneeling beside the bed, his hands coaxed her hips to the edge of the mattress. He pushed her gown up and lifted first one leg, and then her other over his shoulders. Her dusky eyes had become darker with anticipation, and his own locked with hers, as he lowered his head to taste her for the first time.

Mike felt her tense as his tongue circled her. She moaned at the intensity of feeling he brought, and she murmured, "Not there ... not yet." His lips closed around the flesh of her inner thigh. And then he was lapping at her, his warm tongue meeting her own heat, and she relaxed, opening herself to him. Her juices bathed his lips, his chin. The scent of musk engulfed him and he sank into her, receiving all she had to give. Sucking, swallowing, he was gluttony itself, while she writhed underneath him.

Kate clutched at her nightgown, tugging it higher. Blindly grasping at his hand, she placed it on her breast. When his thumb dragged across her nipple, she arched up, wanting more. She groaned when he withdrew his tongue. Gasped, when she felt his fingers enter her. Cried out, when he suckled her swollen clitoris.

She came hard, every muscle in her body quivering with sensation. Before she could come down, he was undoing his zipper—freeing himself—with one hand, as he stood and lifted her to him. He plunged inside her, driving in deep.

Kate watched through eyes at half-mast. She saw his jaw clench, his eyes close tightly, his head fall back. Seeing him in the throes of his passion brought her to the edge once more. Her hands covered his and she begged him to go harder. The second wave of orgasm enveloped her and she repeated his name. When his own relief came, and she could actually feel his hot semen spurt into her, she reached for him, sobbing the words "I love you . . ." over and over again.

He let her hold him. His disbelief that making love could feel like this closed his throat. Before he could stop himself, he was crying and Kate was smoothing his perspiration-soaked hair from his forehead.

"We're a pair, aren't we?" she murmured through her own tears.

He pulled away from her and took her face in his hands, kissing every feature. When he was able to speak coherently, he whispered, "It's been a long time coming,

Katie. And I knew it could be like this . . ." Her eyes smiled at him. "God, I love you so much." His voice dropped lower. "So much . . ."

"Take off your clothes, Mike. I want to feel your skin next to mine."

He didn't notice Julia's lamp until he went to turn it off an hour later. His hand stopped in midair. He looked down at Kate, already well on her way to sleep. Everything and everyone seemed to be in the right place, and he told her that.

A soft smile came to her lips. She kissed his chest and said, "Merry Christmas, sugar."

The barking nagged at him in his sleep. It was a never-ending series of sharp yelps, punctuated with long howls. The sound finally woke him and Mike sat up jostling Kate into semiconsciousness. He listened for less than a second, then shook Kate's shoulder. "Katie?" When she didn't respond, his voice grew loud with worry. "Kate! Wake up. Where's Homer?"

"Huh?"

Mike quickly went to the window and threw it open. Homer's barking filled the room. "Did you feed him tonight?" Mike asked. He had turned to Kate, when something caught his eye, and he spun back to the window and the black night. "Oh, Christ . . . Kate! Wake up!" Mike clambered over her, trying to reach the telephone.

The fear in his voice brought her fully awake, and she found herself crushed to the mattress. "What? What's wrong?"

But he was already talking into the phone. "Fire at number eighteen Frazier Street . . ."

His terse words shot her full of adrenaline, and Kate pushed him aside. She tumbled from the bed and ran to the window. She refused to register what she saw.

Pale yellow flames licked at the tower room's window, and Kate watched, as if seeing a film of something familiar. Yet it had to be fiction. It had nothing to do with her. It was someone else's nightmare.

Mike was suddenly behind her, his tense voice telling her to get dressed, when the tower window exploded and sent a fiery crystal shower into the night. She screamed and stepped back. His fingers tightened painfully around her upper arms and he propelled her toward the chair that held her clothes.

"Get dressed!" he roared. "I'm gonna go get Homer!"

And he was gone, leaving her to fumble blindly with buttons and zippers as her eyes streamed with terrified tears. Kate heard the first siren as she ran down the staircase.

In the gray light of dawn, with the acrid smell of smoke and wet, burned wood filling her nostrils, Kate sat on the curb. Her hand gripped the leash that tethered Homer to her. She watched as the last fire truck reeled in its hose. Watched as Mike shook hands with one of the firemen. Kate had stopped crying some time ago, but her eyes burned as if the fire had somehow spread through her body.

Neighbors, who had dressed hastily and looked like refugees in their slippers and overcoats, stood in small clumps, whispering. Relieved the fire hadn't spread to their own homes, they now took an active interest in the real-life drama they were witnessing. Kate wanted to go back inside. She wanted to hide from them and their furtive looks. Wanted to go back to Mike's bed and pull the covers over her head. But she stayed and stared straight ahead, waiting for Mike to come back across the street.

The tower was gone, along with everything it had held. In its place was a dark, ragged hole that extended into the roof. The firemen had covered it with tarps, but the ugliness of it stayed with her. Tom Dennison, a former schoolmate and volunteer firefighter, had said she'd been lucky. The fire hadn't done any major damage to the second floor because it had moved up. Staring at the smoldering roof as he'd talked, Kate hardly thought "lucky" was the word she would've used.

"We're so sorry. Do you know how it started?"

The voice startled her, and Kate's head snapped to the left. An older couple who lived two doors up the street stood side by side. They weren't looking at Kate, but at her house.

"No, I don't," she replied.

"Lucky you got out," the man said as he eyed the muddy mess that had once been her front yard.

Kate began to say she hadn't been inside when the fire started, but thought better of trying to explain where she'd been at three in the morning. Instead, she said, "Yes . . . lucky."

They didn't catch the slight sarcasm in her tone, and they finally looked down at her and smiled vaguely. The woman said, "Bad time of the year for this sort of thing."

Kate gazed at her for a moment and bit her tongue to keep from asking if there was ever a good time. "Thanks for your concern," she said as she stood. "If you'll excuse me?" And she walked across the street toward Mike, Homer following behind her.

"I want to go inside," she stated.

"Why don't you wait?"

"I don't want to wait," Kate said impatiently.

Mike sighed. "Okay, let's go."

Kate handed him the leash. "No. I want to go in alone."

"No way, Kate."

But she was already walking away from him. Her voice drifted back to him. "I'll just be a few minutes."

"Damn it, Kate!"

She stopped on the front porch and turned to face him. "Just let me do this."

The implacable tone of her voice, and the stubborn set of her mouth that Mike knew well, made him stand still and throw up his hands in surrender.

When she came outside fifteen minutes later, Kate didn't say a word. She simply took Mike's hand and walked back across the street with him.

Mike's phone call had brought Matt to the house, where the three of them now sat around the kitchen table drinking coffee. Kate had tuned out the two men several minutes before. She sat perfectly still, hands cupped around the mug in front of her, her mind drifting from image to image—sensation to sensation.

Smoke-blackened ceilings. The brown splotches of wallpaper in her bedroom where heat had seared through the connecting wall. Water stains already forming on the hardwood floors. A cold dampness invading the upper floor. A feeling that the house had never wanted her there in the first place, and had now gotten rid of her completely.

She shivered and heard Mike's voice talking to her. Her eyes met his.

"Where'd you go, Katie?"

She smiled slightly and tried to shake off her melancholy. "I was just thinking that there's nothing left of Paul anymore. All the tangible evidence burned with the tower." A lone tear spilled down her right cheek. "I don't have anything of his anymore and that makes me sad. It's as if he never existed and that can't be right."

Mike's face fell, and she quickly went on, wanting to explain. Wanting to stop any hurt she may have inadvertently caused him with her words. "Oh, sweetheart . . . no." She took his hand. "What I mean is, that no matter what my life was like with Paul, it was *my life with Paul*. I shouldn't have to forget him completely, should I?"

Matt's voice was tentative, but his words possessed a strength Kate and Mike couldn't ignore. "I'm what's left of Paul. Can I be your memory of him?"

RESTORATION

CHAPTER

FIFTY-FOUR

F rom the window seat, Kate watched the sun rise over the Blue Ridge. The light bathed her in warmth. She closed her eyes and lifted her face to it. An early spring had descended on the valley and, for the first time in years, Kate felt a tremendous joy in the warm temperatures and the yellows of daffodils and forsythia in bloom.

She opened her eyes at the sound of a soft snore and looked around at a sleeping Mike. Homer lay next to him and answered with a snore of his own. Kate stifled a laugh and turned back to the window. The sun glinted off the For Sale sign in her front yard, momentarily blinding her.

For Sale. It was a frightening, liberating concept. The sign had been up a few days, but it still startled her when she saw it. Paul's mother had been a little more than startled when Kate phoned her with the news.

Kate sat at Mike's kitchen table, her knuckles white as she'd gripped the telephone receiver. To her credit, she hadn't slammed it down in Margaret Armstrong's shell-like ear. Instead, she'd calmly placed the phone in its cradle and then shouted every expletive she could think of.

Mike had been standing quietly in the doorway, and after Kate let loose, said, "Went *that* well, did it?"

Kate let go of the phone and turned. "She acted as if I'd taken out a full-page ad in the *Richmond Times* announcing I'm going into hooking, for God's sake!" Mike grinned and Kate said, "It's not funny! She's saying stuff like, how *could* you sell the memory of Paul? . . . the house he grew up in . . . the family home! And when I asked her if she wanted to buy it from me, she couldn't come up with excuses not to fast enough. They want me to keep it, but not one of them's ever offered to help with the upkeep."

"It's your house, Kate. You can do whatever you want with it," Mike said softly, but Kate was rolling.

"And *then* she says, in that holier-than-thou voice, 'And where will you live, Kate? Above that little shop of yours?' " She slammed her hand down on the table. *"God!"*

"You didn't tell her, did you," Mike stated.

Kate blushed and mumbled, "I couldn't do it. I'm sorry."

Mike shrugged and pushed away from the doorframe, but she could see he was hurt. "Aw, Mike . . . imagine what she'd say if I'd told her I was living with you."

"You could've told her we're married."

"But we're not."

"But we will be."

They looked at each other. A slow smile came over Mike's face and Kate felt an intense starburst of desire. He reached for her arm and drew her out of the chair. His hands circled her waist and she was suddenly sitting on the table. Just before he pulled her jeans off, he leaned close and whispered, "Did you at least tell her about the dedication?"

His voice was so seductive that the question didn't register for a few seconds, at which time she breathlessly answered, "It was my lead." At which time Mike said, "Imagine what she'll say when she finds out about Matt."

Kate pushed open the window and took in the dewy scent that promised a perfect day. Her house, with its restored tower and fresh coat of white paint, shimmered in the morning light. The thought of selling had drifted through her mind the night of the fire. Matt's imploring question clinched it for her. *Can I be your memory of him?* It echoed back to her for days.

Mike and Matt had worked long, hard hours putting the house back together for her. Mike hadn't said, "I told you so," when the fire investigation concluded that an animal—probably a mouse—had chewed through the old insulation on the wires, eventually causing the fire. Kate remembered Mike's cautionary offer to check out the tower room, and her refusal. When he saw the report, he'd simply nodded and gone back to the list of supplies he and Matt were compiling.

It had been Kate who finally said, "It's my fault. For not letting you into the tower. I'll never hide anything from you again." She also remembered Mike's smile as she added, "This roommate thing? Can we make it permanent?"

Since that time, nearly three months ago, Matt had left for Florida and spring training. He had made the two of them promise to come down to watch him play after the gym dedication. He'd also made them vow not to get married till the fall, when he could be a member of the wedding.

"Ring bearer?" Mike had teased.

"Hey, you know I'm *the* best man," Matt had parried.

Mike had glanced at Kate, who'd responded, "Not in this case."

Reluctantly rising from the window seat, Kate

stretched and turned back to the bed to find Mike watching her with a sleepy smile. "Come back to bed, Katie." She allowed him to wrap his body around her and, as his arms crossed over her breasts, she took his hands and held them tightly. "By tomorrow it'll all be over with," he whispered. "By tomorrow our lives will finally be our own."

Their unspoken thoughts merged. *And Paul will finally be laid to rest.*

CHAPTER

FIFTY-FIVE

K ate, head bent, leaned against the bathroom sink, the heels of her hands digging into the _____ counter. She took another deep breath and saw reflected her pale, nervous face framed by the institutional beige of the toilet stalls. A wave of nausea made her swallow hard and she closed her eyes and shook her head to clear it. One of her earrings—a gold shamrock with a small emerald center—fell into the sink with a soft clink. Kate's heart stopped for a moment, until she realized the drain was covered with a stainless steel grid. With shaking fingers she picked up the gift from Mike and clipped it on again just as the bathroom door burst open, followed by the high-pitched voices of two girls in the middle of an argument.

When the teenagers rounded the corner and saw Kate, their mouths closed simultaneously and they regarded her with the universal suspicion all fifteen-year-olds employ against adults. Kate tried to smile—couldn't—and quickly walked past them. As she reached the door, she silently said, "You can do this," and then pushed her way out of the new gymnasium's ladies' room.

She slowly made her way down the hall, her shoes

echoing on the virgin linoleum. Her feet already hurt. Kate couldn't remember the last time she'd worn heels. Or a dress. But it had been long enough that she'd had to go out and buy something for this evening. The few semiformal dresses that had been relegated to the back bedroom's cedar closet literally hung on her.

It had been as if the saleswoman in the boutique had seen her coming, and Kate still cringed at the 350 dollars she'd forked over. It was the first dress she tried on. The saleswoman made a huge fuss over her, exclaiming how the color was "*the* thing for your hair," but Kate didn't need any prompting. The emerald-green sheath, with its kick pleat and scoop neck, had been perfect. It had been one of Kate's good days, and she'd liked what she'd seen in the mirror.

She wanted to feel sexy again. Wanted to look like a woman a man might desire. Wanted them all to know she was indeed alive even though her husband had died. But most of all, Kate wanted Mike to look at her the way he had all those years ago in San Francisco on the night of his architecture award. She had taken his breath away then, and it wasn't hard to recall the feeling of power the moment had given her. Tonight, as she'd walked into the living room where he'd waited, Kate hadn't been disappointed.

Now, trying to find her way through the maze that would lead her to the main room of the gym, she cursed the tight skirt and the two-inch heels that forced her to take six-inch steps. Kate had a mental image of the look on Margaret Armstrong's face as she took the podium to read her dedication speech. It would be a look that confirmed all Mrs. Armstrong's convictions about Kate. If she were a character in a cartoon strip, a bubble would hover over that perfectly coiffed head, enclosing the words: *Paul! She's selling*

*the family home! Dressing like a ten-dollar whore! Living
with your best friend. My darling, I'm so glad you're not
alive to see this!* The possibilities for melodrama were
endless.

But Kate would've given her right arm to witness the
exact moment when Margaret learned her perfect son
had hidden a grandchild from her. Despite Kate's loss of
faith in Sheryl, she felt sorry for her.

Kate slowed to a stop in front of the double doors to
the gym. The music that filtered through sounded suspiciously like a sappy Carpenters song, and Kate grimaced.
Wasn't this bad enough without including some of the
worst music of the seventies? Could disco be far behind?

Kate placed her palm against the brass plate, took a
calming breath, and pushed open the door. The voice of
Karen Carpenter assailed her. If she ever needed a drink,
it was now. No such luck on school grounds. She knew
the goblets on the banquet tables were filled with water,
and the two punch bowls held a sickly sweet concoction
of something red.

Donna Estes had gone all out. The tables were covered with linen in the school colors. Centerpieces of daffodils in vases tied with royal blue ribbon carried on the
theme. The table servers were seniors coerced into
working for extra credit. Kate stood at the door and
watched them plunk salad plates on the table with all the
panache of truck-stop workers. She saw a huge pink
bubble emerge from the lips of a bored blonde, who
silently spoke volumes. *I'd rather be anywhere but here on
Friday night.* It made Kate smile for the first time that
evening.

Her eyes searched the cavernous room for Mike, but
he had already spotted her and was frantically sending
coded signals for Kate to rescue him from a former
classmate. Kate made a beeline toward him and, as she
reached the two men, took Mike's arm and said,

"Excuse us, Pete, but I'm starving." Nothing was further from the truth, but the statement propelled Mike into action, and he shrugged at the slightly balding former football player and let Kate lead him to their table.

Seating Kate, he leaned down to whisper, "If you ever need to know anything about annuities, Pete's your man." He noticed the slightly glazed look in Kate's eyes and he quickly sat next to her. "You okay?"

Kate had seen the names on the place cards, and was about to suggest they move to another table as rapidly as possible, but it was too late. The entire Armstrong family, looking like the royalty they thought they were, led by a beaming Donna Estes, were making their way through the crowd and toward the table Kate and Mike occupied.

"God, Mike . . . how am I going to get through this?"

Mike leaned toward Kate, his eyes demanding she look at him. When he had her attention, he said, "They are part of the past, and the past isn't going to hurt you anymore."

She looked at him gratefully. "Kiss me, Mike."

The corners of his eyes crinkled in pleasure at her small rebellion and he brought his hand up to cup the back of her neck. Drawing her in, his lips met hers in a meltingly soft kiss. When he released her, he stood and turned to confront the stunned faces of the mother, sister, and brother-in-law of his best friend.

Smiling broadly, Mike said, "It's been a long time, Mrs. Armstrong. Patricia. Gordon." He reached across the table and heartily shook Gordon Swope's instinctively offered hand. Donna Estes hovered behind the family and Mike nodded at her. "Nice work, Donna."

The irony in his words soared over Donna's head, and she beamed at him, nearly forgetting the scene she had just witnessed.

No one had spoken a word to Kate yet. Mike waited till the Armstrong clan was seated, then said, "And you all remember my fiancée, Kate?"

The question had the desired effect. Patricia's and Gordon's heads simultaneously swiveled to gape at Mrs. Armstrong, who resembled a deer caught in the headlights of an oncoming truck.

Kate nearly laughed out loud when a small delighted squeal issued forth from Donna. The word "congratulations" was barely out of her mouth, when she hurriedly excused herself, unable to wait to convey the news.

"We're planning a fall wedding. My nephew is the best man and he won't be available till then," Mike went on. "Hey, but listen to me. I'm doing all the talking."

Salads sat untouched. Paul's mother finally managed to say, "This is rather . . . sudden."

Kate knew what those four words really meant. As far as Margaret Armstrong was concerned, Kate should still be wearing black. Preferably a nun's habit, if it came to that. But take another husband, after she'd had Paul Armstrong? God forbid.

"Sudden in what way?" Mike asked, his face the picture of innocence.

Kate found her voice at last. "Mrs. Armstrong, I know this is hard for you, but Paul has been dead three years today. I wasn't buried with him. I don't want to mourn him anymore. I'm very happy right now. I'd very much like it if you could be happy for me, too."

Plates of some sort of unrecognizable chicken dish appeared in front of them. While the student finished serving their table, no one spoke. When he was gone, the silence became unbearable.

Gordon finally put his hand out to Kate and said, "I hope you'll be very happy." Kate gratefully took his hand. And then he added, "You deserve it."

Kate looked into his eyes and saw a sympathy that could only come from understanding. "Thank you." She smiled.

The congratulatory words from Paul's mother and sister were less than heartfelt and the next twenty minutes went by excruciatingly slowly, with Mike trying to fill in the enormous conversational gaps on his own.

The background music stopped mid-lyric, and there was a deep, hollow thudding noise as Donna Estes tested the microphone at the podium. The seventy-plus diners grew quiet, and sounds of silverware clattering on plates and throats being cleared filled the gym. Donna spoke into the mike and a squeal reverberated through the room, causing some laughter.

Backing away a few inches, she said, "Sorry, folks. That was almost as bad as that blackboard thing Mr. LaPlante used to pull on us." A sea of grins greeted her as they all remembered the English teacher who truly knew how to get a class's attention. "I'd like to introduce the principal of Staunton High School, Mr. Mark Lewis."

Applause greeted the lanky young man.

"Thanks for coming and thank you all for your donations of time and money. This beautiful new facility is a testament to your hard work and generosity. The state of Virginia paid for half of it. It never would have been built without all of you."

Once again, applause broke out.

"I'd like to ask Kate Armstrong to join me."

Mike squeezed Kate's hand as she shakily stood. All heads turned to watch her walk to the podium.

Shaking the principal's hand, Kate stood back, waiting.

Mark Lewis turned back to the microphone. "Every student who passes through this school is special, in his or her own way. But there are some who seem to stand out. Who make us all proud to say that we shared the same halls of learning. Paul Armstrong was one such student.

"Paul Armstrong died three years ago today, but he left behind a legacy of what one can achieve with talent and hard work. Yes, Paul Armstrong played baseball here before he went on to become a star in his field, but more importantly, he also maintained a three-eight grade point average. We would like all the aspiring athletes who come through this building to know there is a place for learning in sports.

"Therefore, I am enormously pleased and proud to welcome you all to the Paul Allen Armstrong Memorial Gymnasium."

Mark Lewis gestured for Kate to step forward, and as she neared the podium, the applause drowned out her introduction. When it was quiet again, the principal said, "Mrs. Armstrong, we'd be honored if you'd say a few words before revealing the plaque."

Kate gripped the sides of the podium and looked down for a moment as another smattering of applause broke out. When she raised her head, she looked out across the vast room. Her husky voice—steady—reached everyone. "You all probably already know this, but I'm Kathleen Moran Armstrong. Everyone calls me Kate. I haven't been Mrs. Armstrong in a very long time."

She hesitated only a moment, as she sought out Mike's face. When she found him in the dim light, she noticed someone sitting at the table who hadn't been there before. Julia winked at her and Kate smiled. She went on, strengthened by the two people she could truly call friends. "I think I can safely say that Paul would have been thrilled by all this. He loved children of all ages and I know that if he were alive today, he would be spending a good amount of time here doing what he could to help these kids reach their goals.

"I also know that Paul Armstrong, besides being a great baseball player and a brave man, was only human. And those are the only things I can say about Paul with any real certainty. He was just like any of you. He had his moments of doubt. He had his flaws. And even though I knew Paul for seventeen years, I never really *knew* him."

The room had gone completely silent. Kate found Mike's eyes again and saw not only love in them, but pride. She raised her chin, knowing it was time to finish this thing once and for all.

"We are, after all, only human, too. We see what we want to see in those we love. But I don't think we ever really know them. And I believe that's the way it should be. I think everyone needs to keep a small piece of themselves. Something you can say is truly yours. Something no one can take away.

"When Paul died I thought I'd lost that little piece of me. But I've found it again. Paul's life ended three years ago. Thank God I've just recently discovered that mine didn't. So, if you don't mind, I'd like to get on with the business of living."

Kate turned away from the astonished crowd and in a few short steps stood next to the curtained plaque. Whisking aside the fabric, she kept walking until she reached the disc jockey who'd been providing the musical entertainment for the evening. She bent down and whispered something to him. He nodded and flipped through his stack of compact discs.

The gymnasium had filled with the echoing sound of applause, but Kate didn't hear it. As she walked toward Mike, who now stood, she never took her eyes off his face. Her hands reached out for his, and as the clapping died down, she softly said, "Can I have this dance?"

The unmistakable bass notes of "My Girl" filled the room as he pulled her into his arms. Pressing his lips into her neck, he said, "All the dances have always been yours, darlin'. I was just waiting for you to ask."

ABOUT THE AUTHOR

Annette Reynolds was born in Greece, grew up in California, has a degree in arts management from Mary Baldwin College in Staunton, Virginia, and now lives in an eighty-six-year-old house in Tacoma, Washington. *Remember the Time* is her first novel, and she is at work on her second.

DON'T MISS THESE FABULOUS BANTAM WOMEN'S FICTION TITLES

On Sale in July

THE SILVER ROSE

by the incomparable JANE FEATHER,
nationally bestselling author of THE DIAMOND SLIPPER

Like the rose in the haunting tale of "Beauty and the Beast,"
a silver rose on a charm bracelet brings together
a beautiful young woman and a battle-scarred knight.

_____ 57524-4 $5.99/$7.99

A PLACE TO CALL HOME

*A new novel from one of the most appealing voices
in Southern fiction,* DEBORAH SMITH

True love is a funny thing.
It can overcome time, distance,
and the craziest of families.

_____ 10334-2 $23.95/$29.95

Ask for these books at your local bookstore or use this page to order.

Please send me the books I have checked above. I am enclosing $_____ (add $2.50 to cover postage and handling). Send check or money order, no cash or C.O.D.'s, please.

Name _____

Address _____

City/State/Zip _____

Send order to: Bantam Books, Dept. FN158, 2451 S. Wolf Rd., Des Plaines, IL 60018
Allow four to six weeks for delivery.
Prices and availability subject to change without notice.   FN 158 7/97

Jean Stone

IVY SECRETS

They were three women living a lie.
They met within the ivied walls of one of
New England's most prestigious colleges: three girls
from vastly different backgrounds who became
roommates, soul mates, and best friends.
But fifteen years later, it's not the bonds of
friendship that have brought them back together but
the lie they've lived ever since they left
those hallowed halls, a lie that has come back
to haunt and hunt them....

IVY SECRETS ____57423-X $5.99/$7.99
